ADVANCE PRAISE

A skilled writer, Reardon makes Amelia a witty guide through the drama and pain. A former mental health therapist, Reardon infuses the book with a passion for recovery and appreciation of life. Her background brings bona fides to an expansive, engrossing novel. It's an involving, well-written debut.

—Kirkus

Reardon's courageous, unfiltered story about addiction and mental health is a triumph of recovery, certain to inspire anyone struggling with similar challenges.

—Karen S. Gordon, author of *The Mutiny Girl,*
Gold & Courage Series

Hopeful, introspective, and lyrical—a work of literary realism tinged with the grit of recovery. A strong debut with real emotional honesty and a protagonist whose flaws are heartbreakingly human. A book for anyone who has ever had to rebuild, one brick at a time, while learning to live in their own skin. Themes of autonomy, self-confidence, and love as action anchor this moving tale.

—Independent Book Review

If you've ever battled your own demons, numbed the ache, or longed for redemption in the wreckage, this book will feel like someone finally wrote your secret diary out loud. Being a recovering addict myself, Amelia's chaos feels like a familiar mirror, her self-sabotage too close to home — but so does her fight to crawl out.

—Cyn Posner, author of *Escape to Mexico*

Wethersfield Road has the power of optimism. It's Kristin Hannah mixed with the raw openness of *Margo's Got Money Troubles* with a heavy dose of non-preachy self-help. Much like Hope and Amelia, I feel like this book found me. This book left me with so many lessons and strategies for doing the best I possibly can to make my own life extraordinary by finding beauty in the ordinary.

—**Jess Ross**, Bookstagram

Wethersfield Road is such a moving, down-to-earth read. Reardon captures the ups and downs of healing in a way that feels so real—messy, funny, emotional, and full of hope. I couldn't put it down—raw, compassionate, and ultimately uplifting.

— **Jennifer Rollin**, LCSW eating disorder therapist, co-author of *The Inside Scoop on Eating Disorder Recovery*

Beautiful and healing. It's a story of hope and love.

—**Kelsey Johnson**, Booktok

Filled with reflective moments that offer hope and joy in a world of despair, *Wethersfield Road* examines wealth from a myriad of different directions. It's an evocative novel about riches, transformation, and self-defeating manners. Reardon paints the life of a woman who simultaneously has everything and nothing. The darkness that emerges so realistically in Amelia's life is juxtaposed by moments of realization, discovery, and enlightenment that send her into unexpected directions and positive ways of approaching life. Underneath a façade of riches lies a powerful force for her recovery and change. It wells up like tears to transform Amelia's life in unexpected ways, despite her proclivity for self-destruction. Compelling, realistic, and thought-provoking, all in one.

—**Midwest Book Review**

Anna Binder Reardon is a literary mastermind; captivating, intriguing, and breathtaking.

—**Jen Beach**, Booktok

WETHERS FIELD ROAD

a novel

ANNA BINDER REARDON

Printed in the United States.

Cover and book design by Asya Blue Design.

ISBN 979-8-9924198-7-0 Paperback
ISBN 979-8-9924198-8-7 Hardcover
ISBN 979-8-9924198-9-4 Audiobook
ISBN 979-8-9924198-3-2 Ebook

For anyone who "was born and took it personally."
—my friend Barry

AUTHOR'S NOTE

This book contains graphic sexual content and depictions of domestic violence, sexual trauma, substance abuse, eating disorders, sexual abuse of a minor, and severe mental illness. The intention of exploring these topics is to tell the truth about the ways we as humans struggle. If you find the above topics triggering in any way, I ask that you use extreme caution in navigating this story and put your own well-being and mental health first. This is ultimately a story about recovery in all its various forms. Amelia's journey can be messy, but as most of us know all too well, healing is anything but linear. May we all have the time and space we need to heal and feel whole.

With love,

Anna

CHAPTER 1

Amelia Glickman would never admit it, but she secretly fantasized about near-fatal car wrecks and potentially terminal cancer diagnoses. It's not that she wanted to die, per se; she dreamed of being the center of attention among worried friends and family, deliciously dramatic hospital visits, and social media posts about how she "lit up any room she walked into." Amelia had always sensed that she was someone people tended to take for granted, someone you didn't appreciate until they were gone. Or, at least, almost gone. She walked around with a chip of "then they'd be sorry" on her shoulder. Or she *did,* until the crushing reality of an actual near-death experience all but annihilated said chip.

The thing about illness and car wrecks is that victimhood's a part of the package deal. "How could this happen to you?" and "No one deserves this less," would both fall off the tongues of suddenly interested acquaintances, the illusion of importance quenching her thirst for relevance and adoration. But what about the kind of trauma where *you* set the drama in motion? What about intricately tracing your path back to every poor decision and every red flag that you so fiercely painted green?

See, Amelia did the thing you weren't supposed to do. She moved in with her much-older boyfriend at 18, the very second she graduated high school, and started playing house. It was a way to spite her monogamy-resistant father, plus her codependent mother who was dealing with divorcing him by not so much dealing with it. She'd spent the

1

entirety of her senior year splitting time between two houses, all the while watching her dad throw money at well-meaning women on Jdate and helping her mom construct the perfect match.com profile to woo all the other middle-aged divorcés who weren't her dad. In the wake of that mess, she was ready to prove to herself and anyone else who was watching that "family" was still an attainable goal. It had all exploded in a dramatic flash of violence and good intentions. The flash had a fallout that made her yearn for boredom and the mundane for the first time in her 22-year life.

Now in the aftermath, she pulled up a block away from her new house with the knowledge that it took just seven minutes to drive to her new place from her therapist's South First Street office. Seven minutes. For someone whose life was falling apart in such high definition that she could barely breathe, a longer drive to therapy would have been out of the question. The house was supposed to signal a fresh start, but Amelia couldn't help but cringe as she looked ahead, anticipating the daily, painful attempt to be a decent fucking person, all the while feeling like she was rotting from the inside out. That's the thing about depression: When you're in it, it's like you've never felt true happiness once in your life. Like every memory you could have sworn was good is now tinted grey. Every possibility stretched out before you is a preemptive disappointment, bearing a heaviness that even people who have experienced depression themselves cannot fully be with, unless they are currently in it. One cannot simply choose to access such sorrow. Depression's something that must *take* you.

Amelia put her red Range Rover in park and glanced around Old Enfield, smirking at how well her father's guilt-on-wheels gift fit with her new surroundings. Trying to ignore the way her hands vibrated in anticipation, she ground the tip of her one-hitter into a wooden dugout she kept in the center console. When her therapist called her out for being slightly stoned during the appointment last week, Amelia knew she needed to hold off on smoking until after the sessions with Cathy.

Hers was the last opinion of Amelia that mattered, after all. Cathy was the only person who'd warned Amelia that moving in fresh out of high school with her traumatized adult boyfriend was likely the worst idea ever. As the only person who ever told Amelia no, how could she not trust and respect that?

It was hard to sneak things past Cathy. Amelia had been seeing her since she was 16, AKA the first time she had abruptly stopped her medication and fell into a dark, sticky pit of depression. So at 11 a.m., this post-therapy hour was by far the latest in the day she had waited to smoke in weeks. She closed her eyes as the hitter delivered a hazy sense of peace into her lungs, pouring cool water on her smoldering, busy brain. The comforting soundtrack of hushed pop punk, mixed with the sweet crackle of burning weed, lulled her into something resembling serenity. The familiar thick, earthy scent filled the car, and she took her first full breath of the day. Like a meditation—all the way in and all the way out.

Amelia savored these last moments of relative calm before the storm. She fired her mini pipe for a few more hits before dousing herself with vanilla-scented body spray in abundance and popping a piece of gum in her mouth. She pulled around the block, and the sight of her move-in day on Wethersfield Road flooded the dash. Anxiety diluted with buzzing artificial haziness crept up her throat. Cable guys hung cords on telephone poles. Movers hauled the pieces of her old life that survived the chaos, along with hints of shiny new furniture, up the front walkway and through the front door. Upon her father's insistence, a security company installed new cameras and alarms around the perimeter. Amelia couldn't help the pang of guilt in her stomach as she watched Daddy's money pay for these well-meaning people to set up the fragments of her broken life in the delightful façade of a house now inexplicably hers.

The charming red door and quaint front porch seemed to mock her. She pulled into the driveway and prepared to continue her less and less convincing performance as someone who had their shit together. With the thunk of the car door, Amelia spotted her mom, Jen, doing a subpar job of masking her frustration by talking with a particularly cute mover. Mom "could have sworn the scuff in the coffee table wasn't there at West Elm." Amelia easily caught Cute Mover Guy's gaze and smiled coyly.

"Amelia, finally! You need to tell us where you want the purple chairs!"

Jen, as she and her sister Beth referred to their mother both to her face and behind her back, looked like she could be a lot of people's mother—just not theirs. Amelia and Beth had pale, milky skin dotted with brown freckles and blue eyes. Amelia's hair was flaming red, while Beth's was more of a strawberry milkshake blonde that Amelia had always been jealous of. But Jen had olive skin, dark brown hair, green eyes, and a resentment as deep as the ocean because she always got confused as the nanny when her daughters were growing up. The girls were the spitting image of their father, who'd moved from emotionally absent to Jen's ex-husband over the past two decades. No one could blame her for the bitterness.

"Why don't *you* tell us where the purple chairs go," she replied in a cutting tone, "since we all know you already have the entire house layout finalized in your head." Something like hurt flashed through Jen's eyes but was masked quickly by productivity as she reentered her natural state of organizing.

Levity, humor, or any amount of kindness—Amelia kept meaning for her words to have those insulating them. But lately, everything she said was a precise reflection of how she felt: achy and vile. This was no way for a person who just unironically purchased purple chairs to behave. It was also no way to talk to her mother, who had basically dedicated her entire life as of late to helping Amelia start over. Her guilt was made worse by the fact she knew this deeply. She could hear the disdain in her voice anyway. What blew her mind was that most of her anger was directed toward her mom, when it was abundantly clear to anyone that what had happened was all her dad's fault. But Amelia would let Cathy pick that one apart next week.

It was like the friendly, funny girl from before her parents' divorce was locked in a cage deep in her chest and was banging on the metal, trying to get out and treat her mom the way she deserved. Someone else had been in charge for a while now. She first met this person in her sophomore year of high school, and her first love, Trevor, would refer to her as "Shadow Amelia." The shadow would show up periodically in the years to come and thrash around violently, making everyone around her miserable, including herself. But Shadow Amelia had been spending more and more time in the driver's seat since the divorce. In the past month since the incident, it seemed more and more like she was here to stay for the long haul.

In any case, the purple chairs were more of a fuck-you than anything. Amelia had never decorated a dorm room in ridiculous colors and posters, or even picked out an over-the-top bedspread for her first apartment. She'd just sprinted headfirst into neutral tones and feigned domesticity, a state where she resided until 22. Something that she didn't admit to anyone until after her life exploded was how trapped she'd felt from the jump. It wasn't normal to fantasize about her own death or that of her significant other—but at the time, it felt like the only way to escape her lousy decision with any ounce of pride. Now she was free, no matter how she got there, and the floral Anthropologie bedspread and custom purple Pier 1 chairs, while ridiculous, were oozing the femininity and naivety missing from her past four years.

That's why the purple chairs were important, and that's why Amelia carried closest to her chest the most shameful secret of all—she was happy that it had happened. She was relieved that the wheels had come off and the proceeding crash had almost, but not all the way, killed her. Because she got out. And while currently she could barely get out of bed or draw a sober breath, she couldn't help but feel like the new house on Wethersfield was some kind of second chance. Though she had no fucking idea what that meant or what she was supposed to do with it. What she did know was the house with the charming red door and the quaint front porch was no place for Shadow Amelia.

Jen, at last, broke the deafening silence. "Let's put the chairs against the back windows?"

Amelia's guilt deflated slightly as she nodded in response, grateful that her mother could take the constant snark in stride. She wasn't sure what she would do if someone made her address the fact that she constantly acted like a dick; she would probably just give up entirely. But everyone just kept fooling themselves. This was fine, totally fine, everyone was fine; they just needed to get through move-in day and everything would be *fine*.

Amelia looked down at her worn-out chucks and picked at her cuticles before shuffling to her mom and giving her a weak side hug. "Thanks for getting here so early," Amelia offered sheepishly, wishing to God she could just be someone else, someone who was nice to her mom and could be grateful for second chances.

Jen just smiled softly and dipped her head against Amelia's shoulder, almost apologetically. God, she was pathetic; even when she was a brat, people felt sorry for her. The truth was, she needed someone to tell her how to furnish a house. But also, what to wear. What to do, what to say. Who to be. How to wake up every morning, brush her teeth, and take a shower repeatedly like she didn't just do it the day before. *Everything* was exhausting. So, thank God her mom knew where the purple chairs should go because Amelia could barely remember how to feed herself. Jen went back to unpacking boxes and directing traffic, and Amelia took the cue to wander around the new house.

Constructed in 1933, the Wethersfield bungalow was small but bigger than she needed. The original red door opened to a sitting room with a fireplace and built-in floor-to-ceiling bookshelves she was sure she could never fill. The windows, framed by a sea foam trim, let in soft natural light that filtered through delicate white drapes. To the left was a small office space, empty and begging for someone who crafted or did yoga to have their way with it. The small dining room at the center of the house seemed to beg for smiling company and inside jokes that she knew she couldn't provide, and beyond it, a medium-sized kitchen with more cabinets than Amelia knew what to do with. She opened one of them and saw her three dinner plates and two mismatched breakfast bowls stacked in a meager heap. With the opening of the drawer to the right, she found three forks, a spoon, and a butter knife, huddled together for warmth, pleading for friends.

"Me too, utensils. Me too," Amelia muttered, closing the drawer. She looked up to find a lovely window overlooking the kitchen sink. Over the sink stood a large windowsill, upon which someone with a pulse might place a vase of fresh-cut flowers.

Past the kitchen was a large living room with a vaulted ceiling and big bay windows overlooking the cutest backyard in the history of the world. Garden beds overflowed with flowers, and a wooden fence wrapped all the way around the beds except for a gap where a majestic oak older than the house and Amelia combined made up the difference. The oak had a thick trunk and an owl house perched above, the tiny roof of which housed two sunbathing squirrels. A birdbath nestled in the shade of the tree tended to blue jays who splashed and played whimsically as a soft breeze rustled the leaves above. Jesus Christ, she felt like a clinically depressed, bloated Cinderella. Amelia stared out the window with a wry smile, imagining that the fairytale mouse friends would be there to supply ample bud and pinot instead of a new dress for the ball. She shook off the thought, momentarily concerned that she had, in fact, completely and totally lost it.

The sound of four paws, slipping and sliding on unfamiliar flooring and bounding across the house, snapped Amelia out of her haunted Disney daydream. Delilah came into view from where she must have been sniffing and exploring the new digs. A rare, genuine smile spread across Amelia's face as she knelt to greet the medium-sized, yellow mutt that looked more like a dingo or a coyote than a dog.

"My sweet smooshy girl, hello! What do you think of the place?" she cooed. "Pretty good for a super mutt, huh?" Delilah offered kisses and wagged her too-long-for-her-body tail.

Delilah was, quite literally, a super mutt, at least according to the mail-in DNA test Amelia ordered. She and *the ex* got Delilah as a three-month-old puppy soon after moving into their apartment. After four years of taking care of each other, no one could deny their special connection, now made even stronger by the fact that Delilah was the only living soul with her on the night that changed everything. In fact, Amelia probably could have fought her way out of that hellish apartment sooner that night if she hadn't been so hell-bent on not leaving without the barking, terrified pup. She finally gave up, escaping alone, and for 10 minutes, as she waited for the cops at the neighbor's house, she tried not to throw up as she wondered why the barking had suddenly stopped. Delilah was unharmed. Otherwise, there would have been two people in jail that night, and only one would be missing the "attempted" prefix to manslaughter.

Amelia wandered into the bedroom with Delilah at her heels and froze. Until this moment, she hadn't fully considered what it was going to be like to fall asleep alone on her first night in the house. She had gone from living with her family to living with her boyfriend and right back to crashing with Jen—and for someone who preferred being alone, she really hated being lonely, especially where a bed was concerned.

Delilah looked up at Amelia with what could have passed for confusion and annoyance. "Well, not completely alone," she said softly.

The French doors to the backyard filtered in more of that splendid natural light that seemed to melt her like the wicked witch. Part of her couldn't wait to close the blinds and go back into her coffin, but for now, she had to go on pretending she was someone who could tolerate sunshine. The bathroom was large and updated with fancy purple tiling and a waterfall showerhead. The "his and hers" sinks seemed to scoff at her as she considered all the "hims" who would likely be coming through this space in the coming weeks and months. She knew that even if she tried to keep them away, her loneliness would win out, and they would arrive and depart like a compulsively revolving door. Her new neighbors were going to think she was running a brothel, for fuck's sake. She chuckled at the thought and mustered the courage to make herself useful and unpack a box or two.

Amelia retrieved her new bedding and sighed. Would the duvet and thousand-thread-count sheets help her ignore the fact that this was the mattress and bed frame she had shared with *him* for four years? But that was what the weed was for, to forget. Smoking insulated her from the pain and overstimulation of the outside world, an invisible bubble protecting her from the brutal impact of people's thoughts, feelings, and actions, including her own.

She considered her first time getting high as she ambled around the bedroom. At 15, that deep inhale of pungent smoke seemed to reach a deep, aching place at the center of her chest that had never been touched before. She was liberated, broken open, and yet whole for the first time. Like the substance had zeroed in on an itch she didn't even know needed to be scratched, only to leave her wondering how she'd been getting through life so itchy in the first place. But the weed no longer worked when it came to completely alleviating the perpetual discomfort. It hadn't worked in a while if she was being honest. On that depressing note, she made her bed and then went to join her mother, who was now unpacking boxes in the dining room.

Bundled up in a protective layer of bubble wrap was a framed pencil drawing of a large, brown horse's face with a white star on its forehead. The edges of the star bled out beyond the borders of a traditional marking, as if someone had dipped their thumb in the wet paint and smudged it upwards and to the left. Not exactly the most physically attractive horse in the world, her Hope, with her giant donkey-like ears. Her riding trainer, Deb, sarcastically joked about the ears when Amelia commissioned the drawing, but no one could deny the beauty, down to Hope's very soul. Even though Amelia saw Hope almost every day, she wanted the picture somewhere she could see it regularly; just the mere reminder of Hope's existence was enough to pull her back from the edge on a particularly bad day.

One of the only things tethering Amelia to this planet was this love of her big brown mare. Hope had come into her life at just the right time. During high school, Amelia had drifted away from the taxing and heavily structured world of Hunter/Jumpers that her family had historically been involved with, instead trying her hand at theatre. Still, a brush with fate brought her back to the equestrian world just in time for a highly ranked show horse to become available via a fire sale. A family emergency made it necessary for the previous owner to sell the mare quickly and at a reasonable price. Amelia swooned when she heard her show name, "Promise Me," and saw photos of the horse perfectly clearing massive, flowered jumps, the earnest, knowing eyes under those ears focused forward like she was truly trying her very best. Even then, having just moved into the doomed apartment with the ex-boyfriend, she knew that she and Hope were the ones who truly belonged together.

Hope got Amelia back in the sport after she gave up theatre, and the rigor and demands kept Amelia from having enough time to kill herself with drugs and alcohol. Hope was also why, on more than one occasion, Amelia did not decide to check out early from a life that was becoming more unbearable as the years went on. She couldn't stand the thought of someone giving Hope a thwarted explanation of why she had suddenly stopped going to the barn with her two favorite things: old-fashioned red and white peppermints and neck scratches. Hope was her reason for trying to start over in the Wethersfield house. Aside from sessions with Cathy, riding was the only time Amelia made a conscious effort to be sober. It was the only time she could stand sobriety, and Hope was the only living thing that compelled her to seek life's full presence.

As the hours went on, the carcasses of cardboard boxes stacked higher and higher on the curb of Wethersfield Road. Figments of her imagined new life took shape on the bare walls, and shards of the past lodged themselves into the floorboards, pieces of her settling like dust. Movers packed up their dollies, Jen put her finishing touches on the place, and panic muddled with relief began to set in. Soon, she would be alone, something she simultaneously craved and dreaded. She began to quietly walk her mom to the front door.

"Are you going to be OK here all by yourself tonight?" Her mother's voice startled Amelia out of her thoughts.

A pang of panic that she was becoming all too familiar with surged through her body. The sudden, disproportionate scares that were previously reserved for jumps had become a daily occurrence. She was becoming more skilled at stuffing down and covering up the alarm. "Oh yeah, I'll DoorDash some dinner and the dingo I will christen the new TV with *Drag Race*. Home sweet home."

Jen kissed her on the top of the head and began gathering her things from where she had left them in the foyer. "Don't forget to set the security system," she said as casually as possible while she opened the front door and crossed the threshold back into the world.

Not exactly something she was likely to forget.

Amelia leaned against the open door frame with Delilah at her feet and watched the last of the trucks pull away while Mom made her way down the pristine walkway to her car. Even in her catatonic state, Amelia couldn't miss the spectacular sunset that painted the sky above old West Austin in pinks, purples, and oranges that only nature could conjure. It was nice to know that even after everything, fear wasn't the only thing that could take her breath away.

As if she could sense the faint aroma of something like Hope, Jen stopped halfway to her car and turned back. "You know, I think people fall in love in this house," she said at the end of a deep sigh. "The realtor said the previous owner lived here for seven years. Started a career, met her partner, had a baby. They needed more space eventually, but..." She trailed off and looked back at the spectacular view. "I know it's been just awful. More than awful. But I think you'll find happiness here."

And with that, she walked to her car and drove away, leaving Amelia to ponder the words. She stood there a long time as the trees faded to black silhouettes in the twilight, listening to the crickets as Delilah sniffed around her new front yard. It was early April, a special time in Texas when the warm sun, cool breeze, and blankets of bluebonnets lulled you into submission before destroying you with relentless 100-plus-degree summer days.

Amelia's bare feet began to catch a chill, and she wrangled Delilah back into the house. As she shut the charming red door, she felt as though the house itself were taking a deep inhale, breathing her in, wrapping its arms around her, fierce and gentle at the same time. She was finally alone, and it had been far too long since the last time she smoked, which must be why she was assigning humanistic traits to a structure. On that note, Amelia pulled out a joint rolled with a strain her weed guy deemed "green crack" and made her way into the kitchen to locate her trusty pink Bic. She could almost feel the chemicals in her brain shift in delicious suspense as she tucked the thick, perfectly rolled bundle of bliss between her lips.

Just as she was about to light the end and *really* christen the place, she noticed an envelope on the counter. "New Owner" was written on the front in loopy cursive. Amelia's eyebrows zipped together in confusion as she inspected the envelope. Her mom must have gotten it from the realtor and left it there for her. She tore open the sealed envelope and leaned over the counter to read it.

> *Dear new owner,*
>
> *It's not in your head. This is a special and delightfully unusual place. I moved in here seven years ago with a broken heart and no clue how to move forward with my life. The loneliness was suffocating, and the sadness all-consuming. I think most of us have been there at some point in our lives, but I believe this house takes us in when we are down and lifts us back up. She will take care of you if you let her. I think she chooses us carefully. At least that's what my letter said when I moved in. And how true that turned out to be! The love that grew around me here on Wethersfield Road can no longer fit within its walls. I wish you the same healing and abundance in her wise embrace.*
>
> *—Kate*

She stared down at the letter for several poignant moments. Through the haze of her feigned indifference and skepticism, she couldn't help but recall how the house seemed to reach out the first time she saw it. As if inviting her to stay. Maybe it hadn't been mocking her after all. Maybe Amelia's wires were so crossed that good things seemed bad and bad things seemed good.

But she shook those thoughts loose with a dismissive "Interesting."

She stuffed the letter in a drawer, lit the joint, sauntered over to one of the purple chairs, and opened Tinder. She wasn't ready to be "embraced" by a house just yet, and she certainly wasn't ready to spend the night alone. As she gazed out the bay window at the barely dark sky and inhaled that first, immaculate hit, a rare city-sky shooting star leaped across the horizon—as if the Universe, the house, and the Texas sky were conspiring against her indifference, insisting that Hope lived here too.

CHAPTER 2

"I'm going to rape you, and then I'm going to kill you."

Her boyfriend of four years spoke in a dead voice from where he straddled her on the bedroom floor. He sounded robotic, like the talk-to-text function on a phone. Amelia flailed her legs, entertaining a poorly timed notion that she should be doing more weight training at the gym. She threw a desperate gaze at the phone he'd flung across the room after canceling her 911 call. Delilah's sharp, frightened barks quickly drew her attention to under the bed. Amelia's hope wore thin; she was running out of energy to fight.

"Please, Mark," she choked out. "Just stop." His hands moved to her neck. Things moved in slow motion as oxygen became scarce. She tried to recall another time when begging had been her only option. Nothing. Delilah's confused, protective yelps snapped her out of the slow-moving sludge of her thoughts.

"The dog is barking now," Mark said, matter-of-fact. "I'm going to kill the dog,"

"What the fuck is wrong with you?"

"I just need to come." His legs remained tight around her torso, his hands moving to his belt buckle. The shift in his grip catapulted her thinking into overdrive, a survival instinct bursting through the haze of this nightmare. She was overcome by a strength she didn't know she had as her arms took advantage of the sudden freedom. She punched him in the side of the head. With a childlike scream, his legs loosened their grip, and she pushed him off, springing out of the bedroom.

His words, "I am going to kill the dog," echoed in her head as she scrambled to the front door. She eyed the doorknob and then looked to the left where Delilah's leash hung on the hook and in a split-second made the decision to go back into the bedroom, leash in hand. She couldn't leave without Delilah.

"Delilah, please, baby, come here," she said, trying to hold her voice steady. "It's alright. Let's go for a walk." Amelia didn't realize she was sobbing until she heard herself pleading with Delilah from the doorway. The terrified dog slunk further into her protection under the bed, and Amelia let out a sound of distress she'd only ever heard in the movies. The wheels in her head turned to lead as they struggled to spin amongst the sticky goop of fear.

Mark came towards her again, this time chuckling maniacally.

"What the actual fuck?" she said to herself, maybe out loud, maybe in her head. It was all too chaotic to register.

His hostile laugh set her wheels back in motion as her nervous system zapped into fight mode. Her strong horsewoman's riding leg shot upward to nail him right between his legs. He fell back down to the floor with a crash.

Guess that really does the trick. Another poorly timed intrusion of her busy brain. It wouldn't take long for him to recover, and his large body blocked the opening where Delilah still cowered in fear. She knew she'd have to leave the dog to make it out in one piece. With shallow breaths, she forced her body to turn around and head back towards the front door, her steps pulling her away like magnets facing with opposite poles. Looking back towards the bedroom, she prayed to whatever Forces of Good there were that Mark couldn't fit underneath that bed frame. It might give Delilah a few minutes of safety, enough for help to arrive. Finally, she opened the door. Barefoot in her pajamas, she stepped out into what seemed to be a different world, screaming for help as she sprinted down the dark street.

Amelia sprang up in bed with a sharp gasp, clutching her heart as adrenaline shot through her body. Within a few moments, she recognized her new bedroom on Wethersfield. She attempted to regulate her breathing, which was much easier once she found the blonde ball of fur at the foot of the bed. Delilah looked at her with annoyance for disrupting her beauty sleep. Delilah was safe. She was safe.

It was just another dream. Amelia had lived at the new house for over a month and had only spent the night alone a handful of times. Because every time she went to bed without the weight of another body next to her, or every time she tried to fall asleep rather than simply losing consciousness at the hands of a substance, the dream attacked. She was catapulted back to that night, the same chunk of the event playing repeatedly, the meat of the drama unchanging but still just as petrifying each time she jolted awake in what she logically knew was the safety of a different room.

She reached for the preloaded bowl of sativa placed strategically on the nightstand for this exact reason and wasted no time lighting it. She took a deep inhale and turned on the bedside lamp, prompting another sassy look from Delilah.

"Must be nice to have a two-minute memory span." Amelia gazed longingly at Delilah as the dog drifted effortlessly back into a deep sleep. She never found out what made her stop barking so abruptly on that night of terror. Maybe Mark left the room, or maybe something more insidious, though Delilah seemed unharmed when she was finally back where she belonged in Amelia's arms. People hurt other people all the time in this fucked-up world, but Amelia believed in the depths of her soul that only a monster would hurt an innocent animal. Mark was a lot of things, but monster wasn't one of them. Or was it? She didn't even know anymore.

The sativa's buzzing hum of protection sheeted her body. With the smokey bubble of armor between her and the depraved reality of what happened two months ago, her mind began to cycle through the rest of that evening that changed everything. Some things, she was certain, would stick with her forever. The panicked face of her neighbors as they ushered Amelia into their house, having already called the police about the blood-curdling screams coming from next door. The sound of countless different sirens approaching as red and blue lights flooded the street. The confusion in her mom's voice over the phone when she answered the second call in a row from the neighbor's unfamiliar number. The inexplicable urge to tell the cops that she had taken a course on domestic violence last semester, as if to say, "This isn't supposed to happen to girls like me." The police hauling a handcuffed Mark down the front steps and into the back of a cop car. The fact that the only reason they were legally allowed to arrest him in the state of Texas was not that he attacked her, but that he punched an officer. The shock that Mark had been hoarding boxes of ammunition and guns in the closet. Her inappropriate recognition of how sexy one of the cops was as he shook his head and breathed out the words, "You got really lucky tonight."

She knew from her course last semester that the person most likely to kill you is your domestic partner, and she knew the exact statistics confirming what Sexy Cop had said. She did get *really* lucky that night. She didn't harbor the perspective to acknowledge that the word "lucky" could be synonymous with "white" or "rich." What if the color of her skin was darker and the cops hadn't believed her story about the attack they never witnessed? What if Daddy's money hadn't been able to break her lease and buy her a house? What if-What if-What if. Having the last name Glickman in Texas was certainly not an assurance of special treatment. But once again, her immense, undeserved privilege had saved the day. Though none of that mattered in the moments before she escaped. She'd just been a woman trapped in a house with a dangerous man. Privilege was convenient in enduring the aftermath, sure. But as she fought for her life, nothing existed but the sound of her breaths and the sheer determination to make sure they would not be her last.

Amelia sighed as she pushed out the smoke from her lungs along with the remnants of adrenaline from her nightmare. Nightmare? Flashback?

Trip down memory lane? She never knew what to call these hellish twists of the mind that felt so visceral. She was always astonished by the accuracy, the precision, the consistency of these scenes as they played back in her sleep. It was like her brain was hooked to some sort of demented projector. But that's what she got for trying to go to bed alone. Or not nearly fucked-up enough.

Amelia pulled up Instagram absentmindedly and began to scroll as she let the high settle over her bones like a weighted blanket. She looked through her social accounts often, eager to gauge how the rest of the world experienced her. She was having trouble faking it in real life, but damn if she couldn't still turn it on for a picture. In one from graduation, she wore a smile that almost reached her eyes, pointing with glee at the diploma she held in her hand. Social media was spared the argument between her dad and Jen that followed this fabricated snapshot of joy and confidence almost immediately. Also not captured: She just barely graduated. She frequently wondered what an honest caption might sound like.

"Hanging on by a thread! *heart emoji* Hit the like button so I don't kill myself lol!"

Amelia scoffed and rolled her eyes, continuing her scroll until she came across a photo Mark's friend posted of himself playing beer pong. Something twisted in her stomach. Fucking Caleb. He had become Amelia's friend by proxy over the years, but she hadn't spoken to him since he sat her down a few weeks ago over a pitcher of Lonestar and tried to convince her to forgive Mark. The conversation was fuzzy, thanks to the alcohol-infused trauma response, but she heard the words "psychotic break" and "second chance" at least a few times.

It wasn't the first time one of their mutual drinking buddies had made this argument. It made Amelia's skin crawl. "He blacked out," they would say. "He feels horrible. He's lost everything."

But she didn't really care, not the way she pretended to. Morally and therefore publicly, she wished for him the best mental health treatment money could buy and a happy, full, beautiful life. Inwardly and at her most primal core, she felt nothing but hatred. Sometimes an acquaintance would ask how she knew he was *actually* going to kill her. She'd just gawk at them, because how do you explain that? "Um, I just sort of took his word for it?" You see, when someone looks at you and, without an ounce of irony, declares they intend to kill you, you sort of just believe them. Those people weren't there to see that look in his eyes. They didn't watch the ability to connect to another human being drain away from the face of someone they'd lived with for four years.

How fucking dare they.

Amelia closed Instagram and chucked her phone across the room, drawing another exasperated sigh from Delilah. She wished for a different set of circumstances, a life where she could keep Delilah and Hope and change everything else. So many different realities all existed at the same moment in time. That's what plagued her worst of all: At the exact moment her life was flashing before her eyes, someone out there was falling in love, having mind-blowing sex, eating an ice cream cone, watching *The Office*, or laughing at a dirty joke. Why couldn't it be her, then? Why couldn't it be her *now*? None of this was supposed to happen to someone like her. It was some kind of sick joke, and she was waiting for the punch line. Because in what world was it normal for a 22-year-old college senior to sit on the bathroom floor typing out an affidavit?

Such a weird word: aff-a-dave-it. This was required for the protective order her lawyer and father insisted upon. In it, she explained the disturbing phone conversation that caught her attention on the night of the attack, the direct threats to kill her and the dog, the interrupted 911 call, and the restraint. But what she couldn't explain in this objective and factual law document was how suddenly, on a Sunday evening after family dinner at her mom's, the entire world was flipped on its axis.

She'd been too high in the preceding weeks to pick up on the signs of a manic episode. She thought Mark was just smoking too much when he said he'd cracked the code to life and excitedly tried to share his newfound wisdom with her. She was so focused on her own dwindling mental health that she hadn't seen the red flags blazing past her until they were on fire in his eyes.

The protective order would last one year. For 12 full months, Mark was not legally allowed near her or her home, her nonexistent place of work, or Greystone Farm where she rode Hope. He was also not allowed to contact her in any way. Two months down, 10 to go. She wondered who she would be when the order ended. Would she still be the same self-proclaimed stoner slut on her throne of luxurious bedding? Would she still be thinking about Mark at least once every few hours? Would she still feel like a scream looking for a mouth?

She wouldn't be able to hold on much longer to the ledge of sanity she clutched onto. She was running out of steam. Deep down, her options included turning into a completely different person or not being a person at all. Problem was, she wasn't sure which sounded better. If it hadn't been for her girls Hope and Delilah, no one could say how much sooner her will to fight would have dwindled that night. Maybe it would have been better not to fight at all. But something in her did, perhaps the same part of her that the house on Wethersfield Road called out to in the first place.

The question she hadn't dared ask was who Mark might be in 10 more months. Someone who wanted to get in touch with her the moment he was legally able, or would he have moved on completely and all but forgotten her name? Feeling bad for what he did, or not remembering what he did in the first place? Would he have outrun his demons, or would they have cornered him and torn him to bloody, mangled pieces the way Amelia's threatened to do to her? The idea of anyone being mad at her was something that caused the utmost anxiety for Amelia, so the idea that someone could want to harm her seemed like next-level torture.

She took another hefty hit of her medicine and rolled over, leaving her phone on the other side of the room so she'd be forced to get out of bed when her alarm went off in a few hours. She had riding training tomorrow at the barn and some big competitions to prepare for; winning with her horse was the last piece of self-worth she possessed. While Amelia was used to letting down the humans in her life, she wasn't ready to let Hope down just yet. When that day came, she'd really be fucked. The very walls of the house on Wethersfield seemed to whisper a lullaby of creaks and shifts, settling into a natural symphony. She dozed off restlessly, trying in vain to draw pleasant dreams out of the abyss.

CHAPTER 3

To no one's surprise, but respectable adults' shock, Amelia had been sexually active since the ripe age of 13. She never had unsatisfied customers over the years, yet the need to prove herself was constant. Even as a teenager, it was hard to feel appealing if she wasn't getting laid. Unfortunately, there would always be someone classically "hotter" than her and, therefore, always a better hookup option.

If she'd been born in the Baroque Era, she would have seriously cleaned up. But her pale skin and soft curvature were not a sought-after look in the Aughts. This put her habitually on edge, begging to exist in someone else's eyes, auditioning for the role of a lifetime with every sexual favor she performed. There was something powerful in being perceived and desired, and she yearned for it like it was her only sustenance.

The first thing Amelia ever believed in was true love. Snow White, Cinderella, and the rest of that gang all insisted that her one true love awaited and that with him, *everything* would make sense. That first kiss would stop time, and they would live happily ever after. When she watched *Aladdin* as a kid, she thought about how warm his skin must have felt. She was pleasantly surprised to find her next-door neighbor's hand to be as toasty as she imagined, and it thawed her from the inside out.

Maybe this was the reason she had always been desperate for male attention and why physical contact and love had been synonymous for just as long. One might also blame the sleepover in third grade where she watched porn for the first time: She could still see her best friend

Katie's innocent face staring at the glowing screen in wonder as she uttered, "Look how much he loves her." What it looked like to Amelia on the family room's VCR/TV combo was two strangers fucking for money. She still took performance notes. She figured they'd be useful in a few years, at most. Somewhere between Disney and PornHub, sex and love became irrevocably intertwined in a way hookup culture would endlessly shit on. At least that was half of the truth.

The other half was that Amelia always wanted to touch and be touched. Ever since she was seven in Brian Harbor's basement, playing house and holding his body to hers, she wished she could stay in that fort of blankets and broomsticks forever. She wished for the zing of pleasure when she touched her bare knee to Eric Smith's under the art table in first grade to last just as long. Over the years, Amelia chased that sense of security and excitement right into dirty bar bathrooms and poorly lit alleyways. Not places for a princess, but that didn't matter anymore. She found it would never make sense how Cinderella had the willpower to head home at midnight when Prince Charming looked so delicious at the top of that grand staircase. Even when he begged her to stay. The lack of willpower was probably one of many reasons no one had ever mistaken Amelia for a Disney princess.

Amelia was perceptive, even from a young age, so she discovered quickly how much harder she had to work to be noticed. Blonde petite girls like Sarah and Susan seemed to get this attention without even trying—or wanting it, for that matter. It was total bullshit. Completely unfair; the more they pulled away, the more they were chased. Pulling away had never been in Amelia's nature, and every time she held herself back the way she saw the other girls do, the way the boys seemed to *respond* to, it was like stuffing her desire to be loved into a pressure cooker until she blew the lid right off and made even more of a spectacle.

For this reason, she had always wanted to be someone else from the inside out. She'd stare at herself in the security mirror above the tapes at Blockbuster as she walked among the aisles, silently praying to be made over again down to her very bones and chemistry. Then she'd pick out a movie starring an actress with a body she would never have, in a love story she could never emulate, then fall victim to the belief that mutual, swift orgasms were the norm. Over and over and over again.

But the internet was a great place to pretend to be someone else. She used to make up screen names on AIM and chat with the cute boys in her grade, manipulating them into telling her persona whether they thought "Amelia" was hot or gross. Sometimes she would even talk shit about herself to see who defended her.

"Wouldn't it be easier to fuck her with a bag over her head?" she once said about herself under the guise of a classmate. This story was the final piece of a puzzle that later led her therapist Cathy to believe there might be a repressed memory of sexual assault deep inside her. It might explain her sick mentality around sex and attraction, even as a child. Using a fake screen name, she told Toby Garrett, the boy she obsessed over, how hot all the boys at a different school thought Amelia was.

Toby, who knew her well enough at this point through no effort or desire of his own, copied and pasted the conversation to send to the "real Amelia," adding, "You're finally hot! It's what you've always wanted." She died a little inside, but that didn't stop her from bullying herself on the internet every night while the pre-teen male population of Austin watched. Why had this talking shit about herself, and waiting for a knight in shining armor to come to her defense, become a favorite pastime?

By her early 20s, she had an inkling that what she was doing on Tinder wasn't far off from her manipulation games on Instant Messenger as a middle schooler. Sprawled on her couch at Wethersfield like a corpse, legs propped up on one of the purple chairs, she swiped compulsively, looking for her next stranger to invite into her body. She'd convinced herself this was how to harness her power. But somewhere deep down, she knew she was actually giving it away. Ever since she learned that the best method of getting Toby Garrett's attention was to talk about sex, she had been trying to gain a secret power by giving it all away to the person in front of her. Even if they didn't ask for it nicely. Or at all.

In this way, every sexual encounter other than her first love, Trevor, had been transactional, her most recent ex, Mark, included. In fact, she hadn't made a conscious decision to have sex with someone since she and Trevor broke up in her junior year of high school. Nevertheless, she persisted with her endless loop of attention and emptiness.

Trevor lived on the outskirts of Austin those days, and there was a tiny piece of her that yearned for his goofy smile and mop of shaggy brown hair to appear during her nightly swipes. She imagined what it would be like to see him walking in; would they pick up right where they left off? He was her first love, after all. They lost their virginities to each other and then dated between 14 and 17, growing up together.

Throughout their entire relationship, she had this fear that she was going to fuck up the best thing that had ever happened to her. She might have been on to something. She dealt with severe mental health symptoms all throughout high school, and the brunt of this was constantly flung in Trevor's direction. She wound up breaking his heart, even though her entire existence had been plagued by the fear of him breaking hers. She shattered her own soul before someone else could get to it first. She had loved him so much it hurt.

She didn't remember ever being in love with Mark in that way, but she must have been. She could see the memories with him played back, the giggling and snuggling. But she couldn't remember what it *felt* like. With Trevor, it was the opposite. She couldn't picture it; that body and that life felt so far away, but for the feelings she experienced. They were teenagers. He told her she made his heart horny, and they laughed until they couldn't breathe because that was the age where that still came easily and because nothing had ever described an emotion more accurately. That was exactly what it felt like—like her heart was on fire, causing it to beat out of control like an overheated machine. Sometimes it seemed like all she was doing with her life was trying to recreate that same high.

This forecast was getting too heavy for a Thursday night. Amelia swiped left on a particularly cute guy named Tom, and dopamine flooded her brain as the app sprung to life, declaring that it was a match. The early June streaks of sunset filtered into the room, and for just a moment, she felt whole. She sipped pinot grigio from the bottle and typed out her standard dating app greeting: "Heyyyy," because, of course, she wasn't waiting for him to make the first move. Somehow, this one misspelled word always communicated exactly what she needed it to; it said so much by saying so little. In less than 10 seconds, Tom responded, and they were off to the races of preliminary banter.

> Tom: well hey there sunshine :) What's up?

> Amelia: not much, just BORED

> Tom: bored? We can't have that. Any plans tonight?

> Amelia: not yet...

She was shameless.

> Tom: well I was thinking of going down to the bar at the W on 2nd with a couple of buddies, maybe around 9? Bring some of your friends and we can all hang :)

Shit... She twiddled her texting-toned thumbs and took another swig of the pinot, trying to come up with a good reason why all her nonexistent friends would be busy on the same night.

> Amelia: W sounds cool... I think all my friends are working tonight : (

> Tom: bummer.

> Amelia: I hear that I'm fun for the whole family, though.

She swore sometimes things just flew out of her mouth, or fingers, in this instance.

> Amelia: sorry, weird joke.

> Amelia: lol

Amelia: but should I still go or...

She rolled her eyes until she could see the inside of her skull and asked the slut gods to grant her even just a crumb of game.

Tom: lol... all good, I'll see you at 9.

Phew. Amelia shot up like she had been given a reason to live another day and began getting ready. First, she fed Delilah and left the back door to the yard open so the pup could go do her business and have some outside time; she never knew when she'd be home, after all. Then she hopped in the shower and began shaving and moisturizing everything below her belly button, something she could probably do in her sleep at this point. As she slathered her legs in shaving cream, she caught sight of the deep purple bruises on her thighs, and the memory of a recent debauched escapade flooded all five of her senses. She'd tried to forget, but it kept sneaking back into her psyche.

It had been a misty, humid day a few weeks back. The entire area of her face below her nose had been slightly pink and tender because she'd burned off all her pale blonde facial hair and potentially a thin layer of skin with the Sally Hanson removal cream. She'd bought it on one of her stoned late-night snack runs to CVS. Concealer hid most of the evidence, but her skin stung and sizzled in the heat with the reminder. She was drinking so many different kinds of alcohol that afternoon on Rainey Street that she could have opened a bar inside her body and invited all her organs to come to have a drink on the house.

"I'm just a really sexual person." The words were past her lips and hanging in the thick Texas summer air before she could filter them into her "don't be a ho for once" file. It was a day date, for fuck's sake. The 30-something Iraq War vet devoured it, and she knew she had already given up her choice in the matter of whether they were hooking up later. The truth remained that she hadn't made a conscious choice to have sex with somebody in years. It always just *happened*. No wasn't even a word in her vocabulary—as if she was conditioned to believe herself lucky that they even wanted her in the first place. She thought it would be rude to say no, especially after all the drinks they usually bought her, and this dude was no exception.

They checked into the Casulo, a trashy hotel on I-35. Maybe it was because somewhere in her wisest mind, though she didn't have a stop button, she knew this was not a dude she wanted to give her address to. She was pretty sure the front desk guy thought she was a hooker. *Might as well be.* They stumbled into the tacky hotel room streaked by late afternoon light and she kind of left her body after that. All she could remember was the pain and how she wanted to ask him to stop. She just couldn't. She was so quick to sell herself out with suggestive language when it came to someone wanting something from her. But when it was something *she* needed, the words got stuck in her chest, convinced they weren't worthy of coming out. Especially when those words were along the lines of "no" or "stop." If she told men to do something different, how would she ever win the game of "best sex of your life" or "world's most unforgettable girl?"

As she continued to maneuver her trusty Venus razor, her bare skin broke out in the bad kind of goosebumps that made the hair you just shaved off grow back instantly, and she felt consumed by the idea that someday, if she ever had to put herself back to together, it was going to take a while even to find the pieces. She definitely needed to finish that bottle of wine before driving, yes driving, over to the W. Amelia thought her reluctance to *ride* under the influence would be a pretty cute joke to tell at parties. If she ever got invited to one. She had absolutely no perspective. She was the piece of shit at the center of the Universe; everyone and everything else was collateral.

Once she got out of the shower, she scrunched curl cream in her long red hair. She wasn't above going out with it wet, not that anyone would look at her twice in Austin. Though the W was more Dallas-y than Austin-y... But whatever. She hadn't eaten much that day, so she shoved a few gluten-free cookies in her mouth. A nutritionist had told her gluten caused inflammation and could be contributing to her depressive symptoms, and she'd been gluten-free for a few weeks. The epitome of health and wellness. Amelia threw on a pair of jeans and a tank, finished finessing her makeup mask, polished off the bottle of pinot, and ensured Delilah was inside before heading out the door and hopping into the Red Range. As she pulled out of the driveway, she cranked up some Kesha. She could almost feel her charming bungalow roll its eyes as she took off down Enfield Road and headed east toward downtown.

It was one the next morning by the time she struggled to fit her key back into the lock at the side door. Delilah was happier to see her than Amelia deserved, and the glow of the house seemed to usher her inside like a flabbergasted but doting mother. She was bringing men to her home less and less, and she momentarily wondered if the house had set some unspoken rules or boundaries around this that she'd been following inexplicably. She set the alarm system, collapsed onto the couch, and dove back into the box of gluten-free cookies. Delilah was quick to curl up at her feet now that Amelia was back where she belonged physically. Mentally, she was back at the W. She replayed the night, simultaneously titillated and mortified by the images as they flashed by in another one of her brain's demented slide shows.

She had walked into the W with buzzing, nervous energy that always accompanied meeting a stranger from the internet IRL. Her biggest fear wasn't getting murdered but that they'd be disappointed once they saw her in the flesh. That she wouldn't be hot enough, or that they'd think she was catfishing them. But in dozens of encounters, this had only happened once.

But this was a good night. Tom looked absolutely thrilled to see her cross the threshold of the bar. He was tall, thin, and clean-cut in a button-down polo. Way better than his picture. The luck of her swipe was intoxicating, and within five minutes of chatting, she wrapped her hands around his neck and kissed him. Then she gave him *the signal*. It was the same one every time: she'd arch her back, press her chest against them, bite their lower lip, and let out a small whimper. It was like kicking them into high gear. Everything sprang out of hunger from that point on. Faster, breathier, harder, wetter. The signal was always an immediate result of her "fuck it" brain taking over. She thought this was the point at which she took control, but in reality, this was when she gave it all over to her impulses and, in turn, to whoever's arms she was in. Amelia would have bet money on those impulses being pleasure-based, but the truth was, it was all fear.

Next thing she knew, she was leading him into a stairwell and unbuttoning his pants. *Is semen gluten-free?* She sank to her knees, and then her mind went blank in that familiar way as the saga of constantly, and literally, putting herself in that one-down position marched on. When he finished and pulled up his pants, she wiped her mouth with the back of her hand and giggled, asking him if he was going to blow her off and never call her again.

"Are you kidding? After that head?"

It was the nicest thing a man had said to her in a long time.

That realization should have been more depressing, and maybe it was, deep down somewhere. It was just stuck beneath a rotting heap of unprocessed emotions, enough to fill a football stadium. But at least it was just a blow job. She could almost hear her mother ranting about how Bill Clinton had convinced an entire generation that oral sex wasn't really sex, and she chuckled to herself. Monica Lewinski was actually someone Amelia personally identified with. Curvy girls needed to stick together. And she understood how one might find themselves in a situation such as that. She was proud of herself for not going all the way on the first date.

That restraint was far from automatic, or even common. On one date about a month ago, she made a deal with herself that she was not putting out that night for any reason whatsoever. But this was Amelia, so she and the Tech Bro of the week quickly ended up on the roof of a parking garage. He kissed down her body and unzipped her pants, muttering something about wanting to taste her—which was like fucking

Christmas, to be honest, because Mark had always refused to partake in that particular activity. That probably should have been her first red flag.

Tech Bro's tongue tickled her skin and his fingers crept up her inner thighs. *It's just third base, right? I'm not going to go for the homer. That's all that matters.* Then she remembered why she had taken sex off the table for herself that night in the first place. She had a hemorrhoid. The poor bastard was about to go down on her and orally discover a *fucking hemorrhoid.* Arguably the worst way to discover one, though they were all unfortunate.

She was a horseback rider with IBS, so these weren't all that uncommon. But still, it wasn't something she advertised, especially to the guys she was hooking up with. He was much less likely to notice this unfortunate ailment if his face wasn't between her legs, and she was barreling forward too quickly to grasp for anything along the lines of "slow down." So instead, she gasped, "Um, I can't handle waiting? Fuck me instead!" He didn't need a lot of convincing.

She finished off the box of cookies and peeled herself off the couch to let Delilah into the backyard. The little blonde dog trotted out to the lush lawn with glee and Amelia looked at the sprinkling of stars that managed to shine bright enough to compete with the twinkling lights of Austin. A chorus of cicadas and crickets lulled her into deep thoughts about loneliness and outer space, but she was eventually distracted by the discomfort of booze from earlier that night and the full box of gluten-free cookies settling in her stomach and begging for release.

She was annoyed by her body's insistence that she take care of this release in the bathroom before passing out in bed. But she knew her habit of many years always got what it wanted. She called Delilah back into Wethersfield and set the alarm, but the security system didn't keep her safe from the most dangerous influence of all: herself. How cliché. The house seemed to ache for her as she ambled to the bathroom like a slave. Amelia got on her knees to pray to the god of shame, reaching inside to pull out all her sins. Then she flushed them away.

CHAPTER 4

As the door closed on June, July brought with it the promise that darkness can always deepen. Something had shifted, and Amelia had barely seen the light of day unless it was to train with Hope, crack the door open for Delilah to run outside, drive the seven minutes to therapy in her pajamas, or reach her arm out into the abyss to grab a delivery, and that was taking all the life force energy she could muster. All her meals were Doordashed, her fridge and pantry were empty but for remnants of takeout, and laundry was strewn about the house as if she had shed a million bougie skins. The charming Wethersfield house smelled like a cross between a distillery and a dispensary, and she treated it like the loneliest frat house in the world. It still insisted on cradling her as she fractured into a thousand pieces, like an ever-loving container for her chaos.

Amelia would have loved to blame her parents' divorce for damaging her ability to love and be loved. Maybe it was the fact that Mark had sucked the life out of her until there was nothing left, but truthfully, she was ill at heart, and had been for a long time. The hardest truth to swallow had been the role she played in the toxic relationship with Mark. As deeply as the victim role appealed to her, she knew it took two to tango and that she tended to drive people to their breaking point. Of course, what happened to her that night of the sirens was not something she or anyone else ever deserved, but it was also not something that existed in a vacuum. Ever since she was an infant, people older and smarter had been telling her that she was too much, and it was hard not to apply that to this instance.

Even her parents echoed this sentiment. Of course, they didn't mean to. Her mom and dad loved telling the story of how she used to willfully avoid her crib by sticking her stubby little fingers down her throat and puking up a mess once she was put to bed just so she could keep playing with her toys while they cleaned it up. They thought it was a *hilarious* memory. And maybe it would have been if it wasn't something she still struggled with or a blaring example of such an urgent need to constantly change the way she felt. It was as if that need was lodged in her very essence, outshining even her earliest memories. Rumor had it that the moment she was born with bright red hair and vibrant, wide-open blue eyes, she fixed her intense gaze on her dad and then her mom before bursting into a guttural scream as if to say, "Good luck, fuckers."

Amelia held that same potent eye contact with herself now in the bathroom mirror at Wethersfield, marveling at the red splotches on her cheeks, the bloodshot veins looking back at her, and the tears streaming down her face. The next part of her routine included washing her hands and brushing her teeth vigorously, but she always appreciated that gratifying moment of leaning onto the bathroom sink, heaving like she had just run a marathon, basking in the light-headed high. She tried not to let her thoughts linger on the way she could feel her body starting to break down as a result of the drinking, smoking, and purging that populated her life each day. Finally, she shook her head to break the trance and completed the cycle for the second time that day.

Usually, she tried to limit herself more, but she'd just gotten back from her dad's house, and the feelings this brought up usually demanded the stuffing and discarding she'd become so accustomed to. The home on Lake Austin that used to belong to her family now belonged to her father and his girlfriend and was constantly undergoing renovations—probably so that he didn't wake up every morning with the eerie reminder that they weren't a family anymore. Every time she went there, something looked different, and her heart broke a little more. The sanctuary in the upper right corner, where she suffered through school and early symptoms of mental illness, was now a classy guest room. Her dad and his girlfriend were staying in it while he remodeled the marital suite he and her mom used to share. *And no one was saying any of it out loud.*

After completing the purging ritual, she plopped down on one of the purple chairs and lit a joint. Amelia always knew when she was beginning to flail mentally; she played the same movie over and over again on the television in the background, like a soundtrack of all the ways she was a disappointment. It was the movie that had broken her heart by lifting her up out of the depressing droll of normal life, teasing her with the false promise of being *almost* special, and then dropping her. The gods of film laughed as she plummeted back to earth. Whenever this movie was on, no matter what she was doing around the house, she was haunted by the girl who was better than her. The girl who dated NFL quarterbacks and released catchy pop albums to her millions of followers. All while Amelia rotted in irrelevance. She could see and feel the scene of the cattle call audition where they'd faced off like it was yesterday.

Her theatre class attended the auditions for the experience, assuming no one would get a callback. They were a prestigious fine arts academy that prided itself on providing their students with real-life experience for their future careers. But Amelia's intense blue eyes must have spoken to the big-time Hollywood casting director, because she and her family were pleasantly surprised with two callbacks. She didn't get the role, but she heard later she made it to the top 10. Their reasoning for not selecting her? She was too over the top in her performance.

She quit her high school acting after this experience and refused to go through with college auditions, too heartbroken to continue her career. But it was really just an excuse to smoke all the weed she wanted. She slipped into the narrative of being almost good enough like one might slip into a soft, warm bed. It was comforting and suffocating all at once. Amelia was never lacking in potential; the follow-through was where she would float into nothingness like a smokey exhale.

The buzz of her phone on the coffee table sent her bloodshot eyes squinting to read the new text.

Dad: Thanks for coming by today. We always love seeing you.

She didn't respond. How could she? She was still processing the fact that only four and a half years ago, her parents were still married, her family still under one roof. At least figuratively. Amelia's dad had been gone for work 90 percent of the time ever since the Chicago incident.

When her dad hit it big in business, Amelia's family moved to the suburbs of Chicago very briefly. She was 13. She couldn't blame it on the location per se, but ever since Chicago she had dabbled in bulimia et al. Every dysfunctional seedling that had been taking root below her surface seemed to break ground and begin to bloom when they got to Chicago in the dead of her seventh-grade winter break. The flirtatious attention-seeking online became cybersex and naked photos. The light food restriction and research on how to make herself throw up became a daily, practiced exercise. Then the inkling that she was somehow different from the rest of her peers became crippling depression and thoughtfully drafted suicide notes in her journal.

Everyone in the family struggled to live in that place; Amelia just did it out in the open, loud enough for all four of them to feel spoken for. All of their sorrow and doubt filtered through the family system and out through a toiling Amelia. So much so that the Glickman family decided to head back to Austin barely six months into the uprooting of their lives, but her dad would keep the job in Chicago and just, *make it work*.

However, they didn't return to their normal house on the Enclave Mesa cul-de-sac, with the creek running through the back of the neighborhood where Beth and Amelia grew up collecting tadpoles with their neighborhood friends. They moved to the gargantuan house on Lake

Austin simply because they *could*. In many ways, Chicago was both the beginning and the end of everything.

At the end of that school year, before they moved back to Austin, her science teacher had pulled her aside and asked her why she'd turned into "such a bad kid all of a sudden." Though she hadn't even considered her emotional state on the matter, she confessed tearfully that she, her mom, and her sister were moving back to Austin but that her dad was staying there for work. Her teacher's face softened, and he said he was sorry she was going through such a hard time. Of course, she left out the fact that her dad would be commuting back to Austin every weekend...but nevertheless, she went out into the hallway and felt a rush of grief fill her heart and spill from her eyes. This was likely the moment she realized her parents were over, even if she didn't consciously accept the fact until it came out of her dad's mouth years later. When all was said and done, a middle school science teacher whose name she couldn't remember knew about the brokenness in their family before any of them did.

If you had asked her at that point if she thought her parents would ever get divorced, she would have told you to go fuck yourself. Her parents were soul mates. They knew everything, and they were everything. That's why it was so earth-shattering when her dad sat them down in 2011 and said he was just...done. Done with being married specifically, but in turn, done with all of them as a unit. Amelia still couldn't believe that her dad could want to fuck other people more than he wanted to stay a family.

"What, are you getting a *divorce?*" Beth had first joked at the family dinner when their parents said they had something serious they needed to discuss. Amelia laughed along. She'd never forget the way her parents' faces turned white in response. This silent confirmation hung in the air, the family twisting like a ghost on a noose as the world shifted on its axis.

Mom moved out a few weeks later, and the house on the lake had never been the same, both physically and emotionally. Amelia and Beth spent the rest of high school splitting time between the two houses, but Amelia only had to deal with this for nine months before she spread her wings all the way to North Austin three miles up the road to "settle down" with Mark and start college. Amelia always felt guilty leaving her sister in that mess to fend for herself those next few years, but now Beth was finally off being a cute little genius getting her BA in English and gender studies in Connecticut, *actually* spreading her wings in a place where all four seasons, new faces, and adventure sat blissfully at her fingertips.

Meanwhile, Amelia extracted the shards of two broken homes out of her wounds from the divorce and Mark's attack. She'd tried to see through the blood and gore of those gaping wounds. She wanted to see her dad the way she used to. But watching him date around and then finally meet his current girlfriend made it seem impossible. Her mom, Jen, hung onto her sanity by a fucking thread and finally met someone. Both of her parents now lived with their new lovers, acting like idiots in the gauzy new phase of their relationships. And there she was, traumatized, single—and feeling as if the other three members of her family of origin had moved on and not provided a forwarding address.

After the divorce was finalized, Amelia and her dad would meet for coffee, and she made it her mission to understand where he was coming from. All he could offer was that he felt like he was dying in the marriage. Jen had not so subtly implied that there had been other women. Her mom's behavior since the divorce had also been far from perfect, and Amelia was stunned at the sight of both parents toppling from the pedestal she had perched them upon during childhood. The inertia from their fall had sucked the gravity from the atmosphere, and she was still holding on for dear life lest she lose her grip and go floating out into the abyss.

Her reflections halted abruptly when she noticed she had smoked the joint down to her fingertips. On that Sunday afternoon, the harsh rays of the Texas sun cast spotlights on the dusty floor. Delilah napped peacefully in the one closest to Amelia's feet. She and Delilah were leaving for Santa Fe first thing in the morning, and she wondered how she would make the 12-hour drive alone, belted in beside her thoughts, especially when she had already been spending so much time alone in the confines of Wethersfield. She figured that once she arrived in New Mexico, she would be okay because she would be with Hope and Delilah. Greystone Farm, where she competed and trained, had never entered this Santa Fe competition. She loved going to a horse show somewhere new with Hope—it was always exciting to hear a new voice at a fresh ring with equally fresh competition announce, "Next on course is number blah blah blah, Promise Me, ridden by Amelia Glickman."

There weren't many Jewish girls on the show circuit in the South, and Amelia always got a kick out of hearing the name Glickman ring out across the fairgrounds. Growing up, her grandmother shared a one-bedroom apartment with five family members in the heart of Brooklyn. She and Amelia's grandfather worked hard to build a launch point for her father to become as successful as he was, and Amelia still wore the ruby pinkie ring her grandmother bought when she finally made her own money as a young adult. Amelia never failed to consider the journey the ring took from Brooklyn to the show as she cantered into the arena in her expensive show coat, ruby ring hidden under leather riding gloves, lulled by Hope's cadence, on their way to place above horses worth well into the six figures. Because most of those horses and riders, no matter how fancy or experienced they were, couldn't hear one another the way Amelia and Hope could, communicating wordlessly, like a silent dance to the rhythm of the earth as it spun, gliding over flowery obstacles, almost pausing in midair, just to show off.

The same molten need for performance and attention that drove Amelia's short-lived acting career gave her a competitive edge in the horse show ring. After the failed audition, she stumbled through life aimlessly until Hope and a lifetime love of horses swooped in to cushion the coming blows. It was as if something greater, some Force of Good, had sent Hope to Amelia and with specific instructions: "Your job is to make sure things don't get *too* out of hand."

Amelia couldn't wait to see Hope again. The horses from Greystone Farm and her trainer, Deb, always left a few days early. She was eager to press kisses to the smudged, white mark on Hope's forehead and feed her the peppermints she had been stocking up on. The most real thing in her life had always been her connections with Delilah and Hope; in the past few months, it had also been the *only* real thing in her life. Maybe getting away with her dog and her horse was exactly what she needed to break out of the depressing ritual of her life. Maybe she could take a tolerance break from smoking, drink less wine, and avoid Tinder while she was out there. She'd get some good sleep and even journal a bit—like a mini-retreat.

Amelia even decided to leave her stash home in Austin, a bold move for a daily smoker with severe clinical depression who barely took her prescribed medication. *Might as well get good and fucked-up before the little respite.* She opened a bottle of wine and poured it into an honest-to-God glass to kickstart the turning over of her new leaf. But the wine glass didn't stop her from finishing the bottle by the time she was done packing for Santa Fe; it just put a few more steps between her and relief.

The sun was setting as she surveyed her packed bags and a pile of Delilah's essentials: a Tempur-Pedic dog bed, a large bag of unnecessarily high-end kibble, K9 fish oil supplements, and her plush lamby. She had to be the most spoiled super mutt in all the land. The everyday lonely restlessness began to creep in, eating a pit in her stomach. She knew going out to a bar was out of the question; in fact, she hadn't gone out on a date in weeks. Instead, she snatched up her MacBook and flopped onto her bed with it after closing the door to her room for some privacy from Delilah's judgmental gaze. She opened the laptop, yanked down her tank top to reveal the mounds of freckled flesh atop her chest, and went to one of the video chat websites she frequented. This was yet another habit that spanned almost a decade, and the more agoraphobic she became during one of her bouts of depression, the more her thirst for attention and praise insisted on such online rendezvous.

She'd had a love-hate relationship with screens ever since the movie audition debacle but had been exploring the dark corners of chatrooms since well before that. She talked to strange men online long before it was legal for her to do so and hadn't stopped since. When she logged into Chatroulette and shut off her brain to exist in someone else's eyes, unlike the movie magic of Hollywood, there was a twinge of danger involved.

She preferred this way of meeting her needs; she didn't have to leave home or even talk to anyone if she didn't want to. Instead of wasting a night on someone with whom she shared no chemistry due to an unfortunate swipe, she could just click the "next" button and try again until one of the stranger's voices hit the place deep within herself that she was trying to reach. She felt like a puppet master, pulling this string, tugging at that one, watching the peaking and crashing interest in her, playing the game of "Do I exist, now?" with anyone who would follow her rules. She failed to realize she was the puppet. She was *always* the puppet.

She loved being able to precisely manipulate and observe the image she was portraying to these men in a small, digital box like she was a god. But more than anything, she wanted to be airbrush perfect like she was on-screen. She wanted her skin to be the same shade of color all over her body. Smooth and soft and hairless, free of blemishes or bumps. She wanted her breasts to hold themselves up and her nipples to look slightly pink and always erect. She wanted a perfectly bare vulva cut and pasted onto her grown woman's body, two folds of angelic skin hiding what she was taught to be ashamed of unless otherwise instructed by a man. She wanted to be simultaneously subhuman and superhuman. And screens gave her that, even if just for a moment.

She had almost been special enough to crystallize this flawless image of herself on a silver screen and leave her mark on the world indefinitely. As pathetic as it was, she still resented her near brush with fame as a teenager and shamelessly told the story in her 20s. The story of the big audition. She told it to anyone who would listen. She could feel the cringe radiating off her surroundings every time she dove into the tale, but she couldn't stop her recitation any more than she could stop abusing drugs and alcohol.

That danger was enhanced after a close call when she was 19 and a sophomore in college. She had been on an Adderall bender, up for days on end, spending the wee hours talking to a 43-year-old English professor from New England. To be honest, he could have been *anyone*. Amelia was titillated by sending him anything he requested and asked for nothing in return, completely intoxicated by the mindlessness of doing what she was told. About a week into this little arrangement, she ran out of Adderall and remembered the whole live-in boyfriend thing with Mark.

She called it off with Professor Webcam and was shocked when he threatened to circulate her pictures if she didn't continue doing whatever he said. That was Amelia, though. Always assuming the best of the worst people and the worst of the best people. It was a personality flaw dating back to middle school, though she was beginning to pick up on it for what it was: self-sabotage. But the unflattering light of self-awareness did fuck-all to change her behavior. She existed on the worst kind of autopilot. She could still see his menacing message in her mind's eye whenever she logged on to chat with someone new.

> **ProfessorXXX: Listen you little bitch, you send me my pictures, or we will see how far the ones that I already have can go. Who knows? They may even make it to a small liberal arts college in Austin.**

Until that moment, she had not fully understood what it meant to be scared sick. She'd never told him where she was from. She immediately threw up and told Mark everything that happened while he cried and asked why she would do such a thing. Then, she responded to Professor Webcam the way any sane young woman would.

> **GnGer66: Joke's on you, asshole, I'm 16. You do anything with those photos, and your sick ass is going to prison. *BLOCK.***

He never reached out again, but she scoured porn sites for images of herself for almost two years after the fact, afraid she might see herself staring back across the blue screen. At least she looked good in the photos. And those surely weren't the only ones; there must have been hundreds of naked pictures of her out there, pictures in which her face was both visible and identifiable at a variety of ages. Who knew what was floating around in the ether? Certainly not the airbrushed version of herself she had gotten so close to selling during the audition.

Amelia reveled in the dopamine that began to flood her brain as she perused the night's online options. She wanted to act out in every way possible because what was the point? As humans, we were going to have some good days but mostly bad, the fairness of which did not exist, and then one day we'd finally die, and it might as well be alone. She was convinced that if enough people woke up to the truth she was so familiar with, there would be a global mass suicide. So, for now, she was eager to continue living in the foreshadowing of her inevitable mental collapse, a slide punctuated by flashes of desperation and impulse-driven interludes of relief. As she sank into her process, she stared towards the surface of the water, longing for the will to swim up to the lifeboat she was currently calling Santa Fe.

CHAPTER 5

August in the South was like the Midwest in the dead of winter: brutal, oppressive, and downright dangerous. It was the perfect time to fall apart. Amelia had been home from Santa Fe licking her wounds for a week, more or less in the same position under a clammy pile of blankets on her bed. Meanwhile the Austin heat blazed on, surrounding the four walls of air conditioning. Lulled into a restless yet borderline vegetative state by the hum and clack of the ceiling fan, she rotted in bed, watching the blades spin fast enough to cause the house to take flight.

Santa Fe was a disaster, which surprised no one but Amelia. She had spent the first week of the trip making good on her promise to ditch the bud, but the effort felt like gripping onto a greasy doorknob, knuckles white as snow, as the winds of a twister did everything in their power to take her back over the rainbow. Going without was as close to unbearable as she had come. Leg spasm-filled sleepless nights, nightmares, the panic attacks whenever she'd leave the rental casita to go to the showgrounds, the hatred and rage when she looked in the mirror, all amid the empty, desperate loneliness associated with the thought of home and the lack of someone there waiting for her. *No place like home, my ass.* Week two wasn't much better. But at least she secured some schwag to get her through the nights. The strange house in New Mexico couldn't shelter her from the storm the way the Wethersfield house did. She was falling into an endless sleep and then being jolted awake in a loop of mental anguish.

By week three, she couldn't get out of bed in the morning without taking a hit. By the middle of week three, she couldn't leave the house without taking a second and third hit. By the end of week three, she was in the warm-up ring on Hope, navigating equine traffic, trying desperately not to look high. Riding fucked-up was the one thing she swore she would never do. Amelia *drove* high constantly. She had since she got her license. She thought everyone did and just didn't talk about it. She wasn't under the typical stoner delusion that she was completely unaffected by marijuana behind the wheel of a car, but she could keep it together long enough to get from point A to point B in one piece if she really focused. Riding Hope was sacred, her line in the sand. Her well of empathy for other humans had long dried up, but the aching current of connection to animals was the last whisper of a pulse she possessed.

Her trainer, Deb, could tell something was off but figured Amelia and Hope would pull it out in the show ring like they always did. Amelia could have said she didn't feel well and needed to dismount. She could have asked to use the bathroom, at least splashed some cold water on her face, buying some sober-up time. She could have done a lot of different things. What she did instead was ride into the show ring, prepared to point her horse at 3'6" jumps, and wish for the best. A man came over the loudspeaker announcing Amelia Glickman and Promise Me, but instead of thinking of her grandmother's childhood apartment in Brooklyn, she held back tears. Somewhere deep down she already understood how deeply she had fucked up. But even that didn't stop her from crashing Hope into the first jump. *Only a monster would hurt an innocent animal.*

She'd never forget the harsh spray of dirt slapping the base of the wooden fence, the crack of wood under Hope's knees as they came down on the jump, and the way the world literally turned upside down as she was flipped over Hope's neck onto the other side of the obstacle. But most of all, she'd never forget the look on Hope's face as she peered down at a pathetically splayed-out Amelia, the horrific mess she'd managed to make separating them by literal feet and figurative miles. Hope wasn't hurt, thank whatever forces may be, at least not physically. But the deep emotional pain in her big brown eyes bored holes through Amelia's soul. She had harmed the one living thing she couldn't bear harming. She had looked their powerful bond and rhythm in the eye and spit on it. Ruptured it with a mind-altering substance, completely blocking the connection with her soul horse. It was as if the horse whispered, through stunned tears, "Where did my Amelia go?"

Amelia's trainer Deb ripped her a new one, of course. She knew she deserved it and welcomed the harsh words. Thanks to the dark sunglasses Amelia wore and the shadow of her helmet, Deb had no idea Amelia was high, and she had no reason to; she had never been under the influence at the barn before that week. But Amelia had completely disappeared mentally on Hope in front of a towering obstacle. Riders asked so many things of these grand, wise animals, and abandoning them in the last moment before taking flight was one of the worst things one could do in return. So while Deb did not understand the full extent of the situation, she knew something was going on with her riding student that summer, and it had finally come to a head. This likely made her soften at the end of the lecture when she suggested that Amelia call Jen. Her mom used to be at every show and even rode herself but was doing so less and less since the divorce and meeting a new beau. The thought of calling her mom and telling her what she had done, how epically and abysmally she had failed her trainer and horse alike, made Amelia sick to her stomach.

When Amelia put Hope back in her stall on the showgrounds without a scratch on her, she considered what Forces of Good might be responsible. Something bigger. Big enough for capital letters. But she quickly fell back into self-hatred and guilt. She found herself in this pattern often, struck by wonder, connection, and something like gratitude, only to catch herself, stop in her tracks, and flip a violent U-turn back towards self-sabotage. Yet that protection never seemed to let up, no matter how much she retaliated.

She sheepishly unwrapped a peppermint. Hope wearily nuzzled her hand and accepted the treat, and Amelia considered how long and hard she would have to work to regain her trust. When she shut the latch on the stall door and pulled out her phone, she surprised even herself by pulling up her dad's contact info and typing out a text.

Amelia: I fucked up. I think I need help.

Five minutes later, when Amelia got in her car to leave, she checked a new message.

Dad: What's going on? Where are you?

Amelia: Santa Fe. I think I'm not OK.

Dad: I can be there by tonight if you need me.

Amelia stared down at her dad's last message, acknowledging this strange limbo. The expanse of air between the truth and a lie, between embracing the hand reaching out to help her and sinking her vicious teeth into it. She typed out a response about how unnecessary it was for her dad to come, about how she just had a bad day riding and was overreacting, but something stopped her from hitting send. He hadn't even asked her what was happening; he just wanted to be there. If only she could admit she needed him.

She deleted the lie before she could talk herself out of it, sent him the address to the Airbnb, and let her head fall forward onto the steering wheel once the tinny *whoosh* signaled the message was sent. She began her drive home to the rental, a comically magnificent dessert sunset painting the sky as the first tears she'd shed in months streamed down her dirt-stained face, leaving moist paths through the dust on the way down her neck. They were sad tears, sure, but they also signified the relief that was barely beginning to course through her veins; she had finally told someone just how not OK she really was.

Jonathan Glickman caught a flight and was at the rental house within a few hours. Amelia had been harboring an idea of her dad that made him feel like a distant stranger since the divorce, but the man rushing to her aid was the same one who always came to her rescue in record time. She thought back to the night of the incident with Mark months ago. That night Jen swooped in like a beacon of Hope, sifted through the ashes of her incinerated life, and plucked her from the mess to safely carry her home. She organized the move and made sure everything at Wethersfield was ready to embrace Amelia and her new life. Maybe people, her parents included, would be there for her if she simply *let them*.

When she opened the door to let her dad inside, Delilah gleefully bounced around his feet in greeting while Amelia silently expressed gratitude for the extreme privilege in her life. She gave such thanks for maybe the first time ever. She needed him to get there fast because who knew how long her window of willingness and honesty would remain open? And there he was, right on time. They sat on an unfamiliar couch and talked for hours; it was their longest conversation in years. They talked about the ache of depression, the throb of anxiety, and the ways we as humans try to temper our pain.

"I think I used to love to laugh," Amelia muttered, looking down at her hands as she popped her phone case on and off, fidgeting with the waxy plastic. "Sometimes I think it was my favorite thing; to feel like I couldn't even breathe because something was just so insanely funny. Now I'm constantly breathless because everything scares the shit out of me. Most of the time, it's so dark that I think every smile and laugh must have been fake."

"I was there for a lot of those smiles and laughs, honey. They seemed pretty real to me. But I know it doesn't feel like that right now."

"Maybe I'm just a really good actor," she responded wryly. "Did you know I was almost in a movie?"

Jonathon gave his daughter a smile that was somehow laced with both humor and sympathy. "I think I remember hearing something about that."

Her lips curved weakly in response. "The last thing that felt real was Hope. But even she can't pull me back from the edge anymore. The only thing that feels real now is how much I hurt. And I have everything, literally *everything* anyone could ever want, and I know that. I wish I could at least be ignorant of that, so the fact that it's not enough would make me feel less like a rotten princess on top of everything else."

"Regardless of money and opportunities," her father said, "which, yes, you've had plenty of, you've been through a lot, kid. And even if you hadn't, mental illness, depression…addiction…those things don't tend to discriminate or take circumstances into account."

She seized on the word "addiction" and tossed it around the confines of her mind, sifting through the syllables like a kid pushing vegetables around their plate with a fork to avoid taking a bite.

Her father broke the heavy silence. "But you're right. The hardest part of feeling that deep sadness and fear is how it bleeds into the past and the future. If only the present were affected, we'd still have nostalgia and hope, but it tints everything before and after it in that lifeless grey tone. Everything you thought was good about your life until that point now feels painful to look back on, and everything to come is just as terrifying and bleak. When both those things are true, the present becomes truly unbearable."

"Unbearable," Amelia repeated in a whisper, staring down at the floor, absently nodding like a zombie.

Jonathan looked at his daughter and took in her pain. "You know, sweetie, I think that's why sometimes there's nothing as terrifying as being inside your own head. It's why we all do the unhealthy things we do. Whether it's drinking, smoking, sex—anything to shut off the noise. But it's only a temporary solution. The pain only grows the longer we run away from it."

She looked back in weighty consternation at the man beginning to resemble the father from her childhood. The one who did silly dances at bedtime and had a killer Julia Child impression. Maybe she could accept that while he'd been a shitty husband to Jen, he sure was an awesome dad. And maybe in some Universe both could be true at the same time.

"It sounds like you know from experience," she said, barely audible.

But he was intent on hearing her. "We all have our shit, Amelia Bedelia, but only you can deal with it." The old nickname gave her pause. "Even me and your mom can't do that part for you. But if you let us, we will do everything in our power to make sure that *you* can." Amelia choked back a sob as she let the realization marinate that even though her parents' marriage was over, in some ways, they could still be a team.

Her dad took her home to Wethersfield the next morning, and she spent the next couple of days on the phone sitting through intake calls with one of the best psychiatric hospitals and rehabilitation centers in the state of Texas. She had agreed to go to treatment that night in Santa Fe with her dad, and for some reason she wasn't backing out, even though every fiber of her being screamed to stop making plans that were going to get in the way of her medicating with drugs, sex, and wine. Her parents helped her make arrangements, and she stayed high all the while, knowing that the painstaking frigidity of sobriety would drive her to scream a big "fuck off" to everyone trying to help get her treatment ducks in a row.

Sometimes, she tried to play it off like she was going to treatment because her parents were making her. The truth was that she desperately yearned for a life worth living and, better yet, a life worth *experiencing*. A life worth living would be the absence of this dark storm cloud constantly hovering over her. A life worth experiencing? She couldn't even fathom that. But there was a powerful life force energy deep inside her. This Force of Good tethered her to Hope, Delilah, and even the house. It insisted that she never give up on treading water lest she finally let herself drown. She was too paralyzed by bone-chilling despondence to harness that force and get all the way into the lifeboat. Maybe the doctors at the fancy hospital would be able to uncover that piece of her and kick it into high gear. Maybe they could tell her why even though everything hurt so, so bad, she couldn't fully cry. The emotions got stuck in her chest on their way up to her eyes.

So, she lay there on Wethersfield Road, draped in designer bedding like a decaying statue, and watched the minutes tick by. Each second that passed brought her closer to the next morning when she, her mom, and her dad would head to the hospital in Houston, where she would be living for six weeks. Aside from the oncoming wow factor of her parents teaming up on this little heist, tonight would be her last opportunity to get fucked-up, maybe ever, depending on how things unfolded with the doctors and therapists where she was headed. So, she was determined to consume everything she had before waving the white flag tomorrow and letting her parents extract her from the whimsical holding cell she called home. The place where the charming floor-to-ceiling bookshelves were as empty as she was.

Amelia let the promise of her last bottle of wine and the last half bowl of keef resurrect her from the goose-down tomb and lead her into the living room. The purple chairs were stacked high with leggings and hoodies—the rehab uniform, according to Reddit—and her open duffel bag oozed toiletries and coloring books. She sipped and smoked while stuffing clothes inside, the same season of *The Office* playing in the background as always. She had moved on from the endless reminder of her failed Hollywood career, thank God.

No matter how dead inside she felt, Michael Scott could always draw a reluctant smile. "I declare…. BACKRUPTCY!" he shouted over the TV speakers. That line always came closest to making her laugh, and this time was no exception, but when the spark of the sensation lit in her gut, she looked around and found no one to laugh *with*. So, what was the point, anyway? Loneliness can extinguish any flame.

She knew deep down in her bones that she needed to be saved, and she wasn't above believing that her savior would be someone she'd call her true love. After all, she wasn't so far gone that she couldn't recognize an incredible night sky. She just couldn't make herself step outside and look up for the sole reason that she had no one to look up with. No one to hold hands with. No one to look back into her eyes and remind her that although the world spun aimlessly on a tilt, one as subtle but obvious as the sickness in her mind, she did exist, sure as the butterflies fluttering in her gut.

"I just need to find the Michael to my Holly," she muttered to herself. Maybe that was why she resisted the impulse to invite a stranger over to invade her space and her body. Or maybe it was because, on a Sunday night, no one was responding to Tinder inquiries. The pickings in the online chats were slim as well. It was as if those mysterious Forces of Good continued to conspire with the house to protect her from herself, their current goal being to get her out the door and on her way to rehab in one piece come morning. These Forces of Good—some of which she'd begun to suspect were fighting for the life force within her—knew that what she really yearned for was someone to look at the stars with. And at first, it would have to be herself. Amelia would have to become enough for Amelia.

She began to wander the house. She wanted to take in the details of Wethersfield and somehow keep it with her as she ventured to this odd new place of being with herself. She took in the unused dining room table, the drapes that filtered in light from the distant and terrifying outside world, the extra room at the front that had become a storage closet, and the fetching red front door that stood between her and whatever was to come when she opened it tomorrow. Who would she be when she opened the door again in six weeks? Someone different, most definitely. Someone better? Hopefully. On her way back to the living room, her eyes landed on Hope's portrait hanging on the wall, and she sighed. Her eyes traveled to where a curious Delilah followed her through Wethersfield like a bodyguard. A familiar, almost-crying-choking feeling got stuck in her chest.

The hardest part about leaving was saying goodbye to Hope and Delilah. She had never gone more than a day or so without seeing them, and the way her gut caved in at the thought reminded her of her high school breakup. That ending was the truest example in her life of how it felt to have your heart shatter inside you following a goodbye. Delilah was staying with Jen and would get spoiled the way all grandchildren should, and Hope was in excellent hands, as always, with her trainers and barn mates. But she knew kissing Delilah goodbye in the morning would be brutal. She could hardly stand to think about her emotional goodbye to Hope nearly a week ago.

On that morning on the way home from Santa Fe, Amelia had requested that her dad stop off at the showgrounds, and he agreed, though he probably would have agreed to anything after securing her "yes" to rehab. He stayed in the car in the gravel parking lot, the exhaust mingling with the morning fog as the blue-tinted light of those last moments before sunrise crept across the horizon. It was a Monday, the only "off" day in the horse show world. On all other days, there would usually be buzzing activity stretching from the wee hours of the morning before any hint of sunlight. But on Monday morning the barn aisle was dark and quiet. Amelia tentatively walked to where Hope was stabled and peeked in to find her favorite iteration of the mare: curled up in a generous pile of pillowy shavings, strands of hay in her forelock, happily munching on her bale of breakfast. Amelia always loved to imagine that this was Hope's version of breakfast in bed or morning coffee still under the covers, and the vision sent warmth to pool around her icy heart.

Amelia carefully unlatched the stall door and tiptoed into Hope's space, making just enough noise not to startle her. Hope looked up at her sleepily for a few seconds and then went right back to lounging and munching. A ghost of a smile pulled at Amelia's lips as she sat down near Hope's big brown head and began to stroke her neck and scratch lightly under her mane. A soft, appreciative nicker puffed against her leg, the light gust of breath sending a few stray shavings floating away as the first rays of sunlight cast streaks of dazzling dust through the slats on the barn wall. The trust that still flowed between them was a relief but stung just the same; she knew she didn't deserve it. But that's why she had agreed to leave for six weeks in the first place. She wanted to become someone who was worthy of that trust.

Amelia needed to hit the road and face the mess she made. So she pressed her nose into the crook of Hope's neck just below her round cheekbone, the spot that always inexplicably smelled of lavender. She inhaled the scent and let out a shaky breath.

"You are *everything*. And I am so sorry. I will miss you like crazy, but when I see you again, I'll be... better, I think." A lone tear fell from Amelia's eyes and onto her lap, and she touched it almost reverently with the tip of her finger, then brought it to the smudged white star in the middle of Hope's forehead before kissing the same spot. "I'll be back before the heat breaks." She slowly got up, latched the stall shut, and walked to the car without looking back.

Amelia knew at that moment in Santa Fe, just like she knew now sitting in Wethersfield, that she couldn't *afford* to look back. She made her way to the living room and begrudgingly picked up the packing list the treatment center had sent over. She couldn't believe there was a packing list in the first place, like this was just some depressing summer camp for fuckups. She read through it again and checked off the items in her head until she got to the last one: a journal. Of course, they'd put a journal on the center's stupid list. Amelia groaned and began to search the house for something that could pass as a journal. She had just resolved to pick one up on the way tomorrow when she came across a floral notebook in the drawer of her bedside table. On the front cover, the shiny gold script read, "Something Beautiful is on the Horizon." A bitter chortle escaped her as she racked her brain, trying to remember how the hell she came across this floral nightmare of paper. It must have been a gift from someone well-meaning but ever so out of touch with her current vibe.

Amelia absentmindedly flipped through the notebook. The first couple of pages were filled with her own handwriting. She knew she had been under the influence *a lot*, but she continued to underestimate how often she blacked out and vacated the present moment. She began to read.

June 20, 2015

*Let's say you're researching a role. I was an actor, after all.
The role is a pathetic whore with zero self-respect and a
ticking time bomb of self-destruction where normal people
store their souls. Just let your drug dealer ejaculate on your
face with zero warning or explanation, and you'll be good
to go. But let's be honest, "let" is a strong word. "Failed to
scream at in response" more so fits the bill. I'm starting to
think that maybe drug dealers aren't the most stand-up guys.
Shocking. I have lots, because I also have lots of epiphanies
in which I throw out all my weed and delete my dealer's
numbers so that I can become an upstanding adult who
cooks food instead of DoorDashing, someone who goes on
coffee dates instead of dirtyroulette.com. I collect dealers like
Trevor's mom collected acrylic crosses. Anyway, the new guy
recently suggested we fuck in exchange for an eighth. The
worst part was that I did it, even though God knows I have
enough in my trust fund to support my habit. I guess I'm
just really committed to this role. And I'm all like, "Who do
you think you're talking to?" But it's pretty obvious that no
matter how hard I try, I'll still be the girl they assume I am.
Even though I'm "sooooo offended." Yeah, SUPER offended
from where I'm bent over a questionably stained couch. My
therapist, Cathy, keeps saying that I need to feel empowered,
that I need to be reminded that humans are good, that life is
surprising, and that love still exists. And I know that's not
going to happen until I do something that scares the shit out
of me. Like hiking across the country or traveling to India
like those women from the books. Something brand-new
that can crack me wide open so new light can get in. Maybe
I'll find it after I let go of the deep resentment towards my
parents for bestowing on me the inconvenience of personhood.*

Yikes. She could remember the events in question but had zero recollection of writing it all down. She tossed the dainty journal with the not-so-dainty entry into her duffel bag. At the very least, it'd be a good reminder of why she was there in the first place. And it was certainly validating that even black-out Amelia, AKA Shadow Amelia on steroids, knew she needed a change.

What she was beginning to learn, and what she suspected she would continue to learn on her grippy-sock vacay, was that she had felt like shit since before she even knew what feelings were. And she'd do *anything* to help her forget her perceived unraveling of the world and the complete destruction of everything good about it.

She was the girl who slept with you on a first date because she had nothing to say and couldn't tolerate the silence. She was the girl who did whatever you wanted and became whoever you wanted to escape the confines of her own miserable headspace. She woke up every morning astonished that she was unlucky enough to exist. Her flimsy sense of self was ruled by the next fix; the next thing that would turn her into nothing but a puddle of ecstasy, begging not to dry up in the sun after a downpour. She needed something vast and circumfluous to fill every crack and crevice that had been eroded by circumstance and chemistry. And she knew the substances and the mindless sex weren't going to foot the bill anymore. Which was exactly why she was throwing her hands up in defeat and diving into ice-cold water first thing in the morning.

Her departure grew closer and closer, and she was finally out of bud and wine for what could be the last time ever. She walked through the house gathering empty wine bottles, bare Ziplocs, blackened bongs, and sticky pipes like a druggy easter egg hunt. When she was confident she found all her eggs, she tied up the trash bag and walked it out to the dumpster amidst a chorus of clanging. As she tossed it into the bin, she couldn't help but feel astonished by the miracle that she was actually going through with all of this. It was as if the same Forces of Good that protected Hope gently guided her against her better judgment.

She breathed in the steamy August air and lifted her head at the exact moment the dark night sky released another unlikely shooting star over Wethersfield Road. She thought for a moment about how maybe something bigger had been chasing her down and how maybe now she was finally ready to be caught. As she walked back inside, the house smiled down at her softly, knowingly, lovingly, and it rocked her to sleep for the last time on this side of the tracks.

CHAPTER 6

Five years earlier, the Forces of Good were nowhere near catching seventeen-year-old Amelia Glickman. They simply nipped at her ankles as she galivanted toward all the wrong things—until a phone call from a casting agent on a cold Sunday night changed everything. It was all happening exactly the way she'd imagined. She'd walk into the Four Seasons Hotel in downtown Austin, ready and eager to meet the two highly respected brothers who made movies she'd loved for ages. She'd be the best, skinniest, most charming version of herself that day, dazzling them with her mastery of the words. She'd obsessed over every line, practiced with anyone who would give her the time of day, read the script three times, and the novel twice. She recorded herself on the family's boxy video camera rehearsing the scenes until she ran out of tape. She figured she was as ready as she'd ever be to meet her fate of becoming a famous actor.

Famous actors tended to be thin, and though Amelia had never been the largest of her peers, she was a chubby baby, a thick kid, and a curvaceous post-pubescent teen. She was substantial and too meaty for Hollywood, certainly to play the fourteen-year-old girl the character embodied. So, she starved herself in preparation for the big day. She was adamant that purging was not going to cut it this time, and she was methodical in eating the bare minimum to make it through each day. The sickness was shrouded in the disguise of a young woman taking her future in acting seriously and seizing this once-in-a-lifetime opportunity with every ounce of willingness she could muster. Instead of resistance, she was met with support. Purging was something you had to do in secret, but restricting your intake was celebrated if you existed in a somewhat larger body.

For weeks, she tried her best not to exceed 500 calories, and by the time she met with the directors her exhausted body was begging for sustenance. So much so that she binged on Mexican food the day of her audition. After her scheduled rehearsal with the casting director, where she was prepped for the actual audition with the directing brothers, she gave into biology and let her body inhale the calories it had been lacking. It gulped them as if coming up for air. Something about the rehearsal and how the casting agent was changing the way she'd been saying the lines for weeks caused her to panic, and her empty stomach couldn't take it anymore. She had hours before needing to head back to the hotel for the actual audition in front of the directors, so it was safe to assume she'd have the time and space to take care of her little problem and undo the damage of copious amounts of carbs and cheese.

She'd never forget the way the duct tape rubbed her sensitive skin raw under her shirt where she'd smashed her breasts down to appear more like the 14-year-old character and less like a grown woman at 17; how it dug in painfully as she gorged on chips and queso like it was her first meal in over a month, because it sort of was. To her horror, the casting agent called her mom just as they paid the check at the Mexican restaurant and said the directors were ready for her early. So, there she was, frozen inside her incomplete binge-purge cycle, itching for release, hands smelling like salsa even after two hand washes, sporting cheese breath and a bloated belly. Not exactly what she was picturing when she imagined the day she'd burst through the fold and enter the world of fame and excellence.

Amelia looked down at the shiny marble floors of the hotel lobby. Pausing in the center of the big open space, she gazed at the elaborate light fixtures, trying to ignore the mounting discomfort in her stomach. Early February in Austin could be anything from a balmy eighty degrees and sunny to a blustery ice storm, but that day was somewhere in between. The Texas winter sun was bright, and a crisp 50-degree breeze wafted off a sparkling Lady Bird Lake. She might have considered it a beautiful day if it hadn't held so much significance.

Amelia and her mother walked to where the casting director stood with two other teenage girls and their parents, as well as the infamous duo seated atop high bar stools. The brothers set down their glasses of golden-brown liquor and politely greeted her and the other girls reading for them that day. She ogled the amber liquid, wishing she could do a shot, just to take the edge off. Pleasant small talk was exchanged, and Amelia took the opportunity to size up her competition. One of the girls appeared to be a theatre kid like her, mesmerized by her present company and yearning to make a good impression, but nothing Amelia couldn't handle. The other wasn't an actor. But she oozed the rough-and-tumble country girl vibe they were going for, adding a level of pizazz that could pose a threat to Amelia's career plan.

After what felt like ages, the casting agent began ordering everyone around to various corners of the hotel. The other theatre kid was called up to the business suite to read first. She was tailed by an assistant and the directors into the elevator. The casting director brought Amelia and the others over to a waiting area in the lobby before following the chosen ones up to higher ground.

Amelia sat with her hands folded in her lap in a way that communicated to everyone around her just how seriously she took this, and her excitable and oblivious counterpart eagerly made her way outside to play, of all things. Amelia looked out one of the big windows at the back of the lobby and gawked as Country Girl rolled down the grassy hills on the well-manicured hotel lawn out back—she even had the nerve to giggle wildly when she looked down and saw the fresh green stains on her jeans. Amelia couldn't help but wonder if it was an act, a strategy to stand out at the audition. Either way, she couldn't be forced to roll down a hill gleefully, not with a gun to her head. Or without her lunch making its way back up.

She picked at her cuticles nervously as she sat next to her mom in the lobby. Jen didn't seem any more relaxed than Amelia.

"Are you anxious?" Jen asked. Her eyes darted over to the elevator every few seconds as if she were willing someone to whisk Amelia upstairs to her fate and finally break the nauseating tension.

"Nope. I could take a nap right here."

Jen rolled her eyes and huffed a laugh as the two finally turned and locked eyes.

"What if they don't like me? In the rehearsal, it was like they wanted me to be a completely different person."

"You mean the acting?"

It was Amelia's turn to roll her eyes. "Well, yes, obviously, I'm supposed to be a different person, but there's only so much 'dialing it back' I can do."

Jen closed her eyes and nodded in understanding. "That's never quite been in your nature, Amelia Bedelia."

Amelia rubbed her temples and shook her head slowly. "Yeah…"

The conversation dropped away to make space for the hustle and bustle of a downtown hotel at check-in time, and Amelia sank back into her anxious thoughts about dialing it back. She was a theatre kid. All she had ever heard from her teachers was "bigger, louder, MORE, say it to the back row," and that was never something she had a problem with. She loved how her essence could fill up the entire space easily, and she could finally stop trying unsuccessfully to shrink away. Being on stage was like unbuttoning a tight pair of jeans at the end of a long day. Film acting was very different, like sucking it in and tugging the zipper up. Sure, she had stood out in the cattle call and then somehow made it past the first couple of callbacks. But now she had to prove she could be subtle, that she could say what needed to be said with just her eyes. Amelia had never said *anything* with just her eyes.

Jen and Amelia stiffened as the casting agent and the first girl to read exited the elevator. The girl's face was unreadable. The casting lady displayed the same pleasant but no-nonsense smile, plastered to her face at all times. Country Girl came bursting through the glass door into the lobby, panting and laughing with a younger boy who must have been her sibling, and much to Amelia's dismay, she was next on the docket. Amelia leaned her head against the wall and sighed audibly just as the elevator door closed to take Country Girl and the casting agent up to the hotel suite of truth. She closed her eyes and took deep breaths as she silently willed the enchiladas sitting like a boulder in her gut to dissipate before she was granted her turn.

She was just considering how she might never eat Mexican food again when she felt her phone buzz and heard her mom's phone ding in unison. She pulled up the family group chat titled Enclave Mesa Gang, named after their first address in Austin in Northwest Hills. Those had been the good old days before the strain of the Chicago move in 2007. When they moved back in 2008 after her dad hit it big, it was into the fancy new lake house, where it would all eventually fall apart. But the name lived on, an echo of simpler times.

Dad: Break a leg!!!!

Beth: Don't fuck it up

Amelia could hear her mother scoff, and even imagine the roll of her eyes from the seat next to her.

Jen/Mom: Nice...

Amelia: I feel like I'm going to puke, for more than one reason. Why did we go to Guerros??

Jen/Mom: You begged me to go to Guerros...

Amelia looked over to where her mom was sitting beside her. Jen just shrugged in response.

Dad: Rookie mistake

Beth: Did you get me anything?

Amelia could feel the buzz of new messages continuing to pour into the group chat as she opened a different unread message.

Trevor: good luck

Now Amelia was *actually* going to throw up. She stared down at the text and felt her stomach flip flop with joy and regret. She'd broken up with Trevor three weeks earlier in a jealous rage and had been trying to get him back ever since. Up until this point, he'd had her number blocked; he'd finally had enough of her black-and-white mood swings. But even when he was mad at her, he wasn't one to miss the big moments. She knew better than to start a whole conversation with him potentially just moments before riding the elevator up to her fate, so she just hearted the message with a tap. She became a fraction more settled in her seat with Trevor's well wishes tucked carefully in her heart.

She poked at her phone, then opened her final unread text.

Cat: break a leg, girl! We are all rooting for u!

Amelia pursed her lips in suspicion and wondered if Cat's message was genuine or not. On the one hand, Cat was always more or less friendly towards Amelia. On the other hand, they were pitted against each other for every leading role at the theatre academy where they attended high school. Amelia always assumed that everyone she came across was as jaded with jealousy and competition as she was, which made it hard to make friends, trust anyone, or assume the best in people. It had its benefits, though she couldn't think of any right now.

Getting the actual part in the movie would be secondary to being the envy of all the girls at school, finally proving once and for all that she was special—that she had *won*. On that humble note, she allowed herself to be carried away by daydreams of walking down a red carpet at the Oscars, wearing a fabulous gown, hand in hand with a tuxedo-clad Trevor. So grounded of her to bring the hometown sweetheart.

Just as the music began to play her off stage to raucous applause after a moving speech, Amelia snapped into the present moment, where the golden sun began shining its low-angled, late afternoon light across the lake and skyline. Country Girl and the casting agent crossed the lobby towards them from the elevator. The casting director's polite mask was still in place, and the girl appeared unfazed and eager to get back outdoors, which really blew Amelia's mind. There was no room Amelia would rather be in than the one she was about to enter. The casting director nodded in her direction, and she shot up out of her seat, barely looking back at Jen as she tossed her phone onto the empty chair. *Show time.*

A woman in all black waited for them in the elevator. An assistant that Amelia hadn't yet met stared ahead and swiped a special key card that illuminated floor 32. *Damn. Up there.* Amelia tried to think of something charming, witty, anything to say to the casting director as the elevator ascended to the heavens, but she came up blank. Instead, she fought off the urge to pick at her cuticles and thanked the God of Digestive Tracts that she was feeling less painfully stuffed and bloated. Her breath hitched as the elevator door opened directly into the business suite. *Damn it, no prep time.* She thought she'd at least have the walk down the hallway followed by a pregnant pause as they knocked on the door to get herself together. But alas, there she was, thrust into the lion's den. She felt the need to apologize for taking up all the air in the room and stand on her tippy toes all at the same time.

Three men, two of whom were the idolized brothers, plus one woman, sat behind a long table. The brothers smiled warmly, but the others didn't look up. Amelia's nerves sprang up in response and were likely what caused her to exclaim awkwardly.

"Hey, y'all!" she shrieked, her voice seeming to test the limits of the space. *What. Are. You. Doing?* she thought.

"Hello…" one of the brothers replied kindly, pausing to look down at a sheet of paper, "…Amelia! Thanks so much for being here today." She smiled and nodded in lieu of words you might call a reply.

"Alright, here's what you're going to do," the casting agent said, breaking the tension. "Stand on the X. Cheryl over there...Wave, Cheryl." The woman at the table waved without looking up from her phone. "Cheryl is going to read as your scene partner, and you're going to talk directly to her, not to the camera. Got it?"

Amelia's mouth hung open slightly as she stared back, frozen for a moment before snapping herself out of it and replying. "Got it!"

The strained silence that followed felt oppressive until a famous pair of expectant eyebrows broke through the thick air in the room.

"Right! Well, um. I'll just go ahead and, um, get started then." A feeling of profound emotional discomfort in her gut had replaced the intense bloating, but nevertheless, she dove into the scene with the fervor of a thousand suns and the subtlety of a bull in a china shop.

She all but blacked out during the next 10 minutes. Reading through a scene with Cheryl was like acting with a doorknob. She felt like she couldn't get a reaction from her if her life depended on it, which took Amelia's need to be seen and doused it in lighter fluid. The disinterested look on the directors' faces tossed the match. A tap-dancing clown buzzed inside her chest, desperately trying to ensure they didn't miss it, constantly doing jazz hands and shrieking, "Get it?"

The silence that followed the completion of the scene was even more painful than the one that preceded it.

"Good work," said one of the brothers finally. She wasn't sure which one was which.

"Thanks so much, Amelia," added the other brother, writing something down on the piece of paper in front of him. The tap-dancing clown in her chest threatened to lurch forward and jump over the table to see what it said.

"It's still a little bit...Disney," added the casting agent. From the way she said it, Amelia guessed that Disney wasn't a good thing. Amelia thought back to the tone and tempo of the typical movies the brothers directed and then knew for sure it wasn't a good thing.

"Let's go through that last page one more time, and I want you to just pretend you're having the conversation in real life. Don't try so hard." Oof. If that last part wasn't the story of her entire fucking life. She felt the comment like a punch to the gut. Why was it so hard for her not to be over the top?

It was her last chance to fulfill her destiny. Closing her eyes, she took a deep breath and tried to pretend she was having an average, everyday conversation about avenging her father's death. When she was finished, the brothers were even more checked out than before, and the casting agent shot Amelia a placating smile that didn't even come close to reaching her eyes. Amelia thanked the table of intimidating grownups and followed the unimpressed agent back into the elevator. She couldn't help but feel like she'd disappointed her; the woman had been gunning for Amelia all along and even gave her a second chance to do it differently.

The air seemed to shift as Amelia stepped across the elevator's threshold and into the lobby. She walked slowly back toward Jen and took what felt like her first breath in hours. She was back to sharing oxygen with normal, everyday people, and it stung her lungs with remorse as she ventured back out into the real world. She had the sickening realization that she'd never breathe the same air as someone that important again because, deep down, she knew she didn't get the part. She had been in that room, breathing that air, and she blew it. *At least I don't have to worry about all my nudes getting leaked.*

She didn't talk the entire car ride home, and when they arrived, she locked herself in her bedroom with the water bottle full of vodka she'd been hiding in her closet. She drank and watched a pirated, grainy version of *Wicked* on Broadway. It was the first of many times that she'd drink alone, and the last of many times she would listen to "Defying Gravity." This anthem had been her ticket out of the ick in her soul, and she just hadn't been good enough. She was always too much and not enough all at the same time, and it just hurt too bad.

Acting broke her heart, even though it didn't mean to. It was an industry fraught with rejection, and one needed a solid backbone to survive. She hadn't even been fully rejected yet, but she was holding a funeral for her career. She lowered the casket of her talent and potential beneath the ground to the eerie soundtrack of show tunes.

Amelia's mental state deteriorated quickly in the weeks following the audition. The decay was more indicative of mental illness than the audition itself. The movie was only the straw that broke the camel's back, not the whole hay bale. She'd been depressed before, severely by the time they finally put her on medication in middle school. But since the audition, she had stopped taking the meds, stopped showering, and stopped going to school. The gaping hole in her chest made her experiences from middle school seem like child's play.

"Let them think I'm in Hollywood!" she dramatically screamed at her mother one day as Jen tried to get her out of bed and out the door to school. Though she'd sworn off the theatre, the theatrics were far from over.

One particularly brutal morning a few days later, Amelia sobbed into her pillow. "I just need to know. I need an answer. I need closure." Her desperate mother called the casting director and inquired about the role, begging for anything, any answer, good or bad, that may help to break the putrid spell cast over her daughter.

"Oh yeah. She didn't get it. None of the girls from the callback did. They went with a different kid. I thought we called you."

They were never going to call. And Amelia was never going to get over it. She would eventually take her meds again; she'd even get out of bed and go to school again, but she would never, ever act again. Even when her dad asked Jen for a divorce only one year later, a day when a performance might have helped in some way.

But perhaps the Forces of Good were catching up with her more quickly than she knew. The character in the movie was meant to be filmed on horseback for more than a few scenes, and one of the reasons she likely stood out at the audition was because she knew how to ride. After a few months back on her medication, she began to go out to the barn with Jen again, like she did when she was a little girl. It was a way to get out of the house and out of her head. The horses were a balm to her broken heart, and the smell of sawdust, manure, and fresh air was a balancing agent to her brain chemistry.

Eventually, her mom and Deb convinced her to ride in a show again, but she did so only casually and occasionally. Until a brown mare with a white star that resembled smudged paint somehow found her way to Amelia and changed everything. At 17, a door was cracked open that had long been shut, and by 19, the door had been just wide enough to let Hope in. Now, at 22, she was about to find out if she had the guts to open it the rest of the way and step outside, from darkness into light.

August 11, 2015

I finally did it, I landed myself at an inpatient treatment center. Cathy has been hinting at it for a while, but it still feels surreal to be here. They insist that you either journal or read during quiet time, and since none of my books have arrived in the mail, I thought I'd crack open this floral nightmare of a journal and do some soul-searching. I've officially been sober for 12 hours, a new record. When I was doing my intake interview, Dr. Phillips (fine as fuck, by the way) asked me what I wanted to get out of my time here. The only thing that I could think of was that not wanting to die would be nice. I thought everyone here would look crazy, but they all seem pretty normal, honestly. That may be a red flag. Anyway, my goddamn pictures of Hope and Delilah keep falling off the wall because tacks are considered "sharps," and you have to hang everything on the wall with this not-so-sticky putty, and it's making me want to murder everyone. Goodnight.

August 16, 2015

It's barely been a week, and I've read Catcher in the Rye *thrice. I very much relate to Holden Caufield; a rich kid with a ton of privilege who loses their shit, ta-dah. We hate all the same things. Maybe being here will help me improve my choice of literary heroes. But seriously, having a clear-ish mind for the first time in years is kind of bizarre. I am learning that I am actually self-aware but also unwilling to do anything with that awareness. I think that's why I do everything I can to numb the thoughts and feelings; blissful ignorance and all that. When did it stop feeling so blissful?*

But now that I'm not basically hooked up to an IV of mind-altering substances 24/7, that brutal self-awareness has rushed back in. The doctors here have diagnosed me with PTSD, Severe Cannabis and Alcohol Use Disorder, and here's a fun one, Borderline Personality Disorder. As much as I hate to admit it, BPD does make sense when I think back to the black-and-white thinking and toxic relationship skills that haunted even my high school love life. Poor Trevor...What surprises me is the PTSD. I think I forget how bad that night with Mark was. I block it out until it comes rushing in. To be fair, they said I'd no longer fit the criteria for these within a couple of years if I A. stay sober and B. take my meds and attend regular therapy. You'd think that would be a no-brainer, and I'm certainly going to try my best, but I'm skeptical. Anyway, I really like my therapist here, Dr. B. She has me trying to notice my most repetitive thoughts, and so far this is what I've got:

Am I fat and ugly? Are my teeth weird? Why do my thighs rub together when it's hot out? Why do I sweat so much more than other girls? Do people think I'm weird? How long does it take to kill yourself by carbon monoxide poisoning? If I didn't feel so pimply and hairy and awkward, would I stop trying to escape my body altogether?

August 20, 2015

Last night I had a lucid dream. I knew it was a dream, so I used it as an opportunity to let my addictions run rampant. I did drugs, drank, fucked whoever I wanted to, and traveled from place to place on a bicycle. But then the sun started to come up, and I didn't know where to pedal to next. And that's the problem and the miracle at the same time, isn't it? The sun will always come up, and it's nice to be around people who get that it's a blessing and a curse—who understand depression, period, who don't judge you when you suddenly fall into a sullen silence, or ask what's wrong. They already know what's wrong: nothing and everything at the same time. And that's sort of beautiful, huh? To be truly seen and understood in all your gritty glory. I've always wanted to feel a part of something. I just wasn't expecting that something to be a band of misfit toys. But I'll take it. All of us are just a little broken, but a lot brave.

The other day at breakfast, one of the more happy-go-lucky nurses was bragging about her lovely weekend, spewing gratitude and good vibes, when one of the more depressive dudes in the place looked her dead in the eye and said, "You're talkin' to the wroooong crowd." I spit out my shitty rehab coffee, and the whole table of us laughed until we cried and had bathroom emergencies. I haven't laughed like that since I was a teenager. I forgot how good that feels; it really is my favorite thing. I feel a part of the group here. I usually separate from the group, and I think it's because

*I am terrified of being mediocre, but I sure make a mess
out of trying to be extraordinary. The bottom line is I've got
a lot to figure out, but this place is making me fall in love
with humans again. And I'm human, aren't I?*

August 29, 2015

*My therapist Dr. B finally broke the seal. When we were
talking this morning about what happened with Mark, I
started crying. It's nine p.m., and I still haven't stopped.
It's like all the tears from my parents' divorce and the
trauma of that night are finally rushing out. I know
I've been depressed, but this is the first time since I can
remember that I am actually fucking sad. I miss my parents
being married. I miss being a family. I miss being on stage.
I miss the feeling of soaring over jumps with Hope. I even
miss Mark. I miss things I've never even seen or heard of. I
long to look out into the world and see vastness that's never
been touched by human beings. I long to be moved to tears
by love and beauty. I long for this sadness to be sacred. In
its fertile, freshly cleared ground, I want to grow a beautiful
life. And I know the work doesn't stop here. I know I have
to keep working with Cathy when I get home, keep taking
my meds, and stay fucking sober. But for the first time
ever, it's feeling worth it to lean into the discomfort of self-
awareness; to relearn how to live.*

September 5, 2015

*Today, Dr. B asked me what my greatest fear is, and the first
thing that came to mind was that the world would end, and
I'd never be able to experience all of it. And fuck if that's
not a mouthful. Because I want all of it or none of it at all.
The immensity of that pressure is so great. In here I came to*

understand that maybe that's why I dumb myself down and chase these stupid boys. Seeking their approval and shifting from one center of gravity to the next is an infinite loop, while my actual life is so finite that it makes me want to sell all my things and get high under a bridge for the rest of my life. Because it's all going to end someday anyway. As a kid, I used to stress about when the sun would finally run out of heat. I hate the thoughts in my head that tell me all I'll ever be good for is dirty sex. I hate the desperation I portray when, in my heart, I know all I have to offer. I hate the fact that all I want to do is scream and cry and cathartically explode into little pieces. I hate that during this whole time, up to now, I've been waiting for the love of my life to come save me and whisk me away. Really, I'm the only one who can do that. I need to be my own hero, or I will die waiting for one.

September 12, 2015

I really miss Hope. Delilah, too, of course, but I am so eager to get home and show Hope how far I have come in such a short amount of time after everything that went down in Santa Fe. I am officially one month sober! She really is the only living thing that could have gotten me here. That's what is so unbelievable about horses. You always have a teammate with no hidden agenda; nothing but loyalty and trust exist in a healthy bond between rider and horse. There is occasional miscommunication and annoyance, sure, but it always comes from a place of authenticity and truth. As long as Hope is alive with her big eyes and inexplicable lavender scent, all is well with the world. It's like I don't even know who I am without her. It scares the shit out of me because one day, I will have to live without her. I'd give anything to keep her right here at this age and have her forever and ever, because being with her is the only time life truly makes sense to me. When I see her again, I'll be on course to be the person she deserves.

September 16, 2015

My heart is breaking for my roommate Mia. She's anorexic but would never tell you that herself. It was time for her to leave the hospital, and the doctors broke it to her that her BMI was too low and she would have to stay until she gained a few pounds. I had never seen someone my own age (other than me, of course) throw a temper tantrum. I walked into our shared room and saw her lying on the floor completely deflated, a light dusting of white powdery stress ball innards resting on her frail body and the surrounding carpeted hospital floor. Alanis Morrisette screamed from her iPod speakers. She has a preoccupation with visions of throwing herself off tall things and destroying anything beautiful. I think that might be why she is so fixated on the idea of destroying herself. She is so painfully beautiful. Meanwhile, my own eating disorder has hardly been addressed, let alone detected, because I can hide behind my normal weight. Kind of fucked-up if you think about it, right? I'm not exactly being forthcoming with the information, though, and it's not like I have the privacy to purge here anyway.

September 22, 2015

I can't believe I'm going home tomorrow. The journey is far from over, of course. When I get home, I immediately start Intensive Outpatient (or IOP as the cool kids call it), biweekly sessions with Cathy, and have agreed to go to recovery meetings (gag me). I am also starting with a new prescribing doctor in Austin to make sure I stay compliant with my meds. There are so many different names for all the things, it's like its own language. Rehab or Inpatient is the first place, AKA, res; you live as a resident there for a while, so you're not allowed to go home at night. IOP is like a step down from that where you go to a program for a few hours every weekday. Apparently meetings are completely separate, not to mention free, and are just a place you go to be with other people in recovery. Anyway, I met this nice older woman today. She just got here and said this is her tenth stint in treatment. When I was talking to her, I realized that it could so easily be me if I don't take this seriously. I don't want to have to do this again.

I want tomorrow to be the first day of the rest of my life. I want to do all the uncomfortable, healthy things. If I want a life I've never had before, I need to do things I've never done before. This isn't a dress rehearsal, it's my actual life, and I have more opportunities than most to make it a beautiful one. Maybe I can even make other people's lives more beautiful one day, too. Or maybe I'm just on that pink cloud they talked about and soon I'll come crashing back down to earth. More will be revealed, and all that...

CHAPTER 7

Amelia opened the charming red door to her home on Wethersfield Road for the first time in six weeks. She dropped her bags in the room with the bare floor-to-ceiling bookshelves. Her mom, dad, and Beth trailed in behind her. Beth was visiting for the weekend to welcome Amelia home, and the four of them had just finished a hearty meal of Tex-Mex at Maudie's. It was the first meal they shared as a family since the divorce.

As Jen shut the front door, Delilah darted towards Amelia and leaped into her arms as she knelt in greeting. Tears had become a regular occurrence. She stroked Delilah's soft blonde fur and gently kissed the top of her head. "I'm home, my mooshy girl."

While Delilah licked off her salty tears, Amelia thought about what her counselors at the rehab center said about new sobriety. "The good news is you're going to feel, and the bad news is, you're going to feel." Her family began taking her things into the living room to be sorted and unpacked. Amelia regarded the sun-streaked floors, sea foam edging, and the trendy purple chairs as if she had never seen them before.

"I can't believe I live here," she said in awe, as her new friend, gratitude, spread warmth through her body. Her family and the house alike breathed out a soft laugh and gave her an aggrieved but fond eye roll.

"Do you want me to stay for a while?" Beth asked as she scratched behind Delilah's ears. "My flight doesn't leave until tomorrow morning."

"No, no, go get some rest before you head back to school. I'm going to start a load of laundry and pass out. I'm exhausted." Their mom and dad nodded slowly, and glanced at one another, still always maintaining a good six feet of distance. They were learning how to be together relative to their daughters, but moments of transition, back into their separate lives, always brought back the awkward tension.

The four of them stood atop eggshells, threatening to crack until Jen broke the silence. "You sure you're going to be OK?"

Amelia's first instinct was to scoff in response. She softened when she thought of something else she'd learned in rehab: She didn't ruin her life and their trust overnight, and she wasn't going to get it back overnight. She smiled and nodded. "Promise. And I promise I will let you know if that changes."

"Don't forget, Intensive Outpatient starts tomorrow at noon sharp," her dad added.

"I won't forget IOP; in fact, I will be there with bells on. Ten minutes early." Lesson number three from rehab: It was all about a good attitude and punctuality. On time was late and early was right on time. Jesus, was it now her lot in life to have an inner dialogue of recovery slogans?

They all shifted awkwardly in the pause that followed, learning how to be a new kind of family.

"Thank you for everything," Amelia finally said to break the silence. "I mean it. I love you guys." After a hug they each made their way through the red front door, departing to their separate homes and separate lives.

She stood in the doorway, watching a man and his dog walk slowly down the street a few houses down. A young family played with a soccer ball in their front yard across the way. All this time she'd thought she lived alone on Wethersfield Road. A sense of unspoken comradery and community bloomed in her chest. Maybe it was that stupid pink cloud again, or maybe she just wasn't as terribly lonely now that she wasn't the only person on her mind. Her acute self-awareness was growing into an awareness of others around her. It was as if she'd at last found fellow humans after a nuclear fallout in which she presumed herself to be the last one standing. These humanoids seemed to be everywhere.

Her phone buzzed in her back pocket, distracting her from the signs of life filling her heart. More pesky tears stung the back of her eyes when she pulled it out and saw the resurrection of the Enclave Mesa Gang group chat.

> Beth: Let us know if you need anything, Amelia Bedelia!
>
> Beth: I hope this isn't weird. Is this weird? Hope I didn't make it weird.
>
> Jen/Mom: lol. Not weird.
>
> Dad: Not weird.
>
> Amelia: Not even a little weird.
>
> Amelia: But stop texting and driving
>
> Beth: *eyeroll emoji* I'm at a red light...
>
> Amelia: Love y'all. Goodnight. and thank you. *heart emoji*

Amelia smiled to herself and put her phone back in her pocket. Maybe the end of a marriage didn't have to mean the end of a family. Maybe Jen was happier with Chris, and her dad was happier with Maya. Maybe it would just keep getting less and less strained over time.

Once inside, she stopped in the small, empty front bedroom and wondered what it might become in her new life. Was it really begging for a crafting table, or was it more in the market for a yoga mat and a treadmill? Maybe a good old-fashioned home office was more the vibe. Her treatment team insisted on her getting an actual job. Gone were the days of riding and competing as her only obligations. But the kind of get-well job she was in the market for didn't require a home office.

Possibilities for the space continued to swim through Amelia's mind as she made her way to the living room and took a seat in one of the purple chairs. She tucked her feet underneath herself and patted the spot next to her, welcoming Delilah to snuggle up in the crook of her bent knees. Abruptly, Amelia realized that while she used to spend 99 percent of her life in self-inflicted solitary confinement, this was her first time being alone in over six weeks.

This was the moment of truth in a lot of ways. How would she behave without eyes on her? Would she act out or keep on her path of recovery? She flipped through the Rolodex of her toxic coping mechanisms just to try them on for size, like taking a dress off the hanger and holding it up to herself in front of a mirror to see how it might fit now, which Bachelorette she might embody tonight.

Bachelorette Number One had been a fan of the binge-purge cycle. Even at one of the best treatment centers, the eating disorder had flown entirely under the radar. The center's oversight was rooted in the build of her sturdy body and validated by the archaic BMI criteria still used in ED treatment—if you weighed above a certain amount, you must not be that sick. Purging had been out of the question with all the lurking nurse techs, plus she had been on a rigid schedule of meals and snacks, manhandled into a normal-for-now relationship with food.

Bachelorette Number Two would get it on with a stranger. She could certainly use the release. Trying to masturbate in treatment while her roommate slept on the other side of the wall wasn't all it was cracked up to be. Especially when the staff cracked the door open every 30 minutes for night checks. Attempting to stimulate a pleasurable sensation on antidepressants was like trying to rouse the dead. Thirty minutes was just warming up, especially when you were lacking the necessary hardware. The desire itself never left, but the pleasure button in her pants felt like a slab of rubber most of the time. She was definitely eager to reacquaint herself with sexual gratification, but not necessarily as a way of acting out, more like a solo, bedtime activity. Another kind of self-care, her new recovery buzzword.

But Bachelorette Number Three insisted on her undivided attention. Number Two was too hot, Number One was too cold, but Number Three was *just right*. If she was going to act out and blow all her hard work and her parents' rehab money, it would be with drugs and alcohol. It was really the crux of the issue, after all; being fucked-up always made the food work that much faster and the cheap love taste that much sweeter. Weed was usually her go-to, but after six weeks, she was craving her old friend alcohol more than anything else. She sat in the purple chair, looked out into the backyard, and thought about how good the warm splash of liquor would feel as it ran down her throat and filled her stomach with molten goodness. That flip of the switch from white to black where everything felt beautiful again, like a flattering Instagram filter on her view of the world. It was a magical but poisonous elixir.

But the problem with that heavenly moment of the alcohol hitting your system was how quickly it would always pass. Five seconds of bliss would come and go, and then she would need more. And more. And then even more. She would spend the rest of her night—no, the rest of her *life*—trying to get back to the Instagram filter, unable to detect that it was all an illusion in the first place. Bachelorette Number Three would lure her into the depths of dark, dangerous waters only to hold her head under until she drowned.

She looked down at Delilah sleeping peacefully in her lap and shook her head. The dog's pure heart and intentions were opposites of the toxic part of Amelia—the one intent on killing her. That part could convince her to change the way she felt at all costs, even death, slowly or quickly, depending on what the occasion called for. It actively tempted her to mess up and drink, use, fuck, *do anything* to satisfy the craving. Death was ultimately safer than feeling the depths of pain and sadness she ran from. The fractured pieces of her fought to the death for survival on either side of the fault line.

Now that she was home, away from the safety of the pack, those damaged cells battled within her. *So act out. Be bad. Get fucked by a stranger. Slapped around. Disrespected.* Fresh out of treatment, she wanted to throw her life away for one night of ecstasy and oblivion. What she really needed to learn existed in the space between wanting to do something and making the decision to actually do it. It was the difference between her addiction and her wisdom. Between something she thought she desired and the truth about what she needed.

But cravings and urges subside with time. And negative emotions demand impulsivity in the first place—like waves that peak and crash. In treatment, she learned that feelings only last about 90 seconds unless ruminated upon. Problem was, she sometimes didn't want to have feelings at all. Hers felt so real and so strong that those 90 seconds seemed capable of stretching and growing and engulfing the rest of her timeline completely. Like her feelings might devour her flesh and spit out the bones.

She could have sworn that the thing she wanted above all else was to turn the feelings off. But she was beginning to suspect that her truest self wanted something more substantial and serene. Because her truest self understood that as threatening as they seemed, feelings couldn't harm her. The way she dealt with those feelings, however, had the power to cause serious harm, and in some instances, death.

The Forces of Good wrapped their arms around her, shaking away that option to act out as if clearing an Etch A Sketch. It was time to try something different and get a different result. The house seemed to lift her out of the chair and toward the back door, and at first, she didn't know why, but then it dawned on her: This was the perfect time to try out her first meeting. Her discharge team told her there was one downtown tonight. She needed to be with people who "got it" and then cap it off with a good night's sleep. Meetings were there for her when she was feeling lonely or scared or like she needed support, but she still couldn't imagine mustering enough courage to walk into a room full of strangers and let them see who she really was. Why couldn't she see herself the way Dr. B described in her final session yesterday? It was so simple in that room.

Amelia had tossed a stress ball back and forth between her palms in the comfort of that office. "I just wish I could be one of those girls who like, knows how to do winged eyeliner, and responds in the exactly cool enough way to Snapchats, and doesn't send repeat text messages. Just for one day, just to know what it feels like, to know for sure I'm wanted by everyone, like Mia. All the guys here are in love with Mia; she's just so obviously beautiful. She's a 10. People have to squint to find what's beautiful about me. I'm just a six with a decent sense of a humor."

Dr. B smiled warmly. "You know, I think there's something to be said about the difference between an amusement park and a National Forest."

Amelia cocked her head. "Come again?"

"Amusement parks are shiny and fun in an obvious way. You go there, and you pretty much know what to expect. People go there to have a good time, to get that feeling in their stomach when there's a big drop on a roller coaster, to win some prizes, and marvel at the lights on the Ferris wheel."

"Like the girls that can do winged eyeliner."

"Exactly! And there's nothing wrong with the amusement park. Some people would pick going to the amusement park over just about anything else."

Amelia nodded and rolled her eyes.

"But what about the people who aren't fans of the amusement park? What about the people who would rather visit a National Forrest? A place where the beauty is natural, subtle, full of wonder. A wild place that buzzes with the hum of aliveness, that houses something as raw and as real as the force of nature itself. You are a force of nature, Amelia."

She stared back at Dr. B, captivated.

"My point is, there are probably more people in the world that prefer the amusement park, I just don't think those are your people. Your people are the ones who marvel at trees and appreciate the intricacies of the earth. You just haven't found them yet, because you keep trying to be the damn amusement park. You're a life force powerful enough to spring up through the concrete and grow towards the sun."

"So, what you're saying is, fuck the eyeliner?"

Dr. B laughed and rolled her eyes good-naturedly. "There is a whole life for you out there, but it's up to you to plant yourself in the right place and tend to your growth lovingly and diligently. I, for one, believe you could embody an entire forest."

Tears stung the back of Amelia's eyes, and her chin trembled. "I'm going to miss you, Dr. B."

"I will miss you, too. But you are ready to apply what you've learned here to your life out there. When you're feeling doubtful about your path forward, just think of what I would tell you."

"That I'm a motherfucking National Forest."

Amelia grabbed her keys off the hook and hoped she remembered how to drive the Red Range after six weeks of being hauled around in a druggie buggie. She opened Wethersfield's door, willing, maybe for the first time, to just breathe and be a tree. Maybe she'd even find some forest friends in the church basement she was headed to. The address that one of the counselors had written down for her was seven minutes away. Her therapist Cathy's office was also seven minutes away. *A lucky number.* She sat in the car and looked at the house of healing and magic, then pulled out of the driveway as the opening notes of "Defying Gravity" serenaded her for the first time in five years. She was flying high, not a substance in sight.

CHAPTER 8

After a week, Amelia finally got around to shelving the first book in her new collection. The tattered copy of *The Catcher in the Rye* she stole from the rehab library acted as the centerpiece along with a few self-help books and recovery memoirs. Other meager additions included a clay vase she had made in art therapy and her goodbye card signed by the staff and other clients.

The charming floor-to-ceiling bookcase began to sprout life, no longer empty and hollow. Maybe one day, it would spill over with stories and wisdom like the shelves in Dr. B's office library. She sat in front of the towering bookshelf admiring the humble beginnings as she sipped her third cup of coffee of the day, a beverage proving to be paramount in sobriety. Amelia forgot to be anxious for a moment. Despite the inevitable moments of discomfort, she was able to enjoy the first day with nothing on her busy, early recovery schedule.

Show tunes flowed from her phone. Ever since that night enlisting the power of "Defying Gravity" to get her through the first meeting's door, she hadn't been able to stop listening to her old favorite musicals, from *Guys and Dolls* to *Spring Awakening*. *Wicked* broke the dam, something inside her that had long been closed off. It hurt to think of her falling-out with performing. But her soul clicked into place when she let herself belt along to the soundtracks—perfect backing to the rollercoaster of a week since being released into the wild.

Fear gripped her heart in a chokehold when she'd walked into the church basement just seven days ago. She was five minutes late and crept awkwardly to a seat in the back row. She tried and failed not to disrupt the speaker, and a cold sweat broke out on her neck. There were about 15 people in the room. Some even looked about her age, but they might as well have been speaking a different language with how in her own head she was.

As the meeting wound down, she left five minutes early—so she could stay consistent after being late to arrive and disconnected. She was also determined to avoid talking to strangers at all costs. As she disrupted the gathering a second time and made her way for the door, a woman with dirty blonde hair and a smattering of freckles similar to hers narrowed her gaze. Dark eye makeup and a black t-shirt stood out against the woman's lighter features. Though around Amelia's age, something in the stranger's self-assured gaze made her shrink at the extended eye contact.

Back in her Red Range, Amelia breathed a sigh of relief. *First meeting, check.*

Except not really. At her session with Cathy later that week, she promised to go back and make more of an effort to "connect with others." And that meant tonight, Amelia would make the same seven-minute drive to the muggy church basement, and this time actually open her mouth. It wasn't even noon of meeting day, and she was already nervous. At least now she knew what to expect from a meeting after a week of opening up in Intensive Outpatient. IOP, as everyone called it, was one of many recovery acronyms to keep straight.

Inside Wethersfield, she leaned back on her forearms to the finale of *Les Misérables*. That one line was the most beautiful thing: "To love another person is to see the face of God." Had she ever truly loved someone, or knew what that meant? Of course. She'd loved Trevor more than words could describe, and she loved her mom, dad, and Beth like crazy.

But one of those silly self-help books she'd just shelved talked a lot about love as an action versus love as a feeling. What was it like to love someone *in action?* To live life with love as the guiding force? And what in the fuck was all the God business about? That one still seemed well above her pay grade. She knew she didn't believe in a Sky Daddy or anything like that, but there did seem to be some kind of underlying force to it all. A Force of Good, maybe.

Just as a chorus of Broadway's best began to belt the final words of the musical, "Tomorrow comes!" in perfect harmony, her phone buzzed with a text.

> **Cathy: Amelia Bedelia! Don't forget about your meeting tonight. And remember, discomfort in recovery isn't a red light, it's a green light you have to squint to see! :)**

Amelia smiled and shook her head. Her therapist had used the family nickname ever since Amelia shared it with her years ago, so Cathy calling her that wasn't unusual. Amelia thought it was sweet. What *was* unusual was Cathy texting her on a Sunday about something that didn't have to do with scheduling a session. This must be important. In rehab she learned about strength in numbers—how being in the middle of the pack was vital. How allowing yourself to be seen and known by people who understood what you were going through, and trying to get better themselves, was crucial to one's own success in recovery. She supposed she would get this from both the meetings and the other IOP participants. But she knew IOP would eventually end, and if she established a solid enough routine, meetings could support her indefinitely.

Amelia let out a dramatic sigh as she thought back on her first week of IOP. It had been more or less uneventful, at least the first three days of the week. She liked the counselors and group leaders, and the other participants were kindred spirits, much like ones she found in rehab. Would people at the meeting turn out to be that way as well? There was something about the folks she was meeting in recovery that lit her soul on fire. *A little broken, but a lot brave.* Maybe the people who preferred National Forests were just the people who felt things as deeply as she did—the ones who had been through their own shit and come out the other side stronger. Too bad they all had to blow their lives to smithereens in order to find each other.

Some had external explosions: loss of relationships, houses, cars, careers. Some had internal implosions: self-esteem, passions, the will to live. And some of them had both. Implosion was more common for someone as privileged as Amelia. Externally, she had everything she could ever want, and anything she lost could be easily replaced. Internally? She was completely bankrupt, her soul empty. But this made space for the power of the forest to grow in abundance, letting nature replace the trees she'd been chopping down in the name of an amusement park.

On day one of IOP, Amelia met privately with one of the counselors to discuss her goals. She wanted to become more comfortable setting and sticking to her own boundaries and learn how to regulate her emotions more gracefully. Not drinking or smoking weed was the biggest, especially since she was still keeping that whole eating disorder thing to herself. It was currently dormant anyway. It was nice to have specific goals to work on beyond "not wanting to die." That was the main point in residential treatment.

Her time at the raggedy IOP building would be spent in group therapy, psychoeducational classes, meditation groups, yoga, guest speakers, corny games, and art therapy on a rotating schedule. By day three, she had experienced each unique layout of the schedule and was already bored. But the promise of new participants hung in the air. She had become fast friends with the middle-aged ladies, the group of boys her age, as well as the woman in her 30s with the cool tattoos, but she was ready for some fresh meat.

On day four, everything changed. Liam, the not-quite-divorced 39-year-old divorcé walked in and... He. Was. *Sublime*. He sauntered into the room in slow motion. Perfectly weathered Converse carried his tall, well-built frame across the dingy therapy room. A disheveled band t-shirt he had probably bought at an actual show hung effortlessly on his broad shoulders. His worn jeans spoke of life experience, and his blue flannel suggested a rugged sensitivity. His grown-man-sized hand combed through curly golden locks of hair that matched a delicious stubble. He dwarfed the 20-something boys in both spirit and stature. Amelia's mouth hung open as his deep blue eyes surveyed the large group room, and he politely nodded towards the other members in greeting. But when his eyes met Amelia's, they locked on her like a magnet, and the butterflies in her stomach performed acrobatics in response. *Well, fuck me sideways.*

In group therapy that day, she learned all about Liam's ongoing, messy divorce, heavy drinking, lifelong battle with depression, and dysfunctional family. *The perfect man.* Once they had gone around the whole circle and everyone had hurled their baggage into the center for the group to inspect thoroughly, it was time for a smoke break. Out in the parking lot, she had her first real Liam conversation.

"Could I bum a cigarette?" she asked. The tried-and-true recovery icebreaker fell easily from her lips, and while she wasn't a smoker per se, she had been bumming cigs since she was 15, usually when she was fucked-up. At almost two months sober, she was more than willing to partake, especially if it meant talking to Liam.

"Sure," he said with a smile bright enough to burn down an entire village and leave no survivors. His rough, calloused hand brushed hers as he handed her a Marlboro red, sending a surge of electricity through her body, not unlike the kind of sensation she used to experience when taking an enormous bong hit. Their eyes met as she wordlessly put the cigarette between her lips, and he raised his Zippo between them to light it. She took a long drag and blew smoke up into the crisp, early fall air, her eyes closing in gratification.

"Mmmm, cancer," she breathed.

"Oh my god, what?" He followed up with a surprised laugh.

Amelia's eyes widened. "Sorry, sometimes I say really weird shit that seems funny in my head, but it's just... you know, weird."

Liam smiled and shrugged, looking down at his chucks and then back up again at a bashful Amelia. "I like your freckles." He rubbed the back of his neck and tilted his gaze in faux shyness.

Since puberty, no one but her grandmother had said they liked her freckles. She was sufficiently shocked by his compliment. "Thanks. I've heard they're angel kisses, but I must have been gang-banged." When Liam guffawed, she decided she would henceforth do anything in her power to elicit that gorgeously awful sound.

"You're pretty funny, Amelia." Her entire body flushed pink because even after all the introductions in the group, she still didn't remember half the people's names in IOP. He'd remembered hers after the first go-around.

"Glad someone thinks so," she joked, hoping she was disguising the complete adoration taking over her system. Man, she could fall in love fast. Her dad always said she wore her heart on her sleeve. As a result, the wildest shit flew out of her mouth. While she wanted to curb some of her more harmful excesses, she was also starting to like some of the big things about herself. Her own transparency was growing on her—she put all her cards on the table and had so many to play that some of them got flung across the room. She got a kick out of saying things that were off the wall and a little shocking. Liam seemed to get a kick out of it, too.

"So, do you come here often?" he teased.

"For the last three days, yeah, it's pretty much the only place I go. Other than the barn"

"The barn?"

"I—um, I ride horses. Competitively. Hunter/jumpers. Mostly I just spoil and obsess over my horse, though."

"What's his name?"

"*Her* name is Hope."

"God, I'd love to see your horse sometime."

"Yeah?" No one ever wanted to go out to the barn with her, except Jen. "Are you kidding? Absolutely!"

"I mean, sure, anytime. Here, why don't you take my number." *Hallelujah for the perfect opening.* Liam handed her his phone and she entered her contact information, then handed it back just as a counselor poked their head out the door to announce the end of break.

"Looking forward to hanging, Amelia" he said with that same smoldering smile as he turned to walk back into the building. *Oh, she was so fucked.*

Days afterward, Amelia was pulled out of her Liam dream by Delilah's raucous barks as a leashed neighbor dog dared to walk down Wethersfield with its owner. Amelia huffed a laugh and extracted herself from the rug in front of her now partially decorated floor-to-ceiling bookshelves. Making her way towards the back of the house to let Delilah out into the yard, she noticed her muddy boots still on the back porch from yesterday's ride. She felt her lips curve into a smile at the recent memory.

Before rehab, she had gotten so accustomed to the tall boots, fancy breeches, and shad belly coats of the horse show world that she had forgotten the simpler joys: field rides and training sessions at home in plain old paddock boots at Greystone. While she focused on early recovery, she planned to spend more time riding at home than traveling and competing, and to be honest, she wasn't sure she minded. Hope didn't seem to mind it either. She was happy to be sleeping in her own stall in Austin and grazing in the lush pastures. They were both leaving behind the glitz and glamour of the horse show world for a while and going back to basics. The firestorm had cleared the path for more simplicity.

Amelia had been nervous that first time she drove out to the barn after treatment. It was her first time seeing Hope since that morning in Santa Fe. Without the show accident, Amelia never would have gone into treatment, and Hope's unconditional love was the only force strong enough to make her pause and consider recovery and a new way of life. She didn't know how she'd ever be able to say thank you.

She pulled up at the barn just as the sun extended its arms in a sleepy morning stretch across the horizon, incrementally revealing the big, green field. To get to IOP in time, she needed to get her ride in early. Riding wasn't the only thing in her life anymore. She was committed to putting recovery first. She'd heard early on at the treatment center that you were liable to lose anything you put ahead of sobriety. And she wasn't willing to risk losing Hope. Not again.

Amelia parked in the gravel lot near the stables, took a deep breath, and then made her way to Hope's digs. Her heart sank in disappointment when she found the stall empty with the door ajar, but the nest of plush shavings indicated that Hope had only just recently rolled out of bed.

She must be out in the pasture already. She made her way down the barn aisle, smiling at the other horses in greeting. As she came out the barn's other side, she spotted Hope's large bay silhouette in the distance, head down, grazing happily on fresh morning grass sprinkled with morning dew. Ever since Amelia was a kid, she'd always imagined those sparkling drops of moisture made the grass taste better, like butter on a piece of toast or brown sugar on oatmeal.

She paused when she got to the edge of the fenced-in pasture and breathed in the sight of her soul horse just existing. Perfectly content in the here and now without spectators. What a simple yet profound way to live: completely in the moment, unpenetrated by others' thoughts, feelings, or actions. In contrast, Amelia lived her life based completely on how her reflection bounced off others. There was so much that Hope and Delilah could teach her about living and healing. The laws of nature were rich with lessons for humankind.

Amelia continued towards the fence that separated them and let out a choked laugh/sob hybrid when Hope clocked her arrival. The horse stared with an all-too-human look in her eyes, registering Amelia's presence. There was a visible shift in Hope's stance as it dawned on her that Amelia really was there. Hope wasn't like most horses. She knew exactly how long it had been since she'd seen her person.

With an excited snort, Hope trotted to where Amelia stood beyond the fence, tears streaming down her face. She'd once read something about the chemical properties of different kinds of tears for grief, sadness, fear, anger, happiness, relief, gratitude. The tears staining her face as she was reunited with her animals were a clean and cool awakening. A revelation.

As the distance between them shrank, the world righted itself. They stood there for a long while minding the shift, Amelia stroking Hope's neck and planting kisses on her smudged, white star. She was supposed to ride that morning, but instead, she just sat on the fence and told Hope everything about the chunk of life since last being with her. In her new frame of mind, the sport itself was fun—but it was really about her relationship with Hope.

On the early mornings that followed, she did, in fact, ride. The pair hadn't slipped right back into their seamless dance just yet. As training picked up again, it was evident that the crash and the time away had disrupted their chemistry on course. On the ground, everything was as it always had been, but in the tack, Amelia still had some trust to regain. Hope remained understandably tentative at jumps. In all other areas of life, Amelia was insulated by privilege, sheltered from the external consequences she could have been saddled with. But no amount of entitlement could stop her from almost destroying the relationship that meant the most to her. She found that she and Hope could love and trust one another in some ways and still be healing in others. All of it could be true at the same time.

In the present, as she poured a fourth cup of coffee and stirred in the vanilla almond creamer she loved so much, Amelia looked forward to seeing Hope tomorrow. Her hands absorbed the warmth of the refreshed mug and she considered the newfound complexity of her innerworld in sobriety. She'd spent so much time in fight or flight, where only impulses existed: eat, fuck, numb, drink, crash, go, *more*. She sat with this ongoing evolution and took a sip of coffee, instantly charmed by the sweet, caffeinated nectar trailing a warm, golden path through her insides. She'd really perfected her milk-sugar-coffee ratio in rehab.

Just then, her phone buzzed against the countertop, making a horrid sound. Amelia picked up startled and annoyed. She expected it to be Jen checking in or Beth sending a meme, but her jaw dropped in awe and delight as she read the incoming messages:

> Liam: so when do I get to meet your horse? :)
>
> Liam: it's Liam btw, from IOP

As if she didn't know which Liam and hadn't been waiting for this very text message.

> Amelia: lol, when do you want to meet my horse?
>
> Liam: how about tonight? I'm off work at 8.
>
> Amelia: it's not really a nighttime activity...
>
> Liam: damn
>
> Liam: oh well
>
> Liam: another time then.

Amelia stared down at the text thread, and honest-to-goodness considered leaving the conversation at that, having a quiet afternoon at home with Delilah, and then going to the eight p.m. meeting *on time*. She really, truly did. But without her permission, her fingers danced across her keyboard instead.

> Amelia: we could do something else
>
> Liam: we could :)
>
> Amelia: I'd usually say let's meet at a bar, but I guess we don't do that anymore...
>
> Liam: lol guess not
>
> Amelia: what do people do when they don't drink?
>
> Liam: coffee shop?
>
> Amelia: coffee shop it is. Epoch?
>
> Liam: See you a little after 8, Freckles :)

Despite the abundance of smiley faces, which indicated that Liam was closing in on 40 with alarming speed, Amelia blushed and sat in one of the purple chairs. The butterflies fluttered in her gut. She was only 22, and this cool, older guy wanted to hang out with her; she was just that mature. Someone that mature could skip a meeting every now and then. She felt guilty about not following through on her promise to Cathy. But it wasn't like it was her last chance to go to a meeting, for fuck's sake.

Hours later, Amelia was putting the finishing touches on her look for the evening. She sported faded jeans, a Led Zeppelin t-shirt with pre-torn holes in it that she bought for $60 at Nordstrom, and her chucks. What was it she was going on about just a few days ago? Something about wanting to be more than just a reflection of those around her? She was the ultimate social chameleon.

She fed Delilah, let her out to go potty, and checked the mirror one last time. This was feeling a little familiar, and not in a good way, but she ignored the bubbling of intuition in her gut, tousling her long red curls just so and checking her teeth for stray lip gloss. Once Delilah was settled inside, Amelia grabbed the keys and headed for the side door. Her eyes narrowed at the way it stuck as she tried to swing it open and head for her car in the driveway. Either the foundation of the house was shifting, or the house on Wethersfield was asking her to slow down, pause, and examine her next move more carefully. She decided it was the former, finally yanking the door open and closing it again behind her. Doubts crept in when she pulled the Red Range into the street. What if it was too soon? What if this was the wrong move?

She stopped the car at the stop sign where Wethersfield Road ended and looked up at the darkening sky above the edge of downtown Austin.

"God, Universe, whatever you are…If this is the wrong thing, give me a sign, any sign, and I swear I will turn this car around." Saying the words out loud surprised her. Pausing for dramatic effect, the Forces of Good then sent another unlikely shooting star across the horizon, framed perfectly by the windshield of her car.

Amelia's mouth hung open, and she marveled at the sanctity of that moment. The Universe pointing her way back home. She looked down at her hands on the wheel, and a pregnant pause filled the car. She looked up again tentatively, almost embarrassed.

"Thank you," she finally said in a clipped tone, "but if you could just give me, like, *one more* sign, I *swear* I will turn this car around." The house, the Universe, the Forces of Good, even the literal stop sign all collectively threw up their hands in defeat and let out an exasperated sigh. Amelia chewed on her lip and took in the awkward silence. No second sign came. The Forces of Good were understandably insulted because how was a shooting star dancing across the sky right on cue not enough? And so, she was off, driving down Enfield Road toward her first big, sober mistake.

CHAPTER 9

Later that night, Amelia stepped back into Wethersfield with Liam close on her heels. Delilah gave the strange man a once-over before sniffing his shoes. Not a threat. Back on the couch, she tucked her snout under a throw pillow.

"Delilah, don't you want to say hi?" Amelia squeaked. Delilah only breathed heavily. "She's usually so friendly and welcoming."

"This is where you live?" Liam said, ignoring her preoccupation with Delilah. "All this is just for you?"

"Me and my 12 personalities."

He laughed indulgently, lifting his arm to scratch his neck, revealing a tempting sliver of midriff that Amelia wanted to lick. She walked into the kitchen, eager to give her awkward limbs something to do. God, this part felt clunky. They knew they were there to hook up, although still in the phase of pretending that wasn't the case. They were circling the uncharted body of water, splashing around in the puddles of their charged energy, waiting to see who might jump in first, delighting in the "will they, won't they?" But everyone knew. They so would.

As she grabbed two Topo Chicos out of the fridge and dug through her growing utensil collection for the bottle opener, the different parts of her battled it out. There was one part that wanted to pull Liam's shirt completely off after just a glimpse of the bare skin on his waist. Another part wanted to run away screaming. After hooking up with dozens of men, why should this feel any different? Why should her insides twist uncomfortably as she peered from water's edge into the sparkling blue?

Just as she popped the caps off the sparkling waters, the difference hit her like a belly flop. She hadn't hooked up with someone while sober since she was 15. Her sexual encounters had been buoyed by drugs and alcohol. They'd been a magical life vest that kept her safe from inhibitions and self-consciousness. They transcribed the ripples, water droplets whispering in her ear what to do with her hands. Would she even remember how to tread water? She worked up the courage to dive in and doggy paddle enough to keep her head above the surface.

Amelia walked toward Liam and offered him the bottle that acted as a stand-in for the usual liquid courage. He nodded in appreciation, and she stood there in her house with the grown-ass man she'd met three days ago and wondered what the hell to do next. Thankfully, Liam seemed to be an experienced swimmer.

"Before I forget, let me play you that song I was talking about." He plugged his phone into a speaker under the TV and sat on the large couch a good four feet away from a wary Delilah. He patted the spot next to him as a song by Iron and Wine began to fill the room.

Amelia immediately obliged, sitting with her thigh pressed against his, both of them leaning back to rest their heads on the top of the couch. They listened and Amelia fought off the urge to tell him she'd heard this song before, more than once, in fact. But it seemed important to him that he showed her something new. Very Aladdin on the magic carpet ride. *Men.*

As the song ended and another began, Amelia turned her head towards Liam slowly to find him already looking at her, a coy smile on his face. *Well played, Old Spice.* His fingers traveled the space between them to where hers lay and then rested their clasped hands atop joined legs. He began to play gingerly with the ruby ring on her pinkie. A soft sigh escaped her at the contact, and she bit her lower lip in that rehearsed way men seemed to love. It drew his eyes to her mouth. Dangerous sparks crackled in the chemistry brewing between them, and she marveled at the acrobatics in her lower belly. He pressed his forehead to hers and let out a low grumble when their lips were just inches apart.

The proximity of his beautiful mouth to hers sparked the phenomenon Beth fondly coined "pussy dips." No intoxication was needed; this was a drug all on its own. She could feel her brain swimming in the chemicals of anticipation and arousal. *So good.*

Liam looked down at their joined hands. "I was thinking..."

Before he could complete his thought, Amelia's hand curled up Liam's neck, tracing his delicious golden stubble on the way to grip the shaggy, dirty blonde hair at the back of his head and pull his mouth to hers. He tasted like cigarettes and black coffee, and she swallowed the surprised, excited laugh that slipped from his lips as they parted ever so slightly, inviting her to deepen the kiss. She slid her tongue tentatively against his in response, his hands moving to brush her hair over her shoulder and cup her jaw.

They kissed for several long moments until their bodies turned towards one another, both sitting up on their knees. Liam's hands fell at her hips, testing the waters with a tightening grip. Amelia arched her back, pressing her breasts to his broad, hard chest with a breathy whimper as if to say *dig into me before I change my mind.* He immediately answered, hungry hands pulling her soft hips in until her body was flush with his.

He broke away breathlessly, his gaze slipping from her lust-lidded eyes to her kiss-swollen pink lips and back again. "God, you're fun to kiss."

His whisper rode on an irresistible smile that she could *hear* even if her eyes were still closed and not staring back into his dark blue ones from inches away. They both looked down at the place where her pale, freckled cleavage pressed into him, and she tried to catch her breath as she watched him watching her. This was her favorite thing: seeing herself through someone's wanting eyes. A noise between a growl and moan escaped his throat as he wrapped his arms around her waist, pulling her impossibly closer, their lips meeting once again.

He staggered backward and fell to a seated position, pulling her on top of him so she was straddling his hips. Delilah looked over in annoyance from where she had been resting in comfort and headed for the front room, wanting no part of this mess. Amelia fell into him with a giggle and nipped at his lower lip as her hands grew hungrier, looking for their next place to explore. She ground her hips into his hard length where it pressed against his jeans. She marveled at the way her body could affect him this way, ignoring the fact that male erections were a dime a dozen. A barely audible whimper broke the barrier of Liam's lips as he came up for air, and the excitement of breaking him was superb. She had successfully overpowered the man in front of her and had him exactly where she wanted him. Her body always knew this before her brain did.

She was hardwired to assert dominance by constantly putting herself in a one-down position. It made zero sense, but it drove her every thought and action, and apparently, sobriety made little difference in this. She hadn't yet learned that this little dance of dominance and submission was best enjoyed with a true connection steering the ship: conversation and consent being the wind in its sails.

His hands slid down and grabbed handfuls of her Lucky-jeans-clad ass and squeezed in a way that evoked a moan she knew would pull him in even further. It was the kind of sound she'd always heard in porn. She could never really tell if the sounds coming out of her mouth were genuine or just what she knew she was supposed to utter. Moisture began to dampen her panties, as it always did, even when her gut was less than enthused by the man in front of her. The first time that happened, making out with Toby Garrett by the football field, she was mortified, convinced there was something fundamentally wrong with her body. Sometimes, that shame still permeated, thanks to a society built around women's supposed deficiencies.

But she didn't think too deeply about this in the moment, because this was the best part, the part before she'd given anything away to him. The part where she could still fool herself into thinking she had the upper hand. She was still remarkable in this moment, the limbo between being the only person in IOP who he'd deemed important enough to kiss and becoming just another of the people he'd fucked. But as he freed a breast from the top of her bra and swiped a thumb over her hardening pink nipple, she felt the power she had been yielding begin to slip away.

She always wished there was more time in that sweet spot before she was ripped open and exposed like a raw nerve. And it was such a confusing space to exist in, being someone who loved basking in her delicious sexuality, who craved the sensation of being consumed, and yet yearned for the pure kind of love and adoration that defied all reason at the same time. The kind of intimacy that was built upon slow kisses and holding hands but maintained by fervent exploration.

The zap of sensual pleasure versus the feeling of being broken open battled for prevalence. But her greedy body accepted the delights bestowed on her in the physical realm. She couldn't help feeling struck by how easily she fell back into the same song and dance as articles of clothing began to sprinkle the floor between the living room and bedroom. Together they made their way to the king bed that had maintained solo occupancy since she'd arrived home last week.

By the time they were naked in bed, she had completely lost her voice; she became whatever he wanted her to be. This form of selective mutism always made the condom situation interesting. For years, she had put the ball completely in the man's court, never asking for protection, not wanting to break the spell. But luckily, Liam had a condom; unluckily, it looked like it was from the early 90s. *It was the thought that counted.* To be fair, she'd been on the pill since freshman year of high school, so unplanned pregnancy was off the table. It was, however, a miracle she'd never gotten an STD.

Still, she'd never get over how easy it was to let someone inside her body, but how hard it was to watch them leave. Maybe deep down, she was trying to catch one. Not in a psycho pregnancy trap kind of way, just in a "feels too good not to want seconds" kind of way. The actual sex part of sex was a performance, and she wanted to be good enough to make them stay. It was no wonder she always got her feelings involved.

As they lay side by side afterward, Amelia felt empty. She wondered what she might feel like if she had opted for her meeting instead of this. She'd probably be sleeping peacefully with a blissful Delilah at her feet. Instead, she let her head spin out. How could something that felt so good 10 minutes ago feel so shitty now?

"I'm pretty sure that was super against the rules," she muttered, staring up at the ceiling.

"What rules?" Liam said, still a touch out of breath.

"The unspoken IOP rules. I don't think there's supposed to be any... *fraternizing.*"

He huffed out a lazy laugh. "We're both adults. I don't see the issue." But Amelia didn't feel like an adult. Not even fucking close. She chewed on her bottom lip, now in a very unsexy, anxious way that threatened to draw blood. She'd been treating her body like a cheap carnival for many years, and this time she didn't have substances to soften the blow of the post-orgasmic comedown. Not that orgasms were something that happened for her all that often during these little rendezvous, this instance included.

"Hey," Liam said, shifting onto his side and propping himself up on an elbow. "You OK? You seem, like, not here."

"I'm fine. Full disclosure, I've never done any of this sober." She rolled on her side to mirror him, gesturing between their bodies with her free hand. "The during part still felt the same, but I guess I need to get used to the before and after. I'm usually passed out by now, and you'd usually be gone before I woke up. But here we are..."

"Here we are," he said, giving her a genuine smile. "I really like you, Amelia. You just say whatever's on your mind. I never have to guess what's going on with you or try and interpret what you say. You just say it."

She hummed curiously in response.

"But, as you know, I'm going through a nasty divorce."

Here we go…

"And I'm really not looking for anything serious just yet."

"At least this part is still the same," she joked, but she could feel her stomach drop. No one was ever looking for anything serious. And it never failed to amaze her how much the energy shifted after a man had come, the power exchange complete. And why did these conversations about expectations always happen post-coitus, after they could do anyone any good?

In a way that made her want to die, Liam smiled sympathetically. "I really do want to keep hanging out, getting to know each other. But I think it's best if we keep things casual. And to your point about the rules, we should probably keep this to ourselves. I mean, it's really no one's business but ours, right?"

And most likely both of their therapists, but she wasn't about to point that out. "Right."

Her stomach just kept plummeting lower and lower, and soon it would be underground, joining her dead and buried self-esteem. Not that she didn't agree it was better to keep this little affair to themselves. It just also wasn't the first time she'd been asked to be a secret. In middle school there were long phone calls with Toby to plan their secret make-out sessions. She understood why they had to hide it from the adults but never had the nerve to ask why it had to be a secret from their peers. Deep down, she knew it was because Toby was embarrassed by her—by how *much* she was. She'd never felt worthy of being loved out in the open. Like she was someone people loved despite their best judgment.

He broke the silence, "So, how long have you lived here? I don't know many 22-year-old homeowners."

"What makes you think I own and don't rent?" she asked, eyebrows raised.

"The Range Rover…"

"Ah. Fair enough. I've been here since April." She counted the months on her fingers. "So about six months, I guess."

"It's nice. Has a ton of character."

"This house *is* a fucking character," she responded with fondness, thinking of all the important roles the house had played in her new life thus far.

"Partial remodels this close to downtown must cost a pretty penny. How'd you swing that?"

"I'm a tech genius. Sold my start up. The usual."

Liam stared at her blankly and she laughed uncomfortably. "No, I, um… my dad… trust fund."

"Ohhhhh a trust fund kid, looky there!"

"Yeah, yeah, yeah, I'm a cliché rich kid with addiction issues, I get it."

"You said it, not me." He let a laugh slip out. "But I get it. My dad's a wealthy doctor who always foots the rehab bill. And I'm the family disappointment who got kicked out of every private school and fired from every job. And then there's the divorce…"

She was surprised by how quickly he was opening up, but lying there naked without the cloak of booze seemed to have a way of turning them inside out to one another. Was this how people in recovery always talked? *Or was she someone special to him?* "It's hard to be a fuckup when you've been given every reason not to be."

"Yep." He shifted his leg.

"It just feels so weird sometimes. It's not like we always had money or anything. We were a pretty standard middle-class family until I was about 12, and then my dad hit it big." Her words started flowing as she looked at the ceiling, and she briefly wondered why she was telling him all this before continuing. "Hell, my great, great grandparents were born in Riga, Latvia. I'm pretty sure I have family members who were killed in the Holocaust, and my dad's parents were raised in poverty."

"Then what happened? How did it all end up here?"

"Well, they worked their asses off to create a launch point for my dad to live differently. And then he worked hard too, but also got lucky."

"How do you fit into all of that?"

"You know, I've gotten all these really wonderful opportunities thanks to the money he made, but in some ways, it was at the expense of our family unit."

"How do you mean?"

So many questions. His curiosity could only mean one thing: He was falling in love with her, he just didn't know it yet. "Well, when my dad sold his first company, they invited him to run it in Chicago. So, the four of us, my mom, dad, and sister Beth, moved in the middle of my seventh-grade year. When we moved back home to Austin, they built the lake house, but my dad only commuted home on weekends when he could. I think that's what first forced a wedge in their marriage. Even though I know we had problems before all that went down, I can't help but associate the money with the end of our family."

"I guess I can understand that." He reached to touch her hand.

She squeezed back and looked up at him and then back down at their joined hands. "You know, come to think of it, the move kind of marked the end of my childhood, too."

"Damn, 12 is just a kid. Pretty early for childhood to end."

"Yeah, I mean, it was either that or when I sent my first nude. Or when I got tits at Disney World. And no, I will not elaborate. Meh, tah-may-to, tah-mah-to." She looked at the ceiling thoughtfully. "Or was it when my Jewish grandfather got drunk and broke the news about Santa Claus? I couldn't have been more than six at that point."

"Jesus," he said through a laugh.

"Sorry, I don't even know why I'm telling you all this," she said as her cheeks flushed.

"I mean, I did ask," he said with a kind smile. "What about your mom?"

"My mom? Jen's a spitfire. That side of the family is Sicilian. They're pretty great."

"Sicilian and Jewish, that's a hell of a combo."

"You're telling me. My mom's side was working middle class; they were all educators. Still are. Much smarter than me."

"I doubt that."

"I don't know, they're pretty smart. I guess I'm still trying to figure out how I fit into all of it."

"Do you consider yourself Jewish?"

"Culturally? Yeah. I'm like a walking talking loaf of challah bread. But I was never bat mitzvahed or anything. Neither of my parents were religious or traditional, but if you look up Jew or Sicilian in the dictionary, there'd be a picture of each of them. Or at least their auras," she said with a laugh. "What about you? Where is your family from?"

"I'm just a WASP. Nothing super interesting. I come from a long line of rich, white Protestants. I wish I had anything interesting to say about my family. That's why other people's stories have always fascinated me. I don't really have my own."

"That's not true, I think everyone in recovery has a story worth telling." He shrugged off her comment and moved like he might get out of bed. The energy had shifted in a way she couldn't put her finger on.

"Do you consider yourself Christian?" she asked, trying to keep him beside her as long as possible.

"Fuck no." He laughed, and then Amelia joined in. "I am spiritual, though."

"What do you mean? Isn't it the same thing?"

"My first rehab counselor used to say that religion is for people who fear hell, and spirituality is for people who have already been through it. There's just got to be something bigger than me out there. Otherwise, I probably wouldn't be here after all the shit I've pulled."

Amelia furrowed her brow. She had never thought about a spiritual side of things outside of religion; to her knowledge, spirituality and religion went hand in hand. She wasn't a big fan of religion, so she'd never contemplated something bigger, but the Forces of Good that brought her to Hope, Delilah, Wethersfield, and this recovery journey stuck in her mind as she drifted off in thought.

Liam finally broke the silence again. "Well, I'd better get going. Don't want to miss curfew at the halfway house."

"Yeah, of course. See you tomorrow?" He gave her a nod and a wink and began to get out of bed and get dressed. Amelia lay there, looking at the ceiling, and listened as he went on a scavenger hunt for his haphazardly discarded socks and shoes.

Amelia sat up, pulling the sheets over her bare breasts, twisting a loose thread on the comforter as he stood in the doorway ordering an Uber.

He held up the phone. "Two minutes away." He strutted over with all the confidence in the world and kissed her on the flushed cheek. "Bye, Freckles." And then he was gone. The house let out a big exhale before drumming its metaphorical fingers on the countertop as if waiting for an explanation. Delilah finally felt compelled to rouse from the couch. She looked at Amelia from the doorway to the bedroom with a familiar energy of "What do you have to say for yourself, young lady?"

"I don't even know. Don't look at me," she responded. To whom she was unsure, but it felt disrespectful not to answer somehow. On the one hand, she'd had sex with someone who was off-limits. On the other hand, they'd talked about the Holocaust naked. *Was this intimacy?* She pulled a pillow over her head and tried to muster the energy to get up and lock the door before falling into a restless sleep.

The next day in therapy, Amelia confessed her absence from the meeting and her reasoning. She had a raging emotional hangover, even without a drink or a drug in the picture. She told Cathy the whole story, feeling somewhat grateful for the luxury of remembering all of it.

"So, I broke the unspoken rule of not sleeping with the other patients in IOP."

"That's a very much spoken-about rule."

"Huh?"

"Yeah, I'm pretty sure it was part of the paperwork you signed when you enrolled."

"Well, fuck. I won't tell if you won't?"

Cathy narrowed her gaze at Amelia. "Look, I've never been one to tell you what to do…"

Amelia cackled at Cathy in that way you can only do with someone you've known forever. "Oh, come on, you love telling me what to do!"

Cathy paused and pursed her lips, holding back a smile. "I've made suggestions, sure. But you're an adult now. A *sober* adult. You have to do these things because they are the right thing to do, not because you're scared you'll get in trouble if you don't. It has to be self-care instead of self-denial. Otherwise, you'll forever be the rebellious teenager trying to get her way."

"Touché. But it was just so different from every other hookup. We talked afterward, and he asked me questions about myself."

"Oh great," Cathy said. "The bare minimum."

Amelia gave her a look. "It was sort of weird, though—when I tried to ask him the same questions, he kind of pulled away. He opened up but in a very vague way."

"True intimacy needs to go both ways. Otherwise, it's just a battle of our attachment wounds. You have an anxious attachment style, and it sounds like he's avoidant."

Amelia thought back to the shift in energy when she asked him for details about his family.

"Therefore, you're oversharing, and he is pulling back when asked about himself."

"Oversharing? Did you miss the part where he asked me about myself?"

"That may be true, but not everyone deserves your whole truth, Amelia. Not unless they are willing to give a piece of themselves in return." Cathy shifted in her chair, uncrossing her legs and then recrossing them the other way. "And I am sure you have heard that relationships in early sobriety can be a slippery slope. But that has to mean something to you and how you value your sobriety. Otherwise, it's just a saying. What I'm curious about is how it feels to have crossed that line. Rule or no rule, slope or no slope, your gut can guide you. It's how you feel when you lay your head on your pillow at the end of the day. So, how did it feel when you went to sleep last night?"

"Not good?" she said as more of a question, begging someone to tell her how to feel, what to do, who to be. "God, I don't even fucking know how I feel! It's just this big ball of blah energy in my chest that shrinks and expands depending on what's going on around me. I am completely reliant on others, like a needy chameleon."

"Tell me more about the needy chameleon."

"It's like I have a porous sense of self. I soak up whatever it is I'm doing, or whoever it is I'm chasing until nothing exists but what they need me to be." She paused and waited for Cathy to respond, but she just sat there, providing the space for her to continue. "Like with men and sex. I mean, I think I've always known how much I perform for men. I'm constantly auditioning for the role of their next girlfriend, and when I get a callback, I'm all the more ready to ham it up and become whatever they want me to be."

"And how has that been working for you so far?"

"Great, if the goal is to be a shell of a human being who ties all her worth to sexuality. I act like the most important thing I can do for a guy is get him off. The saddest part is sometimes I really do believe that."

"I think that was likely the first way you got a boy's attention and kept it on you."

"But why do I even need their attention in the first place? Why am I so desperate to be lovable? And why does *that* have to be what makes me so hard to love? It's totally fucked."

Cathy let the words linger, nodding compassionately like a caricature of an understanding therapist. "Idealization and devaluation of others, extreme fear of abandonment, rapidly changing sense of self, disconnection from others, feelings of emptiness, self-destructive behaviors..."

"What are you doing?"

"Listing the symptoms of Borderline Personality Disorder."

"Ah. Cute."

"Diagnoses are just a cluster of symptoms, Amelia. It's nothing to be ashamed of. The stigma is just that, a stigma."

"I guess it's just, in a lot of ways, it seems like a death sentence. Or at least a sentence for a shitty life."

Cathy gave her a weak smile. "A lot of people diagnosed with Borderline don't have much self-awareness around their symptoms. That's actually the only symptom of the disorder you don't have. Self-awareness has always been one of your strengths, which is a blessing and a curse. A blessing because you have so much potential to get better and create a life that suits you. A curse because you know exactly what you're doing and why. It's like watching a horror movie but you're the main character, and you're shouting at yourself through the screen to run away instead of checking out the weird noise in the basement."

Amelia huffed out a laugh. "Why the fuck do they always go into the basement?"

"Why do you continue to sacrifice your long-term peace for short-term relief?"

"Damn. Has it been 50 minutes yet?"

Cathy checked her watch but ignored her question. "You're incredibly smart and insightful, Amelia. And everything we've discussed today is important information, but it isn't new information. From what you've told me, this has more or less been your pattern since the fifth grade. Holding the knowledge of your issue but continuing with the same behavior will drive you absolutely mad. And I say this with love, but if you keep making decisions like you made last night, you will eventually use. Because if your behavior continues to be self-harming, you will find it necessary to numb again. Especially now that you know better."

"Jesus, I think in the horror movie I'm the one running away, but I'm also the scary stalker with the knife. And if you're not running from yourself, what's the other option?"

"The other option is you buckle down, and we do the archaeological dig. We do the real therapy work and find what's on the other side of these Borderline symptoms, because they don't exist in a vacuum. We've just never gotten a chance to go that deep because there is always some sort of chaos to clean up."

"Maybe that's the point of the chaos. Maybe part of me doesn't want to see what's behind it."

"Whatever it is, you've built your entire personality around protecting yourself from it. That's what a personality disorder is—your symptoms are defense mechanisms there to keep you safe, and they become so ingrained it becomes who you are." Cathy paused. "But Amelia, sometimes I see who you really are, peeking from behind a curtain. Like a force of nature."

Like a ghost light that refuses to be extinguished after final bows. Or a wildflower that grows back year after year no matter what.

"Like a National Forest," Amelia almost whispered. "You know, I see her sometimes too. But there's a lot of debris to clear out before she can have the space she needs to grow."

While Cathy smiled at the reference Amelia had shared, they both sat in the dense silence that followed.

Amelia finally said, "I'm just going to be honest with you because you're Cathy, and you're the only person I'm fully honest with." Cathy raised her eyebrows. "I'm not done with Liam. I'm not ready to let it go just yet."

"Well, we grow at the speed of pain, don't we?" Cathy got up from her plush therapist's chair and opened the door to her office. "I'll see you next week."

Amelia smiled weakly and walked to her car. As she drove the Red Range towards IOP, she thought not of what she might learn today, or how she might grow, but of what Liam might think of her outfit.

CHAPTER 10

A melia blasted the *Hamilton* soundtrack on repeat most days since arriving home from rehab, and today was no exception. On her way to IOP, she belted with passion alongside the Schuyler sisters. Tending to drive with her emotions, her speed increased at pivotal points in the plot as she imagined how she'd play a given role. Sometimes Hamilton himself. Having family in New York, Amelia had been going to Broadway shows since she was old enough to walk, another manifestation of the immense privilege borne somehow out of her grandmother's cramped Brooklyn apartment. To Amelia, the people on the stage were the most special people in the world. Chosen ones, even more so than movie stars. The people on stage seemed to glow and transcend this realm.

Growing up, she'd wait outside every stage door, fighting her way to the front of every line, and hand over every playbill for signing. She was always prepared with a silver or black sharpie, depending on the graphics of the play's design. Then she'd watch in awe as her heroes made their way from the sacred theatre back out into the streets of New York City. They'd fade into a painting of the cityscape as they walked away until you couldn't tell them apart from any other New Yorker. Her excitement would screech and claw inside her chest as she watched it all unfold.

But she always played it cool on the outside, because she had a secret. A leg up on all the fans flailing about foolishly with their own pens and programs. No one knew it yet, but she was one of the chosen ones, too.

She had to be. One day, she'd be the one coming through the stage door to mingle with adoring fans. She'd apologize for being unable to get to everyone and then disappear down the crowded street, the sound of her sensible heels clack, clack, clacking on the concrete on her way home to the cozy apartment with the exposed brick wall. Not that she'd thought too much about it.

She couldn't accept the idea that she was just another kid in the audience, another crazed theatre nerd with a ridiculous Broadway dream. Amelia couldn't stand the idea of being ordinary. In fact, ever since the first pediatrician marveled at her early milestones and dubbed her as "extraordinary," gushing over how bright she was to her young, proud parents, she'd been trying to prove he wasn't mistaken. So, when Trevor picked her out of everyone else at their high school and they fell in love, only for her to blow it? When Hollywood came knocking on her door only to say never mind? When men picked her up at a bar only to fuck her and forget her? All of that just about killed her.

She would forever be almost good enough. She could never follow through when it mattered; she just stayed stuck in a game of catch and release. She still couldn't force herself to step away long enough to try something else.

The need to be picked, to be the best, hands down, bar none, was louder than anything else. Each time, it was "maybe this time." *What if I picked myself instead?* The thought from deep in her chest was quickly discarded, replaced by the slam of her car door, the beep of it locking, and the sound of her footsteps on the way into the IOP building.

Whether she was winning first place at a horse show, getting cast in her dream role, or being hit on at a bar, the feeling of winning always won out. It drove her crazy that no one in IOP knew that Liam had picked her. As new girls filtered into the program, and the ones that had already been there, took notice of Liam's big blue eyes and elegantly disheveled hair, Amelia fought the urge to mark her territory—or preferably, have the entire room watch as he marked her as his.

But she couldn't deny the salaciousness of their secret two-week love affair. The way they would sneak hungry make-out sessions in the hallway on smoke breaks and brush fingertips secretly during silent group meditations. The way they'd make a show out of saying goodbye to one another at the end of group just for Amelia to pick him up at the corner and head back to Wethersfield for their daily dose of debauchery. The way his opinion became the most important one in her life so quickly. Her days consisted of training with Hope in the mornings, IOP in the afternoons, and nights of rediscovering her body while caging her giant, gaping heart.

Settling into the normal therapeutic programming for the day, she couldn't help but think about the upcoming third act. The sex was OK, and as she got to know Liam better, her body seemed to wake up and reorient to the idea of physical enjoyment in a way she'd once feared would forever delude her now that she was sober. She even got close to orgasm occasionally, but it was becoming clear that it would take more than someone chasing their own pleasure to create enough space for a climax. What she really needed was patience and connection—what she was getting was the bittersweet and underwhelming wake of someone else's release. She whisper-yelled metaphorical pleas to be loved and cherished, trying in vain to be heard by someone wearing emotional headphones.

It was a Wednesday afternoon in IOP, the day after a particularly average evening of sex and pillow talk. Group therapy had just begun. She shot Liam a sultry look across the circle of chairs, but his weak smile and averted eye contact alerted her to the tension in the room. *Interesting*.

Amelia wondered if someone had relapsed again. Last week, the counselors gathered the program participants in a similar way and let them know that one of the younger boys had overdosed and just barely made it to the hospital in time. The boy was back in residential now, and as many times as the counselors assured them that relapse was part of recovery—something they'd have to get used to, even—Amelia didn't think she could ever not be shocked and sad when someone "went out." They made it seem so benign. The fucked-up truth was if the person survived the relapse, it was deemed "part of recovery." But if the person didn't make it back, the relapse was used as an ominous warning. When she looked around the room, everyone was accounted for, so what was all this tension about?

"Alright, everyone, quiet down. There's something serious we need to discuss," the middle-aged, blonde counselor named Chrissy announced. "It has come to our attention that one of the IOP rules has been broken in a way that could compromise the sanctity and safety of the recovery space we've created together." Perplexed murmurs could be heard around the room as Chrissy continued. "Two participants have entered into an inappropriate relationship and have been dishonest about it."

As these words echoed around the dingy group therapy room, Amelia felt her soul exit her body and her heart fall out of her butt. Her wide eyes darted across the room to Liam, but he was too busy staring down at his shoelaces to notice.

"As you all know, it is integral to the therapeutic space that sexual and romantic lines remain uncrossed in the interest of preserving the supportive neutrality of the space. Therefore, we have all participants sign an agreement stating they will not violate these agreed-upon boundaries during the IOP process."

Amelia knew at that moment if she had eaten lunch, it would be on the floor.

"On that note, I'm going to give the floor to Liam."

This just kept getting worse and worse.

"Yeah, um, thanks, Chrissy. I owe everyone an apology. I crossed a line I shouldn't have crossed. I entered a physical and romantic relationship with a group member," he said, clearly repeating what he had been told to say, all the while scratching the nape of his neck like she'd seen him do all those times.

Now his slightly exposed midriff didn't make her mouth water. She was just trying to conjure any amount of moisture to quench the vast desert her throat had become.

"But you know, while I'm sorry for being dishonest and breaking the rules, I'm also glad it happened. Because what this person and I have is really, really special."

Amelia's pulse was out of control at this point.

"In fact, I think I'm falling in love."

In love? Suddenly, her worst nightmare was becoming her ultimate fantasy; forbidden love defying the odds, casual turning into forever because she was that irresistible, public admissions of affection leaving onlookers in shock and awe. Amelia couldn't help the demented smile that spread across her face amid all the tension. *It's happening. He chose me.*

After a thick silence, Chrissy cleared her throat, "And what about you, Cassandra?"

Cassandra? Who the fuck is Cassandra? Amelia's head whipped to the other side of the circle to find the cool, tattooed woman in her 30s going through her own emotional roller coaster. Oh, that Cassandra. Cassandra's hand flew to her mouth to stifle a teary giggle, then clutched her heart as she looked around the circle in delighted surprise, finally landing on Liam's eager gaze. *What the fuck is going on?*

"Oh, Liam, I think I'm falling in love with you, too." He beamed back at her, and Amelia shook her head and closed her eyes, trying to shake herself awake from the nightmarish atrocities at play.

Counselor Chrissy released an exasperated sigh. "You know what this means. The only way you can both stay and finish the IOP program is if you agree to stop seeing each other outside of group."

Liam huffed out a laugh, never taking his eyes off Cassandra. "Not me." Cassandra nodded in agreement, inching to the front of her chair.

"Alrighty then," Chrissy said in a clipped tone. "If I had known we'd be discharging you both, we could have done this in private. So much for the learning moment! Well, before we say our, um...*goodbyes* to Liam and Cassandra, does anyone else in the group want to share how this has affected them or how this makes them feel?"

"Yeah," Liam said, sans eye contact with Amelia, "I mean, it was never my intention to hurt anyone, you know?" It didn't appear that he was actively avoiding her gaze, more that it just hadn't crossed his mind. The rest of the group members shrugged and looked around in the awkward silence that followed.

That's when Amelia started laughing hysterically. A loud, unhinged cackle from deep in her core rang out across the room, bouncing off the walls chaotically. Everyone in the room, Chrissy and the lovebirds included, stared at her in confused terror. She tried to form words, but that just made her laugh harder until tears rolled down her cheeks.

"Amelia, do you want to share what's coming up for you with the group?" Chrissy asked in a concerned voice.

But she simply couldn't. Stop. Laughing. She just covered her damp, reddened face with one hand and waved the other wildly as if to say, "I cannot right now."

Liam had a look on his face like he just remembered that he'd been fucking her every day for the past two weeks. The room remained silent while Amelia tried her best to rein it in. How had he even had time to be screwing someone else in the first place? She thought back to what her sister always said about never assuming you're exclusive with a man unless it has been explicitly stated. If you find yourself thinking, "I know we haven't exactly discussed it, but we see each other every day and talk about our families, he couldn't *possibly.*" Well, yes, he could.

"I have to pee," Amelia finally said through her laughter. "Excuse me." She made her way to the bathroom in the hallway as Chrissy and the other group participants looked on with baffled concern. Once alone in the bathroom, her maniacal laughter seemed to run out of steam. She leaned forward with her hands on the edge of the sink and watched as droplets of water dripped from the faucet. She choked on the familiarity of being almost special enough. The next thing she knew, there was a knock on the door. Amelia's gaze shot up, and she made eye contact with herself in the mirror as she racked her brain about how to handle the intrusion. Another warning knock echoed off the tiled walls.

"Amelia? Are you OK in there? It's Chrissy."

God damn it, Chrissy the counselor was the exact last person she wanted to talk to right now.

"Fine," she replied with a dramatic eye roll, shooting daggers through the door, willing the well-meaning woman to go the fuck away.

The door creaked open as Chrissy came in. She closed it softly, leaning against it to ensure privacy and feign some chill. When their eyes finally met, she offered a sympathetic smile. "You were involved with Liam, too, weren't you?"

She considered lying but didn't see the point. "Yeah. I was. I *thought* monogamously, but…"

"Ah. We've all been there, huh?"

Amelia cocked her head, surprised by Chrissy's candor. "We have?"

"I was young once, Amelia. Although men still act like assholes when you're older, too. Case in point." Chrissy gestured towards the group room.

Amelia couldn't help but laugh at that. "Speaking of," she said, nodding in the same direction, "Don't you need to get back?"

"Nah," Chrissy said, lowering herself to sit on the bench at the edge of the large public bathroom, "I left one of the interns in charge."

Amelia nodded in response and propped herself up to sit on the edge of the sink. "The good one or the bad one?"

"The bad one," Chrissy said with a laugh.

"Oof. You knew which one I meant and everything."

"Is she really that bad?"

"All we hear her say is, 'And how do you feel about that?' Last week, she told someone to stop crying."

"Yeah, that's pretty bad. So how did this happen? You're not in trouble, I just want to understand."

"He just gave me attention, and I liked it. What can I say? I'm a sucker for men who give me the time of day."

"Bar seems pretty low. Why do you think that is?"

Amelia shrugged. "Since I was 13, I've been consistently chasing boys. Even after I catch them, I still chase them until they run away. My love life is like a possessed merry-go-round. I used to think I was just trapped, but I'm starting to realize that I'm the one who keeps buying tickets and going back.

"Sounds like you need to take a step out of line."

Dr. B's kind face entered her mind. "More like I need to leave the whole amusement park."

"Have you considered taking a break from all that? Sex, romance, dating?"

"Would you judge me if I told you it never even crossed my mind?"

Chrissy shook her head, "Look at the world we raise our daughters in! All the Disney movies and what have you. It's all about true love's first kiss saving the day, as if men's lips alone could ever make anything better."

"Except Mulan."

"Yes, except Mulan. And some of the newer ones are getting a lot better, to be fair. But in the 90s, when you were just a bundle of neuropathways ready to be excavated? Love at first sight."

"I don't even know what life would look like if I weren't constantly begging to be loved."

"Well, you'd have to find a new end-all be-all."

"Right. I'm sure I could just run over to the store and pick one out."

Chrissy sighed in exasperation. "Are you going to continue to deflect with humor now that you've been vulnerable, or can we go back to having a real conversation?"

"Jesus!"

"Am I wrong?"

Amelia just shrugged in silence.

"Anyway, what's most important to you?" Chrissy asked.

"My animals, I guess."

"And when do you feel the freest?"

Amelia thought about this for a moment. "When I'm outside with my animals."

"I dare say *nature* may be of some significance to you?"

"I dare say it is."

"You know, there are a lot of people who connect with nature almost spiritually. Many lives are improved by simply plugging in to something bigger, and nature is certainly big."

"I never thought about spirituality outside the confines of religion until *fucking Liam* started talking about it that way. But he's an asshole in my head now, so I'm trying not to give him much credit."

"What did he say about it?"

"That religion is for people who fear hell, and spirituality is for people who have already been through it. He didn't come up with that on his own or anything, but still, I hate him now, so…"

"You know, I don't think it all has to be so black-and-white. What if he taught you some valuable things *and* he wasn't the right person? Both can be true at the same time. And just because someone couldn't love you the way you deserve doesn't make you unlovable. I really need you to hear me when I say this. You're going to have to learn to love yourself before you'll be able to love anyone else, let alone allow yourself to be truly loved."

Well, shit. She couldn't even say it out loud, it stunned her so.

When Amelia got home that evening, she perched herself on one of the purple chairs and tried to enjoy the light fall breeze through the open back door. She looked out the window at Delilah exploring the bushes near the edge of the fence. The sun had just sunk behind the hills across town, and twilight began to seep into the horizon. It would be dark soon. *Time to feel lonely.* Amelia instinctually pulled her phone out of her pocket and went to redownload Tinder. Her finger hovered over the icon in the app store. The dopamine hit lay just on the other side of the glowing screen. Sitting forward in the chair, she took a deep breath, set her phone down on the coffee table, and rested her elbows on her knees like someone mentally preparing for the game of a lifetime.

She stared down at the floor and envisioned the fork in the road as it manifested itself, forming a split trajectory, vivid lines on a map within the very floorboards of the house. To the left, the toxic merry-go-round urged her to hop back on for another few laps around hell itself; to the right, the complete unknown, something different, possibly better. The path to the right was like an illuminated chunk of unclear mosaic. But it lovingly drew her in, promising to reveal more along her journey. She knew where the left path led like she knew the lines in the palm of her hand. That merry-go-round could not, would not be her legacy.

Then her phone died.

The Forces of Good had been at her heels for a while, but in that moment they intercepted her completely. She was relieved that the decision about the path was made for her. She walked into the bedroom, and instead of just plugging her phone into the charger, she reached for the floral monstrosity of her journal, reacting with somewhat less of a scoff than usual to the cover's cursive gold lettering: "Something Beautiful is on the Horizon." Maybe it was, maybe it wasn't, but she couldn't keep doing what she had always done. She took the journal and her pen to the couch and began to write.

October 15th, 2015

Well, I've been home from rehab for three weeks, and I've already had a relationship crash and burn. My instinct is to fuck the pain away, but Chrissy implied that it would behoove me to take a break from the whole song and dance. She said I need to learn to love myself before I can love anyone else. She also said spirituality could help me. I've always found religion and God to be pretty elusive, but

*when I was thinking about it today, I realized something
a little disturbing: My whole life, I have somehow believed
that "God" has a dick. What's even more disturbing is the
realization that if God has a dick, I'd want to be someone
he'd like to fuck with that dick. That is how deep this shit
goes. And if I ever meet the fucker who planted this seed of
internalized misogyny—well, let's be real, at this point I'd
probably hop on his dick too.*

She took another deep breath and cracked her knuckles before continuing
the journal entry with fervor.

*I just feel so much in this moment. I want to eat a thousand
cupcakes and bury the feelings under a mountain of
frosting. I want to be blindfolded and used by a room
full of men. I want the blood in my veins to be replaced
by substances that melt me into nothing more than a
puddle of ecstasy. I want complete oblivion. And you know,
underneath it all, these are the moments when I want to
die. I want to cease to fucking exist. Because no matter
what I find out there, I will always just want more of
it. But despite these gargantuan feelings, I know there's
something better on the other side of all this discomfort—I
catch glimpses of it every day. I'm going to start looking for
a more effective center of gravity; I need something more
substantial to revolve around than someone's opinion of
me. Like the towering trees that outlive human beings. Or
the way the wind sends leaves cascading down the sidewalk
without revealing itself. The way Bluebonnets sprout on
Highway 71 each spring no matter what tragedy occurred
that winter. If there is a God, I think it's in the forest. And
as far as I know, forests don't have dicks. They just are.*

She paused and looked out the window into the backyard. The orange-tinted moon shimmered behind a screen of tree branches as it made its way to center stage in the darkening sky. Every single day, all 365 days of the year, the moon chased the sun around the planet. Amelia would have killed for the consistency of the moon, to replace her chase of the next man with the chase of a real light source, even if she didn't know what that was yet. Maybe it was OK to need the light of something to bounce off your surface and illuminate you, so long as it was worthy of the idolatry. Amelia tapped her pen on the edge of the notebook and unspooled her next words carefully.

> *Jen used to say that you don't truly know someone until you know them through all four seasons of the year. Seen them wither in the fall, rest in the winter, bloom in the spring, and flourish in the summer. If my goal is to know and love myself and connect to the earth around me, I might as well take a full year, all four seasons, all 365 days, to do so. Fuck it. I'm going to do it. I am going to give up sex, flirting, dating, MEN all together for a full year. At this point, what do I have to lose? And who knows what might rush in to fill the space?*

CHAPTER 11: MONTH 1

It was one of those late October days in the South so beautiful it could inspire poetry in the damned. The golden autumn sun warmed Amelia and Hope from the inside, balanced with a crisp breeze that smelled like the transition and release that only the turning of the season could alchemize. In Texas, summer and winter lasted about five months each, and spring and fall were lucky to soak up the spotlight for four weeks before they were pushed off stage by more domineering seasons. Due to their limited engagement and mild manner, spring and autumn evoked a special kind of joy in Texans, as if the people never experienced delightful weather before. Or perhaps they'd just forgotten what it was like to enjoy being outside since the last time it happened, six long months earlier. Amelia ran her fingers through Hope's sun-kissed mane, closing her eyes to breathe in the air that danced through the trees at Greystone Farm.

It was a group lesson day, and Amelia could have fallen asleep right where she sat atop Hope's strong, athletic form, waiting for her turn to complete the course Deb had laid out for the riding students. She could hear Deb's voice as she dictated proper form and pacing. She was barely paying attention, though she certainly should have been. Still anchored in the stirrups, Amelia wrapped her arms around Hope's neck to offer the mare a squeeze. A soft, contented nicker escaped Hope's velvet nose and lightly rumbling lips. Amelia breathed out a fond chuckle in response. She twisted her fingers in Hope's mane, considering the way her grandmother's ruby pinkie ring glistened in the afternoon sun. She never took it off, not even to ride.

It had been a week of no boys. No dating apps, no sexting, no video chats, no dates, no flirting, no nothing. She felt lonely, but on the other hand, she found herself in a passionate new love affair with the wind. She was falling for the way it gathered the dead leaves on the sidewalk and sent them skittering down the concrete in crispy clicks and clacks. She admired the way it tousled the curls cascading down her back during morning walks with Delilah. The way it created rustling sounds in the trees above. The way it needed no color, shape, texture, or weight. These were the kinds of things people pondered when they weren't trying to get laid all the time.

But then someone in the grocery store would look at her the wrong way, and she'd spiral into the pit of existential dread and apathy. Or she'd notice the stars glistening in the night sky and instantly be flooded with self-pity because she didn't have anyone's hand to hold as she gazed up. In one moment, she'd be floating on her pink cloud, noticing the wonders of the natural world, grateful to be alive and sober, and the next, she'd want to yeet herself off a cliff. The endless cycle of pink clouds and cyclones arguably mirrored the real-life Texas weather in that four-week season.

The walks, morning coffee, and the crisp, cool sheets of a bed made every day were the things she looked forward to. These things were a far cry from having a stranger over to dick her down and then exit stage left at two a.m. Each morning, she'd roll her eyes at making a bed she was just going to get back into hours later, and each night, when she folded back the comforter and crawled in, she'd be grateful that she did. She was learning how to tolerate delayed gratification instead of chasing every impulse. To make decisions that felt good after the fact instead of during the act.

That particular morning on her walk with Delilah, her decision to abstain from acting out paid off in the serenity flowing through her.

Sure, she had been bored at times, not reaching for the boy, the drink, or the drug. But as a result, she could really see the masterful painting of scattered shadows on Wethersfield Road and the elegance of the leaves fluttering down like tiny dancers. She could feel warm sun on her skin met with the cool nudge of the autumn breeze. She could experience a true moment of gratitude that wouldn't have been possible had she reached for a vice up to that moment.

But the storm clouds always had a way of rolling in and casting her sunny outlook in the darkness of shadows, and that morning was no exception. Halfway through her walk with Delilah, the phone rang and she had to dig it out of her back pocket to find Liam's name on the screen along with her contact photo of him, a selfie of the two of them that clearly meant more to her than to him. Before she could think any better of it, she accepted the call.

"Um, hello?" Delilah turned her head back towards Amelia and seemed to cock her eyebrow as if to say, "Who could possibly be important enough to interrupt our morning promenade?"

"Hey, Freckles," she heard Liam say through the crunch of her headphones. She hated the way her stomach did a backflip, causing the butterflies to jolt awake from their weeklong slumber. She stayed silent until he spoke again. "Been a while. I miss seeing you at IOP."

"Well, maybe you shouldn't have fucked Cassandra behind my back and gotten yourself kicked out, then." Delilah looked back at her again with judgment as they continued descending the block.

"Whoa, where is this hostility coming from, Freckles?"

"Maybe don't call me that anymore."

"Amelia, we were never exclusive. I thought I made it very clear that I needed something casual. But I really did enjoy your company."

"For sure. You just enjoyed some else's more." The walk came to a complete stop as squirrels and birds scattered from a nearby tree when she unintentionally raised her voice. The pink cloud to storm cloud pipeline was 0-100.

"I guess I just don't see it that way, Freckles. You're both phenomenal women, but I always saw you as more of a friend. I didn't mean to fall in love with Cassandra. It just happened."

"Well, it wouldn't have just happened if you stuck your dick in one person at a time." Delilah began pulling her down the street again, completely finished with the rude pause in the walk.

"Again," Liam said, a little frustrated, "you never communicated that you had expectations of us being exclusive."

She was beyond pissed. "Is this a joke?" All her shitty experiences in the Austin hook-up scene over the past year bubbled up to the surface. But she took a deep breath. She might be overreacting or taking things out on him in a way that was unfair. "Hey, I'm sorry. It's possible we just miscommunicated. I know you're not a bad guy, and I know you probably didn't mean to hurt me."

"I really didn't. I feel like shit knowing I did."

"I'll get over it. And I wish y'all the best, I mean it." She didn't really mean it, but she wanted to.

"Thanks, Freckles." She could practically hear his stupid dimples through the receiver.

"So, why did you call anyway?"

"Well, I have a proposition for you…"

"Okay."

"Me and Cassandra were interested in adding a third in the bedroom, and you were obviously my first thought."

Amelia tried to speak, but all that came out was another one of her hysterical cackles, much like the one from the group therapy confessional last week. "You know what?" Back to yelling, she kept her walking momentum for the dog's sake. "I am *so* sick of this faux free love, fuck-boy bullshit. And it's not even your fault that I'm so sick of it! I put myself in this position over and over and over again and act shocked and appalled when someone looks at my behavior and assumes I'd be down to be their third. So, no. My answer is no. Maybe this whole new age thing works for you, but it just doesn't fucking work for me, and I have to stop pretending it does."

"Okay?"

"Bye, Liam. I'm mostly frustrated with myself. I do wish you the best."

"You too." She shook her head and stared at the ground. It wasn't just his audacity, it was something else. It was the idea of being with another woman, threesome or otherwise—a desire she had long buried under her compulsive need to impress and woo men. Trevor had his suspicions back in high school when she'd get "jealous" of other girls. She'd accuse him of wanting to fuck them and he'd ask if it was just that she wanted to fuck them herself. It usually didn't go over well.

Later on her ride with Hope, Amelia picked at the pilling leather on the edge of her saddle as her brain lured her into memories of girl-on-girl experimentation at middle school sleepovers. She had enjoyed them a little too much at the time to chalk it up to "practice." It could have just been hormones. Deep shame titrated with terror seeped through her pores as she tried to push away the complicated feelings and desires of her past. This was the kind of reflection that her break from boys and sex was creating space for.

That wasn't a bad thing, but now certainly wasn't the time. "Amelia and Hope, let's go." Deb's stern voice broke through the swirl of her thoughts.

Amelia gently squeezed her heels into Hope's barrel, and they began to move from their spot on the rail in the sun. Hope's gait sprang up into a peppy trot and then slid gracefully into a fluid canter after a few moments, her steps languid yet powerful. The feeling of dancing with her in the arena could beat any high. As they rounded the corner to the first jump, Amelia felt Hope's ears dart forward, and the horse's gaze clocked the obstacle as she balanced herself on four powerful legs and calculated the number of steps to the fence like a sentient computer. This was Amelia's favorite part. She'd gently yet firmly hug Hope's sides with her legs, follow her bouncing neck with a flowing arm, and watch the world disappear behind her as they glided over the obstacles in their path.

Amelia had what equestrians called a "good eye," meaning that she could usually see or feel where she was on course. The ideal launch point from where the horse took off to jump existed in a sweet spot that was not too close but not too far from the base of the jump. Too close or too far could range anywhere from an ugly jump to truly dangerous, depending mostly on the size of the jump.

The day in Santa Fe when she smoked before riding, the weed had completely blinded Amelia's good eye. On that day when she crashed Hope, she pushed past her comfort spot and gotten much too close to the jump, getting them both tangled in the poles. The size of the jump made it all the more miraculous that there was not a scratch on the mare. Since that horrible day, which acted as its own launch point for Amelia's new life, she had been working diligently with Hope to rebuild their trust and reestablish her "good eye."

There was no way to apologize to a horse. Amelia couldn't simply sit down with Hope over coffee and own up to where she'd been wrong and say how sorry she was. The only way she had to clear the air was through her actions. Showing up to the barn early and staying late for extra quality time, long drawn-out grooming sessions followed by Amelia hand-leading Hope out to graze in the best patches of grass, plus hours of saddle time going back to basics. During that perfect fall day a month after returning home, all the pieces came back together. She felt Hope determine the distance to the jump, and instead of overriding her spiritual calculator out of anxiety, she supported her mount as they flowed through the course almost effortlessly. It turned her brain to jelly in the best way, the truest form of connection between two beating hearts.

"Nice, Amelia. Beautiful." Deb called from her spot, seated on the railing of the ring as they cleared the final jump. "Beautiful" wasn't a compliment a trainer like Deb tossed around lightly. She could be a little rough around the edges—great with animals, not as great with humans. Amelia breathed all the way in and all the way out and gave Hope an appreciative stroke on the side of her muscular neck as they slowed down to a trot and then a walk. Of course, she was thrilled to be working back to their normal cadence, but more than that, she was grateful to be on the road to healing their special relationship. Their bond could outlast any trauma or addiction. It was everything.

After the lesson ended, and after spending ample time brushing Hope and feeding her not one but two apples, Amelia led her back to her stall and kissed her goodnight on the nose, whispering "See you tomorrow, Perfect."

As Amelia made her way out of the stables and back to her car, she looked across the expansive green field beyond the arena, a patch that appeared to be shimmering in the brilliance of golden hour. The sky was lit by glittering low-angle sunlight, and birds soared across the horizon, pausing their wings in midair, letting the breeze simply carry them where they needed to go. The smell of hay and earth tethered her body to the ground just as the invisible wind held the birds in the sky. For a moment, she thought of how nice it would be to share this moment with someone she loved. Someone who she saw as a partner, someone who wanted to fuck her and then not forget her.

The next thought didn't even feel like her own. *The view was just as beautiful with no one else there to confirm it.* It was like that old saying: If a tree falls in the forest, and no one hears it, did it really make a noise? Of course, it did. Just because she was experiencing something wonderful and beautiful alone didn't mean it wasn't happening. Just because no one was in love with her didn't mean she was unlovable. Even if she wasn't bearing witness to it, the birds would still be airborne, and the field would still exist. In that moment, her five senses were enough.

When she turned the key to start her new Toyota Rav4 hybrid, she couldn't help but feel more at home and more comfortable than she ever had in the Red Range. She had traded the Rover in last week on day one of her "no more bones or boning" experiment, because the fancy SUV, while very pretty and slick, was not very National Forest. She was trying to shed all the excess bullshit that didn't align with her truest self. It was impulsive to trade it in on a whim, but this kind of impulse beat ones like the unsafe hookup fueled by drugs and alcohol kind—a varietal with notes of bulimia.

The sun was setting as she pulled up the big hill to exit Grey Stone Farm. A familiar sensation of gratitude coated her tired, sated bones after the afternoon of riding and doing barn chores. Rich hues bled across the Texas sky as the sun began to slip by and make way for the moon. Neither took away from the beauty or importance of the other or would ever try to. She wanted to exist this way among the other seven billion people on the planet, shining within herself while appreciating how others shined as well.

She glanced at the digital clock on the dash. Damnit, there was time. She promised herself, if she made it out of the barn in time, to head to the church where the meeting was held. She was hoping she'd miss it and have a good excuse for continuing to avoid it, but she would make it just in time if she wore her breeches and boots. Choking on her reluctance, she drove toward the church basement of misfit toys.

She hadn't attempted to return since her first awkward experience the night she got back from rehab, and she was more nervous than she could admit out loud. They'd find out she was more broken than they were, too broken to join their club. What if they all-out rejected her? Like a theatre troupe taking the stage enthusiastically, the torments of middle school began to seep through the walls of her mind until she was drowning in them.

A Jewish star drawn in Sharpie on the chest of her gym shirt. The school's refusal to issue her a new one when it wouldn't come out in the shitty school washing machine. The way they insinuated it was because she must have drawn it herself for attention. The Myspace comments boys would write on each other's pages that simply said, "God, Amelia Glickman is ugly." The way Toby Garrett never stood up for her, but continued to feel her up in secret behind the water fountain in the English hallway before joining his friends in ridiculing her. The way she'd let him.

Jesus, did all roads lead back to fucking middle school? It was where she'd learned that being different was not only frowned upon, but was also dangerous. No wonder she considered it a miracle of epic proportions when a guy wanted to fuck her. No wonder she leaped at the opportunity to feel wanted without considering what she wanted herself. No wonder it meant so much to her when she sat in the audience of that theatre at age 13 as Elphaba from *Wicked* defied gravity before her very eyes, despite being weird and green. Green like her, like the National Forest. Would the people who attended these meetings be green, too?

When Amelia pulled into the church lot, her heart pounded in her chest, pumping adrenaline through her body like she was about to go into battle. She never felt this way about IOP—why was this different? Was it because everyone was there by choice? Was it because, in this setting, no one had to be nice to her or hang out with her based on any rules or counselor supervision? Something in her knew she had to face whatever was inside. She got out of the car and locked the door with a beep.

She pushed through, not away, the feelings of fear and discomfort as she made her way to the door. She'd been thinking a lot about a book her parents read her and Beth as kids, *We're Going on a Bear Hunt*. This family was searching for a bear, and every time they reached an obstacle or a new threshold of adventure they must cross, a line came up that she and her family would recite throughout the years when something felt hard. "We can't go over it, we can't go under it. Oh no! We have to go through it!" Today, she was going after the brave, strong, woman she knew was inside of her—she was finally chasing something real.

The closer she got to catching her elusive bear of truth, the more wisely she'd have to hunt. The only way to get to the other side of those tough moments was through them, feeling and experiencing them fully. There was no up and over, or down and around. Catch the bear? Maybe you just tried over and over to get as close as possible. She had to try something different—not just once, but every time she wanted to run and hide.

Amelia made her way down the stairs. When she reached an empty chair just in time for the meeting to start, the blonde girl with the freckles from her first meeting winked at her and said, "You're back! We've been saving you a seat." She took a deep breath and sat all the way down.

CHAPTER 12: MONTH 2

Amelia stared blankly at her new friend across the table at the coffee shop where they'd been sitting for over two hours.

"So, was he going to rape you and then kill you? Or kill you and then rape you— 'cause there's a big difference."

She'd just regaled Sadie from the meeting about the tale of Mark. A dark smile spread across Sadie's face, and Amelia let out a sigh of relief followed by a chuckle. "Jesus, your humor is as dark as mine is."

"Have to laugh, or we'll cry, right?"

Amelia raised her mostly empty coffee mug in agreement as if to say, "Here, here." Sadie tucked a strand of dirty blonde hair behind her ear and dove into her own traumatic saga. Though it was their first time to talk outside of the meeting, they'd been trading fucked-up stories for hours, giggling about the depravity of it all.

Sadie was also at the meeting the night Amelia first got out of rehab, gawking at her with a raised brow from the front row. When Amelia finally stayed through to the end a few weeks back, Sadie was quick to approach her and exchange numbers. Though full of snark, shrouded in black eyeliner, and elevated by her combat boots to a respectable 5'2", Sadie was genuine, kind, and welcoming. So much so that Amelia stopped pretending to be busy when Sadie asked her to coffee. Unlike IOP, socializing outside of a meeting was normal, even encouraged.

Amelia hadn't had many friends since her high school theatre days, so she'd been nervous about meeting for coffee. But the pauses in conversation were comfortable, and all the laughter put her at ease. It was the first she'd really spoken of Mark and the incident since coming home. She was relieved Sadie could make a joke and then launch into their own sordid tale, rather than looking at her like she was damaged beyond repair.

Sadie struggled with substances, depression, trauma, and even an eating disorder, although Amelia had not yet divulged her ED. In fact, she hadn't talked much about her relationship with food and her body over the past month, not even in therapy. In the absence of male attention, she was beginning to think she might need to start. She had to admit she was struggling. Recovery was starting to seem like a game of coping mechanism whack-a-mole. She'd hammered down the sex and drugs, but the eating disorder popped up with a vengeance. The game was rigged.

"So yeah, basically, men are trash," Sadie said with a shrug. "I'm glad you went with the protective order; that's the way to go. Has he tried to contact you since?"

"Nope, thank God. I can't imagine dealing with that and trying to be sober and get my own shit together."

"Heard. It does get better, though. Keep talking about it in therapy and keep being honest with your support system. Time alone doesn't do shit, but time plus intention really does heal all wounds." Sadie was already a few years into her own recovery journey, and Amelia considered if she'd ever be able to accumulate the same level of wisdom. The idea of inspiring someone the way Sadie inspired her was enough to evoke a new host of butterflies entirely separate from those of attraction or romance.

Amelia checked her phone. "Shit, the time. I've got to go," She downed the last of her latte.

"Where are you off to?"

"I've got a dog to walk."

"Is this the famous Delilah I've been hearing so much about?"

Amelia smiled at the mention of her name. "Nah, she already had one this morning. I'm working part time at a dog-walking service. My care team said it was time to start my get-well job."

"That's a pretty badass get-well job."

"Agreed. Gives me plenty of time to train at the barn plus see the long list of professionals who are trying to keep me alive and sober. Animals are like a million times better than humans." Sadie chuckled. "We should definitely do this again sometime. It's nice to talk to someone who, you know, gets it."

"Oh yeah, good luck getting rid of me now. You're my kind of crazy, lady." Sadie seemed to mean it, and Amelia's smile reached up to her eyes. She'd made her first real friend in years, and it hadn't even been on purpose.

Amelia made her way toward her first dog of the afternoon. Susan the Dachshund was one of her regulars. When she arrived, she made small talk with the owner in the living room. Lots more human interaction these days, and it wasn't as physically painful as it was pre-sobriety. It was almost as if she were a normal, functioning member of society. Almost.

As they made their way out the front door, Amelia inhaled the sweet, airy floral scent of the lush garden pouring from the beds beneath the house's front porch. She wasn't sure she'd ever get used to discovering all five of her senses and the way they took in the world around her. In some ways she didn't want to get used to it. She wanted to stay in awe of the world around her. Like a kid who just got glasses and realized that those green blobs on the trees were actually clusters of individual leaves.

A smile broke out across Amelia's face like a wave meeting the shore as the sensation of a single raindrop washed over her. She watched the tender moment just before the sky broke open and water tumbled down from the heavens. It was magical, the way the clouds cradled the moisture until they could no longer hold it in, then released the raindrops to dribble their way from the clouds to the earth all because gravity pulled everything back home to center. Each droplet felt like a revelation on her skin. By the time a damp Amelia and her charge made their way home, the shower had ceased. The sun shone on the wet grass, creating a blanket of sparkling green across the lawns.

Amelia headed to her car to drive to her next walk, Chunk, a goofy pit mix. The dog had two dads just about her age, but usually only one was home during the walk. He was usually on a call in what appeared to be a home office, but he always poked his head out and gave her a kind smile.

She slipped her headphones in, banking on the fact that she didn't have to do much peopling at this house. *Codependent No More* was her current audiobook recommendation from Cathy. Amelia opened the door to the charming Hyde Park cottage and, even through her headphones, immediately heard the click-clack-slide conundrum of Chunk making his way to the front door with enthusiasm. She couldn't help the wry smile that spread across her face and the fond chortle that erupted from her throat; his goofy, pittie smile was just too fucking cute. As the lady in her headphones rattled on about healthy relationships, an unintelligible male voice from the other side of the house abruptly filled her gut with familiarity and a touch of fear.

"Who's here, bud? Is it time for your walk?" As the man turned to face her in the front hallway, Amelia froze, and his eyes widened almost comically. Her high school boyfriend's jaw hit the floor to mirror hers. "Amelia?" he exclaimed. "*You're* Chunk's dog walker?"

"*You're* Chunk's other dad?" She ripped the headphones from her ears. A gleeful Chunk looked between the two of them, none the wiser to the tension filling the space. His thick pittie tail just smacked in rhythm against the floor while he eyed the front door and panted, slobber dripping from his jowls.

A flabbergasted Trevor shrugged in response as if to say he was guilty.

"You're gay?" It flew out of her mouth before she could think any better.

Trevor rolled his eyes. "Can you keep your voice down, please? Josh is on a work call." He whisper-yelled like they'd seen each other yesterday instead of more than four years ago.

Amelia rolled her eyes back and tilted her head toward the front door. Trevor nodded, and she clipped Chunk's leash onto his collar and led the three of them onto the front porch. Once outside with the door closed, she continued. "You're gay?"

"Jesus, Amelia. I'm good. How are you? How's the family?"

Amelia scoffed in response. "Pardon me for being a little shocked to see you."

"And I'm not shocked? You're at my fucking house!"

"Touché." She folded her arms. "Are you really going to make me ask again, though?"

Trevor folded his arms as well and narrowed his eyes. After a very pregnant pause, he sighed. "If you must know, I'm bi. I realized it when I met Josh my junior year of college."

"I mean, I gave you my fucking virginity, and you've met all my living relatives, so yeah, I'd say I must know." Chunk's leash dangled from her hand as the pittie grew more restless to begin their neighborhood jaunt.

"Jesus," he huffed. "You're just as ridiculous as ever." He sounded exasperated, but a fond smile pulled at the corner of his lips.

She smiled back and then laughed. "I'm sorry. I know I'm being rude. I just cannot believe I am standing in front of you right now. Outside you and your husband's house, no less!"

"Boyfriend," he corrected. Chunk was starting to pull on the leash, and Trevor and Amelia both looked at him. "Why don't I join y'all today?" he asked. "We can catch up a bit, and Chunk will be placated."

"You don't have to do that, y'all are paying me and everything."

"Amelia, I haven't seen you in years, and you weren't just my high school girlfriend, you were my best friend, too. I want to hear how things are." Amelia was moved by this sentiment but shook it off and motioned for them to begin their walk. They hit their stride effortlessly, as if no time had passed.

"I don't know what to ask you first, why you're walking dogs for money with a trust fund sitting in the bank, or whether you're still dating that creepy older guy who came to our senior musical."

Amelia cackled. "Fair, but both have long answers."

"Hit me." The street was quiet as they walked, and for the second time that day, she launched into the story of her rock bottom with Mark and her stint in rehab that led to the get-well job. She told him about the terrifying night with the cops and the big breakup, the house on Wethersfield Road, Delilah, Hope, and early recovery from BPD and substance abuse. She had forgotten how easy it was to talk to Trevor, and she was struck by how much lighter she felt each time she said it all out loud.

"God, it's been an eventful four years, I take it."

"That's an understatement."

"I'm really glad you're OK, though. Sounds like there was a lot of potential in there to not be OK, and it's pretty amazing you are. I know you've struggled with some of this stuff for a long time, and I'm happy you're getting to the bottom of all of it."

A pit formed in Amelia's stomach as she thought of how fresh some of her wounds were back then. How the bloody mess had drenched Trevor as well. How he never would have left if she hadn't pushed him away. "I do want you to know I'm sorry," she said, reeling in Chunk's leash. "I've wanted you to know that for a while now. I'm learning a lot about the way my brain works. In high school, I knew fuck-all, and you got the brunt of it. I was constantly lashing out at you, and you were so patient and kind."

"Well, I loved you, Amelia. I think I always will in some ways. But loving you wasn't always easy. I can't tell you how exhausting it is to love someone so intent on ignoring the ways they're amazing."

"What do you mean?"

"You were just always so funny and out there, so different from everyone else. It was refreshing, but instead of owning it, you'd shut down and lash out when you felt too vulnerable." Trevor stopped moving and furrowed his brow as he considered his next words. "It's like, the same fire that makes you so incredible fuels your self-destruction. You're constantly existing somewhere in the space between generating energy and nuclear fallout."

Instead of getting offended, Amelia smiled softly. She forgot what it was like for someone to know her so well. It was a different kind of intimacy. The romantic feelings, comfortable in the past, made space for a new kind of friendship. "Can I ask you something, at the risk of sounding rude?"

Trevor smiled and shook his head. "Well, I know you're going to anyway."

"Were you really attracted to me back then? I always kind of thought bi was just a pit stop on the gay train."

"What is this, 2005? Bisexuality is completely real and valid. And, yes, I was attracted to you. You were my first love in all of the ways. And if you have any more questions about being bi, you might want to look in the mirror, sweetheart."

"I *knew* you were going to go there."

He cocked his head. "Am I wrong?"

"I...I don't know, to be honest. For the past few years, I haven't had much room to think about anything other than making boys want me and numbing everything else." It was the first time she said it out loud. "But can I even really say bi is possible, if I've never dated or hooked up with a girl?"

"Of course. Your identity is yours, no matter what. Would you tell someone who loved doing theatre that they weren't an actor just because they'd never been on Broadway?"

"There are some holes in your logic there, but I see what you're getting at. It doesn't really matter right now anyway. I just began month two of my year sans dick. I hadn't really considered it, but pussy should probably count, too."

"Sounds like a solid enough plan. I took an addictions class in college, and the professor talked a lot about how detrimental relationships and sex can be in early sobriety."

"Yeah, so I've heard..." she said sarcastically. "Wait, addictions class? Why did you take an addictions class? Seems like a weird elective for a theatre major."

"I decided early in undergrad that I wanted to be a therapist. I stepped away from theatre after my freshman year. I'm in grad school now, getting my master's in counseling."

"*That's* why you sound so smart about this stuff..."

Trevor chuckled while the afternoon sun tucked itself behind the trees to the west. They rounded the last corner of their walk, his house coming into view.

"Do you think Josh is your forever person?" She asked it abruptly, sensing their time together was ending.

Trevor smiled warmly. "Yeah, I really do. It's always been so easy with Josh. I think, in most ways, love should be easy, even when it's hard."

"I'm happy for you. You deserve all the love in the world. And he seems amazing. I liked him even before I knew he was your baby daddy," she said, gesturing towards a sated and panting Chunk.

Trevor laughed, pushed his shaggy brown hair back from his forehead, and glanced over at her as they reached the front porch. "You're going to find your forever person, too, Amelia Bedelia."

Her throat clogged with emotion. "Maybe."

"And you're not going to have to convince them to love you." He continued. "They'll fall all on their own."

A couple of hours and two other walks later, Amelia unlocked the door to Wethersfield and ambled into its loving embrace. She'd had an exhausting day. It wasn't a *bad* day, but she was certainly drained. And starving. She'd forgotten to eat again today. It had happened a few times in the past week.

She stumbled to the pantry with shaking hands and cold sweat pooling on the nape of her neck and started in on the bread, balling it up and shoving it into her mouth, one full piece at a time. When she'd made it through the entire loaf, she began eating the jar of peanut butter, one heaping spoonful after another. She hadn't figured out the art of grocery shopping just yet, so her options for this binge were scant, but she'd already lost all control and care. The weather could change fast in recovery, from pink clouds to storm clouds.

When people talked about eating disorders in detail, it was usually about the starvation aspect, which was more or less celebrated in girls with her body type. When the pendulum swung back, it swung into darkness and shame. This breathless gorging hijacked her entire body. The shame blended the survival instinct to be fed and the need for complete mental oblivion, the stuff, stuff, stuffing of any feeling other than the mounting fullness. The excess was mirrored by the chaotic nature of emotional instability. She was beginning to sense a totality in the blank state of mind amid the possession of the body. In the past she'd always waited to be done with the binge, but she was beginning to realize it was about waiting until it was done with her.

As the binge loosened its grip on her neck and the food in the kitchen dwindled, tears were already streaming down her face. She knew what came next, and she hated it. She had abstained from purging since rehab. The constant discomfort in her body that vibrated at a low frequency was humming to life. She was never free from thoughts of having a body, but this level of awareness felt unbearable. That was the beauty of being high on something or someone. The sweat, itch, poke, spill, contract, ache, and bloat could melt away into nothing. Without the option to soften the blow of her pain in the other ways, Amelia felt the eating disorder enslave her in the pantry.

She felt like humidity, as if the thickness of her clouds held onto rain before a downpour. She was so painfully full that when she first stood over the porcelain portal, she threw up without any effort. When she got on her knees and reached down her throat, that old familiar feeling of numbness spread through her body, and every way she'd ever been disappointed in herself spilled into the toilet bowl. She usually would look at her glassy, bloodshot eyes in the mirror afterward. She could marvel at their blue in a sea of blown-out-blood-vessel red, searching for some sick sense of approval from herself.

But this time, when she ran her hands under the cold water and rinsed out her mouth, she couldn't look up at the mirror. She felt light and empty, tingly and vacant. She wasn't proud of herself. As the tears continued to flow, the house wept with her.

CHAPTER 13: MONTH 3

At the end of her seventh year of personhood, Amelia Glickman realized with great displeasure that she had a body, and that body took up physical space. Not only did she have a body, but a rapidly changing one at that. The fluorescent hotel bathroom lights at the hotel in Orlando did some horrendous things to her pale complexion. She couldn't put her finger on it, but she was pretty sure this wasn't how a body was supposed to look. The family and her grandparents were all in Disney World that December to celebrate birthdays, her eighth and her sister's fourth. Even closing in on winter, Orlando was muggy and warm. While that sometimes felt stifling, Amelia was grateful she could wear her favorite Limited Too jean shorts with the pink flower embroidery.

She ran her stubby fingers through her damp hair and tried to decipher what was so different about her reflection today. Beth was already asleep in the adjoining room, and her parents and grandfather had gone out to dinner, leaving Amelia at the hotel with Grandma Glickman, who lounged on the hotel bed just outside the bathroom door, watching something on the television. The hushed buzz of the TV filtered into the bathroom and harmonized with the drip, drip, drip of the leaky shower faucet. She stared in the mirror, trying to merge with the reflection in a way that might make her feel real.

Her father had not yet hit it as big as he would, but he was doing well for himself nonetheless, hence the family trip to Disneyworld. It was the evening after their third day at the "happiest place on earth," an ironic backdrop for the existential crisis Amelia found herself in. How was it possible to be thrilled to the core by Cinderella's castle and come to terms with the mortality and imperfection of her physical form within the same 24 hours? Of course, she didn't have words for the quandary, just a nauseating pit of impending doom infiltrating the center most part of her. If someone had told her the truth then—that the impending doom would take root and plant itself firmly in her gut for the next fifteen years—she probably would have given up right then and there.

Her eyes caught on the swollen blush-colored buds on her chest as she brought her trembling fingers up to touch the tender, puffy skin. She'd been warned by her cousin about the bugs, lizards, and even crocodiles in Florida. The innocent teasing had manifested itself as debilitating anxiety in the form of her whispered question, "Mommy, will a crocodile ever eat me?" She asked each night before bed for weeks leading up to the trip. Finally, she knew what plagued her pale, aching skin: a poisonous bug bite, obviously. Hot tears ran down her red cheeks, and the desperate fear of giant lizards and an unnamed existential dread tore its way through her small but steadily expanding body.

Sobbing, she entered the bedroom, announced by the dramatic crash of the door careening into the wall. "Grandma. I'm dying," she choked out.

An alarmed woman who could pass as Amelia's twin, but 60 years her senior, scanned Amelia's naked form, looking for blood or bruising. She quickly registered the lack of danger, and her face broke into a gentle smile. She tucked her dyed red hair behind her ear and stood up from the bed, making her way past Amelia to the bathroom. She returned to the room with a fresh towel and wrapped it around her granddaughter's vibrating shoulders.

"Why are we dying, Amala?" Grandma Glickman was affectionately dropping the end of Amelia's name and adding the Yiddish diminutive, a common form of endearment in Jewish families, Bethala not excluded.

"I got bitten" was all she could get out at first. "By a giant, bad bug. Or something."

Slightly more concerned, her grandmother tilted her head and furrowed her brow. In response, Amelia gulped and let the towel slink off her freckled shoulders, gesturing toward her chest. Another knowing smile from Grandma Glickman. She made her way to sit on the edge of the bed and patted the spot next to hers. Amelia wrapped the big, soft hotel towel around her shoulders and padded over to the bed to take a seat next to her. She wiped her eyes and nose with the edge of the towel and looked expectantly up at her grandma, preparing herself for the confirmation that this was, in fact, the end.

"Sweetheart, I think you're getting breasts."

"I thought only chickens had breasts."

Her grandmother laughed. "So do people. They're also known as boobs or boobies."

"Oh. I know about boobies."

"Oh yeah?" she asked with a friendly, somewhat amused grin.

"Yeah," Amelia said softly, deep in thought. A month ago she'd had her first experience with body panic. It always appeared in a bathroom. In the mirror at home, she'd noticed a smattering of coarse, wispy hairs sprouting out of the mound of flesh her mom always referred to as private parts. Jen hadn't said much at the time, but she did wordlessly plunk the early 2000s cult classic *The Care and Keeping of You* courtesy of American Girl down on her Pottery Barn Kids bedspread. Amelia hadn't read much of what was inside the book, but she had studied the daunting, cartoonish images of genitals, nipples, body hair, and feminine hygiene products. Nowhere in that damn book was there a picture that anywhere near resembled her current situation, pubes and all.

"It's perfectly normal, Amala. A little early, maybe, but perfectly normal."

Amelia's lip began to quiver again. "But why don't they look like the ones in the book? Or like my mom's?

"Because yours are baby boobies, sweetheart. They're just beginning to grow."

"Well, mine are ugly, and I hate them," she said through tears.

Her grandmother smiled in sympathy. "I know you don't believe me right now, but you'll like them one day." She paused and then mumbled sardonically, "And so will everyone else."

It was no grand secret that the Glickman women had huge tits. But even her mother's side was notably well-endowed. She was just destined to have an awesome rack. Regardless, there would always be a better way to be than the way she was. Sitting on her grandmother's hotel bed, the Florida moisture hanging in the air, she came to terms with this for the first time.

Amelia wrapped her towel around her body like a dress, the way she'd always seen her mom do when exiting the shower. She might as well start acting like an adult now; childhood was fun while it lasted. Once wrapped up tight, she let out an exasperated grunt and flopped down onto the bed belly first. A soft hand began to rub her back a moment later.

"Talk to me, sweetheart. I promise you aren't going to die. It's not a poisonous bug bite, and I'm not going to let any lizards or crocodiles anywhere near you."

"It's just... I already feel so different than everyone else at my school," she muttered into the pillow. She turned her head so that she could stay sprawled out on the bed but face her grandmother. "How many 8-year-olds do you know with boobies?"

Her grandma stifled a laugh. "Come here, sweetheart." Amelia roused herself to go sit on the edge of the bed once again. "Being different isn't a bad thing." She took Amelia's hand in her lap and squeezed tight. Amelia began to twist her grandmother's ruby ring around her pinkie, basking in the comfortable silence.

After a few moments, Grandma Glickman pulled her hand back and removed the glistening pinkie ring off her own hand, placing it lovingly on Amelia's little thumb. Amelia looked up with question marks in her eyes.

"I want you to have it. It's precious to me, just like you. When I got a real job in the city, this was the first thing I bought for myself to celebrate. It has reminded me every day for 40 years I am an independent woman, and now I want you to look down at it and remember that you are as well. No matter what anyone says or thinks."

Little Amelia looked down at her thumb in awe and began to twist the ring just like she had when it was on her grandmother's finger. Just like she would do every day for the next fifteen years. And over those years, she would indeed grow fond of her breasts. She'd particularly like the attention they drew, and sometimes she'd even enjoy their soft bounciness and how it felt to bask in her own femininity. But mostly, they would feel heavy, sweaty, and oppressive, especially in the Texas heat and especially when riding. Girls with small boobs seemed so free and easy, clean and carefree, with their braless spaghetti straps and perky appendages.

Now, closing in on the end of her twenty-second year, Amelia was just as vexed by the consistent and painful awareness of her physical form. With plenty of AC and the right amount of cleavage, she still enjoyed her chest. However, the small but constant changes were enough to make her skin feel like a prison. She stared in the mirror at Wethersfield at the freshly sprouted stretch marks that adorned the mounds of her thick, creamy hips. Her fingers traced the bright reddish-pink indents as she floated through a foggy bubble of cognitive fallacy, believing that the first seven days of Hannukah alone had done such a number on her physique.

She shook her head in her same old "clearing the etch-a-sketch" way and refocused on her makeup. She tried in vain to line her eyes with the black pencil she kept in her makeup drawer for whenever she was feeling ballsy. It was the eighth night of Hannukah, and she and Beth's first holiday meal with their dad and his girlfriend demanded a full face of makeup. At the end of the day, all that mattered was that Instagram would see how deeply she had her shit together. Because nothing screamed stability like a perfectly executed smokey eye.

It was mid-December, and the promise hung in the air of her birthday on the 21st, followed by the rest of the holiday season. It had always seemed fitting to her that she was born on the shortest, darkest day of the year. Sometimes, she felt the absence of light mirrored what could truly be found in her soul. Other times, though she'd never say it out loud, she believed she was summoned to earth to light the night itself. Two sides of the same overly dramatic coin.

After giving Delilah extra holiday kibble, she made her way to the lake house where her broken foursome of a family used to spend every holiday together, playing board games and laughing until they couldn't breathe. The best part was how competitive Jen was. She'd once compared a game of Sorry to the movie *Sophie's Choice* when she had to choose between bumping one of Amelia or Beth's pawns back to start. The memory triggered the grief in her gut as she turned off Wethersfield Road. She'd go through the same rollercoaster of emotions at Christmas at her mom and her fiancé's place. One thing at a time, as Sadie liked to say. At least her mom's house was new, not the place they'd spent their final few years as a family.

Just as her musical of the week, *The Last Five Years*, began to filter through the car's sound system, she noticed a Milky Way wrapper crumpled in the cup holder. She'd skipped breakfast and was ravenous by the halfway point of her dog walks for the day, a rookie eating disorder recovery mistake. She had no way of knowing this yet, trapped in the binge and restrict cycle. She thought it was simply what it meant to be a woman, living in intervals of doing whatever it took to be thin, then cursing her waning willpower when she inevitably failed.

She'd stopped at Walgreens for chips, mini candy bars, and a jar of peanut butter and then promptly sat in the parking lot gorging on the snacks, fully aware that this was a binge and a bad one at that. It had felt good to be numb to everything except the sound of her teeth grinding and chewing her trans-fat-laden medicine until she could swallow it, then adding another greasy layer on top of her long-buried feelings. She stuffed the loss, fear, and shame she could never find the root of. When she had finally worked up the strength to drive across town to the next dog walk, she did so while compulsively stuffing her face. It was like breathing; she couldn't *not* have something in her mouth.

That's when she came across a homeless lady on the side of Airport Boulevard. Without thinking, she grabbed three last mini candy bars and one final plastic spoonful of peanut butter, then handed the woman the grocery bag of her binge remains. The comedy and the horror—she was the rich girl handing an impoverished woman her excess mental health issues, and no one was more disgusted than her. She couldn't even begin to spin it into a Hannukah mitzvah. She made herself throw up when she got home, of course. It was pretty much daily now. But that was a problem for future Amelia.

Soon enough, she arrived at the lake house and was greeted by Beth, Dad, and his girlfriend, Maya. The hardest part of the two potential stepparents thing was how much she liked her parents' new partners. Every time the spark of a bonding moment began to light the path forward, she'd recoil with guilt for betraying the parent they were meant to replace. It was reflexive.

After spinning, squealing, and hugging Beth, she hugged her dad and Maya as well, like a happy fucking family. Maya made some fantastic latkes with all the sides, and Amelia made a mental note to thank the J Date app for that little bonus. A dating pool of only Jewish women was sure to mean incredible food. She also noted the lack of alcohol on the table. Instead, there was a bottle of sparkling cider waiting to be poured. It was important to her that her family members not abstain on her behalf, but the attempt was a sweet thought at her first holiday dinner post-rehab. She didn't feel like it was the time to bring it up anyway. It was one of those things that you never think about until you must: wine or no wine? How did one make it normal while also respecting a family member's newfound sobriety?

After Maya poured the sparkling cider, her dad raised a glass. "To my beautiful daughters. Beth, you are an absolute star out there on the East Coast, acing your classes and making us all proud. Amelia, you and Hope were phenomenal on the show circuit all year. But more importantly, you chose yourself and your long-term health and happiness this fall. I could not be prouder of the women you are both becoming."

"Aw, Dad," Beth said through misty eyes.

"That's very sweet, Dad. It means a lot to me," said Amelia. And it did.

They made pleasant conversation as they dug into the delicious food. Amelia felt contented with this cluster of people, old and new. The accompanying guilt for that contentment was less brutal than it had been before.

"There's one more thing I'd like to say before we light the menorah and do presents," her dad said after a brief pause in the conversation.

"Presents!" Beth and Amelia squealed at the same time, like little kids ready to dig into new toys. It was always when Amelia got her birthday presents from her dad as well, since the day was close to Hannukah each year. Their dad smiled fondly at their silliness.

"Maya and I wanted to share something with you," he said, pausing and taking Maya's hand. He looked like the heart-eyes emoji personified. "We've decided to get married."

"Where's the rock?" Beth shot back after barely a lick of a pause.

"It, um, it's upstairs," Maya said sheepishly. "Jonathan and I, I mean, your dad and I, wanted to tell you first. Seemed less abrupt."

Beth shot her gaze to their dad and pointed her finger accusingly, "Rock, or it didn't happen." Jonathan raised his hands in surrender and marched upstairs, presumably for the ring.

"I know this may come as a shock," Maya said, "but I want you girls to know I'd never want to impose on your relationship with your dad. And I have the utmost respect for your mother." The words sounded nervous, which Amelia honestly appreciated just the slightest bit. Her jaw hung open as she searched for a reply, which seemed to be coming much easier to Beth at the moment. Maybe she could let her do the talking for the night.

"I can't talk about this until I see the rock," Beth said. Amelia and Maya giggled as Jonathan rounded the stairwell with a velvet box in his hand. He popped it open to reveal an absolutely enormous diamond set on a glistening band of smaller diamonds.

"Holy fuck!" Amelia said.

"Damn," Beth chimed in, standing to get a better look. "Good work, old man," She patted him on the shoulder, and he huffed out a laugh.

Amelia couldn't believe it, but she was…. happy for him? What was this madness? Sure, she'd probably feel a little weird about it as she continued to process this—seeing your parents move on and fall in love with other people was inherently hard. But in this moment, she was happy they seemed happy. She wasn't sure what about his new marriage would work when the last one with the mother of his children did not. But she was starting to understand a very important fact of life: Not everything was her goddamn business in the first place.

The rest of the night was filled with the glow of Hannukah candles, the crunch of wrapping paper, the sweet taste of rainbow cookies from the New York-style bakery in town, and a chorus of laughter she hadn't been sure would ever fill that house again. At about nine, just as she was thinking about heading out, Amelia received a text from Sadie. They'd hung out a couple more times after their initial coffee date, and she was slowly but surely easing back into the groove of having a friend.

> Sadie: I'm at Bennu with Lucy. She's cool you'd love her.
> Same fucked up sense of humor. You should come meet us.

It was a miracle she'd made one friend, and the idea of going out and meeting two people at a coffee shop would usually send her running as it teetered on the edge of social gathering. But the Forces of Good must have had other ideas because she found herself replying.

> Amelia: She sounds great
>
> Sadie: She is! wyd?
>
> Amelia: Just finishing up Hannukah at my dad's
>
> Sadie: MAZEL TOV, BITCH! So are you coming to Bennu or what?

Bennu was a coffee shop on the east side open 24 hours a day. After such an emotional evening, it would likely be a struggle not to purge when she got home, and getting coffee with friends would be a good distraction from that. She preferred to stay to her one-a-day purging rule, after all. Fuck it, this was her season of saying yes.

Amelia: I'll be there in 20

Sadie: *thumbs up emoji* *heart emoji*

After Amelia said final goodbyes and congratulations to her dad and Maya, Beth walked with her out to the driveway. As the door to the house shut, the sisters immediately made eye contact and let out a deep breath.

"So how do we really feel about this?" Beth asked.

"I would love to be able to tell you," Amelia said through a laugh. "There's this part of me that's just so, so, so happy for both of them. I mean, Maya is fucking awesome."

"But there's this other part that hates yourself for liking a woman that's not Mom."

"Exactly."

"So confusing, dude."

"Truly a mindfuck." Beth pursed her lips and surveyed the front yard in deep thought before bringing her gaze back to Amelia. "You know, I think we've had this idea in our head of how it's supposed to be—happy together, the four of us. But we were all pretty stuck, if you think about it. Maybe now we can still love each other but find our happiness separately."

Tears blurred Amelia's vision. "Yeah. I mean Mom is super happy with Chris as well. But I just always have this feeling when I'm with them, like if Mom or Dad could see us bonding with this fresh new version of themselves, they'd be so hurt and upset."

"That's a pretty surface love. Isn't truly loving someone supposed to be about wanting them to be happy, even if it's not you there to see it all the time? Plus, family is different from marriage. One can fail while the other thrives."

"When did you get so wise?" Amelia asked, wiping a tear from her cheek.

"I've always been wise. You've just been too high to notice." She said it like a joke, but there was some bite to it.

There was a part of Amelia that wanted to clap back with a snarky comment or brush it off, but instead, she told the truth. "You're right about that. I've been too self-obsessed and too hung up on trying to change the way I feel to tell you how incredible you are, and I'm really sorry. I basically abandoned you the moment our family started to fall apart. Even before that, I made everything about me. You deserved better than that."

"Well, shit." Beth said, her own eyes turning glassy. "Didn't expect all that."

Amelia grabbed Beth's hand. "Things are going to be different now. It feels like I have my head out of my ass for the first time in over a decade, and one of my goals in life is to be the big sister you deserved all along. No one deserves a shitty sibling. Especially you, kid. But if there's anything else I can do to heal what I've broken between us, can you let me know? Because I can't lose you. You're my favorite person in the world."

"You're my favorite person in the world, too. And the only thing you can do is continue becoming the person you were always supposed to be. And that means continuing to get well, to stay sober. Because I can't go back to watching you slowly kill yourself, Amelia."

She pulled her in for a tight hug. "I know."

An hour later, Amelia sat with Sadie and Lucy at the east side coffee shop, sharing cigarettes and vanilla lattes and laughing about stupid shit. Sadie was right. Amelia and Lucy got along splendidly; they were fast friends, just like she and Sadie had been. Now she had, not one, but two friends she could invite to her birthday dinner. She just had to work up the courage to ask them. A casual "if you're not busy…" text in the next day or so would do the trick. Making friends as an adult was like dating; asking them to hang out, hoping they called you back.

Lucy slammed her phone down on the table. "My stupid roommate says if I have the New Year's party at our place, she'll call the landlord. Says it will get too loud and disturb her cats." Lucy took one last drag of her cigarette as she rolled her eyes before putting it out in the ashtray.

"Fuck, that sucks," Sadie said.

"What kind of New Year's party?" Amelia asked, trying to sound casual. She hadn't had New Year's plans for years. She always got too sloppy to secure an invitation to events that notoriously revolved around alcohol.

"It's a sober New Year's party for some of the folks from the meetings around town. I just want to party hard in a safe, sober space, you know? But we might as well cancel it now."

Sadie sighed. "Yeah, you know my place is too small for all those fuckers, or I'd throw it myself."

"I have a house." Amelia's words hung in the air before she could even fathom what they meant. The two other girls looked over at her with expectant smiles.

"Yeah?" Sadie asked.

Lucy clasped her hands under her chin like she was pleading with Amelia. "I'll do all the work! I'll buy all the energy drinks and snacks; you just provide the space!"

Amelia couldn't even believe she was considering this. "Can I invite friends from IOP? None of them drink or do drugs either; they probably need a safe, sober place to go on New Year's as well."

"Fuck yes, bitch!! The more, the merrier, within your comfort level, of course. There are probably so many people dying to go to a safe party where they can relax and not worry about drunk assholes. Oh my god. This is going to be the most legendary sober party ever. It's going to put the wet New Year's parties to shame!"

Sadie smiled and winked at Amelia while Lucy pulled a pen and notepad out from her giant purse. The girls drank coffee and chatted about party decorations and mocktail options into the wee hours.

Ever since meeting Sadie, Amelia found herself smiling more often than not, and her face was still building the muscles to support her new habit. At home later that night on her back patio, with Delilah sniffling around the moonlit yard, Amelia tried to imagine sober people filling her house in just a couple of weeks. Would anyone actually come? Maybe, maybe not. But even if it just ended up being her, Delilah, Lucy, and Sadie ringing in the new year together that night, she'd be one happy girl. She whispered to the house, the dog, and the big tree in the backyard. "We're having a party on Wethersfield Road."

CHAPTER 14: MONTH 4

The early January chill seeped through the old glass windows framing the front room of Wethersfield. She was grateful for her fluffy new Ugg sleep socks, one of Jen's famous stocking stuffers from Christmas. It was two weeks into the new year already. Amelia's first sober Christmas had exceeded her expectations. She didn't have the elixir of wine and pot to numb the big feelings that came up, but she made it through relatively unscathed. The tough moments were punctuated by spells of laughter with her mom and sister, and even bonding moments with her mom's fiancé Chris and his sons. Each time she found another thing to like about one of her future stepparents, the twinge of guilt dulled. Maybe someday those feelings would cease to exist completely.

Amelia wiggled her toes in the butter-soft socks and continued to organize the remnants of her very first sober New Year's Eve party: one pile for trash, one pile for keepsakes, and one pile for next year's party, because a party as successful as that one demanded a repeat performance. Now that she'd graduated from IOP, she was getting around to sifting through the smaller items. Friends like Sadie and Lucy were more than gracious in their help cleaning up the big stuff, further earning the trust Amelia had inexplicably placed in them to handle party invitations after only a month of friendship. When it came to the extra shit they had stuffed into the front room, better now than never.

The room had metaphorically auditioned for the role of craft spot, office space, home gym, and storage closet, but two weeks ago, it had finally landed the role it was born to play: bedroom to a real-life roommate. A real-life male roommate. A roommate with no intention of fucking or being fucked by Amelia Glickman. She continued the task at hand, organizing piles into shoe boxes and trash bags. The night of the party and the meet-cute with her platonic love at first sight played like a film reel.

On December 31, 2015, Amelia looked around the Wethersfield in awe, because by 9:30 p.m. on the last day of the worst year of her life, at least 100 people filled her house with smiles, laughter, and enough energy drinks to send a small Victorian child into cardiac arrest. She'd been concerned no one would come. She'd thought at least a dozen times of making an excuse and canceling to save herself the shame and embarrassment, but she held onto Hope for fear of letting Sadie and Lucy down. And thank the Forces of Good that she did, because People. Fucking. Came. Not only did they come, but every single one of them appeared sober. Sober and happy. Wethersfield was bursting at the seams with the perfect balance of security and excitement, its walls buzzing with joy and connection. She could feel the house spread its motherly arms and embrace the crowd of people who needed a safe, sober place to go on one of the biggest drinking nights of the year.

The most shocking part of the evening wasn't the way actual humans filled her house at a party she threw on purpose, but rather the way her anxiety declined the invitation. Sure, it was out in the driveway doing push-ups, but it was thoughtful enough to take the night off. It would have been impossible to learn everyone's name and find out who invited them, but she shared eye contact and warm smiles with most guests and pleasant conversations with plenty of others. She danced with Sadie and Lucy on the kitchen table to Queen's "Don't Stop Me Now" singing into the Monster can turned microphone like a teenager alone in her bedroom. She laughed at the game of Red Bull pong happening on the back patio. She hugged strangers when they thanked her for opening her home to the misfit toys of Austin. She watched blithely as Delilah happily roamed around the house extorting belly rubs and chunks of charcuterie cheese.

It was like an apparition. Surely this was her life, but where had it all come from other than the unseen Forces of Good? Taking a note from the long list of recovery acronyms, she'd started calling it the FOG. Because hadn't it floated in without a sound and changed her perspective on the entire world like smoke and mirrors? Maybe it was her willingness to work with the current instead of against it that brought on the FOG—the fact that she'd finally let go of control and moved away from the cycle of shame and isolation. Maybe something smiled upon her for no reason at all, and luck alone was the culprit. Or maybe it was all of the above. But at the end of the day, she simply reaped the benefits of trying something different: saying yes instead of no, building connections rather than dependencies. Perhaps she was finally beginning to understand that the why or how of it was above her pay grade.

All she knew for sure was that she'd spent last New Year's Eve on her couch feeling completely alone with a bottle of wine and an absent partner. But at that party, she couldn't feel alone if she tried. Perhaps the people at the party had once been lonely too. Yet there they were together, finding ways to build community and care for themselves and each other at the same time. Like separate chunks of glass in a mosaic coming together to make something beautiful. *A little broken, but a lot brave.* Most of them were likely in recovery like she was, somewhere on the path between complete implosion and healing. Some, perhaps, to support their loved ones. A few maybe didn't even know why they were there.

As midnight drew closer, the energy began to climb, and Amelia made her way to the purple chairs. She wanted to watch the last moments of the year unfold in her once-barren house. Delilah was at her feet and just as awe-struck as Amelia. The three of them, person, dog, and house, stood beside a chair and took it all in.

The magic seemed to give way to something new when Amelia stepped back to take a seat and found herself in the lap of a man she did not know. She sprang up immediately, mortified to find an impeccably dressed dark-haired man sitting in the purple chair she had assumed was empty.

"Oh my god, I am so fucking sorry, I totally did not see you there!"

The man gave her a genuine and kind smile. "All good. I saw it coming and could have warned you, but I thought it would be funnier if I didn't. But I will say, I wasn't expecting a lap dance so early in the evening."

His joke put her somewhat at ease. Instead of running away to hide in the bathroom, something unnamable urged her to sit in the chair opposite his. As she leaned back, the man sighed and crossed his suede loafer over a sharp pair of slacks. He was gorgeous; any man, woman, or child could tell. But as she scanned her body for an initial attraction, a sensation in pussy dips or belly flutters, she came up empty-handed. *Interesting.*

"You know," he said, "the last time I went to a New Year's party with this many people, someone passed out in the bathroom. Of course, it wasn't a sober party, but…" The young man glanced at her, a warm glow of embers in his deep brown eyes.

"Jesus," she replied, cutting him off with a nervous laugh, "Hope no one passes out in my bathroom tonight. Or ever, for that matter."

"Oh, so this is *your* house. Very cool. Thanks for having all of us."

"Are you kidding? Thanks for coming. I can't believe this many people are here. I'm newly sober, and I wasn't exactly surrounded by friendly faces towards the end."

He laughed and nodded like he knew exactly what she meant. "I've been sober for almost four years, and I've never been to a party like this. Community is so important. Not feeling alone. Pretty special to feel a part of something like that, especially on a notoriously hammered holiday."

Her brow furrowed as she thought back again to last New Year's Eve. How desolate it felt. "Wow. Four years, that's incredible."

"One day at a time, and all that."

"That's what I keep hearing. But I am so happy to have everyone, and Sadie and Lucy really handled the invites. It's not like I know all these people. Fuck, I barely even know the two of them. We just met a few weeks ago, but for some reason it feels like I've known them my whole life."

"That mystifying, almost instant connection is common in recovery circles," he said. "Which is why I guarantee people won't forget you did this. And you may have let your friends handle the invites, but you provided the space. And it is an *amazing* space."

He seemed to take in all of Wethersfield's charming details, and Amelia felt something settle in her gut. Maybe she didn't do anything to deserve the privilege associated with living in a house like this, but she could create meaning out of that cosmic joke by sharing it with others.

"So," he asked, "do you have a roommate?"

"Just Delilah." She gestured across the living room to where the pup was currently eliciting belly rubs from a large, tattooed man. Close by, Lucy shotgunned a Red Bull as a group of onlookers cheered.

Her eyes scanned him again. His dark, almost black hair was perfectly styled, and an impeccably tailored button-down hugged all the right crevices of his lean muscles. Still, nothing in her body was registering this as a potential partner or fuck buddy. Was her nervous system finally picking up on her dickless intentions, or was it something else? *Oh my god. He's gay, you idiot.* "So, did you come alone tonight, or did you bring a date?" She was determined to get to the bottom of this.

He smiled in a way that confirmed he could see right through her bullshit. "I came by myself. And to answer your real question, I am neither gay nor am I hitting on you," he said with a wry smile.

When she choked on her sparkling water, causing it to go down the wrong pipe and set off a chain of coughs, the man's hands flew to her back and patted gently as if he were burping a baby. *Kill me now,* she sing-songed in the confines of her mind.

"I'm sorry," he said with equal parts amusement and concern. "I'm just giving you shit."

"All good," she said in a raspy voice, multiple octaves lower than usual "I deserved that." She smiled at him and wiped her eyes. He couldn't help but laugh, which made her laugh as well, despite the burn left in the wake of her wrecked vocal cords.

He shrugged. "A lot of people do assume I'm gay, though. But I love women. I just know how to dress."

"Love that." She was relieved to have overcome that hurdle in the conversation. "So, are you from Austin?"

"New York, actually. I just got back from visiting my folks up there for Hannukah. But I've lived in Austin for the past couple of years."

"You're a New York Jew? Me too!"

"No way! You know, there aren't that many of us here in the great state of Texas." Their conversation flowed easily as they uncovered the fact that both of their families were Mets, Jets, and Rangers fans. This was her kind of dude. Somewhere in her brain, she must have wondered what his name was, but it likely felt unimportant amidst all the things they had in common.

Time got away from them, and before they knew it, a countdown to midnight and next year was echoing throughout the house.

Ten! Her eyes met her new friends, from across the room and a childlike gasp passed her lips as the chorus of cheerful voices bounced off the walls.

Nine! Lucy and Sadie waved at her excitedly, gesturing towards the people around them, chanting in bliss as if to say, "Can you believe this shit?"

Eight! Delilah trotted over to her feet with glee, tail wagging excitedly.

Seven! The fact settled in her soul that being a part of this community and the gift of this moment was more than any silly New Year's kiss could ever be worth.

Six! The realization washed over her that she had not once stopped to ask herself where Liam was.

Five! Her mind sifted through vocabulary and tried to come up with an adjective that meant the complete opposite of loneliness as she fondly watched the young guys from IOP party with the rest of the kids from the meetings, opening up for what may have been the first time.

Four! The energy filling Wethersfield seemed to cause it to levitate, lifting the crowd of joyous attendees into a different realm.

Three! The incomprehensible truth presented itself that she never had to drink or do drugs again to change the way she felt, even if she wanted to.

Two! She made the decision to let go and allow the FOG to carry her from here on out—because she couldn't take credit for all this even if she tried.

One! She felt a distinct ending to the chapter of Mark, of Liam, of numbing with substances, reckless sexual behavior, and self-sabotage—and surrendered to the inevitability of whatever came next in this surprisingly beautiful life.

Happy New Year! Everything exploded in the best way.

Sometimes, making it through a year as a human being is the hardest thing you could possibly do. It was worth celebrating. She made the rounds, hugging her new friends tight, basking in the energy as Wethersfield gently set them back down to earth. The party showed no signs of dying down now that they'd crossed the threshold into the new year. Evidence of this could be found in the group sing-along to "Get Low," the millennial middle school dance classic. But she brought her focus back to the purple chairs where her newest friend still sat.

"So, what do you have on the docket for the start of the year?" he asked her as she got settled back into the chair.

"Well, my last day of IOP is next week, and then it's just a bunch of dog-walking gigs, therapy, meetings, and training with my horse. What about you?"

"Definitely going to need more info on the dog-walking and horse training," he said with wide, curious eyes. "But I'm mostly going to be looking for a new apartment before classes at UT start back up. My lease is up soon, and I've been procrastinating. Then it'll be back to the same old stuff: class, meetings, therapy, you know, the recovery drill." She nodded in response.

Just then, the lamp on the small table between the purple chairs caught her attention as it flickered ever so slightly. Delilah sauntered over to where they were sitting and plunked herself down, resting her head on her new friend's suede loafers. Something tickled the back of Amelia's brain as she turned her head in the direction of the spare room at the front of the house. Was she really and truly losing her mind, or were the house and the dog trying to tell her something in this moment? The house seemed to conspire with the FOG to sway her. The walls always tried to squeeze Liam out like a pimple. This felt like the opposite. But the question remained: Had she simply evolved enough to begin to hear the house more clearly, or was she getting crazier?

Ultimately, she made the game-time decision: believing in magic wasn't crazy. Miracles existed when you wanted them to. *Goodness* existed. "Would you ever want to move in here?" It flew out of her mouth before she could feel self-conscious about it.

"What? Are you serious?"

"I'm totally serious. Unless you're completely weirded out, and in that case, I'm totally not serious."

He huffed out a laugh and ran his fingers through his hair. "I mean, I would love to live here. What do you charge for rent?"

"I don't know. Never had a roommate before. Why don't we just do some research on what the average rent is in the area?"

"Yeah, that makes sense. Are you sure, though? I mean, you just met me, and everything."

"But you're a Jewish Mets fan, how badly could this really go?" He laughed hard and she looked down and picked at her cuticles ever so slightly. "There is one thing, though." He looked at her expectantly and took a sip of his sparkling water. She was learning that in the sober social world, energy drinks were the equivalent of hard liquor, while sparkling water was the equivalent of beer. She took her own sip of a lemon-lime fizzy water. "We can never, under any circumstances, have sex."

It was his turn to choke and sputter. "Oh my god, that's not what I expected you to say." He tried his best to clear his throat. "And I mean this in the least offensive way possible—I don't want to have sex with you."

"I don't want to have sex with you either! Which is wild because I usually want to have sex with everyone."

He barked out a laugh. She was already loving the dopamine shot associated with eliciting that sound from him and the way it paired with his crinkled, sparkling eyes. "I've been there. And yeah, you're adorable, but I'm 100 percent not attracted to you."

Amelia waited for the pang of rejection, the panicked shame, but it never came. It was the first time in her whole life that she didn't take someone's lack of interest personally. In fact, it was a relief. The lack of sexual or romantic chemistry created space for something even better: friendship.

"So, are we doing this?" she asked, standing up and holding out her hand.

"Under one condition." He stood up. "No Yankees or Giants fans at the house on game days." He extended his hand as well.

"Deal," she said as they shook on it. They excitedly discussed move-in dates and logistics before exchanging information, then went to plug their numbers into each other's phones.

"Wait!" she said. "What's your fucking name?"

Amid their laughter, he replied, "Ethan. And you are?"

"Amelia. Welcome to Wethersfield, Ethan."

Back at sorting her piles, she carefully tucked away the last of that night's memories, readying the space for her first-ever roommate. He'd be arriving with a U-Haul to fill the nearly empty room any moment now, and she was nervous. Her therapist was skeptical about the plan. Cathy pointed out that Amelia had a history of making poor decisions with men—and that having a man in her living space might add fuel to the fire. But she also trusted Amelia to make the decision that was right for her. Someone having faith in her ability to make a healthy decision was completely new.

"You're learning how to make decisions with your capital S self in the driver's seat rather than your little s self," Cathy said in session.

"Say what now?"

Cathy laughed. "Capital S self is the part of ourselves that is connected to the greater good, intuitively plugged in, the part able to receive messages from our innermost wisdom. Little s self is the part fighting for instant gratification and relief, regardless of whether it negatively affects long-term happiness and stability."

"Are you adding multiple personality disorder to my list of diagnoses, because to be honest, I'm one diagnosis away from throwing in the towel and going to live in the woods."

"First of all, it's called Dissociative Identity Disorder, and it's not a joke."

Amelia threw her hands. "Jeez, sorry."

"Second of all, human beings are made up of parts. Some are more mature than others. The longer you stay sober, go to meetings, take your meds as prescribed, and meaningfully participate in therapy, the stronger your capital S self will become. And the less your slew of diagnoses will even resonate. Except addiction. That one's kind of a lifer. That's why the best option is abstinence."

"Okay, let's say all of that happens and I become the best version of myself," Amelia said. "Does my little s self just get thrown out in the cold?"

"Your little s self will still be there. But she won't be running your life and making the big decisions. And it will become easier to differentiate between the two. You can learn to nurture that part of yourself, give it what it needs instead of what it demands in moments of fear. Kind of like self-parenting."

Amelia considered the younger version of herself, how she manically attempted to get her needs met with little to no success. For the first time ever, she felt something like compassion toward that young girl.

The sound of a car pulling up in front of the house brought her back to the present. There were natural doubts coming up about having a roommate, here in these final moments alone in Wethersfield, but she trusted in her inner wisdom and the FOG surrounding her. A knock at the door made Delilah wag her tail in anticipation. Her canine companion's openness and generosity of spirit inspired Amelia to develop the same qualities within herself, the animals in her life constantly teaching her about how to be a human.

She made her way to the front, hot on Delilah's heels. The next time Ethan entered Wethersfield he'd have a key of his own. She was about to really and truly let someone in, both literally and figuratively. Scary, but worth it. Because life was only truly worth living when you allowed yourself to share it with others, and the more she let people in, the brighter and bigger it got. With that, she swung open the charming red door for the newest resident of Wethersfield Road.

CHAPTER 15: MONTH 5

Dream Liam smiled down at a lust-drunk Amelia from where his body hovered over hers on a brown suede couch. It was the couch all single men had, as if there was a rule about bachelor pads having shit-colored furniture to mask any questionable stains. She so easily gave up her year of celibacy and self-discovery for those 10 minutes of mediocrity with him. This must be a dream, though, based on the hazy edges of the room and lack of grey in his beard. Though only dreamland, she felt guilty about blowing it. Stranger still when Dream Amelia realized she'd forgotten to pluck the weird black hair on her left nipple as Dream Liam took off her bra.

In the actual world, it was February, and she still hadn't so much as kissed someone in five whole months. She didn't want to be the girl who threw it all away for the boy anymore, so when consciousness seeped into her awareness, relief quickly followed. She hadn't blown it. Not in real life.

Amelia Glickman peeled open her groggy eyes as streaks of late morning sun began to splash light across the walls of the living room. She lifted her head to find a sleepy Delilah at her feet on the end of the couch and a passed-out Ethan. Her new roomie had pushed together the two purple chairs to make a sort of loveseat and appeared relatively comfortable with the top half of his body on one chair and the bottom half on the other. His arms were folded haphazardly on his chest, and he made an adorable little frowny face as he slumbered on. Amelia smiled to herself and rubbed the sleep out of her eyes. It was the third time that week they'd fallen asleep like that, too comfortable and too tired to turn off *Grey's Anatomy* and make it to their respective bedrooms.

"Push one of epi!" one of them would yell, their standard call for pressing play on another episode of the medical drama. Then they'd doze off, waking the next day to solve the mystery of what part they fell asleep on, only to do it again the next night and the night after that.

"Arguably not the best show to be watching when you're trying not to bang anybody," Ethan had joked last night as they queued up another episode. Amelia made all her new friends aware of her resolution to fly solo for a year, and having these friendships to fill the void she once filled with meaningless sex was satisfying in a new and wonderful way. But she still couldn't understand why these people wanted to spend time with her as well. Was it possible that she fulfilled something in their lives too?

Amelia didn't understand why, what with Ethan being so funny and outgoing, but it seemed like he might have been just as lonely as she was. When he agreed to move in, it never occurred to her that he might need her as badly as she needed him. They clung to one another as if they were walking through a haunted house, only the haunted house was their 20s. Life's jump scares seemed easier to manage hand in hand.

She wiggled her toes, careful not to wake Delilah, and registered the ache in the soles of her feet, presumably from her big night out dancing with her sober friends. What had started out as a master class in crippling self-consciousness evolved into a not-giving-a-shit mentality. By the time the third Lady Gaga song thumped through the speakers of the wildest LGBTQ club on Fourth Street last night, she was dripping sweat and moving to the rhythm. Passionately belting out the words to every song made her feel connected to that crazy little girl at the center of her chest.

Queer spaces, she was finding, felt the safest when it came to both sober fun and not feeling judged. Everyone at the club was just happy to be there and let loose; no one cared that she and her friends weren't drinking or that her hair wasn't perfect. It reminded her a bit of high school theatre. The sober and queer communities gave her everything she loved about the camaraderie and creative expression of theatre minus the pressure to measure up. She could just *be*, free like the National Forest.

She saw all the amusement park girls downtown before they entered the sanctity of the LGBTQ club—the ones with cute, blow-dried hair and flawless makeup, not breaking a sweat in their tight little dresses and heels—and for once, she held gratitude for being exactly who she was. Jeans, sweat-dampened t-shirt, and a messy bun. She sent compassion to the girl she used to be, the one who tried everything she could to be someone she wasn't, only for her blowout to frizz 20 minutes into the night.

After dancing, the group went to Magnolia Café on Lake Austin Boulevard. They laughed obnoxiously and packed way too many people into one booth. Confused onlookers wondered how they could possibly be so happy about queso and shitty coffee. She couldn't believe how good it felt to be a part of a group like this. It was reminiscent of the post-show meals at the Chili's on 45th and Lamar with the cast and crew, where the big chorus numbers were encored to the derision of all other diners.

Last week, she'd gone with her friends to see a band. It was the first live music show she'd attended since getting sober. She had hated live music when she was drinking, quite a statement for a girl from Austin. But it was too hard for her to stand in one place for that long; she felt so sick and fucked-up all the time. Before starting sober life, the only place she really felt OK was on her couch. And a show meant countless judgments aimed at her from all directions, discomforts both physical and emotional.

But she'd made it out of that night not only unscathed but joyful. It was the dripping sweat, the chaos of the mosh pit, the cathartic screaming of the lyrics from the crowd of misfit toys to which she belonged. It was the knowing and loving herself on a night out despite not having a boy to flirt with. It was the crazy idea that she felt thrilled to be alive and the wild notion that she could have happy, healthy, supportive people in her life to share it with.

Last night at the club was no different. Her heart was so full it could explode. When she and Ethan got home, they snuggled up in the living room to debrief and fell asleep at some point while reminiscing about carpool karaoke and Lucy's twerking. Though the evening was free of substances and alcohol for the group of friends, the hangover from the dancing, energy drinks, and lack of sleep still radiated in her bones like a fond ache. She quietly extracted herself from her cocoon and made the short journey to the kitchen to start a pot of coffee. The smell of home-brewed Dunkin' coffee filled Wethersfield Road.

Amelia leaned against the counter and watched, mesmerized as the nectar of the gods alchemized in the thick glass pot and drip-drip-dripped its way into existence. By the time Amelia poured a hefty helping into her new favorite mug—the one with a unicorn who was pole dancing that said "Life Sucks Better Sober"—a dazed Delilah did a histrionic stretch and made her way into the kitchen with the expectation of breakfast. With the steam dancing on the surface of her coffee, Amelia filled the bowl with kibble and looked on as Delilah munched happily.

Inside the cupboards at Wethersfield, dishes and cutlery were multiplying and coming to life with regular usage and imprints of happy memories between Amelia, Ethan, and their friends. Newly acquired knick-knacks, art, and other nods to the habitant's personalities sprang up on the walls, shelves, and countertops like the first signs of new growth after a forest fire. In her most depressed state, the tedium of everyday occurrences like making coffee or doing the dishes brought dread, but as with everything else, it could be so worthwhile when shared with others.

When Delilah finished, Amelia tiptoed through the living room toward the back porch, snagging one of the blankets from the couch on her way. The cold morning air nipped at her ears, and she perched her bundled-up self into one of the patio chairs and watched as Delilah sniffed around the yard.

The warmth from the mug seeped into her veins, and she closed her eyes in gratification. The comforting sensation brought her a peace she was becoming more familiar with. Ethan was good at bringing out that part of her. As she sipped, her mind wandered back to a couple of weeks ago when Ethan saw a different part of her that no one had ever seen before. The ugliest part. He could've run away, but he didn't.

On the night in question, she and Ethan ordered pizza and watched the first two *Twilight* movies. Amelia had skipped lunch and was starving by the time the food arrived. In turn, she stuffed herself painfully full. She hadn't purged since Ethan moved in, too afraid of her secret being discovered, but this occasion demanded a visit to the bathroom. She thought she'd go undetected with the sink running and the movie playing.

She sank to her knees before the bowl in devout worship and prayed fervently to be restored. As her sins poured out of her, relief took its place, and she flushed away her pain. Then she rose anew, still unable to look at herself in the mirror, though this used to be an important part of the ritual. She didn't want to fucking do this anymore. She waited the appropriate amount of time for her eyes to stop leaking and for the sheen of clammy sweat on her forehead to dry. Then she emerged as if nothing happened.

"Are you OK?" Ethan looked up at her with concern from his normal spot on the purple chairs.

"Fine, why?" she tried for a nonchalant tone.

"Amelia...that didn't sound fine. Are you sick?"

Her heart sank. In the decade since mastering her disappearing food act, she'd never once been caught. Or even almost caught. Tonight's shame was potent. She'd never let anyone close enough to catch her in the act before.

"Amelia, are you sick?" he asked again. "What's going on?"

She considered lying, saying it must be food poisoning or the stomach flu, but something about his earnest expression conjured the truth. "I'm not sick. Or, at least not like that."

"What are you saying?" He paused the movie and gestured for her to sit on the couch. There was nothing domineering or intimidating about the way he inquired. She made her way back to the couch to sit next to Delilah. Fresh tears sprang up and threatened to break the dam of her eyelids as she searched for words she couldn't find.

"Amelia, do you have an eating disorder?" No one had ever asked her that before. Except Cathy.

"I don't *not* have one."

"What does that even mean?"

"Well, it's not like I've been diagnosed with an eating disorder, and I definitely don't look like I have an eating disorder, that's for goddamn sure." Her hands found the soft pillows of flesh encasing her hips. She felt her convex lower belly, the way the soft flesh on her back dimpled and rolled under her bra strap, the way it had ever since she first needed one in the first place. She was average, curvy, soft.

"Yeah, I'm pretty sure that's not how it works. So, no one else knows about this? Not your parents? Not your therapist?"

Amelia shook her head. "They might know that I used to, but they think it's been a while."

"What about in rehab? Did they know?"

"No." She shrugged. "It's my best-kept secret."

"How long has this been going on, dude?"

His concern confused her. "Since I was 13. So, I guess, like...."

"Ten years." When he said it out loud, it sounded like a really long time.

"Yeah, 10 years, I guess. On and off."

"How is it possible that in 10 years, no one has said anything?" He ran his fingers through his hair in a way that made it stand up a bit.

"I mean, maybe it's because I've maintained a normal weight, arguably with a little extra fluff in some spots. Or maybe I'm, like, an insanely good liar, like a sociopathic caliber liar. Or maybe I've just gotten super lucky, and the bulimia gods have blessed me ever so ardently." The words poured out of her. "Maybe my energy has had such a fuck-you vibe that I've been pushing people away ever since I started. Maybe I just haven't let anybody close enough to see—for fear that they'd take away my biggest vice. Or maybe no one gave a shit in the first place." She gave him the answers to the question she'd been asking herself all along. Because she trusted him implicitly.

Ethan paused to consider her words before speaking again. "Amelia, do you have any idea how dangerous that is? How damaging it can be to your body? To your mind?"

"I mean, it's not like I'm scary thin or anything," she said with an ice-cold laugh.

"That doesn't even matter! It's about your health, dude."

Health. H-e-a-l-t-h. She'd never thought much about that word. She'd never even considered it when it came to her eating habits. It was all about how she'd looked. Maybe that's why her self-harm was always of the vainer variety and not something that might leave behind scars. The only visible scars she had to speak of were the ones in the name of beauty, namely the traces of burn marks that still ghosted her hands from when she'd wake up at 5:30 a.m. every morning before school to straighten her frizzy coils of red hair. She'd wield the flat iron like a sword against herself, meaning to fry out her fullness once and for all. The handle of the tool would become so hot from the hours of use that she'd wince and recoil each time she dragged its clenched mouth down another strand of hair. Sometimes, her locks would steam and hiss, begging to be left alone. Was it possible her body wept in the same way as she tried to maneuver and manipulate it into something it wasn't? "I'm sorry," she said in a small voice.

"I'm sorry you've carried this for so long by yourself."

Once her tears began to flow, she couldn't stop them. Her heart pounded as the reality filled the room. Someone knew her most shameful secret. "Do you think I'm weird and disgusting?"

"Not even a little." He scooted closer to her and wiped a tear from her freckled cheek. "But I am concerned. And I'm going to have to insist that you tell your therapist about this as soon as possible."

"Yeah, I figured that's what you were going to say."

"When do you see her next?"

"She's on a family trip, so a couple of weeks. Two Mondays from now, I think."

"Perfect. Plenty of time to hype yourself up to tell her." Amelia stared blankly at him. "And I'll be here for you every step of the way. One cathartic car-riding power ballad at a time."

She laughed, but the crazy part was how she believed him. "Why are you so perfect?" She considered again the FOG and how the forces carried him in—just dropped him in her path like a dew point at dawn.

He laughed. "I am far from perfect. I just promised myself I would always be there for my friends the way I needed someone to be there for me."

"I want to be there for you too."

"You are, Amelia. You talked me off a ledge with school just last week. And the way I can be myself with you, no questions asked? That's more than I could ever ask for."

"Ditto."

That night was two weeks ago. Now, on a blustery Sunday, she looked in at a still-sleeping Ethan, and her lungs filled with gratitude. Sure, she was terrified to tell Cathy tomorrow, but she couldn't help but note her relief at letting the first person know. Imagine *two*. Imagine actually getting help. As she tried to picture a life without binging and purging, she felt panic but also Hope. She was ready to start whacking at the last mole.

CHAPTER 16: MONTH 6

Nothing and everything had changed in the year since Mark's attack. Amelia was still the same short and stout ginger. She still had a horse named Hope and a dog named Delilah. Beth Glickman was still her sister, Jen and Jonathan were still her divorced parents. She still wore her grandmother's ruby ring on her pinkie finger every day, she still struggled with advanced eyeliner, and she'd still do just about anything for the perfect grilled cheese sandwich.

But as she sat in Cathy's office on the anniversary of almost losing the biggest fight of her life, the resemblance came to an abrupt stop. From her dwelling to her group of friends to her sense of purpose and serenity, she could barely recognize this life compared to a year ago. She was building a life from the ground up, learning the powerful difference between an existence of simple fullness and chaotic emptiness.

She and Cathy spent the first 30 minutes of their session that afternoon checking in about Amelia's eating disorder (or ED) recovery. Amelia had agreed to work with a specialized dietician as a supplement to the therapy work.

"I really think you're going to like Tamara. She comes highly recommended."

"I mean, I'm sure she's nice and everything, but the word 'dietician' just sounds so intimidating. How does this work? Like, is she going to put me on a diet?"

"Pretty sure it's the opposite. She's going to help you find freedom with food and your body."

Amelia huffed out a disbelieving laugh. "I'll believe that when I see it."

"I'll believe it for you in the meantime."

"I haven't purged in almost a month," Amelia said, downplaying it with a shrug. "I've gone that long before, but not on purpose." She still struggled with the binging and restriction aspect of the disorder, and not undoing her mistakes in the bathroom was a white-knuckled effort at best, but she'd promised Ethan. And she'd do just about anything before breaking a promise to the first friend who saw her at her worst and stayed. "I also haven't hooked up with anyone in six months. I'm halfway through my year of abstinence."

"That's wonderful, Amelia. Those are huge steps!"

"Isn't it sad that just the absence of doing something that could kill me is such a win?"

"Says the girl with almost seven months of sobriety and the chips to prove it."

"Touché." She nodded in respect. "So, elephant in the room. It's been a year since *the incident, w*hich means the protective order is up. And I shouldn't be surprised, I guess, but Mark emailed me this morning asking if we could talk."

The air in the room shifted. "Mmm-hmm."

"And part of me wants to hear him out. In a public place, with many witnesses and my support system intact, of course."

"Mmm-hmm," Cathy muttered again, less stealthy in hiding her disapproval.

"It just feels like there may be some stuff we both need closure on. It's not like I'd let him back into my life or anything."

"You know you don't owe him a conversation. You don't owe him *anything.*"

"I know I don't owe it to him, but I owe it to me."

"Fair enough."

Amelia didn't overlook the skepticism in Cathy's reply.

A week later, Amelia Glickman sat alone at a table for two, sipped her vanilla latte, and waited. Lucy sat at a nearby table with Sadie, both keeping an eye out for the signal. Three consecutive tugs on her ear meant Amelia was uncomfortable or afraid. She'd arrived fifteen minutes early to ensure she could settle in and feel safe.

She stared at the milky flower art drawn with the foam of her drink and tried to picture what the conversation might sound like. She wasn't sure what she wanted out of the encounter, but she suspected it was something along the lines of closure. But how to attain that?

Should she tell him how, in the last few months of their relationship, no matter what she was doing, she kept one eye always on him as his behavior became more erratic? Should she tell him that while she logically understood that she had done nothing to deserve the attack, she also knew that she'd been quietly pushing people to the breaking point ever since her first taste of oxygen? Should she tell him how scary it was to know that a state-of-the-art security system meant little if someone really wanted to harm you?

Rather than continuing to should all over herself, she grounded with thoughts of safety and comfort. She imagined Jen's fierce motherly love and protection in her mind's eye. The primal look of fear and guardianship when she'd lunged across the caution tape to envelop Amelia in her arms that night of Mark's assault. Amelia always associated this side of her mother with the smell of clean leather. One night as a kid she needed stitches in her lip after a fall during a game of hide-and-seek tag. She'd been at a sleepover at her friend's house, her mother returning from a nice dinner in a black leather coat. Her dad drove, and she lay in Jen's lap in the backseat, taking deep breaths of the coat's woodsy scent.

She wondered if she'd ever again feel as safe as when the glow of streetlights stretched out to pull them down each block—soothed by the soundness of her mother's embrace, while the only other person who could ever love her as much carefully piloted the car. She hoped one day, when she took her final breaths, it would feel like this. Like being carried safely up to bed after falling asleep on the couch during *Hey Arnold*. Like those last moments before descending into the depths of slumber, wrapped in a comforter that smelled like home, with a nightlight and a monsterless closet.

Deep-seated contentment and faith in the Forces of Good sent the next calming breath through her body when Mark walked through the door. He gave her a weak smile and made his way to the table. She didn't get up to greet him, just nodded in acknowledgment. He looked older—more than just one year older—but healthier, too. A smattering of grey hairs dusted his temples and facial hair, but life filled his eyes, and color tinted his cheeks.

He sat down across from her with a simple "Hi." His familiar voice woke parts of her brain that had been asleep.

"Hey," she said back.

"How's it going?"

"Fine. You?"

"Fine."

An awkward silence. It was to be expected. And low on the list of things that could go wrong.

"What's new?" he asked, clearly trying to fill the spaces.

"Well, I've been sober seven months." Might as well get right down to it.

"No shit? That's cool. Guess we were starting to get a little out of hand there towards the end."

Her mouth opened on instinct to do her part in filling the gap, keeping up the cadence of a normal conversation, until she realized that this wasn't a normal conversation—and more importantly, she didn't have anything to add. *You don't owe him anything.*

"In more ways than one," he continued. "Can I get you anything else from the front, a tea or a scone or something?" He moved to get up from the table, but she stopped him with a shake of her head.

"Um, no, that's OK. I honestly don't want to be here for very long, but I wanted us both to get a chance to say anything we need to say."

He settled back in his seat. "Yeah, Okay. That's fine."

Amelia looked across the coffee shop to where Sadie and Lucy kept a close but discreet eye on things. Sadie offered her an encouraging nod.

"Mark, why did *you* want to meet up? What do you want to talk about?" she asked.

"Well, I really wanted to apologize. I honest to God don't remember anything from that night. You have to believe me. But that doesn't mean it wasn't fucked up. And I'm really sorry. But I guess I also just wanted to ask why you never reached out. You never even called to end it. You just cut me off completely."

For the first time in a year, she wondered what Mark had been going through in the weeks and months following the incident. Then she told the truth. "You scared me to death, Mark. I've never been that scared in my whole life. I... I didn't know what else to do."

They made extended eye contact for the first time since he'd arrived, twin tears glistening like mirrors. "Me too," he finally said. "But not as scared as you were, I'm sure."

She brushed away a runaway tear with the back of her hand. "Do you know why you can't remember?"

"So, I found out I've been struggling with undiagnosed bipolar. All the weed and booze weren't helping either, obviously, but according to my doctor, what happened that night was some sort of mental break."

"Makes sense, and I heard something similar through the grapevine. It sounds like you're getting the help you need, and I'm glad. I'm getting some help, too. You weren't the only crazy one in that apartment," she said with a wry smile.

"Yeah?" he asked on a breath. He seemed relieved at the hint of humor.

"Oh yeah. Look, I'm not over what happened that night. I'll be processing it for a long time. But the more I look back on it, the more I know it didn't come out of the blue. We'd both been struggling mentally for a long time. And let's be honest, we were toxic as fuck, on both sides. Takes two to tango, and all that."

He nodded.

"I didn't deserve what you did that night. And I believe I did the right thing by leaving and cutting off contact cold turkey, as abrupt as it must have seemed. But I am sorry for the ways I hurt you, too."

"I'm so sorry, Amelia." He shook his head and squeezed his eyes shut as if willing with all his might for it to have all been a bad dream. "I never wanted to harm you in any way. And I don't want to harm you now."

Her breath caught in her throat. She didn't realize how much she'd needed to hear that until he said it. "I forgive you. I really do. But I will never forget what happened. That's just the truth. I wish you the absolute best in life, and it took a while for me to mean that, but I can't, I *won't,* be a part of your life moving forward. I ask you to respect that and not try to be a part of mine either."

He nodded. "How are Hope and Delilah?"

Her heart stopped. For some reason, she wasn't expecting him to ask about the girls. Delilah was partially his at the beginning, but Hope had always been Amelia's alone. Hearing him say their names made her skin crawl. "That's the exact kind of thing I don't think we should talk about," she said with more gusto than she felt.

Mark held both hands up before looking down at the table. "You know it was my life, too," he said without lifting his gaze. "The one we lost." His eyes flitted briefly up to hers and back down again.

"I know," she said softly. "But at the end of the day, I pushed you into that life, and it wasn't the right one for either of us. I think that's evident in how much better we're both doing."

"I agree we are better off. I just wish you weren't, like, afraid of me." His eyes pleaded with her.

"I wish I wasn't afraid of you either." She gave him a forlorn smile.

"If you wish hard enough that something didn't happen, do you think it can go away?" he asked with melancholy grin.

"I think that would make us God. Sometimes, we can't control what happens. And I don't think we usually have much control over how we feel, either. But we do have control over what we do with how we feel. And I have to pay attention to my intuition—I've ignored her for too long."

"You're pretty hard to ignore, Amelia. You must have been working really hard to keep the volume down."

"Denial is a hell of a drug. Drugs are also a hell of a drug, but I digress. I'm sober now, and I can hear her loud and clear, and I don't want to see you again."

"Okay."

"But I do want to finally say goodbye," she said, tentatively reaching for one of his hands, then thinking better of it and putting both hands in her lap. "And to thank you for the good parts."

"You think there were good parts?" he asked with a glum chuckle.

"I don't think we would have tried to make it work for as long as we did if there weren't at least *some* good parts."

"I guess you're right."

"I think it's kind of cool though, you know? We don't have to hurt each other anymore. We get to be free. Move on. Send each other light from wherever it is we end up."

"And where do you hope to end up?" he asked.

"That's not your business anymore, but even if it were, I don't have an answer yet."

Though she was more confident than ever that she was on her way to figuring it out.

CHAPTER 17: MONTH 7

Working diligently to remain thin was an unspoken rule of utmost importance among the Glickman women: a value passed down from generation to generation. Appearances had to be maintained not only to avoid judgment and criticism but also to stay safe in a world that stigmatized anything that wasn't perfectly palatable. For that reason, Amelia Glickman truly believed that the most tragic fate was one of being fat and ugly. She'd lived her whole life in a constant state of fear that by being too much, she was not enough, believing to her core that if she wasn't the best—the prettiest, the thinnest, the funniest—why should she even bother existing? Which was why she was stunned into silence by her new ED dietician's next question.

"Is it possible that the body you get when you're manipulating food so aggressively isn't the body that you're meant to have?"

Amelia stared back at Tamara across her quaint office filled with natural light and food items made from crochet. The stuffed strawberry and smiling avocado patronized her from the bookshelf by the window. Her brain stalled, recognizing and then rejecting the need to rearrange every belief she'd ever had about bodies. Tamara waited with patience, legs crossed professionally, until Amelia finally spoke.

"I guess I've never thought about it that way before." She made eye contact with a plush piece of smiling pizza and then shifted her gaze back to Tamara. "Everyone I've ever known has just always tried to be as thin as possible. I thought that was what all women did. We bond over how 'bad' or 'good' we've been that week, obsess over the number on the scale and all that."

"Well, you're not wrong about that. A lot of people live that way. Women, especially, are taught from a young age that they need to make themselves smaller at all costs. In all the ways, not just our bodies."

The film crew in Amelia's head set up the projector and began screening a memory from eighth grade. It was the first day in all of junior high that she'd slept past her alarm and didn't have time to straighten her curly red hair. When she got to school, the same boys who made fun of her "giggly thighs" laughed and told her not that her hair looked bad, ugly, or lame, but that it looked disgusting. She felt disgusting. Everything from her hair to her jeans size was too big. Food was what she used to self-soothe, and she felt like a magician the way she had learned to make it all disappear after the fact, like a theatrical poof through a trap door.

"So then," Amelia asked, "what's the alternative?"

"Divesting from a culture that creates and then profits off your insecurities."

"And I'm sure that's just as straightforward as it sounds, right?"

Tamara laughed for the first time during their session, and some of the rapport-building tension dissipated. "It's definitely not easy. Unlearning something that's been ingrained since birth never is. But it does beg the question: How free do we want to be?"

A potent energy pooled in her chest as she looked out at the vast and hopeful horizon where freedom rang, but her perspective zoomed out quickly to reveal a treacherous path between here and there.

"God, I feel this like...sense of impending doom. What is that?"

"It's impending doom," Tamara deadpanned.

Amelia burst out laughing. "Oh, good."

"Sometimes you have to burn one thing to the ground in order to build something new."

"I get the feeling you're not just talking about food and bodies anymore. That sounds almost political."

"Bodies are inherently political, Amelia, especially for folks with a uterus. Think of it this way: How much money, time, and energy have you spent trying to make your body smaller? Think of the power you'd yield if you let that go and made space for something else. You might change the whole world. And to our society, a woman with the ability to change the world is the most terrifying thing imaginable. So, they put us on diets instead, and frequently those diets turn into eating disorders."

Amelia contemplated the words while staring at a crocheted eggplant. "I mean, it does make sense. It's like I put on this front all day of being normal and friendly and functional, and it's exhausting, and then the second I'm alone, I'm ravenous and ready to unbutton my too-tight metaphorical pants and let loose with Hey Cupcake and the rewind button. I'm like a time-traveling supervillain existing in two realities: pre- and post-gorge."

"Yes, you're using up all your energy on shrinking and restricting. So, let's start simple. It sounds like you try really hard throughout the day to restrict your food intake, and then your literal survival instinct kicks in later in the day, and you binge because your body doesn't take kindly to being starved. That's when you panic and purge, because, of course, you eat too much for one sitting, because your body overrides everything else and tries to get as many nutrients and calories as possible in before you harm it by restricting again."

Amelia gawked at her. "Okay... so how do I fix that?"

"Three meals and three snacks a day. Nourish yourself regularly and allow yourself the foods you enjoy. Much easier said than done, but that's why, in our sessions, we'll process the roadblocks that inevitably present themselves."

"God, it's so fucked! When you have a problem with drugs and alcohol, you're not expected to moderate—you get sober. But you have to eat food every day—it literally keeps you alive. What a mindfuck."

"A mindfuck indeed. But your body is wise. She knows what to do. We just have to clear out some of that noise in order to hear her."

Tamara's office was in the Northwest Hills neighborhood her family lived in before the lake house. She drove toward the heavily wooded Enclave Mesa Circle and contemplated bodies, food, and sex. Something about all of this generated a sizzling energy at the base of her spine that she felt compelled to release. Maybe she was just horny? She silently made a plan to watch porn and touch herself later once she could be sure Ethan was asleep. With headphones, of course.

She didn't want to watch it that often, but when she did want to, she wanted to really bad. And then, as soon as she was finished, she'd shut the laptop in complete disgust and horror, like her perverted energy generator had shut off. She'd never tell anyone, but she fantasized about being a porn star. The life of surface-level encounters, partying, and being objectified had always appealed to her on some level, but only in the "I'd try it for a week without consequences" kind of way—like picturing herself as a star in a pop music video. Only she pictured herself getting railed by an abnormally well-endowed gentleman under the glow of camera lights.

She figured she would need a different body for her secret fantasy career. Okay, maybe she really did need the work with Tamara to give her a new perspective on her body and desire. But unless they were filming some Baroque-style, Renaissance-type porn, or playing to an audience with chubby angel baby fetishes, she didn't exactly look the part.

As she stopped at a red light, she considered the fact that she got razor burn every time she shaved anything, which really put a damper on the whole "look, I naturally just have, like, no pubic hair" phenomenon that was so big in modern-day erotic cinema. She did, however, feel like her acting skills would be much appreciated. She believed there should be a requirement of at least a high school theatre background to star in a porno. It wasn't necessarily about having star quality, but believability went through the roof if the participants at least vaguely understood the concept of character building. Acting is reacting, and all that. She always wondered how the girls in porn weren't terrified of their mom or dad seeing the video.

Whenever her mind went off on that tangent, she was better off just giving up on porn for the night and letting her mind wander while she masturbated amidst the background noise of *The Office* leaking from her laptop. Better than having Ethan hear the buzzing of a vibrator that belonged to someone he was basically related to at this point. She was certain she wasn't the first millennial to have Dwight Schrute intrude on her fantasies, the pleasantness of which was somewhat surprising.

Bringing her thoughts back from their usual vast digression, she wondered how much time and energy she actually spent trying to manipulate her body the way Tamara was talking about? Amelia did it all so she wouldn't be an afterthought in everyone's mental game of who in the room they wanted to fuck. If her tits were the same size, her ass was firmer, her face more chiseled, her teeth straighter, her freckles less splotchy... maybe she wouldn't really be a stripper or a porn star or any of those things, but having the option would be nice.

She didn't know why she couldn't let it go. It all came down to the fact that she had to be the winner in all things—even things that weren't a competition, and even when her competitors didn't know there was a competition in the first place. But underneath that layer was just another "why?"

Power. A soft voice that sounded like her own echoed in the confines of her mind as the light turned green to cross Mesa Road. She was really close to her first Austin home. Without thinking about it, she turned on her blinker and made a right towards Enclave Mesa Circle. Meanwhile, she chewed on the intuitively revealed word like a piece of tough taffy. *Power. Power. Power.*

She pulled up at the curb across from her childhood home, trying her best to go undetected by the new owners. Looking up at the window to the far right of the house, she felt closer to the little girl who slept within the room's 132 square feet than ever before. Those first pangs of loneliness and impending doom had washed over her as she stared up at the lavender, *J14* magazine-postered walls. It was where she played with Barbies and Breyer horses on the floor with her neighbor, where she sang along to the *Grease* soundtrack and played all the parts, and where American Girl Doll's hair went to die at the hands of kitchen scissors.

But it was also where she made out with someone for the first time, a girlfriend at a sleepover who never talked to her again. Where she touched herself for the first time and then thought she'd broken open a trove of chills and electric jolts exclusive to her own body. Where she sent her first dirty instant message to Toby Garrett in pink Arial font, not knowing what the words really meant.

"Is your pussy wet?" he responded in comic sans blue text with a lime green background.

Not understanding why that would even happen or how this could possibly be a good thing at the ripe age of 12, she replied with a winky face followed by, "Not at all." Later that year, she gave him a blowjob in the handicapped bathroom at the movie theatre, and at 13 was surprised to learn that sucking dick was nothing like sucking a milkshake through a straw. It was more like a bobbing-for-apples kind of vibe. As unpleasant as it was, she did learn about pussy wetness that day, making it all click into place.

"Jesus Christ," she huffed out loud, sitting at the curb, the sounds echoing off the confines of her empty car. She thought of the 12- and 13-year-old girls who rode horses at the barn. They were just kids. Some of them still had ponies, for fuck's sake. At age 23, looking back on her sordid middle school years felt almost predatory. She had no business doing the things she'd been doing at that age, yet she was a willing participant and usually the instigator, for that matter. Had she unknowingly traumatized herself? For what?

Power. There was that word again. Maybe at 13, wielding power was as simple as making Toby Garrett listen to what she had to say. Maybe it wasn't necessarily that power felt most accessible on her knees in a public restroom. Maybe in the wake of powerlessness and mounting depression, feeling desired to the extent that it became a primal need was the most forceful, vital sensation available.

But she wasn't a blonde girl with tan, flawless skin and Britney Spears abs, so her power was kept secret. It begged the question, was any of it even real in the first place? Gazing out the window, she wondered what the word power meant. Her iPhone delivered the definition: the ability to influence behavior or events. So basically, to have control over food was nothing more than a survival tactic. She lived in a world where the value of a woman's existence was rooted in how desired and cherished she was by men.

She glanced back out the window. Attached to the lavender room was the bathroom where she shaved her legs for the first time. Where she smeared the first teen spirit stick in her armpits. Got her first period. Learned how to use a tampon. Made herself puke.

Ten years. She'd been at this bullshit for a decade. She'd said it out loud the night Ethan confronted her about her purging. But parked on Enclave Mesa Circle, she finally understood just how long she'd been giving her power away, all while believing she was generating it herself. Her sex life and her eating disorder were almost the same exact age. It could be a coincidence.

And what would it all even mean? What would happen if she radically accepted herself the way she was, fell in love with the space she took up, grew confident in her physical form, and did things for the sake of health and pleasure rather than appearance? She had no idea. Maybe that was part of the adventure.

"Fuck it," she decided.

In a world where it was seen as a weakness to love and accept herself, she would do the unthinkable and enjoy her own life, on her own terms, in her own skin. Or she'd try. She'd learned in sobriety that however long it took to learn something, it took twice as long to unlearn it. But she had a feeling she was in it for the long haul. Giving up the other stuff had seemed scary, too, and look at her now.

She made one final loop around the Circle before heading home to Wethersfield Road, where a million things had died, and a million more were being reborn.

CHAPTER 18: MONTH 8

To remember something is to relive it in the context of what you know now. Memory is rarely 100 percent accurate, always seen through a different lens than the one with which it was experienced. Scents and sounds from the present can elicit recollections without explicit permission. Something about the lavender-scented candle in Cathy's office made her think of Grandma Glickman, black-and-white cookies, and old movies. She basked in the safety of these associations.

"How are things going with Tamara? How has food been?" Cathy's voice pulled her back into the room.

"Surprisingly good. I mean, not perfect or anything, but I'm sticking to my meal plan and haven't purged in almost two months now." She twisted Grandma's ruby ring around a finger. "Month eight of no banging, too."

Cathy smiled and gave her a nod of encouragement to continue.

"But without the disordered eating, sex, or booze, I've had a lot of time to, uh, think I guess." Her fidgeting became the slightest bit more agitated.

"Tell me more."

"Well, before going to treatment, I had my pick of the litter when it came to turning off my brain. Then, when I got out, it was just sex and food left. Once I started the year off from sex, the eating disorder was all that was left. And now that I'm focusing on that—the final frontier if you will—I have no way to avoid the thoughts and feelings I've been running from for so long."

"What have you noticed coming up?"

"Anger. So. Much. Anger."

"Anger about anything in particular? If not, that's alright too. It's OK if it just… is."

"I haven't gotten that far yet, to be honest. I think somewhere down the line, something made me feel like I lost my right to anger. It's been super uncomfortable. Like, all of my emotions have a fire lit under their ass for sure, but anger feels different somehow. Like if I let it out completely, it might burn my whole life down or swallow me whole."

Cathy nodded and shifted her gaze out the office window. "How would you feel if we did something a little unconventional today and tried to tap into that anger in the safe container of this room? Would you be open to that?"

"You're the boss, boss."

Cathy smiled. "If at any point you feel uncomfortable or would like to stop, you just say the word."

"Word."

"Alright then," she said with a chuckle. "Make yourself comfortable, lay down, sit on the floor, lean back, curl up in a ball, whatever feels right."

Amelia shifted lengthwise onto the inviting cream-colored couch, stretching out her legs and clasping her hands across her belly like a Freudian patient. "Paint me like one of your French girls," she said to no one in particular.

"Amelia," Cathy said, suppressing another laugh. "Are you going to be able to take this seriously?"

"Yes, yes. Absolutely. Sorry."

A few breathing exercises and visualizations later, Amelia found herself in a borderline hypnotic state. "The anger is burning hot. And everything bad that's ever happened to me is melded together in a frozen ice block somewhere deep in my chest, creating a mass of anxiety and depression."

"Tell me more," Cathy said.

"It's like something inside me is in a deep freeze as a way to protect itself, and it's dying to thaw, but I won't let the flame anywhere near it, so it can't do its job."

"And the anger is the flame?"

"Yeah. My Borderline shit protects the iceberg from the flame. But the fire's only trying to help. And the protection works more like a pressure cooker, anyway."

"Why can't you let the flame be?"

"Because if I did that, it could burn down the whole world."

"That's a lot of pressure to put on yourself."

"Yeah, no shit," she said, still in a daze. There was a quiet, reflective pause. "We're talking mass destruction. Habitats destroyed, species extinct, an extinction-level event."

"Your anger isn't dangerous, Amelia. It can't hurt anyone unless you let it. It's safe to feel it now." As Amelia blinked her eyes open, Cathy sipped her tea. "You know, I've heard trauma defined as either too much too soon or too little too late."

"Yeah, I mean, I think it's obvious that there was something in my childhood that I was desperately needing but not getting. No fault of my parents. I mean, I was pretty intense right out of the womb."

"What might you have been missing?"

"Maybe just like validation? My emotions were so big, and no one seemed to understand why."

"That explains the too little too late. What about the too much too soon?"

"That's where I'm hitting a roadblock."

"Close your eyes one more time for me. I want you to imagine you're carrying a lit candle toward the big ice block you described. One foot in front of the other. As you get closer, what do you notice?"

"Curtain down. A deep burgundy theatre curtain whooshing closed. It doesn't want me to see behind. The more the flame threatens to melt the ice, the more I have to perform. Like the Wizard of Oz. 'Pay no attention to the man behind the curtain' or whatever."

"Why does the curtain draw closed? Do you know?"

"Because whatever is back there could mean the show doesn't go on."

Amelia peeked open her eyes to find Cathy's brow furrowed in thought.

"And…"

"And the show must go on."

When she opened her eyes, Cathy looked at her with an unreadable expression on her face. "At what cost?"

"So far? Everything."

Instead of making the seven-minute drive home to Wethersfield after therapy, Amelia found herself turning off South First Street onto Barton Springs Road and pulling into the parking lot on the edge of Lady Bird Lake. The last gasps of tolerable weather hung in the trees, the warm May air textured with a pleasant breeze. Spring's newest creations found their legs.

As she stepped out of her car, the beep of the door locking rang through the green waves of an empty Zilker Park on a random Tuesday. She began to put one foot in front of the other, making her way to the hike and bike trail. Cathy always went on and on about bilateral stimulation, how walking, one foot forward and then the other, helped our brains process and chew on information that was heavy or rich with emotion.

Her feet finally hit the gravel trail to begin the loop around the lake, and she thought back to the blood-red theatre curtain that blocked her during the therapy exercise. She looked out at the glittering lake as some bold, brave part of her dared to peek behind the burdensome bulk of the draped cloth. With one tug on the golden rope at the center of the mammoth barrier, it was curtain up. A new kind of show began, fully contextualized memories taking the stage as she walked.

Left, right, left, right, left, right.

You're walking back from the bathroom 20 minutes into AP English, except not really. You're actually walking back from your car, where you just hit your pipe to take the edge off the day. Sweat licks at your temples because the heat hasn't yet broken at the beginning of your senior year, and you come across the music teacher that everyone loves. The one who works on all the musicals. He clearly picks up on the earthy bud scent on your breath, and you play it cool and casual, friendly and charming.

"You know I had a dream about you last night," he says with a sly, flirtatious smile that you pick up on right away. It makes the most sense to act oblivious to it at first, give him one last chance to snap out of it, to backtrack, and not be a creepy piece of shit.

"I seriously doubt that," you say. Your brain is baking more and more by the minute as the high really starts to kick in.

"No, no, I really did," he says back, head tilting downward, eyes peeking up to meet yours in a way that suggests a sexy and knowing confidence that is wholly unearned.

Fucking asshole. "Well, was I doing something awesome, like skydiving or tap dancing in a clown costume?" *Come on, dude, take the out.*

"Don't be demure, Amelia. You know what kind of dream I'm talking about." He reaches for your hand. You freeze and pull back, but you don't say no. You wish you were more surprised it was happening, but the truth is he's given you special attention over the last four years, which you didn't exactly discourage. And it's far from the first time you've seen a grown man act like a shithead. "I found a way up to the roof last week," he continues. "It's a really cool view of Austin from up there. Do you want to come check it out?"

"Um, no. No. I have to get back to class. We have an essay, and uh, my pen is still in there, and um, I've got to go." You smile politely and head back to the English wing. You never speak of it again.

Left, right, left, right, left, right.

You're in a cold classroom after third-period sophomore biology. The majority of the class has filed out, headed to the cafeteria for lunch, but your lab partner is cleaning up the materials from today's experiment— and he doesn't seem to notice how the teacher is sliding his hand up your thigh, higher and higher, stopping only at the crease between your limb and the centermost part of you.

It must not be as weird as I think it is. You remind yourself that your lab partner remains unfazed and would clearly say something if this was out of the ordinary. You don't want to be a baby about it. The teacher was just asking about your weekend plans, after all.

Except when you walk out into the hall and put your head in the crook of your boyfriend Trevor's neck, your whole body energetically crumbles because deep down, you know the difference between good touch and bad touch. Trevor's touch is good; that touch was not. He insists you go to the administrators and report this, but they call it a miscommunication.

You go back to class the next day and spend the rest of the school year cheating off your lab partner's homework and tests, looking the bastard in the eye while you do it, and he never says shit because you both know exactly what happened. It's the last A you ever make in a math or science class in your academic career.

Left, right, left, right, left, right.

You're on a cruise with your family the summer after sixth grade, and you just left the Carnival Teen Social Club's dance on the Lido Deck. You've made a few friends at the club throughout your voyage across the Gulf, and this particular night, one of their adult brothers happens to be stumbling around drunk in the same vicinity as your makeshift group of friends when you're on your way to the 24/7 ice cream bar.

It doesn't take much for the drunken man to convince your group to go to his cabin and try Kahlua for the first time. Next thing you know, you're sitting on a bed in a strange room next to a dude who looks kind of like your dad's coworker. The room is spinning, and everyone is giggling while he rubs your leg and professes to the group of minors, "If this one weren't so young, I would tear her to pieces." You know it's a little weird that you're flattered, but it's something to hang onto when the boys make fun of you in seventh grade next year. Nevertheless, you wonder whether the fall into the ocean alone would be enough to kill you as you sneak back to your family's cabin across the ship—it's the first of many things you picture yourself careening off of in the years to come.

Left, right, left, right, left, right.

You've been a pain in the ass in your eighth-grade math class, and you know it. You were in one of those talking-back moods where your filter dissolves into nothing but wishful thinking. You know you've given off a certain amount of flirtatious and attention-seeking energy, so it seems like your fault when your 40-year-old married algebra teacher runs his fingers up and down the crack of your ass in a room full of bustling students on their way out to study hall.

It was so quick, and in the midst of so many people, you wonder if you made it all up. Throwing up in the school bathroom after lunch is a welcome reprieve from the nausea and feverish chills plaguing your body the rest of that day. Or was it really the rest of your life?

Left, right, left, right, left, right.

Then come the short snippets, each like a flash photo in a pitch-black room, unfolding for a millisecond; the evidence is blurry.

You meet a guy from Tinder on a Saturday night. He's from Philly, in Austin with friends for a bachelor party, and you cannot believe you both like the same cliché millennial emo band, but the truth is, everyone likes them. You're already drunk, but you drive to an Airbnb occupied by a group of strange men without a second thought.

You remember playing beer pong. You remember wondering what kind of girl the groom was marrying. And you remember multiple bodies over your own, like rapid-fire snapshots, a glitch in the matrix, but the matrix is some nightmarish rendering of PornHub, except no one here is getting paid, least of all you.

Left, right, left, right, left, right.

You're at a sleepover, and the girls in your fourth-grade class try their hardest to stay up until sunrise, but you're the last one standing. Staring at the ceiling, you're determined to win the game, but eventually, you let sleep pull you under. After an undetermined amount of time, someone bigger and stronger, likely your friend's older brother, tiptoes into the living room you're all sprawled across and kneels beside your sleeping bag.

He fondles your barely-there breasts, and you use all your willpower to keep your eyes closed and feign sleep rather than meet this humiliating situation head-on. When you sit around the table the next morning with your friends, rehashing the night and gobbling up pancakes, you figure you must have been dreaming.

Left, right, left, right, left, right.

The earliest one is the fuzziest, but it's the origin story. You can't be older than four because your family is still in New York, and you still wear pull-ups to sleep every night. The neighbors have a daughter your age, and you're in their basement playing. The above-ground barred windows allow streaks of afternoon light to highlight the dust in the air, the only visual evidence attached to this memory.

The only other puzzle pieces are the looming presence of an adult male, likely your friend's father, your missing Little Mermaid underwear, and a sense of deep unease that is disproportionate to your age. It's the beginning of something insidious and all-consuming.

Amelia's legs went on with the left-right dance despite the uncomfortable and knowing pang from her roots. Before she knew it, she was back, crossing the pedestrian bridge from the south to the north side of the lake. She stopped at the midpoint, hands on the railing, watching the lake glisten in the late afternoon light. The skyline had changed so much since she was a kid. The cranes still rose up with no signs of development slowing. The splashing rhythm of the UT rowing team's oars broke the surface of the water mixed with the thump, thump, thump of runners' shoes on the bridge's concrete.

A light breeze tucked a strand of flyaway red curls behind her shoulder, and she gently lifted her chin to gaze across the water at the famous graffiti bridge. The art had changed over time, but right now, it was spray-painted with Pac-Mans and tags that said "kung fu grip," "breathe," and "don't give up." As in, "Hey, Amelia. Hope this email finds you well. Let the fuck go of your iron-clad control, breathe through the hard moments, and keep moving forward. Always here to assist. Best, Forces of Good."

She smiled and shook her head, eyes catching on the big green lawn of the Four Seasons Hotel where her audition had played out all those years ago. Its manicured grass overlooked the water and was sure to offer a beautiful view of where she now stood. No wonder the promise of being special, adored, and celebrated had meant everything at the time—she was running away from so much. The danced-out memories lit up the tumors of trauma lodged throughout her body, a cancer threatening to eat away at her. Acknowledging them meant admitting they were real. Instead, she'd forged a protective personality so rigid that it had cracked, creating a mess of Borderlines.

With a new, quiet understanding, she continued her walk, wondering why today was the day it all came together. It was as if a long-forgotten part of her had banged a gavel and said, "You've always wondered why you are the way you are. We think you're ready now, so here you go."

With each step on her trail, she understood more deeply that there were pieces of this puzzle she might never fully put together. It was worth letting the ice thaw, even if doing so meant igniting the flame of her anger. Cathy often talked about the stages of grief: denial, anger, bargaining, depression, and acceptance. She said they occurred in no particular order. Amelia had denied with drugs and alcohol, bargained with sex, and spent most of her life depressed. All that was left was anger, followed by the release of acceptance. It was the ultimate energetic purge, acknowledging the pain and building a life worth living in its wake.

Because the truth was, Amelia was a fire in and of herself. And for some fucked-up reason that only misogyny itself could explain, her liveliness, exuberance, quickness to laugh, and tendency to say things out loud that others kept inside made those men think she was encouraging something that she simply was not. That was a problem within them, not a problem within her.

Even if she had explicitly asked for something, the right answer was, "No, and what happened to you that made you think that was even on the table?" And anyway, she didn't ask for shit. She suspected no young girl ever did. Not really. Yet in every city in the country, more than a few middle-aged men insisted the 15-year-old came on to them first.

Amelia pulled up to Wethersfield a half hour later. She walked through the side door and was greeted by a giddy Delilah. In that moment, she knew for certain that her anger wouldn't burn the house down. Only the bridges to what no longer served her. And some things needed to burn.

CHAPTER 19: MONTH 9

In June of 1951, 11-year-old Rose Glickman dragged the edge of an old kitchen knife against the skin of a bright green apple with the tremendous focus of a surgeon performing lifesaving open heart surgery. Engrossed with the task at hand, the tip of her tongue poked out the corner of her mouth in concentration as she attempted for the umpteenth time to peel her grandfather's apple in a perfect coil of unbroken skin. She'd gotten close a few times, but no cigar. This time felt different, though; she'd mastered her technique and could feel her heart pound and beads of sweat prick her forehead as she neared the bottom of the apple. A spiral of waxy green skin hung like a party favor. She prayed it wouldn't tear harder than she'd ever prayed for anything before.

Her grandfather had promised young Rose that if she could successfully perform this trick, he would give her a quarter. She swiped the knife around the last globus edge of the fruit. Visions of her own copy of the newest issue of *Vogue*, or candy cigarettes, pulled her across the finish line in triumph.

"I did it! I actually did it! I didn't think it was possible, but I did it!" She shouted and held out the knife and apple in one hand, the spiral of a peel in the other.

Her grandfather grunted in response without looking up from his newspaper. Rose lived with him, her mother, and her three siblings in a tiny Brooklyn apartment. She placed the proof of her success for his inspection on the small smoking table between them.

His sigh, barely audible, was muffled by the sports section before he peeked over the readers on his nose. Something like surprise swam across his features as he took in the helix she presented, but he replaced it with his usual disinterested scowl. "Hmm," he finally said, putting the paper down on his lap. Without looking up at her, he leaned down and picked up the peeled apple and the knife and quietly cut the fruit into four even pieces. His eyes didn't bother to meet hers when he handed her a chunk of apple with a smattering of seeds dangling off the core. "A quarter," he said.

The first-class plane fare that carried Amelia Glickman from Texas to New York in June of 2016 was a far cry from the quarter that tricked her grandmother. Also well beyond the quarter was the sleek black car escorting her from the airport to her grandmother's giant house, the one her father had purchased for his parents when he sold his first company. The skyline rushed by her window like the opening credits to a corny movie. The glittering lights pulled her thoughts to the theatre, and she checked the time. The chosen ones were likely making their way to the theatre district for their six p.m. call times. Every night at eight Eastern Time, the curtains on Broadway opened. And every night at seven Central Time, a young Amelia Glickman in Austin, Texas, willed the theatre gods to project her onto a Broadway stage before a buzzing crowd of expectant attendees just before the lights came up. The magic of creating live theatre thrummed through her being like the most potent dose of life itself.

The daydream always called to her like a siren song. She still pictured the casts preparing to take reality and light it on fire. This was especially true in the month following her trauma hike around Lady Bird Lake. A red-hot anger ravaged her nervous system like a wildfire as it made up for lost time and innocence. She'd imagine channeling her wrath into art via the likes of *Medea* or *Who's Afraid of Virginia Woolf?* Then maybe it would feel valid. But each night by seven o'clock in Austin, there was no stage in her line of sight. And the truth was, that was OK. Even when it was hard. Even when it felt like her anger might rip her to shreds. Real life was good enough in the seat of the sleek car, watching the lights, just knowing the theatres existed in the first place.

As the road from the airport to Bubbe's house stretched on, the buildings became shorter, stouter, and farther apart. And as the miles remaining on the navigation system went down, Amelia's blood pressure went up. She'd arrived to help Grandma Glickman around the house while her aunt was out of town for a few days. Her husband, Grandpa Haim, was in the hospital with pneumonia and was now in the clear, but still couldn't come home for a couple of days. Grandma couldn't be alone. An in-home caretaker was starting next week, but Amelia volunteered to step into the gap.

Logically, Amelia knew that grandparents were inherently old and constantly getting older, but something young and naive within her still didn't fully believe it could be true of *her* grandparents. Especially the only two she had left. Amelia never met her mom's mom Gianna, who'd died when Jen was just 25—a fate Jen said she wouldn't wish on her worst enemy. Amelia was quick to agree, shuddering at the thought of going through any part of her life without a mother. Amelia's Grandpa Sal, Jen's father, had passed when Amelia was a senior in high school. In some ways, Grandpa Sal was the family member she related to the most. His last years had been muddled with depression and dementia, and it was the first time she'd seen someone share the amount of mental anguish that her brain was capable of. There was a kinship—only his anguish was in his longing to remember, while Amelia's was in her need to forget.

But Grandma and Grandpa Glickman hadn't seemed to age an inch since the day she was born, until suddenly, they got old overnight. The medical issues seemed to appear like clockwork as soon as they hit their mid-80s. Not unique, but it still shocked her when the people it affected were her own. Living in Austin, Amelia's main source of information in New York was her aunt, who lived 10 minutes down the road from Bubbe and Zeyde. Now she was about to see Grandma's decline for herself.

As Amelia rolled her comically large suitcase up the walkway, she prepared to be greeted by a stranger. But the woman who answered the door before Amelia could even knock was not a stranger; she was Grandma, just slighter.

She wore a colorful scarf wrapped around her head to cover her thinning hair and was just as beautiful as ever. "Amala, my love. It's so good to see you, sweetheart. Come in."

Amelia shut the door and took in the familiar lavender scent. She made her way around the walker between them to greet her grandmother with a gentle embrace. After their hello, Amelia insisted that Bubbe sit as she made them each a cup of tea.

Ten minutes later at the kitchen table under the warm lights, the sun had set outside the window. The steam from their mugs danced and mingled in the glow. They each sipped their decaf Earl Grey and let out their signature "ah" before spending a few moments in comfortable silence.

Grandma Glickman was the first to speak. "Now, it's not a big deal, but I fell trying to go to the bathroom last night. Hit my head, cut my arm. Went to the ER today to get patched up. I'm fine, but they agreed I really shouldn't sleep alone anymore. Would you mind sleeping in my bed with me tonight?"

Would she *mind*? Amelia had been obsessed with her grandmother's gigantic, downy bed since she was a little girl. She would look out the window on the airplane home from New York as a kid, thinking of how the pillowy white clouds must feel exactly like the fluffy throws and blankets covering Grandma's bed.

"Of course, Grandma. We can watch *The Young and the Restless* and tell ghost stories like when I was little."

"Twist my arm," Grandma said with a wink. "Hope I didn't forget to tape this week's episodes." She had taped every episode of Y&R for the past 40 years. She'd clung to the VHS method with an iron grip until Dad finally forced her into a smart TV, teaching her how to save episodes into the cloud. She picked it up surprisingly fast.

As they sipped their tea, Amelia told her Bubbe about Ethan, Sadie, and Lucy and, of course, gave a lengthy update on Hope and Delilah. Her grandmother's contented smile radiated love at the picture of the new life. When Amelia dove into the tale of her sobriety, Bubbe paused.

"You won't drink at all? Not even Manischewitz for Pesach?"

Amelia smiled. "Not even then. I can't safely use drugs in any form, including alcohol. I use it as a means to escape and become addicted to the trapdoor of it all."

She nodded slowly in response, then said, "Proud of you. Always."

Soon, they made their way up the stairs hand in hand, and Amelia provided support and encouragement along the way. She hovered, ready to step in if her grandmother needed her as she prepared for bed. Once Grandma Glickman was comfortable with her reading glasses, her phone, and the hum of MSNBC, Amelia got herself ready for bed and unpacked before crawling in next to her.

The bed was just as plush and amazing as she'd remembered, and the calming ripples in her childhood heart spread through to the rest of her soul. "I'm just as liberal as the next Glickman, but don't you ever get tired of the echo chamber of MSNBC?"

"No."

Amelia laughed. "How?"

"I just love Rachel Maddow. So sharp, that one. Beauty and brains."

"Fair enough."

A commercial for a new movie sparkled across the screen. It starred the actress who got the role that Amelia auditioned for, but the old pathetic pang of shame and envy had all but disappeared. She thought back to all those times she sat on her couch in self-pity, smoking weed and watching the movie she'd lost. In Bubbe's bed, all she thought was that the movie looked worth seeing. Maybe she'd ask her friends if they wanted to go next week.

But Grandma Glickman didn't miss anything, not even the tiniest look on Amelia's face. "Do you ever think about going back to acting? You were so good at it."

"Nah. I'm not cut out for it. Too much rejection and competition. I do miss it sometimes, but I've found ways to incorporate it into my life. It's still an art form I love and appreciate. But it sucks, because I haven't found anything I'm quite as good at. Like riding is so special, but that's mostly because of Hope's skills. I'm only so-so at the sport."

"Amala, your effervescence is what made you an artist, not the other way around. And the creativity and light that made you such a wonderful actress is also what makes you a good human. You make people feel at ease with your sense of humor and openness. You create fun, pleasant spaces for people—just by being yourself. That's the best thing in the world to create."

"I think I might want to be a therapist." It was the first time she'd said it out loud, though it had been bouncing around her mind ever since that trauma trek around the lake. People's stories were always worth listening to. She'd even looked up graduate programs in Austin and fiddled around with the applications.

"Oh, that's wonderful, sweetheart. You could help so many people."

"You don't think my own craziness would get in the way?"

"I think your experience will be valuable."

"I never thought about it that way." She looked over at the quietly humming TV. "Do you remember Trevor?"

"Of course! Such a Bubbelah. What is that sweet young man up to these days?" Grandma Glickman had always loved Trevor, and she still told the story of the time she was in Austin when he got Amelia a sack of potatoes for Valentine's Day because they lasted longer than flowers. "Just like his love!" she'd say. "What a mensch."

"Well, funnily enough, he's doing his clinical hours to become a therapist. I'm meeting him and his boyfriend for dinner next week. I'm planning to ask him about the process of going back to school for my master's."

"Hmm. Boyfriend. Who would've thunk? Good for him."

Amelia giggled. "You know, Grandma, I appreciate the fact that you don't even bat an eye at that. Pretty badass for an 85-year-old."

"Oh please, your great-great-grandmother was a wardrobe mistress for a drag show in the late 1890s. The gays and the Jews tend to have each other's backs."

"Fair enough."

Grandma Glickman turned back to the TV, leaving Amelia to ponder quietly. She wanted to stop pruning her own queerness blooming since childhood. Maybe it was something as deep and as true as her genes. Maybe being queer, or at the very least queer-adjacent, was something as steady and tangible as the blood running through her veins. Maybe the way her soul ached for queer art and history over the course of her life held the answer. The way her heart expanded to fit the restlessness of the Stonewall Riots when she learned about them in school. The way the gay triumph in the Supreme Court brightened even her darkest hour of addiction. Pride had always felt so personal. But could something that society deemed so complicated be as simple and inevitable as her curly red hair? A piece of her heart that had been floating around seemed to click into place, validated and whole.

After a few more moments of silence, her grandmother spoke without looking away from the screen. "You know, I really think you should go for it. Being a therapist. I think you make people feel safe to be themselves. Tell their stories."

"Yeah?"

"Yeah. And you're smart to boot. A master's degree would put that big brain of yours to use."

"Well, where do you think I get it from, Miss *New York Times* Crossword Queen?"

Grandma smiled and glanced at Amelia sitting up in bed. "I would have loved to go to college.

"Why didn't you?" She knew it was a stupid question the moment it came out of her mouth. It was such a different time, but something nudged her to ask, sensing her grandmother's desire to process and express.

"I really wanted to. I even tried to sign up for a college prep course in high school. I was 16 and had a million dreams no one had bothered to shatter yet."

"Would your grandfather not let you enroll?" Amelia asked, remembering the stories about what a piece of work the man was. Always undermining and belittling her. Playing mean tricks.

"No, actually. He was uninvolved by that point. Usually drunk or asleep. Or both. But the principal of the school called me and my mother in for a conference. Said I was better suited for home economics. Secretarial classes if I really wanted to get fancy with it."

"What? Why would he do that?"

"Not sure why he singled me out specifically, but it was a better bet for a woman to earn a husband than a degree back then. I'll never forget the way he grabbed my chin and said, 'Look at this face. She'll be married by 18. Don't waste your money.' I ended up dropping out and getting a job in Manhattan. After my first few paychecks, I bought the ruby ring." She took Amelia's hand in hers, brushing her fingers over the deep red gemstone on her granddaughter's pinkie finger. "I guess I wanted to prove to myself that beautiful things could be powerful, too." Her grandmother's hands were impossibly soft; the skin covering her deep blue veins seemed tissue-paper-thin.

"Bubbe, you *are* beautiful. You always have been, and you always will be. But that is the least interesting thing about you. And that guy was a fucking asshole."

Grandma chuckled, shifting to turn toward Amelia. "Being beautiful, desirable, thin, palatable…It was a means of surviving by being important. I think that's why it's so hard for me now. The wrinkles, the hair loss, all the shifts."

"I get that."

"I'm realizing that bodies are just shells. They hold machinery that will eventually reach the maximum number of repairs and renovations."

"Very wise, Grandma. And a little morbid." She squeezed her hand gently.

Bubbe squeezed back harder with a wry smile. "I'm not dead yet, Amala." She turned off the television. "Let's get some sleep, sweetheart." Amelia dozed off to the cadence of her grandmother's deep, restful breaths.

The next four days were full of old movies, soap operas, takeout, and important conversations. The most important talk was the first real conversation with her grandmother about her parents' divorce.

Amelia cleared the table after dinner. "I think when their marriage ended, the thread that had been holding me together just completely snapped." She started the dishes, adding "But if it hadn't broken, I never would have had the opportunity to heal."

"Are you angry?"

Amelia considered this as she rinsed the plates. "You know, I definitely *was* angry. Like *super* fucking angry. I'm kind of being reacquainted with anger in the traditional sense, but yeah, I would say I was angry in my own way. First more so at Mom, which didn't make any sense, because from what I gathered, it was really Dad's fault." Amelia stopped what she was doing and turned apologetically to where her grandmother still sat at the kitchen table. "Sorry, I know that he's, like, your son."

Grandma Glickman flicked her hand. "Keep going and get to the good part."

"I realized it was just literally none of my business. And besides, they didn't get divorced *at* me, you know?"

"Still, it must have been painful. So painful."

"But they did the best they could. And as weird as it used to be to see them with their new people, they both seem happier.

"Bashert."

"What?"

"Bashert. It's Yiddish for everything happens for a reason."

Before she knew it, she was looking out the window at fluffy clouds on the plane back to Austin. So that was what it meant to care for someone near the end of their life, to tuck in someone who held you in the hospital the day you were born. Someone who changed your diapers. She didn't want to wait for a crisis to tell her people how much she loved them. Whatever might happen in the coming months or years, she'd told her grandmother how much she loved her. And the sense of peace that brought her was immeasurable. Tomorrow was never promised.

She'd also told her grandmother that her beauty was the least interesting thing about her. Why was it so difficult to apply the same sentiment to herself? Since the start of her journey with food freedom and body positivity, she'd gained some weight. Allowing her body just to be a body without forcing it to be an ornament of the smallest possible variety was the final stage of allowing the FOG to hold her. All she had to do was resist the urge to run away when things felt overwhelming.

She wasn't sure exactly how much weight she'd gained, because Tamara had insisted she get rid of her scale. Which, of course, she did in a dramatic and destructive fashion with the help of a sledgehammer. If she was doing this, she was doing it big. But still, she'd gone up a size in her jeans. While she was definitely having scary moments around that, and while there would always be a part of her that wanted to say fuck it and go back to her old ways, she felt liberated at the same time.

She'd gained weight, yes, but she also gained energy, the space for new ideas and pursuits, fresh creativity, and a deepening desire for connection with her people. Healing wasn't linear, but she was headed in the right direction, planting seeds in her National Forest. The amusement park still beckoned, insisting on substances, trying to convince her that if she were not her thinnest, she might as well be dead.

But the truth had already taken root, and it was becoming easier and easier to discern who she really was from who she always thought she should be. The truth was that her body had the wisdom to decide what size was healthiest for it to be. Taking care of herself meant nourishing herself with food, movement, and love that made her shine from the inside out. You didn't tell a tree how large it should grow; you just gave it what it needed to do so. She wished she could share what she was learning with everyone on the planet, but she also knew that most weren't anywhere near ready to hear it.

She pressed her forehead against the cool glass of the window overlooking the clouds. A career in counseling might put her in a position to help others the way Tamara and Cathy were helping her. If she got her grad school application in by the end of the month, she'd be able to start classes as soon as the fall. Assuming she got in, of course. She looked forward to meeting with Trevor and asking more questions.

Amelia could no longer hide beyond feigned disdain; she was *excited* about the future. Human beings—their stories, their resilience, their capacity to heal—fascinated her. Character development was always her favorite aspect of acting, after all. Her life was becoming everything she never even knew she wanted, and she didn't want to miss a second of it. Only a year ago, a cute boyfriend and a lower THC tolerance were all she would have asked for, and man, would she have been selling herself short.

CHAPTER 20: MONTH 10

Suddenly it was July. Amelia watched the stifling heat dissipate in the rearview mirror as she made her way to Santa Fe once again, this time with Sadie, Lucy, and Delilah in tow. Ethan couldn't get off work to join them, so he'd called five times since they left Wethersfield six hours ago to let them know how bored and lonely he already was. Delilah napped happily with her head on Sadie's lap while she read something on her phone in the back seat next to the pile of luggage. Lucy snored softly with her mouth open, the hot pink hood of her sweatshirt completely obscuring the top half of her face. She couldn't wait to see how her friends reacted to horse show life; it was certainly out of the ordinary from what most people knew. It was likely one of the only places on earth with more horses than people per square foot.

As they drove in comfortable silence, Amelia compared this year's trek to Santa Fe to last year's. That putrid smell of fear had radiated from her pores then as she sat with her own thoughts for 12 hours, trying not to panic about leaving her stash at home. Once she got ahold of some bud, she made the decision to ride high. Then, she hit her bottom with the force and magnificence of a supernova. That ache of loneliness felt bottomless as she sat alone the night after crashing Hope, waiting for Dad to come to the rescue, wondering if she was even worthy of being saved. It was crazy to think that the very next summer, she was making the drive with her two sober girlfriends after almost a year sober herself. So much could change in 12 months.

Sober July had been a mindfuck. In therapy, she'd finally gotten to the bottom of all that anger just to unearth a deep well of sadness. Sadness was distinct from depression—it had a reason and a purpose, a weight to it. Depression was like negative space, and she was learning not to bury her sadness in a way that bred depression. Instead, she shared it with the Sunday night meeting. She talked about her rock bottom in Santa Fe, that she was going back soon, and the truth that she was a little scared. She got more vulnerable than she ever had with the group.

"You know when you feel so full of fear you could explode but also so empty you could collapse in on yourself? That's how I've been feeling since some big stuff came up in therapy. But I also haven't taken a drink or drug in 11 months. Though to be honest with y'all, the past couple of weeks, I've thought about it. Not in an 'I'm actually going to do it' way, just in an 'I wonder if using would make me feel any better' kind of way. But I know it wouldn't." The meeting attendees seated in a circle around the room nodded in understanding.

"It's just days like today, the veil between sane and insane feels thin. Like I'm on the edge of barely functioning. Like one inconvenience could push me over the edge into bedridden. And then I secretly wish for a horrible illness, a broken bone, or an earth-shattering phone call. Anything external that could justify the internal chaos. Otherwise, it has nowhere to go."

To her surprise, knowing smiles filled the room. This was her nastiest part, the part that wished for the worst. The part she had hidden carefully. Yet people were nodding and smiling. She continued.

"It feels like the perfect version of me is just *less* of me. I feel fake and phony and empty but also too full. There's nothing scarier to me than the idea of absolutely nothing. So, I make waves in my life and the lives of others. I create chaos to avoid figuring out who I actually am and what I really want out of life. Anyway, like I said, I leave for Santa Fe next week, and I'm scared to be there alone with my thoughts. I'm scared of the chaos I may try to create. So, I guess I'm just saying it out loud as a way to hold myself accountable or whatever. But that's it. Thanks for letting me share."

"Thanks, Amelia," the group echoed. "Glad you're here," a few people added. To her relief, no one called out, "Keep coming back," AKA the sobriety edition of "Bless your heart," which was code in the South for, "You're a fucking idiot." After the meeting, she was met with hugs and celebratory back slaps. One older gentleman who smelled like cigarettes and coffee, a walking recovery caricature, slapped her back so hard she almost fell over. It was good-natured, though.

She was still getting used to the idea of vulnerability being celebrated rather than shunned. But that was the special thing about these church basements and rec center halls; the deeper you dug, the more people related. And it didn't take long for Sadie and Lucy to make their way over to where she gathered her things after the meeting. To her surprise, they insisted on joining her in Santa Fe.

"What about work? And school?" she asked, trying to rein in her hopeful excitement.

Lucy shrugged. "I can work remotely whenever I want. As long as they have Wi-Fi in the state of New Mexico, there shouldn't be any issues."

"And I have a three-week break between summer classes and the fall semester," said Sadie.

"It's kismet, bitch," Lucy added.

The truth was, she would have made it through the horse show weeks in Santa Fe if they couldn't go along, and even with their company, hard things would still feel hard. But she was learning she didn't have to face any of it alone if she didn't want to. One moment, she was feeling sorry for herself, and the next, she was holding her hand out the window of the Rav4 somewhere outside of Lubbock, singing Demi Lovato with her best friends, smiling at the warmth in her chest brought about by an unshakable belief that she was exactly where she was supposed to be.

But the sing-along was hours ago by now, and the peaceful hum of miles passing under tires lulled her into meditations about the nature of grief. This type of sadness was sacred somehow. And as painful as it was, she was grateful she'd been brave enough to let the anger run its course to make room for the deep throb that was left. In June, she'd walked and walked Wethersfield Road and the surrounding streets, focusing on one breath at a time as visceral anger tore its way through her system. For the first time in her life, she wasn't trying to change the way she felt; she was just *feeling* it.

Lucy unleashed a raucous yawn, bringing Amelia back to the moment. "Good shit," Lucy said through another yawn. "Nothing like a little road trip nap." She looked out the window wearily. "Where the fuck are we now?"

"I believe the technical term is Texico," Amelia said. "Right on the border, baby."

"Between Texas and *New* Mexico, correct? You didn't take us south on accident?" asked Sadie, only half joking.

"Yes, dear. *New* Mexico."

The chime of her phone ringing through the Bluetooth speakers split the air. "Trevie" had a contact photo from the 2009 junior year play. She clicked the green button to answer. "Hey! How did it go?" Amelia and her high school sweetheart had been in touch since she'd met up with Trevor and his boyfriend Josh last month to discuss grad school. Trevor had walked her through the process. He was planning to propose to Josh last weekend, and Amelia insisted he tell her when the deed was done because, well, she was Amelia.

"Amazinggg," he said, drawing out the word as long as humanly possible.

"Oh my god, oh my god, oh my god, tell me literally everything! You're on speaker. I have friends with me. Say hi, friends."

"Hi!" Lucy and Sadie said in unison.

"Um, hi!" Trevor then launched into a seventeen-minute retelling of the most romantic proposal in the history of the world. All three girls were on the verge of tears by the time he finished. And the crazy thing was, she felt his happiness with her whole soul. Her capacity for holding joy for others' joy was one of the many gifts the last 11 months had granted her.

"I am so fucking happy for you, dude," Amelia said.

"Thanks, Amelia Bedelia. I'll need lots of help with wedding planning. My eye for this shit exists on the straight side of my brain, I guess."

"It's fully on the gay side of my brain, so let's fucking go."

"Y'all know that's not how it works, right?" asked Sadie from the back seat.

"Enough about me," said Trevor. "All your stuff is submitted?"

"Yup. All my essays, transcripts, and even some recommendations from the two professors in college who actually found me charming, even in my constantly stoned stupor."

"Did you really go to class *stoned*?"

"Yes," the three girls said at the same time. They looked around at each other and cackled.

"Jesus. Well, keep me posted. When do you hear?"

"Early August. If I get in, I can start as soon as September."

"That soon? I thought you'd have to wait until the spring."

"Apparently, a couple people who were accepted for the fall deferred, so rumor is there are a few immediate openings. Fingers crossed."

A few hours later, the girls and Delilah arrived at a charming pale-yellow casita tucked away on a quiet street near the main plaza. Amelia chose to rent a different Airbnb this year, mainly due to the added guests but also because some places simply brought back too many painful memories to endure. As they unloaded their luggage, Amelia admired the large front porch that overlooked a vast expanse of desert vegetation and the start of one of those famous Southwestern sunsets. She felt empowered to use her privilege to make others happy, breathing it all in as she watched her friends gaze at the scenery and anticipate a three-week vacation in a beautiful house.

Everyone opted to share the second bedroom, with its two sets of bunk beds, rather than split up and have someone stay alone in the master.

It was more fun that way. Lucy claimed a top bunk, and so did Sadie, leaving the bottom bunks for Amelia as well as Delilah, who adopted a bottom bunk rather than her dog bed they'd brought along. After ordering pizza and watching the sky put on a dramatic and colorful show, they stargazed and drank chamomile tea while Delilah rooted around in the yard, clocking all the new smells.

Dinner on the porch as the sun tucked itself in for the night, or "dinner and a show," as they decided to call it, followed by tea under a blanket of stars, became routine over the next few weeks. In the mornings, Lucy would work from the Wi-Fi at the casita and keep Delilah company while Sadie went along with Amelia to the show.

A week in the world of horse showing was like chaotic clockwork. Monday was a setup or rest day when you either got all the horses settled in or let them chill in their stalls if you were already at the show. Tuesdays were schooling days, otherwise known as practice, when riders and horses would get some exercise and explore the fairgrounds in preparation for the competition. Wednesdays through Sundays were various competition classes, depending on that show's specific schedule. Most horse and rider teams could only compete for two of the five days, which was part of why many riders had multiple horses. Then the whole thing started all over again on Monday.

Amelia didn't expect Sadie to enjoy watching her train. Sometimes she forgot how unique it was until someone saw it for the first time. Jumping over obstacles on a live animal was pretty wild.

Sadie asked her about the fear one day as she walked with Amelia and Hope back from the arena. They'd had a decent round, ribboning somewhere in the middle of the pack. Amelia cared less about winning these days; just the chance to be with Hope was a gift. "Don't you get scared?"

"Not really. I mean, I've been doing it on and off since I was five. It's kind of like riding a bike at this point."

"But dude, those jumps are huge."

"Meh, not really. They're nothing compared to what the professionals do in the big jumper classes."

"Still...I don't know how you keep such a level head while doing something so scary. Not to mention dangerous." She shook her head. "So, you're just, like, used to it then?"

"I mean, that's part of it. I think it's also the fact that nothing will ever be scarier than what I put myself through that last year of drinking and stuff. Especially those moments when I felt compelled to end my life. I think it's the same faulty risk assessment from my addict brain that makes me forget the potential danger in the sport."

Sadie nodded, silent for a moment. "Has it changed since you got sober?"

"I've definitely felt some of my self-preservation come back, and I'm way more aware of the risks." Silence again. "But at the same time, I don't think anything will ever seem as threatening as Mark pinning my arms down. I've been through hell and come back twice as strong—this is just a sport. And at the end of the day, it's nice to have a healthy respect for the laws of nature." She shrugged and patted Hope's neck. "Plus, Hope takes good care of me." They rounded the corner onto the barn aisle where Grey Stone Farm horses were stabled for the show.

She untacked slowly, taking her time to groom Hope and give her lots of treats. Sadie went to grab coffee at the fairground's café, and the rest of the barn had gone to the jumper ring. Deb was training the next rider of the day, which left the barn aisle still and quiet. Amelia led Hope out to a grassy area on the other side of the stables and stood patiently while she munched on the grass.

One of Amelia's favorite things about riding Hope was how much the horse clearly enjoyed her job. Standing in the quiet breeze, gazing out at the deep blue sky contrasted with the red rock mountains in the distance, Amelia admitted for the first time what she'd known since their first ride last week: Hope was slowing down. At 17, her horse was young to consider retiring her, but Amelia always promised herself that the second Hope didn't love it anymore, she'd give her the most kick-ass, bougie retirement possible. She wanted to partially cover the cost herself rather than relying on her dad's money to take care of it all, and she'd been saving since she started the dog-walking gig. It was the principle of the thing. It wasn't necessarily that it was the time right now, but something in her gut, a gentle nudge in that moment, told her it was coming.

"I hear you, lady," Amelia said softly, head resting on Hope's shoulder. She breathed in Hope's slight, inexplicable lavender scent. "I think this might be our last show."

Hope paused her munching and took a deep breath, her big brown barrel belly expanding and contracting with the sound of a sigh.

"I'll bet that within the next year, grazing will be your full-time job." Tears welled up as Amelia considered what it would mean to transition from this part of their relationship to the next. Maybe their connection wouldn't be as strong without the riding aspect, but that question was answered definitively just a few days later.

After her rounds on a sunny Thursday, Amelia rounded the corner of the show stables with an iced vanilla latte to find a pretty blonde woman around her mom's age standing outside of Hope's stall. She looked in lovingly at the big brown mare. The barn aisle was quiet again, with most people out at lunch and Sadie having opted to sleep in that day and spend some time in town shopping.

Amelia approached the woman and her horse curiously.

"Hey, can I help you find something?" she asked the woman.

The woman turned to her, watery blue eyes red-rimmed with recent tears meeting Amelia's. "Hi. I'm Hope's mom."

Amelia didn't say a word; she just launched into the woman's arms and hugged her like she would a long-lost relative. When she pulled back a few moments later, her cheeks were wet with tears of her own. Amelia and the blonde woman laughed as they fully took one another in for the first time. There was so much in between the two women and this horse that didn't need an explanation.

"My name's Astrid. Your family bought Hope from me all those years ago."

Amelia's heart sank as she remembered the circumstances under which she bought the mare. *Fire sale, family emergency.* She couldn't imagine the heartbreak in letting go of a horse like Hope. She didn't have the words, so she just hugged the woman again.

Astrid pulled back this time and took both of Amelia's hands in hers. "You are just lovely. I couldn't be happier that this is where she wound up. Your love for her could be felt from a million miles away. And hers for you."

"Thank you so much for her. She saved me," she said through tears.

Astrid nodded. "She saved me too. She was my emotional rock throughout my divorce. But lawyers cost a lot of money, so…"

"That's awful. I'm so sorry."

"Sweetheart, she knew where she was needed next."

Amelia nodded and wiped her eyes.

"Besides, everything bounces back eventually. I'm here with my new horse, Beau.

"Baby Beau. I'm sure he's amazing."

"He's a couple of aisles over. Such a doll. But this one," she said, turning to look at Hope inside her stall. "She's everything good in the world wrapped up in a not-so-small package."

"She really is. Please tell me everything you know about her! When did you get her? What's her story?"

Astrid and Amelia went into Hope's stall to share stories about the special mare. They talked and petted her as she ate hay and took naps. Astrid rode her for five years before selling her to the Glickmans. A year before that, Hope had been imported from Germany. Astrid didn't know much about Hope's life before she came to the States other than that she was pregnant at the time. "A few months after she got here, she gave birth to a beautiful, all-black colt, but it only survived a few hours. She and the foal hadn't been cared for the way they needed to be before she was brought over." Astrid told the tale solemnly.

Amelia's stomach collapsed in on itself. "Oh my god."

"I think that's why she can hold space for all of us when we're grieving. She knows about it from personal experience. And it's why she's grateful for each day, each jump, each apple, and each ear scratch."

Amelia was crying again, leaning into Hope's shoulder and letting the tears soak into the fur just like she had a million times. "She'd never have been able to tell me that story. Thank you," she said, lifting her head to look at Hope. In that moment, Amelia could have sworn she heard a voice—maybe hers, maybe Hope's, or maybe some metaphysical hybrid of the two—deep down in her chest whispering, *I'm so glad you know that now. I needed you to know, and now you do.*

The moment was getting beyond surreal, so she leaned into it. "I think it may be time to retire her soon. I've always said I wanted to do it sooner rather than later, give her as many years in a big fancy field as possible." Astrid listened intently, stroking Hope's mane. "And this sounds crazy, but now I'm wondering if she'd want to have a baby. Like a do-over, you know? Seventeen is on the older side for breeding, but maybe it would help her heal in some way. I don't know. I'm sorry, that's so weird. I just feel like she'd be such a good mother. She may love to take care of someone like that."

Astrid smiled, fresh tears sparkling in her eyes, ready to fall. "Don't you see, sweetheart? *You* were that for her. She raised *you*. Took care of *you*."

Amelia's breath stuttered as she caught Hope's gaze again. Her reflection shined in Hope's big glassy eye, and a whisper from that same deep place for just the two of them murmured softly, *You are mine as much as I am yours.* She wasn't sure who said it to who, but it was infinite. They belonged to each other because the Forces of Good willed it so. Competing or not, riding or not, their connection was the truest thing in the world.

Astrid and Amelia talked for hours in Hope's presence, learning more about the person this unique horse connected them to. To make things even more bizarre, it turned out they were both in recovery.

Astrid shook her head with fondness. "Twenty-five years this fall. I've stayed sober one day at a time."

"Okay, now I have chills," said Amelia. "What a crazy coincidence!"

"Is it, though? This is a spirit horse, Amelia. I've always known it, this just confirms it." Hope's eyes twinkled in the fading sunlight.

Amelia could almost see the FOG silently descend in the barn aisle. She couldn't make something like this up if she tried.

As Amelia drove back to the casita, she knew she needed to begin planning for Hope's retirement. The first step was having a conversation with Deb, which wasn't the world's easiest task, but like everything else, she knew the timing would present itself if only she believed it would. The watercolor desert sky, filling her windshield like a masterfully designed canvas, agreed enthusiastically.

CHAPTER 21: MONTH 11

To: drb@mcclinic.net

From: aglick1992@gmail.com

Hey Dr. B!

I can't believe how long it's been since rehab, and I miss you so much! I'm sorry it's taken me this long to send you an update. Stuff has been crazy! I want you to know I think about you all the time and that the things you taught me continue to change my life for the better. I feel like I become more and more like the National Forest every day, and the first step was letting go of the amusement park in the first place. I didn't even know I was holding on to it until I met you. Or that there was even another option!

I have two major updates: First off, I CELEBRATE A WHOLE YEAR SOBER THIS WEEK. Wild, huh? Even wilder is the fact that I have friends who are throwing me a party to celebrate. My family is coming, even my future stepparents. Everyone has been getting along surprisingly well. I used to get so anxious when they all had to be in the same room, and there was almost always some awkward tension. But these days, it's been pretty chill.

Which brings me to my second major update: I'm starting grad school next month! I'm going for a master's degree in mother-freaking COUNSELING. I want to be a therapist and, hopefully, one day, help someone as much as you've helped me.

I can't believe how much can change in a year, me most of all. I used to spend every moment of my time trying to blast off from reality, desperately searching for some kind of meaning, some kind of bigger answer. In sobriety, the layers peel back naturally, and I get closer to knowing what I need to know and accepting what I never will.

OH! And one more thing. I haven't so much as hooked up with a guy in almost 11 months! ON PURPOSE! Can you believe it? No hands, mouths, or other organs. Not even virtually! My goal is a whole year, and I am sooooo close. I'm also working with a dietician to heal my body and my history of disordered eating, but that's a topic for another email.

I hope you're doing well, and I hope you know what a difference you make.

—Amelia

One year, 12 months, 52 weeks, 365 days, 8,760 hours, or, according to the cast of *Rent*, 525,600 minutes. An entire year sober, including holidays and weekends. Every breath she'd drawn, roughly 75 million, had been free from drugs and alcohol. *Fucking wild.* Especially for someone who seldom drew a sober breath for much of the last decade. Last August, she couldn't even get out of bed without getting high. Even when she had to operate heavy machinery, or heavy animals for that matter. She thanked the FOG every day that she hadn't hurt anyone, especially Hope. But that was how she'd existed in the previous summer: spiritually, emotionally, and physically bound to her pipe and her mattress. Today, she was free.

It was certainly something to celebrate. As was her acceptance into the counseling graduate program. It was a relief when she finally got the email offering her admission to the program at the liberal arts college in Austin.

She'd spent the month anxiously checking her inbox and teetering between self-doubt and overconfidence. The acceptance rate was high because it wasn't a hard program to get into, but anxiety didn't take days off.

Wethersfield had become accustomed to large, celebratory gatherings; the friend group enjoyed commemorating moments and accomplishments big and small, and the bewitching house was the perfect place to do it. But today's party was all about her, and the friends and family that filled the space just to congratulate Amelia made her surprisingly uncomfortable. Everyone she loved and cared about within a 50-mile radius was there, except for Cathy and Tamara. Because boundaries, and all that.

"I think I only like being the center of attention when it's inappropriate," she joked with Ethan. He laughed and shook his head, grabbing a Red Bull out of the fridge. It was rare to have all your people in the same room, so she tried to breathe in the gratitude that she had so many people in the first place. She leaned against the dining room table and took in the scene before her. Atop a large, round, homemade vanilla cake with strawberry icing and rainbow sprinkles sat a large number one candle, primed for lighting. Empty boxes of Home Slice Pizza threatened to topple over the edge of the kitchen counter. Drained Red Bull cans overflowed from the recycling bin. The blasting AC did its best to rival the body heat and August temperatures amidst the constant opening and closing of the door to the patio out back, where friends from the meeting smoked and laughed.

Mom and Chris chatted casually with Dad and Maya, the two engaged couples sharing space like they would among any other group of adults. It was a significant difference from the first time they all attended the same event. Mom and Maya even seemed cool, Jen's hand absently grabbing Maya's forearm in friendly exasperation. Beth swapped stories with Sadie and Lucy as Delilah waited patiently at their feet for a chunk of pizza crust or a rogue pepperoni. Deb and her husband talked quietly about horses and competitions with some of the Grey Stone Farm crew. The house was filled with a grounded type of joy, and Ethan stood by her side in the kitchen as she took it all in.

More of her recovery friends from the meeting were trickling in. Maybe it was the free food or just the excuse to hang out, but her brain sidestepped the discomfort and accepted the Oscar gratefully, chanting in the confines of her mind, "They like me, they really like me," Sally Fields-style. This time, Amelia joined the spirit of Wethersfield in a fond eye roll at herself.

For so long, she'd kept people at arm's length. In her work with Tamara, she realized it was a function of her eating disorder, the constant competition that no one knew about but her. And when everything is a competition you're scraping your way to the top of, people are acquaintances at best. But the folks filling Wethersfield now were actual friends. The ones who were a little broken, but a lot brave.

She'd never understand why the best, most sensitive, and intelligent people always experienced pain so deeply. But understanding why was above her pay grade anyway. She used to torture herself with the why of it all, but the people in recovery who seemed the most at peace were the ones practicing radical acceptance. She was grateful for the amazing teachers who surrounded her.

"OK, it's time," Ethan said, digging a lighter out of the kitchen junk drawer. Amelia's stomach swooped in excitement and embarrassment as Ethan pulled her into the dining room and got everyone's attention. Friends and family circled around the dining room table as he lit the single candle and led everyone in an off-pitch rendition of "Happy Birthday." The grand finale was the way they sang "Keep coming baaack," to the tune of "And many mooore." A deep pink flush crept up her neck and filled her cheeks.

"Speech!" shouted Lucy.

"Yeah, how'd you do it!?" Sadie asked, beginning the classic call and response for when someone picked up a sobriety chip, which she'd done earlier that day.

"Y'all already heard my spiel at the meeting," she said.

"Um, we did, but your family and barn crew didn't," Lucy replied.

"Speech! Speech! Speech!" Beth began chanting, and several of her friends from the meeting joined in.

"Oh, fuck me, fine! Fine. Speech."

"YAY!!!!" Sadie, Beth, and Lucy cheered in unison.

"I know there are lots of things you could've done with your Sunday afternoon, and it means a lot that you're spending it with me. If you're in this room, it means you are a huge part of why I have been sober for one year today."

"Prove it!" joked Lucy. Sadie just laughed and rolled her eyes.

Amelia giggled and continued. "Some of you got me here, some of you kept me here, but all of you make me want to do it all again tomorrow and the day after that." She wanted to be done there, but when she looked back at Ethan, he gestured for her to keep going.

After a deep breath, she said, "Sometimes, I feel like I haven't done much in the past year, like I'm not really getting anywhere. Then I look at where I started, and it's almost like I'm a completely different person. Love, I'm learning, is transformative, healing, all-powerful, even. And the love I have in my life today continues to change me from the inside out."

Her people surrounded her, smiling and nodding. She could have sworn her parents had matching glints in their eyes.

"So much of recovery has been about a shift in perspective that allows reality to be good enough. And when I choose to believe in the Forces of Good all around us, I'm truly amazed. Like gravity, the force that literally keeps us tethered to the planet. It used to be a fact of life I took for granted, but in sobriety, when I allow myself to be full of wonder, the power that grounds us and keeps us from floating off into space is enough to floor me. So, I'll keep trying to let the world amaze me in Year Two. Love you guys."

The gathering of people clapped politely, and some of her friends and family stole hugs as Ethan cut the cake and began dispersing plates and plastic cutlery. Soon, everyone was spread out across the house, enjoying their cake and each other's company. As Amelia made her way towards the back of the house with her own slice, she noticed Deb sitting on the back patio with Delilah. A large gathering like this wasn't exactly her riding trainer's thing, so it meant a lot that she had come at all. She must have found the animal and the outdoors a welcome reprieve from the boisterous celebration.

"Hey," Amelia said, making her way through the side door. The air was heavy and warm. Sweat immediately licked her temples as she sat in one of the patio chairs across from Deb.

"Nice speech," Deb said, looking up from where she scratched a grateful Delilah behind the ears.

The piece of Amelia that felt more comfortable in the presence of animals basked in the peaceful silence with the woman she'd known almost as long as her own mother. The woman who showered her with tough love and no-nonsense throughout even the darkest years.

Deb had had the same short, curly haircut since the year 2000, and the way it tousled in the summer breeze conjured up an image of her five-year-old self in braids and jodhpurs learning how to ride a white pony named Wendy in the big open field at Grey Stone Farm. Deb held the end of a short lead line, the pony making an obedient loop around the woman as she coached Amelia on posting trot. "Up, down, up, down, up, down, up, down. Change your diagonal. Remember: outside leg up, inside leg down." Every so often, a bored Wendy would steadily slow to a walk and drop her head down to take a large bite of grass, and Deb would click her mouth lazily, communicating to the pony that it wasn't time for munching but for teaching little girls how to ride.

Amelia smiled as she felt warmth pool in her chest and tears prick the backs of her eyes. "I actually wanted to talk to you about something," she said, swallowing it all back. "It's about Hope." Deb nodded in a way that made Amelia think she'd been expecting this conversation. "I know she's pretty young still, but I've noticed her slowing down…"

"And you want to retire her."

"Well, yeah. She's been so good to me. I always promised myself I'd retire her early, give her lots of years to enjoy the big open field, and just be a horse."

"Some would think that it's a waste, you know. A nice horse like that. She's got at least a few years left if you push her a little."

"But that's the thing, I don't want to push her."

"Okay."

"Okay? I kind of thought you would fight me on this more."

"She's your horse, Amelia. It's your decision. Could she do another few years? Probably. Would she prefer it to grazing in the sunshine? Probably not."

"And part of what makes her so special is the way she truly wants to be out there. So, if she's not going to be happy doing it anymore, I guess I don't see the point."

"I get it."

"You do?"

"It's always been more about the horses for you than the actual riding. You've always been good at it, but since you were a kid, I had to fight you to stop cuddling with them long enough to train."

Amelia smiled. "So, how do we go about this?"

"Well, my suggestion is that you keep riding her at home throughout the fall and winter. Keep her fit with light exercise and smaller jumps. Come spring, we can get her acclimated to the big field, and she can ease into the summer as part of the pack, so to speak."

"Makes sense."

"And what about you? Do we start looking for another horse for you, so you can keep showing and competing?"

Amelia's stomach fluttered. "I don't think so."

Deb nodded without lifting her gaze from Delilah.

"Like you said, it's always been more about the horses for me, and Hope more than any other. Plus, I'll start grad school soon, then hopefully a career. It just sort of seems like it's... time." Deb's eyes met hers, and they both smiled sadly. "And I know you don't love talking about emotional shit, I get it. But I have to say this while I have the chance, and now seems as good of a time as any." Deb's smile shifted as she started just barely to shake her head. "The way you've been there for me, for my whole family…Thank you. Through all our drama: the divorce, my bullshit, my getting sober, you've never judged us. You've always just loved us and taken incredible care of our horses. Sometimes, your tough love and high expectations were the only things that kept me from going completely off the rails. So yeah. Thank you."

They again basked quietly in the early evening colors of summer, sounds from the party filtering out through the back door. "You know, Amelia. Riding will always be here for you. Horses will always be here for you."

She looked at the big tree rustling gently in the breeze. "I know."

And with that, she started in on her one-year sober celebratory slice of cake.

As Amelia and Ethan cleaned up the remnants of the party, something dangerous lurked in the shadows. One year sober, almost one year without sex, no more binging and purging, positive relationships with family and friends, a potential career on the horizon, a plan for Hope… The water was calm. A gremlin, previously obscured by the darkness of her life, peeked out from around the corner and, in a voice dripping with the disdain of the ungrateful, said, "I'm bored. Now what?"

She was designed to create waves when the surface was glassy and still. So, would the quiet ever feel like enough? She certainly fucking hoped so—it'd be a shame to burn it all down now.

CHAPTER 22: MONTH 12

The warm September air swirled deliciously in the late-night breeze as Amelia and her friends made their way down 4th Street to their favorite club. The big, bright Texas stars were aligning perfectly. Lucy flawlessly executed her winged eyeliner on the first try when she did Amelia's makeup and the street parking they found was only a block away from the venue. The Universe had their night laid out ahead of them like dominoes ready to fall in a masterful pattern. The streetlights glowed off magical puddles from the early autumn rains. The night was aiming to be the cherry on top of an amazing start to her graduate studies.

A fabulous bouncer named Julian, wearing big fake lashes, bright pink lipstick, and a fishnet top, checked IDs and collected cash at the door. Amelia's nervous system settled down two notches as she joined the crowd of people existing outside the typical box. By the time they got to the front of the line, it was 9:55, just five minutes before the Friday drag show. They snagged some Red Bulls at the bar and then settled in a spot on the second-level balcony railing that looked down on the dancefloor turned stage.

"Happy birthday, bitch!" Lucy shouted over the noise.

"Thank you, guys! And thanks for taking me out to celebrate," said Ethan.

"Of course!" chimed Sadie.

Amelia leaned over and pecked Ethan on the cheek. "Glad you were born, sugar booger."

Amelia smoothed out the back of her black minidress where it clung to her sheer charcoal grey tights and glanced down at the worn black Converse on her feet. She felt like wearing the outfit when she was getting ready, listening to Bowie with her friends at Wethersfield, but now that they were out at the club, she felt more exposed. While she was no stranger to sexual exploits, she wasn't used to showing off her curvy body in a way that insisted upon her own desirability—in fact, she'd always questioned whether she was hot enough to dress that way at all. But she was learning to push past the discomfort and do what she wanted for the simple fact that she wanted to. Even if she had gained a few pounds.

"You look great," Lucy said with a knowing smile. "Hot AF."

Amelia smiled back and basked in the warm sense of safety and belonging. Lucy wore a hot pink leather miniskirt, a black crop top, and combat boots; her newly blue hair hung low on her shoulders in smooth rivulets. "You look amazing too, obviously."

"What about me?" Sadie asked in mock offense. Her black jean shorts, lacey bralette, and dark flannel screamed the effortlessly cool grunge she was famous for. She tossed her dirty blonde hair over her shoulder.

"Flawless, my dear," Lucy said in a corny British accent.

"And I know I look good," Ethan said, gesturing to his dark wash jeans and stylishly floral button-down.

"Truth," Amelia said.

The emcee of the show, Patsy Glitterbottom, took the stage for the opening number, "I'm Coming Out" by Diana Ross. She was met with raucous applause as she finished up her performance and announced the next queen, Mentally Jill, who, to no one's surprise, was lip-syncing Alanis Morrisette. Just as the preliminary notes of "You Oughta Know" rang out from the club speakers, Amelia's eye caught on an attractive blonde woman around her age ascending the stairs to the second-floor balcony.

This had been happening more and more: the whole checking out beautiful women thing. She'd even mentioned as much to her three best friends and Trevor, but that was as far as it had gone. She was trying to remain curious and open to new possibilities, especially with her year off sex ending next week. Time away from the love game had done its job of providing some much-needed perspective about sexuality and desire in general.

Her first couple weeks of graduate school had been enlightening, particularly her sex and relationships class. Maybe her sexual cravings for a different kind of satisfaction were not necessarily toxic in nature, but instead a thirst that had yet to be quenched by the right kind of connection. The cravings were a deep, dormant, rock-solid core waiting to be alchemized into magma. The molten heat promised to hurt and liberate her at the same time. She wanted to feel something so solid and primal that the dull ache of depression would seem completely inconsequential. She wanted to shake, convulse, *erupt* into a new way of being. She just needed to be more mindful about who that was with and what it all meant to her. And then maybe one day she'd evolve enough to ask herself what it meant to the other person as well. Humans were more than a surface off which to bounce her reflection, after all.

The blonde woman wore a deep purple velvet spaghetti strap dress that cut off mid-thigh and a pair of knee-high black leather platform boots. Her glossy, straight hair hung softly in front of one shoulder and behind the other, showing off a long, slender neck and a small birthmark above where her clavicle rolled into an elegant shoulder—a birthmark shaped like a broken heart.

Wait. Where did she know that birthmark from?

Without warning, she was tumbling through the time-space continuum to be plunked on the floor of her high school theatre dressing room. A place where Aqua Net and hormones beat the crap out of oxygen every time. Her 16-year-old self applied makeup touch-ups at the vanity, sitting next to a blonder, thinner archnemesis named Cat. They prepared to return to the dance call portion of auditions for the spring musical. It was one of only three chances to dazzle the panel of underpaid theatre teachers.

The first chance was always sixteen bars of a song that showed off your vocal range. Second was reading from a scene or performing a monologue. It always pissed her off that the boys simply had to be tall and prove they weren't completely tone deaf, but the girls were forced to belt out notes higher than the Chrysler Building without making a weird face. The third, dance, was at the bottom of Amelia's talent barrel, but she tried her best to distract from her missteps with plenty of charisma. Dance was Cat's strong suit, and she didn't have many weak spots to begin with.

Young Amelia glared competitively into her handheld mirror, annoyed by the fact that Cat seemed unbothered in the seat next to her and, in fact, shot a wink her way when she found her staring. Amelia's eye caught the cracked heart birthmark, not for the first time, as Cat dusted bronzer on her jawline. She'd noticed it several times before in the dressing room—but only once did she wonder how it tasted. The blonde would walk away with the lead that time, but it was always one of them. The way the moon chased the sun.

Years later, 23-year-old Amelia gawked at the blonde, trying to remember why she'd hated this arrangement so much. Especially with the way Cat's sparkling green eyes lit up when they met hers. Amelia's jaw hung open as the woman made her way over to Amelia's group of friends.

"Amelia? Amelia Glickman? Holy shit, how are you doing, girl?"

"Cat, hi!" Amelia accepted her enthusiastic hug. *Damn, she smells good.* "What are you doing here? I thought you moved to New York."

"I'm here for the week for my stepbrother's birthday."

Amelia introduced Cat to her friends, and Cat introduced them to her stepbrother Jake, his boyfriend, and the rest of their crew. Amelia was surprised at how well everyone got along. They talked and laughed and sang along to the incredible performances for the next hour or so. Cat and Amelia's eyes locked more than once until one of them would smile bashfully and look away. Once the drag show finished up and the makeshift stage gave way to a dance floor, Jake and his friends said they'd head to another club.

Cat looked over at Amelia tentatively and then at Jake. "I think I'm going to hang here. If that's OK with you, of course," she added, turning back towards Amelia. "I don't want to crash your evening or anything."

"No, no, totally, stay and hang with us."

"OK, cool," Cat said with a smile.

Lucy, Sadie, and Ethan had already made their way to the dance floor and Amelia lingered as Cat and Jake said their goodbyes for the night. "Nice to meet you, Jake," Amelia shouted as the group made their way out. He blew her a dramatic kiss and sashayed towards the front door of the club.

"Good God, they are *wasted*," Cat said with a chuckle as the rest of the group stumbled out the door after Jake. "I love that for them, but it just isn't my vibe tonight. I want to dance and wake up sans headache tomorrow."

"Well, you definitely chose the right crowd, then. None of us drink."

"Yeah, I noticed that. Any reason why?"

"Yeah, um, we're actually all in recovery. I've been sober a little over a year now." She took a mental snapshot of how beautiful Cat's glowing green eyes were in the shifting, colorful club lights. Were they always that green?

"No shit? That's so cool. Is that how you all met?"

"Yeah, at meetings and stuff."

"You know my mom is in recovery. Fifteen years clean next month."

"That's amazing. I never knew that."

"Yeah, she's super proud of it. And we all are, too, of course. But it was pretty dark for a while. The road to recovery isn't exactly paved with unicorns and rainbows."

"It certainly isn't."

"So, I guess you're kind of a badass bitch then, huh?"

Amelia barked out a laugh. "Me? What about you? Drama school, New York, actually getting jobs. You're who we wanted to be when we grew up."

Cat rolled her eyes. "Oh, please." Her megawatt smile could rival global warming. What if it was more than just jealousy? What if it was something else?

"But you have to tell me. Is it everything we dreamed it would be?"

"I don't know, dude. At the end of the day, it's work. It's fun, but it's a job. Unless you're in that .001 percent that reaches the stars, you're mostly just making ends meet and trying to remind yourself why you love it. So, I guess it's better than a desk job, but it's not glitz and glamour or anything."

"I always thought if anyone were good enough to make it, it'd be you. And me, obviously."

Cat laughed. "Maybe we were 'good enough to make it,' but so much of it comes down to dumb luck. That's why, at the end of the day, you just have to do what makes you happy. And trust me, there's plenty of overlap between show business and addiction, I've seen it firsthand. Then there's the addiction to the business itself."

"What do you mean?"

"Just like, the need for approval and praise running people's lives and shit. It never pans out well, so I see a lot of people turn to drugs and alcohol to numb that pain."

"Cool," Amelia deadpanned. "So, like, basically my life story."

Cat laughed and took a sip of her club soda. "Do you ever miss it?"

"You know, it's funny, I think I did miss it before getting sober, though I never would have admitted it. I will always love theatre as an art form. And now it can be part of my life in a way that's more sustainable. I'm realizing I can enjoy and appreciate it without torturing myself." She paused and sipped her Red Bull. "But yeah, my psyche is too weak for the rejection."

"That all makes sense. It really is true what they say, 99 percent of it is doors getting slammed in your face."

"Yeah, I don't think I'd ever have gotten sober or gotten any of my mental health shit figured out if I had gone down that route." Amelia's surprise at the depth of their conversation waited eagerly in the wings.

"Well, I'm glad you did. You seem... happier."

"Really?"

"Really." The space between them had somehow shrunk, and Cat's intoxicating scent seemed to be all she could focus on for a moment. Like vanilla and citrus.

"Oh my god, I love this song," Cat said, breaking the tension as a mix of Rihanna's "Bitch Better Have My Money" poured from the speakers. "Do you want to dance?"

Before Amelia could respond, Cat was dragging her by the hand to the middle of the floor. Fingers laced, mind you. None of that hands-cupped shit. When they reached the center of the room near the rest of the group, Cat began to move. Dance was her strong suit when it came to the theatre, but Amelia had never seen Cat let loose just for the sake of doing so—she danced like both no one and everyone was watching. It was the practiced lines of a dancer's body that couldn't help but comply with years of training. The soft smile and heavy-lidded eyes of someone thrumming with natural rhythm. The cellular level on which her heartbeat seemed to merge with the music, her face veiled by euphoric bliss.

Ethan smiled over at them and shot Amelia a wink. Lucy and Sadie squealed in excitement at their arrival on the floor. In the wake of their greeting and Cat's effortless luminance, Amelia began to move her body as well. In no world was she a good dancer, not like Cat. But the way Amelia now moved was unmissable and genuine. The performance aspect of dancing in front of a group always sent shivers down her spine, but as she watched her movements play out across Cat's gorgeous face, she could have sworn this was what making a Broadway debut might feel like. Then the one-woman show expanded into something more dynamic as Cat's hands found Amelia's hips and began to rock their bodies in tandem. A performance was so much more dynamic when you could share the stage.

Amelia draped her arms around Cat's neck in a way that made their bodies seal together like a Ziploc. Rocking and grinding and laughing, they lost themselves in the music. As "Scuse Me" by Lizzo began to play, Cat spun Amelia around and rested her hands in the dips of her waist, pressing her chest to Amelia's back. She had done her fair share of bumping and grinding, even with girls when she and her college friends would get drunk enough and want to show off, but this felt different. The performance was secondary to the connection, the chemistry.

After several more songs, the group made their way to the bar area to take a breather and Cat announced that she needed to use the restroom. After she'd drifted off, Amelia spun on her heels to face her friends. "How would y'all feel if I invited Cat to Magnolia Café for our post-club debrief and pancakes?"

Ethan lifted an eyebrow, and Sadie smiled knowingly.

"She's dope. But you know that if she makes it anywhere near the house, y'all are fucking, right?" Lucy bopped Amelia on the nose.

"What? Why would you even say that?"

"Jesus, Bambi, relax with the wide eyes," said Lucy.

"Maybe it's because you've been dry-humping each other to Beyoncé mashups for the past 20 minutes," said Sadie, pretending to examine her nails.

"You're clearly attracted to each other," Ethan added. "If you invite her to hang out after this, there's a good chance something will happen."

Sadie touched Amelia's damp forearm. "And there's nothing wrong with that! It's just... don't you have a week left of your year off? Are you sure you want to sacrifice your promise to yourself?"

Amelia considered this. "I mean..."

Lucy chimed in. "I don't know," Lucy said. "Man, a week is like nothing. You made it most of the year, I say follow your heart, or your vagina, or whatever."

Ethan and Amelia cackled while Lucy and Sadie began their own side argument. Sadie waved her hands around in exasperation. "That doesn't even make sense. You don't celebrate your birthday a week early!"

"Unless you do, because the Universe gave you better weather on the weekend before."

"That is the dumbest argument I've ever heard. You can't celebrate something that hasn't even happened yet."

Lucy scoffed. "Then explain baby showers."

Sadie just stared. "You are a ridiculous person."

"Get your dick wet, Amelia," said Lucy, turning her way once more. "Though life be but short, may your orgasms be long and in multiples."

"Honor your commitments, dude. Your integrity is what matters," Sadie added, playfully nudging Lucy's arm.

Amelia shook her head. "Y'all are like the psychotic angel and devil on my shoulder."

"So, then I will be the neutral voice of reason," said Ethan. "Invite her to Magnolia. You clearly want to spend more time with her. Just take it one thing at a time. This is ultimately your call. You're an adult who gets to make her own decisions. And we support you no matter what. Right, team?" Lucy and Sadie agreed.

Well into the wee hours of the morning and satiated by two hours of laughter, pancakes, and diner coffee, Ethan, Amelia, and Cat made their way up the driveway toward Wethersfield while Sadie and Lucy headed off to their respective homes. Amelia practically vibrated as she wondered whether Cat would just order an Uber once she got inside. She wanted her to stay. She'd known ever since Cat ordered chocolate chip pancakes at the diner without a second thought. Even if there was no sex involved, she wanted to spend more time with her.

Ethan unlocked the door for the three of them, said a quick hello to Delilah, and then let out an overly dramatic yawn. "Well, I'm wiped. I'm going to head to bed. Night, y'all."

Amelia smiled and rolled her eyes. "Night, dude."

Cat was already swooning over a bouncing Delilah. "Oh my god, stop. You are so precious." She scratched the dog behind the ears and sat in the middle of the floor with the pup. How could Amelia have ever disliked this person?

"Delilah, meet Cat." She knelt and kissed her furry head.

After a few moments and sweet nothings, Delilah made her way to the back door and looked back at Amelia expectantly. Amelia took a deep breath as she went to let the dog outside, and with her back to Cat let the words spill from her eager mouth. "You know, it's pretty late. You're welcome to just spend the night. I can drive you to your brother's tomorrow." She let the cool evening air greet her flushed face as she stood in the doorway. "If you want to, of course."

"I'd love to."

When Amelia turned around, the huge smile on Cat's face set her mind at ease. "That's my bedroom," she said pointing. "Make yourself at home, I'm just going to let her do her thing then I'll meet you in there." *Holy shit, did I just invite her to sleep in my bed?* She slept in the same bed as her friends fairly often, but this felt less sleepover-y and more scissor-y.

"Can I get a glass of water?" Cat asked.

Amelia snapped out of her bi panic. "Of course! Cabinet to the left of the fridge, there's a Brita thing in there."

Cat made her way to the kitchen and Amelia stepped out onto the porch. She just needed a moment to collect herself. Was she really about to do this? What if she was completely misreading the signs? And what in the fuck was she going to do with her hands? The dog did her business quickly and Amelia hyped herself up before going back inside the house.

Delilah trotted in with her and nestled into a corner of the couch. The FOG Amelia long ago ceased to deny seemed to coax her into the bedroom. Cat was sitting on the edge of her bed, looking up at her from across the space. God, her eyes were like sparkling emeralds. Amelia mustered every ounce of courage she possessed and sat down on the bed next to her.

"Hey," Amelia breathed, barely audible.

Cat scooted ever so slightly closer. "Hey." The warmth of Cat's thigh sent a shiver down Amelia's spine, and she felt something deep inside of her do a back flip. Her heart lurched like the first big drop on a roller coaster. Cat bit the corner of her own lip without breaking eye contact to make Amelia's breath catch in her throat and her chest flutter as if in a free fall. Her veins began to fill with an aching need.

Being aroused was like being in a completely altered state. The sensations that flowed through her body and brain were deliciously all-consuming. She felt like she was soaking her vital organs in the chemical compound of lust itself. How could something as simple as skin-on-skin send a quake down to her very core? A friendly touch or pat from a peer, mentor, or family member differed from the live-wire nerves that writhed under the hand of someone who wished to consume every piece of you. How could these sensations be the same but so different? Maybe it was as simple as energy, and she loved the way a sexual charge seemed to defy all logic and reason, like borderlines themselves dissolved into warm, inviting goo. But it was somehow all more vulnerable and raw with a woman. There would be no hiding from a woman, no embellishing or faking. No trickery. Sitting on the edge of her bed, she felt laid out bare, and Cat's warm scent, that blend of vanilla and citrus, was electrifying.

Amelia broke the silence. "I really want to kiss you."

Cat flashed her a seductive smile and ran a smooth, manicured hand up Amelia's arm. She dragged her nails softly across the back of her neck and through curly red strands to grip the back of her head with an exquisite pressure that was somehow both tender and hungry. The next thing she knew, Cat's impossibly soft lips were pressing against hers, answering her question in a way that was impossible to misconstrue. When her tongue traced the seam of Amelia's mouth, seeking entry, Amelia quickly granted her access and deepened the kiss, tilting her head and sliding a trembling hand around the dip of Cat's waist. She loved the way the supple curvature dimpled under her fingers as she tested the heaviness of her touch. As she squeezed more firmly, deliciously compressing the flesh just above her sultry hips, Cat released a gratified whimper, knotting the hair at the back of Amelia's head in approval.

Cat soon broke the kiss and pulled back, eliciting a groan that made them both giggle. "I just want to be sure we are on the same page before we go any further. I live in New York, and I don't really vibe with long-distance, so this would just be a tonight thing."

The slightest hint of disappointment plucked a cord in her chest. Maybe she had secretly hoped for more than this one time, but something told her this one-hit wonder could hold its own kind of meaning. "That makes sense," Amelia said, trying to hide the way her breath heaved with excitement. "I should also probably tell you. I've never done this before. Been with a woman and all," she added, face flushing.

"Ooooh, fun," Cat said, dragging a hand down Amelia's thigh. "Any limits or boundaries? We can totally go at your pace."

"No," she said a little too quickly. "Um, no limits, and I'll let you know about boundaries. I want to... I want to do all the things. I mean, as long as you want to do all the things, of course. I just might not be, like, you know, *good* at them."

"Trust me, Amelia, I've wanted to do 'all the things' with you since high school."

"Really? I always thought you just wanted to steal all the lead roles from me." she said with a laugh.

"I know you did," she said with her own wry smile. "Competitive little brat."

Amelia let out a gasp in faux outrage that was quickly swallowed by Cat as she crashed their lips together. *God, making out is fun.* She was astonished that the whole "what is this" conversation had happened before it went any further instead of in the fumbling aftermath. While this couldn't go anywhere beyond a fun time, this was a safe person who knew how to communicate effectively. It was a breath of fresh air and beautiful way to reenter the sex and dating pool. Even if it was a week early.

That single moment was all that mattered. There was a way to take it seriously while also keeping it casual; Cat was proof of that. Amelia began to kiss along Cat's jawline, making her way to the crook of her neck, where she licked and sucked and nibbled hungrily in a way that elicited the most angelic moan she'd ever heard.

"Can I touch you?" Cat breathed.

Amelia slid her dress off. "Anywhere." She was down to her sheer grey tights—she forgot she opted for no underwear, but Cat didn't seem to mind.

Soft hands, smaller than she'd ever had on her body before, traced up her back and unclasped her bra with the expertise of someone who wore one herself. Soft kisses sprinkled her neck and chest before a rosebud mouth closed around the peaked flesh of her nipple. And she fell the fuck apart.

"I need to see you, too," Amelia offered up with a shudder. "Please."

"Keep saying please like that and you can have anything you want." She stood to pull her dress off, leaving her in nothing but lacey black panties and her knee-high leather boots.

"Jesus Christ."

Cat giggled and nudged Amelia's thighs apart with her knee, stepping between her legs, hands resting on her shoulders. "What?"

"I just can't believe I ever thought I was fully straight." Cat laughed and lifted Amelia's hands to her own supple breasts. They were different from her own, smaller and with darker nipples. They fascinated her as much as they turned her on. "Leave the boots on. Please."

"Yes ma'am," Cat said teasingly as she pushed Amelia back onto the bed. "Scoot back a little bit."

Amelia never wanted so badly to follow directions. She shifted back as Cat climbed over her.

"Lift up," she said, smacking the side of Amelia's ass. Up she went, and Cat began to peel off her rapidly dampening tights, her face hovering above the very root of her. "Is this okay?" she asked, tentatively walking fingers towards her center.

"Yes. God, fuck. Yes."

A chaste kiss on the outer flesh made way for a warm, wet bliss just beyond the vulnerable threshold. Cat teetered her towards the edge of explosive pleasure faster than any man ever had. And whereas the men she was used to would give up after a few minutes, Cat. Kept. Going. It could have been 10 minutes, it could have been two hours; the pleasure she was receiving was a gift, not a transaction, and she forgot to worry about how long she'd been down there. Eventually, Amelia broke out in convulsive pulses of heat and rapture, and delight spread through her body like the opening of a million sacred doors. Sounds of all-consuming ecstasy fell from her mouth, a far cry from the performative moans of her past.

But Cat still didn't stop.

"You know I came, right?" Amelia said, slipping her fingers through long strands of Cat's hair.

Cat looked up at her, pupils blown. "But you could come again." And that was it. Her head dropped back down, and Amelia's back arched so far off the bed she could have sworn she was levitating.

After her second orgasm of the night, Amelia was raw and sensitive but no less turned on. "Okay. My turn." She'd pulled Cat up and showed her just how far from done she was with a passionate kiss. "But I may not be good at it."

"I can show you," she said, laying down beside her and guiding Amelia's hand.

"Yes please."

What Amelia lacked in experience she made up for in enthusiasm. At first, Cat lead her, showing her what she liked, and Amelia paid close attention to the instructions and the varieties of pressure and tempo that made her partner squirm in delight. Bringing a man to climax was like hitting the jackpot on a rigged game at the fair, but bringing a woman genuine pleasure was like mastering the sexiest puzzle in the world. Once all the pieces were accounted for, Cat shattered so exquisitely it took Amelia's breath away. Watching someone fall apart for her was beautiful, even if it was temporary.

A while later they lay there, satiated and spent, breathing in the reorganized air. The comfort of their conversation at the club felt obvious now. They had a real connection. Maybe this was the beauty of really letting someone all the way in. She was glad to break her streak a week early if it meant doing so with Cat, though the sex bar had now been set ridiculously high.

Amelia finally caught her breath. "That was… awesome."

Cat rolled onto her side. "Better than a dude?"

"Um, yes. I've always wondered about my sexuality, but it's good to have the confirmation."

Cat considered the words. "I get that."

"Plus, it feels like I can finally call myself queer or bi or whatever and not be a hypocrite."

"Well, your sexuality is valid no matter what. Even if I'm the first and last girl you're ever with, your queer identity is yours to define however you want. Hell, even if you'd never even kissed a girl, it would be valid. You don't owe anyone shit. Especially not an explanation about who you know you are."

"You're ridiculously cool, you know that? Even for a theatre kid."

"Hey, once a theatre kid, always a theatre kid. I didn't miss your *Hamilton* magnet on the fridge."

"Fair." Amelia looked up at the ceiling.

"I still think you may come back to it one day. Theatre, I mean. Or maybe just storytelling in general."

Amelia absentmindedly traced fingers down Cat's forearm. "Maybe."

"And it might not be in the way you that you expect," Cat added. She reached over and threaded their fingers together. "But we both know how therapeutic it can be when you do it for the right reasons."

"Creative expression for the sake of creative expression."

"Exactly."

Amelia turned her face towards Cat and smiled softly. "I'm really fucking glad I ran into you tonight."

"Me too." She leaned in and kissed Amelia on her pulse point, sending shivers down her spine.

"Even though you stole my hopes and dreams."

Cat rolled her eyes as a wry smile spread across her face. "Once a brat, always a brat."

CHAPTER 23

That October, Dakota Bryant came crashing into Amelia's life like a freight train. The un-therapized man of her dreams entered stage right on a perfectly pleasant evening at the regular Sunday meeting. Dakota was a slight man with light brown hair and a beard two shades lighter. He shared that he was trying to stop drinking and needed community, opening up about his work in the music industry and the difficulties that posed to sobriety. He was authentic, kind, self-deprecating. He seemed to fit into the fold easily—so much so that by the end of his first post-meeting hangout, the crew planned to see him play with his band, Bob and Weave, at a bar on Sixth Street.

It didn't escape Amelia that as Dakota invited the folks from the meeting, his light blue eyes flitted repeatedly to hers, chancing a twinkle in the glowing string of lights that adorned the coffee shop patio. It was flattering, of course, the way those eyes checked in with her.

She sauntered into the Sixth Street dive bar on that random Tuesday evening. In early October the city was unseasonably warm, so she donned cut-off jean shorts, a fitted black tank, and her grey Converse low tops. It was her uniform for the warmer months. As the Austin air cooled, she'd add a flannel and call it autumn.

She was the first of her friends to arrive right on time at nine, and she looked forward to letting loose after a grueling first month of grad school. A few sips of Red Bull later, she made her way through the bar dwellers as they bopped their heads and swigged their beers. The bass from the speakers began to rumble through the center of her in the way that only live music can.

But she was unprepared to take in the sight of Dakota Bryant on stage with an electric guitar slung over his shoulder in a way that made him look like the coolest person alive. His soft curls bounced playfully, dampness soaking the ends of the clumps falling around his forehead. His brow was furrowed, lips just barely parted, and his hand made its way up and down the neck of the guitar like a choreographed dance, as the other hand strummed with a precision made up of raw talent backed by decades of study. She was so fucked. Competency kink: unlocked.

Even when the rest of her sober crew arrived, it was like he performed just for her. And she performed right back, dancing and laughing animatedly with her friends, tossing her long, curly red hair from one shoulder to the other and batting her lashes in the direction of the stage.

During an impressive guitar solo, Sadie leaned over, lips curled into a smirk. "How are your panties doing? Moist?"

"I've never really understood the whole musician thing," Amelia said. "But I think that's just because no one has ever played *at me*."

The night passed quickly, and each time one of her friends filtered out of the bar, she considered calling it a night. But something kept her planted in place. By the end of Bob and Weave's last set, she was the only one of her sober crew left. Something in the air shifted as she considered what this meant and what came next.

Amelia leaned against the wall and watched as Dakota packed his guitar case and joked with his bandmates. It had been a year since she was infatuated with a man in this way, and as she watched him in his element from across the room, she wondered how long it would be before she was completely under his spell. While the year off had allowed her life to flourish in some ways, it appeared to have done nothing for her balls-to-the-wall approach to men. Before even talking to him that night, she could feel his energy sapping her essence, permeating her still very permeable membrane of self.

It was close to midnight as he hopped off the stage and made his way across a mostly empty bar. "I'm so glad you're still here," he said. He touched her forearm lightly and dropped a kiss on her cheek. "Are you doing anything right now?"

"Um, I mean, I was going to go home and sleep," she said.

"Want to stop somewhere and get a Coke and a snack?" he asked.

"Sounds great, but I'm pretty sure most things are closed this late on a Tuesday."

"True...you could always come by my place. I have Cokes and snacks." And there it was. The moment of truth. Could she be the girl who went to someone's house for a Coke and snack, or was that as delusional as thinking she could smoke pot recreationally?

"Sure." It seemed to come out of her mouth without her permission. But the next thing she knew, she was plugging his address into her phone and climbing inside the Rav4.

Before long, he led her into the house, which looked like the movie set of a 20-something tortured musician's home. Guitars and amps filled the space, along with sheet music, keyboards, and music stands. It was messy but somehow homey. When she sat on the far end of his large couch, he sidled up next to her despite the abundance of space left over, getting close in a way that left no room for debate about why he'd invited her back here. The feeling was intoxicating, a high of being wanted that was comparable to the bottle and bong.

It was completely different than the way it felt with Cat, but this was what always happened with men. She'd get all self-conscious about whether they wanted her, and then, when it turned out they did want her, she'd act all surprised. The excitement of being wanted overshadowed her own motives and desires. Being wanted was her only criterion for "meant to be." She gave up all her power at the first sign that someone was asking for it. He inched closer in a way that revealed his intention to kiss her.

Every first kiss with a dude started out the exact same way.

Step one: Look each other in the eye and settle silently on a mutual agreement that it's time.

Step two: Lean in together simultaneously, deciding in a wordless conversation who will tilt which way.

Step three: Depending upon how steps 1 and 2 go, you may choose to test the waters with a slightly agape mouth and wandering tongue.

The usual played out on Dakota's couch. Except Amelia never really let steps one and two determine the intensity of three. In other words, she hadn't opted for a chaste closed-mouth moment since fourth grade. She took the plunge without any consideration of when she'd come up for air.

Not even twenty seconds into the kiss, he tried to take off her black tank top. Echoes from her night with Cat bounced off the walls in her head. *Can I kiss you? Can I touch you?*

"No," she said quietly. Had she just said no? As soon as the sound of her own voice registered, she was overcome with an overwhelming sense of ickiness.

"Why not?" he asked with a sly smile. *Shit.* It was a miracle she had even said no in the first place, and that was apparently as far as she'd gotten in her line of thinking. Just no. She was lost for words beyond that. Did a no mean anything without backup?

A voice that wasn't hers, the one she had come to know as belonging to the FOG, whispered the truth: *No is a complete sentence.*

She made herself speak again. "Well, first of all, aren't you supposed to ask permission before you take someone's shirt off?" She was lost, maybe in the middle of a joke, maybe not.

"I've never really asked anyone that before." He looked mystified.

"What do you mean?"

"Well, guys don't ask for permission before they do that stuff because they know the answer will always be no." He chuckled and intertwined his fingers with hers where they met on his lap. "Not that I'd ever pressure you to do something you don't want to. But I've never thought to ask first. Wasn't taught to."

Amelia choked on the thick air surrounding them. He didn't mean anything bad by it, but wasn't that the problem? The way society normalized this for men in that "get laid at all costs" kind of way? But much like the night she ignored the shooting star beckoning her home, she turned her back on this very deep message from her capital S self.

She ripped her shirt off and straddled a pleased Dakota. It seemed like the path of least resistance. Why set a boundary that may disappoint someone when you could leap into performance mode instead? Let the show begin.

Afterward, she felt empty and hollow, like a lone Russian nesting doll. Did she just get herself into yet another casual sex situation?

Her voice feigned humor and levity. "So, is this like a hit it and quit it kind of thing, or am I going to see you again after this?"

"Of course, you'll see me again. You're a down-ass bitch, Amelia. I want to keep getting to know you. But you should know I'm not looking for anything serious or exclusive." A familiar panic rushed in for the first time since the Liam fiasco. Why must these conversations always happen after she let these men literally inside of her?

But she didn't want to unpack all of that at three a.m. in the stranger's bed she'd willingly climbed into. "Word," she said, like the down-ass bitch she was supposed to be.

When she got home that next morning, she gave Ethan the lowdown over a much-needed cup of coffee.

"So, you're fuck buddies," he deadpanned. Amelia stared back at him blankly. "It sounds like you've found yourself in a good old-fashioned situationship."

"How did I fuck this up *again*?"

"Well, dude, when you're wearing rose-colored glasses, red flags just look like decorations." Ethan made his way over to the kitchen cabinets and pulled out the necessary tools for scrambling eggs.

Amelia's head fell into her hands as she collapsed onto the kitchen counter, allowing it to hold her up. She watched as he took the carton of eggs out of the fridge, cracked four into a bowl, and began to whisk. She went on, "I can't believe that I'm in the same position as always, even after everything I felt like I learned in my year off from dating."

Ethan didn't even look up at her when he responded, just calmly proselytized amidst the sizzling backdrop of breakfast prep. "That year off was incredibly important for you, probably in more ways than you realize. But dating is kind of like flying a plane. You can read the manual and reflect on how it should go all you want, but nothing is going to fully prepare you for what goes through your head during takeoff." Ethan popped four pieces of bread in the toaster oven. "You have to learn the mechanics through experience. It doesn't make the time spent reading the book about it any less important. It just means you still have some hands-on learning to do." Ethan dished the scrambled eggs onto two plates.

Warmth pooled into her chest. Even when she was being ridiculous, he loved her enough to make her food.

"So, what's next, Amelia Bedelia? Are you going to test the waters of friends with bennies, or go back to the drawing board?"

"I mean, I've never been a quit before the miracle kind of girl. The go-with-the-flow thing hasn't worked for me in the past, but maybe this is different? And you never know. Maybe it could grow into something more serious."

"Famous last words, dude." He shook his head somberly. "Famous. Last. Words." The toaster dinged in warning.

October 19th

Dakota: hru?

Amelia: Good...you?

Dakota: Good. had fun last night :) Are you and your crew doing anything tonight? I'm still getting used to this whole sober thing. I don't know what to do with my hands when I'm not playing music.

Amelia: Well, I never know what to do with my hands, so...

Amelia: It can be hard to find your groove, but the meetings help. And hanging out with everyone afterward is a good, healthy distraction.

Dakota: good to know I'm not alone in that. I'll see y'all at the meeting tonight.

October 25th

Amelia: Sorry! My phone died last night! Just got out of class.

Dakota: It's Ok, we'd already been on the phone for two hours, so it was probably for the best lol

Amelia: truuuuuu

Dakota: Are you still coming over later to watch The Shining?

Amelia: Yes, but Delilah wants to come.

Dakota: Is that a dog or a person?

Amelia: Dog lol

Dakota: In that case... obviously.

October 30th

Dakota: Are you still mad at me?

Amelia: I'm not very good at staying mad at you, in case that hasn't been made obvious.

Dakota: Is it my charm or my good looks?

Amelia: Well, it's definitely not your fuck boy tendencies.

Dakota: Ouch *crying with laughter emoji*

Amelia: Fuck boys like you who do yoga and meditate are a different breed, though. New Age Fuckboy Energy.

Dakota: Well, at least I have that going for me. Speaking of which, do you want to meet me for a 3 p.m. class, we can get tacos after.

Amelia: Will your Tinder date be joining us?

Dakota: no, this is strictly a BFF date

Amelia: BFF, huh?

Dakota: Duh *heart emoji*

November 5th

Dakota: I'm sorry.

Amelia: Me too. Feel free to just ignore me when I'm like that.

Dakota: Well, you get like that a lot.

Amelia: Well, you go out with other girls a lot, so...

Dakota: Can I come over? I hate the world and everyone in it except for you.

Amelia: Yeah I'll finish this paper tomorrow. Door is unlocked.

November 11th

Amelia: Did you have a good birthday?

Dakota: Yeah, thanks to you. Planning dinner with the sober crew meant a lot to me.

Amelia: Of course! First sober bday can be weird AF. I'm glad yours was good.

Dakota: I honestly never would have made it this far without you guys

Dakota: But especially you, Amz. If I had a nickel for every time you talked me off a ledge this last month, I'd have many nickels.

Amelia: Well, if I had a nickel for every time you made me come, I'd have one nickel.

Dakota: It's not my fault your clitoris is like Fort Knox.

Amelia: LOL it's the meds!!!!

November 17th

Dakota: Hey

Dakota: Hello?

Dakota: Amz?

Dakota: I'm sorry I texted her in front of you, that was shitty. It won't happen again.

Amelia: It's OK.

December 1st

Amelia: I made you a key. Ethan reluctantly agreed to it lol. It's under the mat. Just figured it'd be easier...

Dakota: *heart emoji* OMW to Wethersfield, if I beat you there, I'll order the pizza

"I don't understand why it's important," Dakota said as he paced the length of the back patio.

She'd known for weeks he was still sticking it in other people. "It's important because I don't want an STD!"

"I use a condom with everyone that's not you! How many times do I have to tell you that?"

"Wow, you know that really makes a girl feel special." He had said he didn't want to be exclusive, and she was driving herself insane trying to force this situation into something it simply wasn't. "I just don't understand why I can't be enough. Like, don't we have fun together?"

"Of course we do, Amz. I'm just not looking for anything serious. And to be fair, you said you weren't either."

"Well, I lied, maybe I am!"

He scratched the nape of his neck and shook his head as if he had no idea where to go with the talk. "Look, this has been really great, but maybe it's just run its course." Something tender flitted across his eyes. "Regardless of if we're having sex, you've become one of my best friends. But if it's hurting you, maybe we should stop hooking up."

What was that saying? Love is like friendship on fire. Amelia stood at the ready with a book of matches. Proving she could fuck this man into submission through her own series of submissive acts was as powerful as any survival instinct.

"No. I don't want to stop. I'll get over it."

"Okay, but you can't keep doing this, Amelia. It's getting old."

"I promise I won't get jealous and weird again." She might as well have crossed her fingers behind her back like a petulant middle schooler.

He crossed over to where she was sitting on a lawn chair and kissed her cheek and then Delilah's head. "I've got to head out. I'll text you." And then he was gone, into the night from whence he came.

She wanted nothing more in these moments than to be the chill girl. Couldn't she just be the amusement park this one time? National Forests could take themselves so goddamn seriously. If only she were good enough, pretty enough, thin enough, funny enough, just *enough*, he'd want only her. So, she would keep trying, and keep having sex with him.

She couldn't even pretend the sex aligned with her values anymore. While she objectified herself, she despised the way women were treated as a whole. She was impossibly angry about the ways women were either minimized or sexualized. And the longer she stayed sober, the more she had to deliberately ignore how different she wanted this part of her life to look.

But a chilling voice in the back of her mind was gaining volume, and the more she pushed it away, the more insistent it became. The reason she so desperately searched for love and companionship in the traditional sense was because she was terrified of the fact that she craved a radical independence that had never been modeled for her. Not by her parents, who'd leaped from their marriage into replacements, not taking the time to figure out who they were as individuals before they remarried. What if a lover could be an "in addition to" instead of an end-all be-all? Maybe the independence she craved meant being one whole person who found another whole person—and they made a pair of whole people, instead of haphazardly completing each other?

But that would mean rearranging her insides and overriding everything she'd ever thought about personhood. And that sounded like a lot. Performative sex and being the codependent chameleon seemed way more straightforward.

Amelia was distracted as she trained with Hope the next afternoon. They were winding Hope down for retirement, but it was still important that Amelia be attentive anytime she was in the saddle, and Deb was not one to mince words when she was falling short of that. Amelia was somewhere else entirely during that lecture, waiting with bated breath for Dakota's next directive. She compulsively checked her phone for his usual "WYD?" text to come in as she untacked and groomed Hope. It was easier to ask this man who he thought she should be rather than figure out who she really was.

She breathed in the dusty barn air and tried to be present with her soul horse. She ran the soft brush down Hope's long, muscular neck in a way that made the horse stretch out her head and lean into the touch. It was her favorite part of being groomed, especially when Amelia took the small brush and stroked the inside of her big ears—and as she did so now, Hope closed her eyes and let out a long breath.

After putting away the tack, Amelia returned with a juicy red apple that elicited an excited stomp and huff. She giggled as Hope's whiskers tickled her hands, and foamy apple chunks fell from her mouth and into her open palms. Amelia just held out her hand to make sure she could enjoy every bite, even the stuff that didn't make it all the way into her mouth the first time.

Amid the confusion of romance, Hope remained the constant and secure attachment in Amelia's life. When she was lost, the smudged star on Hope's face led her home. The next three months meant preparing Hope for the big green retirement pasture, the most exciting of which was allowing her winter coat to grow all the way out.

When the apple goo was no more, Amelia led Hope back to her stall for the night. She wished she could sleep in the shavings with her head resting on Hope's big barrel belly instead of facing her own mess.

When Amelia got back to Wethersfield, she took Delilah on a short walk, chatted with Ethan, and took a shower. Dakota didn't text. *He's probably just happy to be free of my craziness for the night.* Amelia had begun to think her love life was just a long string of hostages who got comfortable.

Like, "What's your love language?"

"Oh, it's Stockholm syndrome, teehee."

She threw on her favorite pajama pants and sweatshirt combo and joined Ethan and Delilah on the couch.

"Thai and *Grey's*?" he asked without looking up from his phone. There were plenty of leftovers from her birthday dinner a few nights before.

"Fuck yes."

The weeks to come just added to the confusion. There was no conversation about exclusivity in sight, yet Dakota acted like a man falling in love. And fuck her if she wasn't already there herself.

You're slow dancing at midnight in your bedroom to a D'Angelo song. He spins you, and you laugh because the sensation of your heart exploding feels an awful lot like being tickled mercilessly inside your chest cavity. As your eyes meet, you wrap your arms around his neck and sink into his body like he's your center of gravity. You sway and kiss and vibrate on the same frequency, and he whispers against your ear, "Maybe this will be the song we dance to at our wedding one day," and you positively melt with your head resting on his shoulder.

Then, one night, you've fallen asleep on the couch, and he lets himself in after a gig. A kiss so soft it leaves no sound in its wake delicately extracts you from your sweetest dreams, and you wake to find reality even more desiring. A deliciously scratchy face brushes against your cheek as his barely audible words dance through your awareness like a mythical being. "I missed you," he says, his body hovering over yours. "I think I always miss you when I'm not with you."

So, you peel your buzzing body from the couch and lead him to bed, where you both remove your clothes, not to have sex but to have as little space between you as possible. He crawls under the covers behind you, chin resting in the crook of your neck, arm draped over your waist, and gently sings Ella Fitzgerald in a whisper an inch away from your ear, the sound only for you. When someone who makes music for a living makes it just for you, you feel like the most important person in the world. You while away the next morning with coffee and real bagels from the New York bakery, jazz music echoing through the house like a movie montage, but your version lasts for hours.

Finally, you're on a road trip to see one of his favorite bands, the bright colors of the Texas winter sunset casting both your faces in warmth. Your feet are up on the dashboard, and his hand is on your thigh. You were nervous about so much windshield time and the potential for awkward silences, but the conversation flows and deepens naturally with the hum of his playlist in the background. He tells you details about his parents' divorce and his struggles with substances. "I've never told anyone that before," he says like a revelation, gazing meaningfully out at the open road. Then he turns towards you and sings along to the most meaningful lyrics of the song that's playing, words that sound like they were written just for you. "When I'm with you, I feel like I could die, and that would be alright."

You are scary happy. These will be the moments you play on repeat in your head when you begin to ask yourself if any of it really happened in the first place. Because there are also moments that make you shrink.

"You don't really need those, you know," he said one morning as she dosed out her daily medication. "If you just did yoga every day, you'd be fine." *Maybe I should try tapering off, just to see.*

"Something black may be more flattering. Maybe a sweater, too," he suggested a couple of times when they went out to dinner. *I'm getting older, I should really stick to sensible cardigans and muted colors.*

"God, you were such a slut," he joked one night when they were both sharing old dating stories, the jab tinged with venom. *I need to keep quiet about my past if I want to be respected.*

Then there were the glowing names on his phone screen: Allison, Catherine, Jackie, Mona. The list went on in a manner that could rival a game of gender reveal bingo. They had never had the "exclusive" or "official" talk, but he must have found it easier to start lying about it anyway.

"Colleagues," he'd say. "Potential artists to record or collaborate with."

"You must have a real vendetta against male musicians," she joked.

But none of those girls got to be with him in the way she did, or at least that's what she told herself when the jealousy and suspicion felt like too much to bear. She learned to swallow it. When you looked to someone else to tell you how to feel, you lived in the fragile space between euphoria and despair, sometimes teetering between the two multiple times within an hour.

The transitions between the different parts of herself were jerky now. She wished she could be sexual, spontaneous, and relaxed on Saturday with Dakota and then spiritual and grounded on Sunday at a meeting. Motivated and diligent at the barn with Hope on Monday, then silly and open with her friends on Tuesday. But she'd never learned how to drive a stick, and life's gears were too rusty; each shift was a jolt that shook her off center. If you insisted that your partner tell you who you should be, you forgot who you truly were. Everything around her got smaller and smaller, while Dakota got bigger and bigger.

Then it was the night of the second sober New Year's Eve party, the year that wrapped up 2016. The seeds of friendship she'd planted at last year's party had blossomed into succulent greenery—despite not tending to them properly since Dakota entered her life. Her friends loved her even when she fucked up.

Wethersfield was just as packed as the New Year's before, and joy bounced off the walls as energy mounted in the cheerful space. Everyone was excited to be there except for Amelia. Because musicians tended to work on New Year's Eve, it left her without a midnight kiss. But she put on a happy face and wandered around the party as the hostess with the mostest, asking if folks needed anything and saying hello with a big toothy smile.

Lucy yelled over the crowd, "Five minutes until midnight!" Her newly purple hair was pulled up into a sky-high pony, and her pink sparkly dress was almost blinding. Amelia checked her phone and tried to hide the panic building like a roaring fire in her gut behind a smoke screen of simple irritation.

Sadie adjusted her lacey black minidress. "Nothing yet?"

"No, but I'm sure he'll call any minute now. He said he'd call before midnight. I'm sure their set is just running long."

"Hmm." Sadie didn't look up from carefully pouring Martinelli's sparkling cider into plastic flutes.

Ethan came out of the kitchen in an obscenely fitted and completely fabulous midnight blue suit, Delilah on his heels. He put his arm around Amelia's shoulder and kissed her head through a nest of big red curls. "He'll call. If he knows what's good for him, he'll call."

She gave him a weak smile, then stalked away to check on the guests on the back patio. They all chattered happily, sipping Red Bull and readying their midnight noise makers. "T-minus three minutes to midnight, folks," she announced.

The partygoers out back, including Amelia, shuffled in and prepared themselves for the ball drop on the television. She trudged to the kitchen where her friends handed out flutes of the Martinelli's, Delilah happily lapping up the excess as it sloshed onto the tile floor. She picked up a flute of her own and, with her midnight toast secured, found a spot on the edge of the room where she could lean against the wall and feel sorry for herself while everybody else broke into merriment and saliva-swapping in the name of new beginnings. Before she knew it the countdown began.

Ten! She pulled out her phone for the millionth time to find her texts to Dakota unanswered and her tally of missed calls reading zero.

Nine! Her heart rate peaked and then crashed in an instant at the incoming Happy New Year text messages in the Enclave Mesa Gang group chat.

Eight! She wondered self-indulgently if anything would ever matter again if she weren't important enough for him to reach out that night, completely ignoring the love in the room and on her phone, because it wasn't from him.

Seven! She looked from her phone to the group of boys from IOP, now sober a whole year, laughing and dancing their way through the countdown, ready to explode at midnight.

Six! Ethan picked little blonde dog hairs off his velvet suit coat before joining back in the raucous chorus.

Five! Lucy wrapped lithe arms around a cute boy's waist and looked up at him suggestively as the seconds brought them closer to what was sure to be a spellbinding kiss.

Four! Sadie smiled contentedly with both hands covering her heart as she took in the sober joy, seeming to have a moment just for herself.

Three! Delilah sat in the center of the action with big puppy eyes and an open-mouthed mutt smile to match as she looked around for more spilled cider.

Two! The scene felt incredibly far away like she was looking on from another dimension, the one for better people who were good enough for moments like these.

One! It all became clear how much her situationship had distanced her from the things that only last year she swore she would never, ever take for granted.

Happy New Year! The room burst into cheers as 2017 took center stage. Surrounded by people who loved her, one man's lack of a phone call had the power to make her feel completely, and utterly alone.

CHAPTER 24

Amelia stood barefoot on the cold pavement in the middle of January and thought back to the last time she'd found herself shoeless and afraid, running across a driveway. She'd been 22. Here she was again at 24. At least there were no sirens this time.

It all started when she woke up at Dakota's place in the middle of the night to pee. The blue glow of his phone cast a menacing light across his face, and he didn't even try to hide the way he swiped on Tinder while she slept beside him. Could it be called a moment of clarity if one just simply ceased their willful ignorance? She sprang up from bed and demanded to know what was going on.

"Cut the shit, D. What is all of this?" She stood there naked and expectant in his bedroom doorway in the middle of the night.

When he spoke, it might as well have been 2014, the way everything crumbled around her.

"We're not…"

"If you say we're 'not exclusive' I swear to fucking God…"

"Well, we aren't! You act like we had some conversation about being in a relationship, and we never fucking did!"

She shook her head and rolled her eyes. He had her there.

"I'm just not feeling this anymore, Amz. I love you, but there's just a lot that's not working for me."

"What exactly 'isn't working' for you?" She framed his phrase with air quotes, her bare skin lit only by the moonlight through the window.

"You fucked me twice last night, and now you're shooting your shot on Tinder while I'm asleep next to you?" He kept staring down at the comforter, dazed. "Not to mention the bullshit of New Year's and all the other instances with your precious colleagues or whatever the fuck you want to call them. So, what is it, then? Why aren't you 'feeling this' anymore?"

He looked defeated but somehow relieved it had come to this. "It's a lot of things, Amelia. Namely, your promiscuous past being a big turn-off for me."

She thought back to the jokes about her being a slut and the sideways looks when she'd opened up about her history with men. "Is this a fucking joke?" she yelled, gesturing to the phone in his lap.

"It's not just that! It's also your meds. How am I supposed to consider having kids with someone who takes psychotropics? It doesn't sit well with me."

"Doesn't sit well with you?"

"And if we're being completely honest—"

"—no, go ahead, bring it home, D. What else is wrong with me."

"I thought I could get past the fact that you're not conventionally pretty, but it's been really hard for me." She gawked at him, speechless. "I mean, you're beautiful in your own way."

"But?"

"But maybe if you took care of yourself more with diet and exercise, I could consider something exclusive."

Toby Garrett and middle school secrets flooded her 24-year-old brain. "What does that even mean?"

"I usually go for slimmer sexual partners. Which is probably why I've felt so compelled to talk to other girls," he said as if citing their different tastes in music or movies. "And I'm not trying to be mean; I'm just trying to speak my truth."

"Well, your truth fucking sucks."

But there it was. All of Amelia Glickman's worst nightmares, one thing after the other. Her sordid past, her mental health issues, and her body. Right in a row, bang-bang-bang, he confirmed her greatest fears. It all rendered her completely and utterly unlovable. She started packing her bag without another word, wanting desperately for him to stop her. Tell her he loved her. That they would work this out. That he didn't mean any of it. But that didn't happen.

Less than an hour later, she parked at a comically peaceful Wethersfield with a broken heart. As fucked-up as the whole situation was, the tiniest bit of serenity crept into her heart as she walked into the house's warm embrace. Delilah and Ethan were asleep on the couch, and Amelia collapsed in one of the purple chairs and just watched their soft, even breaths for a moment, wondering if she'd ever be able to sleep deeply again.

A few hours into restless dreams, her phone rang.

"Hello?" she grumbled.

"Sup bitch," Lucy greeted her.

"Sleeping," she replied.

"Well, I need to run something by you. It's time-sensi."

Amelia grumbled nonsensically. She didn't bother to explain why this wasn't a good time. Why she was basically subhuman and should be left to rot in her own filth. There'd be plenty of time to fill her friends in on the drama they were getting so sick of.

"Me and Sadie are starting an abuse survivors peer support group. And we were wondering if we could use your living room while we get it up and running and find a more permanent space."

"What?"

"Before you say no, I want you to think of all the women we could help! It's one night a week for an hour, and it's temporary. Wethersfield is such a safe place. I think it could be really special to host it there. Plus, everything that went down with your ex a couple years ago…"

"Yeah. Fine. Let's do it." It was like she'd breathed in the FOG and it was speaking with her own voice, agreeing to something that sounded sort of awful in that moment. A group of traumatized women in her home every week? When she had just essentially been gutted and left to die? But her reservations got stuck in her throat.

⌒

She and Dakota had a few different phone conversations that afternoon. One where they screamed, one where they cried, and one where they planned on meeting up that evening to discuss the matter like adults. She thought maybe they would kiss and make up once he laid eyes on her, but instead, he just came over and said that even though he loved her, he wanted to have sex with other people more. The pang of her parents' divorce, of her dad leaving, radiated through her body like a tremendous and unyielding ache.

She told Dakota that she was trying to taper off her meds, that she was sorry for all the men she'd slept with before, and that she'd go to yoga every day and become a vegan. She felt her dignity dissolve into thin air and her heart crumple up and die when he handed her back the key to Wethersfield. It was as if placing it back in her possession cracked something open inside him, and he collapsed onto the kitchen counter. His voice broke. "God, I am so fucked up. I'm scared that if I walk out that door, it will be the biggest mistake of my life."

"You're goddamn right. But I think you're going to do it anyway."

When he left, the true storm rolled in. It felt like her vital organs were failing. Heart, liver, kidneys, connective tissue. She cried like she did the day she broke up with Trevor and wondered if music would ever be the same again. She woke up before eight the following morning and drove straight to his house barefoot in her pajamas, just like the night she left. He opened the door and let her in like he had been expecting her, and they crawled into bed together, where she let him fuck her lifeless body.

He admitted he had already slept with someone else, and he didn't hold back when he told her how much better it was than what they'd just done. That was the nail in the coffin. She curled into the fetal position and let everything inside her crumble. Sex was the thing she was supposed to be best at. The thing that was supposed to make him stay.

She wouldn't move from his bed for hours until she finally called Ethan to extract her from the twisted sheets. Ethan stood in the doorway with a protective arm around her trembling shoulders. "This," he gestured between his decrepit roommate and Dakota, "is fucking over." He stared into Dakota's eyes pointedly. "Enough. No more."

But it wasn't over. Because growing at the speed of pain means you're done when your wounds say you're done. They went back and forth for months. Six more, to be exact. No matter how gnarly the emotional self-harm, she kept going back for more, the knife cutting deeper each time, getting dangerously close to the artery.

"If you keep going back to him, you will find it necessary to drink and use again," Cathy would say in therapy. "You're making your own life unbearable. He is not your person."

"I know," she'd say back.

"I truly believe that you could live a life completely free from Borderline symptoms, but not if you continue putting yourself through such extreme relational stress. You're triggering your own attachment trauma."

"I know," she'd say again.

She reverted to daily binging and purging, porn in the middle of the afternoon, and four-hour naps. She hadn't taken her meds in months, and she hadn't attended a meeting since January. She knew how bad it was. The only thing keeping her from drinking or using again was the FOG. And the group of 10 or so women who met at her house every Tuesday night without fail. When she'd inexplicably agreed to host the support group, she never thought she'd be the one it'd save.

The house on Wethersfield Road cradled her broken heart and welcomed women each week as they processed their past and healed with one another in the present. A woman sitting in one of the purple chairs on a Tuesday in March taught her that just because the pain isn't physical, doesn't mean it's not real. Another sitting on the couch in April taught her that love wasn't supposed to hurt the way it did with Dakota. And another, cross-legged on the floor rocking a sleeping newborn as Delilah watched in tender curiosity, taught her that trust and respect were the building blocks of any healthy relationship, sexual or otherwise.

Part of her believed that if she could make this one person love her, she would finally win the game. She was stuck back on the merry-go-round, clinging to the shiny plastic horse's neck for dear life. Sometimes, she'd fall back on her cool-girl persona, saying Dakota was no big deal, just sex between adults. Sometimes, she'd cry in Hope's stall, begging the Universe to see herself as her animals did. And other times, she'd send text-message novels she thought there'd be no coming back from.

> Amelia: I feel guilty about how angry it makes me to get a text from you, but how many times do I have to ask you for space? You've caused so much damage. The second I get space from you I remember how fucking mean you were to me. But you still call me and fuck me all the time and act annoyed when I assume that means you may want to get back together. Just leave me the fuck alone, please, God. I know you have everyone else fooled with the wonderful character you present to the world, and I'm not here to shatter that image for other people, but seriously, dude. I don't want to hear your music or hear your dark jokes. I don't want to see your favorite memes. I don't want to have my heart broken this bad ever again. I know I have my part in all of this, but Jesus Christ, all of it was because I love you.

A week later, she'd be naked in his bed, asking herself how it happened again. The capable grad student in her could barely recognize the girl on all fours, crawling back for more. Though nothing's more painful than seeing through a delusion and doing it anyway, she couldn't stand the idea of being wrong. She had decided on him.

All her friends knew about the bad stuff, but God bless them, they never told her to shut up. They just listened. Then on a mild Tuesday in late July, Amelia sat languidly in the backyard, sipping iced coffees with Sadie. Soon they would go back inside and set up the living room for the weekly women's support group. But for now, they spoke casually about dating and romance, sex and intimacy.

"You know, once Dakota told me that guys don't ask girls for consent because the answer would always be no." It passed Amelia's lips and clicked into place, her words hanging in the tepid air. It wasn't that he was bad. It was that the system in which boys and girls were raised had made them both believe that clear, verbal consent was optional. Aside from Cat, she'd never fully given her consent to anyone—nor had she ever been asked for it. Or asked for it herself, for that matter. A lack of no was not a yes.

Tears began pouring down Sadie's cheeks as she reached for Amelia's hand and scooted beside her. "That is not okay," she said quietly. Amelia didn't realize she was crying as well until a tear splashed on their joined, sun-warmed hands. "That is not okay, babe." The leaves of the big tree on Wethersfield Road rustled in agreement.

Amelia dissolved into a puddle of sobs in Sadie's lap. It all poured out of her eyes: every silent yes that meant no and every harmful situation with men from her past that lacked enthusiastic consent. Her tears seeped into the earth around them, watering the thirsty grass. This wasn't about one singular man. How could she not have seen it before? The merry-go-round was haunted.

Sadie repeated the words like a lullaby. "That is not okay. That is not okay. That is not okay."

After the women arrived for group, they just held her while she cried. "I know," they said. "I know." *I see you.* Amelia felt so seen she was transparent.

The next day, when Dakota texted her to meet up, she told him it was over—really over. Something in her had permanently shifted. Within the immense pain and grief for the girl who never knew what to ask for, she found the centeredness that led to no longer wanting to harm herself. Ten months was plenty of time to spend on a man who could only love her halfway.

Moving forward, yes would mean yes, no would mean no, and the number one person on her list of people to honor would be herself. And she'd never look back. Except to ask herself why the brightest, funniest, most brilliantly effervescent women kept running back to the kind of love that hurts. Tale as old as time. System as sick as a cancer. It was why women needed each other. And it was why the women gathered in the living room on Wethersfield Road and bore witness every Tuesday.

CHAPTER 25

She was almost there, almost whole. And it hadn't been quite as draining getting there this time around. On the first day of 2018 Amelia lounged in bed, sipping a cup of coffee and perusing the two open browsers on her laptop while Delilah dozed dreamily at her feet. "Il meglio della Sicilia!" one sang about its destinations. "Sveicieni no Rīgas!" chimed the other. She looked at photos of the rich, sun-kissed Italian coast of her mother's side, as well as the elaborate art deco Eastern European streets of her father's.

Ever since last July, when she finally let go of Dakota, she'd talked with Tamara and Cathy about roots and a desire to understand the places she came from. She believed that the healing process she started in 2015 could level up only when she breathed the air of her origins. She needed to connect with her heritage, and that meant travel. While the pieces of her life were finally back in place, she was convinced a trip would seal the deal. So, she diligently researched her *Eat, Pray, Love* moment.

There were a few reasons why putting herself back together had been fractionally easier than it was the first time. One reason was that she had the proof, as impossible as it felt, that she could find her way back to center. She'd done it before, and she could do it again—even if her brain insisted she couldn't.

The second reason was the love and support she'd accumulated on her first trek to soundness. Sadie's dark humor and loyal heart. Lucy's quick wit and contagious joy. Ethan's profound wisdom and loving patience. She had Beth and Jen and her dad, and even her almost stepparents. Amelia Glickman was a lot of things, but lonely was no longer one of them.

The third reason was that no matter how dark it got, she didn't take a drink or a drug. So, while she'd felt like she was dying from a sadness so big and full that it was seeping out of her pores, she was still physically sober, and to be sober was to be free, no matter how trapped you convinced yourself you were.

"I guess I just honestly thought that once I got sober, everything would work itself out," she said to Tamara. "I don't think I was expecting to get depressed ever again. But here we are."

Tamara just smiled. "Life will keep life-ing no matter what. The freedom is in the fact that you don't *have* to escape with substances and disordered eating anymore. Even when you *want* to."

Amelia considered this brand-new kind of freedom as she poked around on her laptop, dreaming of long flights and new faces. Foreign yet familiar tastes, sounds, textures, and encounters. This new freedom was one of seeing and experiencing a world that existed outside her own sphere of knowledge and influence. She couldn't control and explore at the same time.

And hadn't the mess with Dakota been a result of her bullshit control issues in the first place? Her incessant need to change how she felt even when it meant demanding to be loved and wanted at all costs, up to and including her dignity? As the coffee went cold in her mug, she thought of all the lines he crossed and all the ways she'd compromised her boundaries to accommodate him. Suffering was the result of the bullshit she did to avoid inner turmoil. It wasn't the loneliness itself that was dangerous; it was the thing she did to circumvent the ache. Things like forcing a relationship that was never meant to be.

On that note, she exchanged the salve of self-destruction she'd been spreading onto her most tender parts for the sincere balm of sacred grief. Grief for who she didn't want to be anymore. Grief for all the versions of herself she'd tried to shrink and manage into something more palatable.

Grief for the knight in shining armor that didn't exist and was never coming. Alone at night, she wondered if her rescuer was a warrior princess with long, glossy blonde hair, instead of a knight in shining armor. Maybe that was why nothing else had worked out, but she knew the knight was just a fantasy.

Speaking of swoon-worthy royalty, she'd be lying if she said she hadn't considered reaching out to Cat to ease the agony of the breakup with a fun little jaunt in New York City. But Cat had recently been cast in an Off-Broadway musical; she was digging into her New York dream, and Amelia couldn't be prouder. She couldn't taint their perfect night together with her usual clinging and chasing. Cat, a woman, had shown her what it was supposed to be like. Sex, intimacy, the whole shebang. It was too special to let things like jealousy, fear, or even a repeat performance ruin it.

Nobody was on their way or waiting in the wings to swoop in at just the right moment. Once again, she had to save herself, and when what you're saving yourself from happens also to be yourself, the simplest things in life become monstrous and foreboding. Things like drinking enough water, eating three meals a day, brushing your teeth, washing your hair, or swallowing pills could feel impossible.

The first day she took her meds again in early August, the small pills seemed to weigh 1,000 pounds, but she still took them. The water tasted foul on her unbrushed tongue as it coaxed the SSRIs down the channel of her throat like a stream attempting to move a fallen branch. Day in and day out, she waited for the chemistry in her brain to right itself, and gradually, the pills became right-sized once more.

Under intense relational stress, the Borderline symptoms came back with a vengeance, and along with them, her struggles with food. Not to mention her overall unwellness of the mental and emotional variety. It was a miracle she didn't drink, but the ED had a field day with all the extra room to spread its legs. Through Cathy and Tamara's support and insistence, she got back on her meal plan and began attending meetings—as soon as she could peel herself from the sweat-slick sheets of despair.

During that first month, she allowed herself to rot in bed so thoroughly that her insides almost turned to mush. The endless scrolling on Instagram, the unwashed sheets, the sweatpants she put back on even after reluctant showers. She'd stand like a zombie under the hot spray, willing the soap to come alive and have its way with her. But she persevered, and as the heat broke, so did the spell in her head.

Now today was the first day of a new year. She breathed in the smell of fresh linens and her own shampoo with gratitude as she dreamt of adventures abroad.

Going into the new year, she would keep doing the things that *worked*. That was the bitch about mental illness. Once you were better, you didn't want to take your medicine anymore. But the medicine, the therapy, the meetings, the meal plan were what made you better in the first place. The concept of "I'm better now. I should stop doing the things that made me better" was ludicrous and yet a literal symptom of the things that ailed her. She supposed you had to fall for the joke once or twice before you could anticipate the fucked-up punchline.

"I feel so stupid. I completely screwed up all my progress and allowed myself to get sick again," she'd said to Ethan one day as they walked Delilah down Wethersfield Road.

"That's not even close to how it works, though," he said. "All of recovery is just three steps forward, two steps back. You don't lose everything you've learned just because you make a mistake and regress a little."

"So, you don't think I should go back to swearing off sex?" she asked, sort of joking, sort of not.

"I think you should take it all one day at a time. We always want to make it black-and-white. Most of life is in the grey. Especially when you're trying to live a sober life. In some ways it gets harder as the years go on."

"Why do you think that is?"

"Well, life gets bigger. You start having problems in areas that didn't even exist before. But isn't it great to have any areas to speak of in the first place? I was shit out of areas when I got sober. We have such rich, beautiful lives today. We're blessed." Their walk and talks were an important healing agent as her heart put itself back together again.

But perhaps it was really the applause that saved her. When she finally extracted herself from her billowy coffin on Wethersfield, splashed her face with cold water, and gargled mouthwash, it was to get her two-year chip at her regular Sunday meeting. Her friends clapped good-naturedly then told her it wouldn't count unless she kept coming back to meetings. Her first weeks back were humbling, but she found out firsthand that this was the only group of people in the world who, when you completely ghosted them, would be genuinely stoked to see you when you came back.

By shattering once again she saw the truth. There was a part of her, the *innermost* part, that was pure as fresh snow. It didn't matter if the other parts were battered or broken, rotting or sloppy, because there was this unsullied core of each and every human being, and it was love in its simplest, most potent form. An untouchable flame. No one and nothing could extinguish it. She was already as whole as she would ever be. *Could* ever be. *A little broken, but a lot brave.*

It was those months when she felt more broken than brave that she learned the most about herself. Such was life—you learned how to deal when you had shit to deal with. It was during those sleepless nights that she finally learned how to untangle the ball of anxiety in her chest thread by thread, feeling by feeling, moment by moment, until she could fall asleep.

She'd recite the process in her head almost robotically. "Here is one thread. The thread is sadness. I felt sad when I saw Dakota with another girl on his Instagram story. Here is another thread. The thread is fear. I felt afraid when I thought about starting school again. This thread is shame. I felt ashamed when I couldn't muster the energy to cook dinner." It was clunky at first, because it was vulnerable to be present with emotions she'd repressed for over a decade. But the progress was evident each time she untangled the mess, like a clump of necklaces at the bottom of a jewelry box.

Amelia roused herself from her New Year's Day cuddle session with Delilah and peeled her eyes away from the travel blogs and flight price trackers to check her school email. She'd begun her clinical work in the fall, meaning she was working with real-life clients—highly supervised, of course, but still real. Jen had taken Amelia shopping for some business casual outfits in preparation.

As wealthy as Jen had become, she still swore by Dillard's over places like Nordstrom or Saks. "Just as sturdy and half the price," she'd said under the severely unflattering fluorescents in the dressing room. Amelia, eager to convince her first clientele at the student clinic that she was a professional, and not a depressed and panicky recovering addict with weak enamel and a nonexistent gag reflex, stood before the mirror transformed as her mother looked on.

"When did Amelia Bedelia become so grown-up?" Jen said, standing behind her and making eye contact in the mirror. There was no age limit for mothers and daughters in the same dressing room. "If you told me what was wrong with me while I laid on a fainting couch in a session, I'd listen to you."

Though a fresh pair of slacks certainly made her feel like a boss bitch, she soon found out that the messiness she was so worried would get in the way of being a therapist was what made her uniquely qualified to hold the space for those who were struggling in the first place. It was surprising—the sense of ease she felt in the room with these people. "Yeah, I've felt that way before," she'd find herself saying to clients. "How can I support you?" Instead of getting fired or chewed out for how unprofessional this was, her supervisor would remind her that the more human a therapist allowed themself to be, the deeper the work could go. And the client retention rate spoke for itself.

The first client she ever saw was a teenager with severe trauma and anxiety, one who trusted her implicitly after just a few sessions. Her professors assured her that this kind of rapport-building was not something that could be taught in school. At the end of this client's allotted sessions, the teen confirmed in the exit interview that she had found therapy helpful.

"What made it helpful?" Amelia had asked, ready to take notes on the coping skills they'd gone over that were most effective. The teen scrunched up her nose as she thought about it. "I don't know. You were funny. Made me like you."

She also learned in the first semester of her internship that money really could buy happiness. Or rather, privilege and access could. When Amelia was at her worst, hadn't her parents enlisted the services of the best, most expensive doctors and therapists to hoist her from the quicksand? Hadn't she always known where she was going to sleep that night, where she would get her next meal, and how to access very costly treatment options when she was ready to do so? Hadn't drowning been horrific enough without the added stress of someone calling out from the rescue boat, "Your monthly balance is due!" or "Is your insurance up to date?" This was why it was important for her to work at a nonprofit and understand the system that 99 percent of the world struggled through. She felt a profound gratitude for all the wonderful things in her life that she did nothing to earn.

Some days as a therapist were heavier than others, and learning how to hold space for people in pain while dealing with her own heartache could be exhausting. On particularly hard days, she found herself driving out to Greystone Farm just to sit on the fence and watch Hope graze. As planned, the horse had been moved to the big retirement field with the older horses that spring. She acclimated to the pasture and took over the herd quickly as its queen bee. Not exactly surprising to anyone who knew the mare.

Hope always seemed to know it was her pulling up the big hill as soon as the Rav4 crested the horizon. She'd trot over languidly, put her head in Amelia's lap, and happily pluck cookies from her open palm. Then she'd nurse the patch of grass closest to where Amelia was perched, and together, they'd enjoy the golden glow of the hour just before sunset. As the ball of fire in the sky crept below the vanishing point of the soft green earth, Amelia would tell Hope what had happened since their last meeting, sometimes out loud, sometimes through silent telekinesis.

She thought of their special bond as she shut her laptop and brought her coffee mug to the kitchen sink. Maybe she could drive out to the barn this afternoon and wish Hope a happy New Year. Maybe Ethan would want to come. Lucy and Sadie, too. As unsociable as she'd been during the dark months, she was back to craving as much time as possible with her friends.

The power of friendship came rushing back one night in October when she finally agreed to go out. She put on dark purple lipstick and a pair of tall black leather boots that reminded her of Cat and left Wethersfield for her first night out since the heartbreak. She and Ethan jammed cathartically in the car to corny pop songs and middle-school-era hip-hop and laughed until she felt like she was going to puke chunks of happiness. She played pool with friends old and new and felt comfortable in her own skin—like she knew who she was again. She even made it through a full hour without thinking about Dakota at all.

At some point in the evening, the group went outside to smoke, and she looked up at a patch of night sky just in time to see a falling star glide across the deep blue canvas. *Hey, you.* As the rest of her friends chatted, their gazes remaining earthbound, she lingered on the great beyond with a smile and shook her head. *Of course.* What had heretofore been a charming coincidence had become an unspoken but very real thing between her and the Forces of Good. The FOG used their shooting star thing to whisper reminders like, "It's going to be OK," or, "Maybe this isn't the best idea," or "Yes, this is exactly where I want you to be right now."

The group eventually made their way inside and began to take over what had previously been an empty dance floor. Amelia thought of Cat as she swayed to the beat of "Dancing On My Own" by Robyn. She tried to dance just like she saw her do that night: like no one and everyone was watching at the same time. And whether it was no one or everyone, she felt sexy—she didn't need anyone to confirm or deny it. By the time she and Ethan made their way back to Wethersfield, they were sweaty and exhausted and drunk on the energy of the evening alone. She smiled at the memory as she rinsed out her mug and placed it on the rack to dry.

That November and December, she took a page out of Robyn's book and decided to try some things on her own. Whenever she wished she had a partner she could do things with, Sadie and Lucy encouraged her to take herself on dates. She took hikes, watched movies, and even went to farmers' markets. She took herself out for romantic solo dinners. They'd put her at tables with less elaborate dining settings than the ones prepared for couples, but she never settled for anything less than date night done right. "Can I have a Diet Coke and a candle?" she asked the server on more than one occasion. She even asked once for a better table altogether, more comfortable in advocating for herself.

She made her way through Austin, learning how to enjoy and value her own company. She drove around with "All Too Well" by Taylor Swift on repeat, roaring down Mopac and delighting in the way she could scream "Fuck the patriarchy," at the top of her lungs. Unfortunately, this was well before the blessing of Taylor's Ten Minute Version, but she made do with what she had at the time.

Then, on December 21, the darkest, shortest day of 2017, Amelia turned 25. She felt as though she had already made it through the worst of her quarter-life crisis. And it was always darkest before the dawn. The days slowly brightened and lengthened after the winter solstice, making room for more light. On this New Year's Day, the earth was 10 days closer to sunshine and wildflowers.

As she slipped on her favorite slippers and opened the back door for Delilah, she thought back to last night. The sights and sounds of her third annual sober New Year's Eve party rang out across Wethersfield. Everyone looked amazing and so like their genuine selves. Lucy wore a bright red sequined dress, her freshly jet-black hair in a messy side braid, and Sadie wore a black leather miniskirt with a matching turtleneck, her hair sleek and blown out. Ethan looked as fabulous as ever in a flashy button-down and perfectly disheveled hair.

Amelia bought a forest green velvet babydoll dress for the occasion. It made her eyes pop, and she'd done nothing that night to tame her thick red mane. She was shiny and effervescent; the look said, "I'm allowed to take up space."

An hour or so into that party, as she finished up a conversation with some of the people from her regular meeting, Ethan approached from across the living room with a man a few inches shorter than he. The man's height was not what caught her attention. It was the way he unironically wore an oversized Tony Romo jersey and a ball cap to a New Year's Eve party.

Ethan's hand casually clapped the stranger on the shoulder. "Amelia, I want you to meet my new friend. It's his first New Year's Eve since getting sober."

The man smiled in a way that made the corners of his eyes crinkle like tissue paper in a lavish gift bag. "Hey, how's it going?" He didn't wait for a response. "Is there any way I could turn the game on? Beautiful home, by the way," he said, looking around. "Cozy."

She stood there with her mouth open, registering everything he'd said so quickly before snapping out of it a moment later. "Based on your getup, I'm assuming there's a Cowboys game on?"

"Playoffs. You mind?"

"Knock yourself out," she said, tilting her head towards the coffee table where the remote sat in its usual place. "Yay, sports," she deadpanned.

"Thanks!" He made his way over to turn on the TV and then stood so close the glow from the screen bounced off his face.

Amelia gawked after him and wondered if he always seemed this strangely at home. She turned to Ethan. "Who is that absurd human?"

Ethan laughed. "Tate Reynolds. Met him at one of the meetings across town. Big football guy."

"I gathered that," she said, eyes wide. "So does that mean he's, like, a total dude-bro, then?"

"No, no. Definitely not. He's kind of an anomaly, actually. His love of football is like, the only manly thing about him. The dude studies philosophy at UT with a focus in feminist theory."

She studied him from across the room, not in the vein of sizing him up, but more of a quiet recognition. She wanted to ask a million more questions. "Master's program?"

Ethan laughed again. "Nope. Undergrad. He's 21."

"OK, I like, *fully* thought he was a grown adult."

"I know, that's what I thought too. He seems older."

"Yeah." She shrugged. "Great beard."

"He's also bald under the hat."

"No shit?"

"Yep. Completely shaved all his hair when it started thinning, apparently. He pulls it off."

"No kidding," she said, slowly nodding and looking over to where other partygoers were beginning to gather around the TV to check the score and watch a few plays.

Amelia chatted with friends and refilled snack trays. After a while, she noticed that Delilah was absolutely stoked by the way that this Tate fellow became more and more animated as the game went on. Delilah hopped around his feet, wagging her tail and jumping up with glee each time he shouted at the television. When the Cowboys did something good, he'd kneel down and scratch behind her ears, sharing in the celebration. It was... pretty fucking cute.

Regardless of his interesting fashion choices, no one could deny Tate's kind blue eyes, charming smile, and infectious laugh. He may have only been 21, but his big brown beard and confident manner of speaking insisted he was mid-thirties. He was the opposite of her usual type, yet for the first time in her life, she wanted to understand what second-and-goal meant.

Midnight snuck up on them. Amelia and Ethan poured sparkling cider into plastic flute after plastic flute just in time for the countdown to begin. That captivating chorus of dozens of people chanting the same thing at the same time filled the walls of Wethersfield. The numbers, though, counted off something new.

Ten! Something in Amelia's chest inflated as she looked around the room at all the friends she would ever need.

Nine! She zeroed in on her three best friends across the room and held their three years of joy, inside jokes, stupid arguments, and dried tears close to her heart.

Eight! Sadness bubbled in her belly for the girl who couldn't enjoy this moment last New Year's Eve—because she was so possessed by fixing something she hadn't broken.

Seven! Anger pushed the sadness aside; anger for the learning and unlearning she had to do around real love and respect, something that should be inherent and obvious, the bare minimum, even.

Six! She breathed all the way in and all the way out, grateful for the reminder that sadness and anger were there to inform her of a boundary being crossed or a value being ignored.

Five! Lucy wrapped her tattooed arms around Amelia's center and rested her chin on her shoulder from behind while Sadie reached for her hand.

Four! Ethan made his way across the room to stand at Amelia's other side and wrap his long arms around the three of them at once.

Three! Delilah sat at their feet, perched happily on the top of Amelia's foot.

Two! Amelia's eyes met the sparkling blue orbs in Tate's head, and it was as if the sound was sucked out of the room and turned up to max volume all at the same time.

One! He smiled at her—a real smile that revealed the simple goodness of him—and subtly lifted his plastic flute of Marinelli's, as sober a celebratory drink as ever.

Happy New Year! Total mayhem, as always. Cheek kisses, jumping, spinning hugs, screeches, and squeals. Because, as she'd been reminded yet again, sometimes making it through another year as a human being was the hardest thing you could possibly do. It wasn't the same kind of hard it was three years ago. She was in on the secret. You always needed backup, no matter the nature of the mission ahead.

After the countdown, Amelia, Sadie, Lucy, Ethan, and Tate sat on the back patio talking along with a few others as the last of the city's fireworks boomed and sparkled in the night sky. The glow from the house tethered them to its safety inside. Tate's warmth from where he sat beside her on a lounge chair seemed to mimic the toasty comfort of Wethersfield herself—like they were made of the same stuff somehow.

"News Year's resolutions time!" Sadie sang, breath visible in the crisp night air. "I'll go first. I want to read a new book each month this year." She nudged Lucy next. "Your turn."

Lucy didn't miss a beat. "Easy. Pole dancing. I'm going to have a six-pack by 2019. Next?"

As it went around the circle, Amelia thought about the conversations she'd been having with Cathy and Tamara: the ones about roots and heritage and the things we remember only in our bones, at a cellular level. Not everyone could consider Sicily and Riga. She knew this now better than ever, thanks to her time at the clinic. She could do it, but could she really *do* it? It's not like she could call Jen to send her directions if she got lost or grab lunch with Ethan if she felt lonely. She'd have to figure it out on her own. No matter what it was. Could she really leave her comfort zone for multiple weeks and just…see what happened?

"Okay, Tate, your turn," Ethan said.

"I want to spend more time with my brothers this year. I wasn't a good influence before I got sober. I want to focus on being the big brother they deserve."

Lucy and Sadie cooed in unison. Amelia knew all too well about falling short as an older sibling. She could relate to his desire to be better than he was. To be the person they deserved.

Tate faced her, a soft smile on his lips. "What about you, Amelia?"

She took in an icy cold breath. "I'm going to take a solo trip abroad." Now that she'd said it in the shadow of Wethersfield, it was real.

Tate smiled. "That's amazing."

She smiled back, getting caught for a moment in the pretty pools of blue that filled his irises.

Ethan butted in. "Where are you going to go? When do Delilah and I finally get our romantic time alone?"

"I think Sicily, the Italian coast. And Riga, Latvia. Probably this summer before my last semester of school and clinical hours. It's where both sides of my family are from. I want to see it and feel it for myself. It's a part of me, after all."

When she woke up on New Year's Day, she let herself dream of passports and airplanes and the way the fresh air greeted you in a place you had never been before, somehow insisting on its newness. Spending the morning overcaffeinating and browsing online, she did the research and made plans for her big adventure. Wethersfield and the people who filled the space with Hope year after year had inspired her to take this chance. Because the chorus of voices in a space that had once held such isolation and despair still left her speechless. And if someone who was as alone as she had been could now be so insulated by love and support, why shouldn't she explore this world and trust the magic in it?

She made her way back into the bedroom and opened the browser she'd had up on her laptop. She could do this. Her breath caught in her throat as she clicked "confirm." When an animated airline employee gave a pixelated thumbs up, she smiled inwardly. *Bon voyage, byotch.*

CHAPTER 26

As much as Amelia wanted her *Eat, Pray, Love* moment, when her sister Beth offered to go on the trip with her, she jumped at the opportunity. Close enough. Now she sat stark still in the second-row window seat and stared at her phone.

Tate: Tell the pilot to fly safe. Precious cargo.

Beth looked at her curiously on their Rome-bound airplane. "What's up? Who texted you?"

"Um, a friend of mine." She tilted the phone for her to scan.

"Friend? I don't tend to call my friends precious."

"I know," Amelia said. Since meeting at the New Year's Eve party six months ago, she and Tate had been spending a lot of what she considered platonic time together. Sure, they texted daily, but that was because he had seamlessly charmed his way into the friend group. He was a welcome addition. As if he'd been there all along. He spent a lot of time at Wethersfield with Ethan, either playing video games or watching sports. The group of them, Amelia, Tate, Ethan, Sadie, and Lucy, had become famous for their fearlessly competitive and boisterous game nights. Between rounds of Coup and Secret Hitler, maybe she'd missed something about Tate.

Beth looked away again and scrolled through the movie options on the screen in the seat back. But Amelia continued to stare at her phone and contemplate the sweet yet unexpected text message. Her mind caught on a night in mid-February. A big group had come over to Wethersfield after a meeting, hopped up on shitty coffee, and decided to play the hormonal version of Russian roulette.

"Truth or dare?" Lucy had asked.

Tate made a production out of his contemplation. "Umm, truth,"

"If you could pick anyone in this room to bang, who would it be?"

His eyes were wide as saucers. "I'm not answering that!"

"Why not?" Lucy gasped in faux outrage.

Tate laughed. "Oh, I don't know, like, boundaries maybe? 'Dare' I mention consent."

"Okay fine, who in the room are you most attracted to, then?"

Tate turned bright red. "Do I have to answer this?"

"Yes." Ethan and Sadie said in unison.

"Unless you want a dare…." Lucy added.

"Okay, okay. Fine." He looked down at his tightly clasped hands. "Amelia," he said without looking up.

Everyone giggled and cheered in response.

She wasn't shocked, but she was delighted, and that required some element of surprise. "Me?"

"Yeah, you," he said with a shy smile and an eye roll.

She crawled across the circle and almost knocked Tate over with a hug. "Oh my god, thank you for healing my middle school trauma. No one *ever* picks me!" Even at her hottest, thinnest, most popular, she was always the second choice at best. But she was Tate's first.

His eyebrows drew together. "You're welcome?"

On the flight, she fiddled with the tray table in the armrest, a silly habit from when she was a kid. That game of truth or dare probably should have been more obvious. But she'd been honest-to-goodness trying her best to "date herself" and not focus on flirting or external validation. She'd been enjoying this process; her almost-year-long hiatus pre-Dakota had done wonders for her ability to tolerate herself, maybe even like herself, but solo dating was edging her towards something near loving herself.

Maybe this was why she didn't file the Tate memory away under romance at the time. Or maybe it was because she was starting to realize it was sort of sad to be that excited someone wants to fuck you.

The stewardess's voice broke through her befuddled analysis. "Anything to drink before we take off?"

"I'll have a ginger ale, please," said Beth.

"Diet Coke would be great, thanks," added Amelia.

When the stewardess nodded and moved on to the next row, Beth turned her full attention back to Amelia. "You're really in your head about this."

"I know, what the fuck, right? Like, why, though? It's just a text. It's not a big deal. Why am I making it one?"

Beth shrugged. "A truly awful breakup can rearrange your insides."

A thoughtful frown formed on Amelia's lips. "I mean, the last time I fell in love I almost lost myself completely."

"Whoa, whoa, whoa, who said anything about falling in love? You got one sweet text message, psycho."

Amelia laughed through a groan. "Why am I like this?"

"*Daddy Issues, the Musical*. It will run forever, like *Phantom* or *Les Mis*."

Frustration coursed through her veins. She had spent the whole second half of last year crawling on her hands and knees from Dakota's bed back to normalcy. And since January, she'd focused on nothing but school, her animals, and her friends. So when would *Daddy Issues* finally close? "Well, the reviews suck. Zero of five stars."

"Hey, just because the show will always be there doesn't mean you have to buy tickets."

"Can you explain outside the context of this depressing metaphor?"

"Just because a problem isn't totally fixable doesn't mean you're at the mercy of the problem. Like, as long as you're aware of your tendencies to, I don't know, fall in love quickly and become over-attached, you can watch for them and work with them to make them manifest in a healthier way."

"You sound like Ethan. And my therapist."

Beth smiled and shrugged. "I'm just repeating what my own therapist told me."

The pilot came over the intercom. "Flight attendants, please prepare the cabin for takeoff. Ladies and gentlemen, sit back, relax, and enjoy our 12-hour and 47-minute flight to Rome Fiumicino Airport." Several passengers cheered, which made Amelia and Beth squeal with excitement.

Amelia opened the window shade and looked out at the Texas sky for the last time for the next two weeks. She toyed with the idea of dropping everything and starting a new life in Italy, having her things shipped over and never looking back. A daft fantasy. She shook her head loose of ideas about abandoning her increasingly wonderful life and banished any thoughts of Tate and potential romance. That was enough of all that. This trip was about self-discovery, heritage, sisterly bonding, adventure, and independence of spirit. She pulled her phone out and quickly hearted the message from Tate before shutting it off as the plane rounded the final corner to the runway.

As the plane defied gravity, she thought of *Wicked*, as well as her own saliva. A few months earlier, Amelia hocked a loogie in a little plastic tube and sent it off to the Ancestry.com people. Just to make sure she hadn't been switched at birth, deeming this a lavish waste of her time and trust fund. Though how wasteful could any journey abroad be, really? The Ancestry results came back within a few days. Two big blue dots on a map. Sicily and Riga. Her people waited for her there.

The plane sliced through the sky towards those big blue dots, and Amelia watched the trees and the streets and the houses get smaller and smaller. Would something in her know she was home when her feet touched the ground in these places? Would it be the same sense of inner recognition as when she walked into Wethersfield? She couldn't wait to unpack all of it in her trusty journal, the same one she'd brought to rehab. The floral monstrosity with the gold lettering that said "Something Beautiful is on the Horizon LOL." It didn't say LOL, but it might as well have. She'd been writing in it more and more.

Amelia dozed off thinking about vials of spit and DNA, the most rudimentary building blocks of humanity, and was asleep well before her Diet Coke ever arrived. She'd wake somewhere above the Atlantic hours later, Beth fast asleep beside her, and feel more like herself than she ever had before.

June 5, 2018

Three days into our trip, I'm officially in awe. Pompeii was actually insane. An ancient city, completely frozen in time. Romans preserved in magma. Human lives stopped in their tracks—most of them positioned to do what we do best in a crisis: protect ourselves.

Things like this always make me think of how much time we spend sleeping. Go lay in bed for hours on end? What if this is my last day to master being myself, and a volcano erupts while I'm passed out in a weird fetal position under the covers—and hundreds of years later, people are looking at my rock carcass in a museum, wondering who I was or what I wanted out of life? But like Cathy says, "You can't live the rest of your life fully without a good eight hours."

But volcanos are pretty amazing and this part of our trip has brought back my childhood obsession. We learned about them in fourth grade science, and I just remember being like, hold on, it erupts fiery rocks? Mount Vesuvius is the one that towers over Pompeii, and you can't see any magma or anything. But Mount Etna, which we saw next, frequently steams and even has small eruptions. I felt like a kid again as the lava turned the night sky into a deep reddish-purple glow. It reminds me that there is so clearly something bigger than us—because if a mountain with a hole that connects the sky to the core of the earth through a chamber of fiery molten rock isn't proof that there is magic on this planet, then I don't know what is.

Up near Mt. Etna, there were hundreds of ladybugs. When we asked the tour guide why that was, he said (in the most adorable Italian accent ever, by the way) that there were fewer predators on top of the mountain. He said it was also on the migration path between Tunisia and Italy, and the mountain air currents likely carry them upwards. There's a lesson there somewhere, but I'm too tired to figure it out. Something about going with the flow, which has never been my strong suit.

Anyway, something about the way they whimsically flew around and landed on our arms made me feel free. So, in the name of freedom and ladybugs, I took out a string of biodegradable prayer beads from the secret zipper in my backpack. It was a chunk that had broken off Dakota's favorite necklace. New-age fuck boys who wear biodegradable jewelry are usually sure to make you aware of the fact that it's biodegradable. I hadn't told anyone that I still had it, let alone brought it with me, but I knew it was important for me to leave him behind somewhere on this trip, and this seemed like the perfect place. And not so much him as what he symbolized: the idea that I need to beg for love, or that it's my job to convince someone I'm worthy of it. I will never again work that hard for love.

I found a big rock and put the string of beads in the earth underneath, and I left him on the mountain. I truly loved him, but it almost destroyed everything I'm trying to build. Real love isn't supposed to do that. As I walked away

*from the rocky grave of my failed relationship, I felt like a
ladybug on the wind, ascending to the heavens, untethered
from the limits of unconditional love.*

June 7, 2018

*I'm moving to Capri. I'll be eating fresh seafood pasta and
baking in the sun for the rest of my days. The weirdest
thing is that sometimes when I lay in the Sicilian sun, I
don't even feel hot. Even today, under the blistering rays,
instead of the phenomenon of frying, it was like I was
harnessing new energy, refueling if you will. That's got
to be the Sicilian blood in my veins—because, as a ginger,
wouldn't it make more sense for me to burn?*

*I really love being here. And I really love traveling. Always
have, even as a kid on trips with my family. Something
about breathing foreign air into my lungs makes me feel
so alive inside. It reminds me how much I have to look
forward to in my life. How much I have to explore. There's
so much life to live.*

*Beth and I are having the most amazing trip. This time
together has been healing for our relationship. I sucked the
energy out of every room when I was growing up. Refused
to make space for her. Ignored her at best and bullied her at
worst. Experiencing the amazing, beautiful, awe-inspiring
moments together is, of course, worthwhile. But also, the
tedious, exhausting, ridiculous, jet-lagged laugh until you
pee your pants moments, which usually happen on our way
from one place to another, like the hellish ferry ride the
other day. But the world's greatest treasures are never easy
to get to. So, you have to have a sense of humor along the
way. The payoff is always worth it.*

There I go saying "always" again. Beth mentioned how I tend to speak in absolutes. Always, never, completely empty, impossibly full, best, worst, etc. It's the classic Borderline black-and-white thinking, I suppose. Some habits really do die hard. Though sometimes I wonder if Borderline Personality Disorder isn't just the human condition, but turned up to max volume.

The scenery is gorgeous, but it's just as beautiful to have simple conversations with the people who live here. I'm beginning to see that understanding and exploring human nature is maybe the whole reason I'm here having a human experience in the first place. So it makes sense that I was drawn to counseling. But for me, it's about the stories, not the science. Fuck, maybe I'll be a writer one day. My thoughts and feelings seem the most organized and straightforward when I'm expressing them on paper.

Long story short, life today is the greatest gift I never thought I wanted. Not so long ago, I didn't even want to be here anymore. I guess suicidal would be the clinical term— but I'm pretty sure daydreaming about moving to Capri is the opposite of that. If someone could kindly let me know whose life this is, I'd certainly appreciate it. It simply can't be mine. It's too good.

June 9, 2018

I can smell the fear and pure aloneness as I look out my hotel room window in Sicily. All I can think about is Jen. My mom had me when she was 26, a fact that blows my mind as I inch my way through my 20s, closer and closer to the dawn of her motherhood. My dad was 28, and I was a "surprise," apparently. They'd gotten married the year before when Mom was 25, the age I am now. Two months after their wedding, Mom's mom, my grandma Gianna, died of lung cancer. There's something cosmically fucked about not having your mother there to show you what to do when you're about to become one yourself.

My dad traveled for work the week after they brought me home, and sometimes I picture my mom in the New York house I barely remember. She was sleep-deprived, trying to figure out how to keep a human alive, aching for her own mom to say all the things moms were supposed to say.

In grad school I've learned that those primary attachments at the beginning of our life lay the groundwork for our relationships and sense of security in the world moving forward. My primary attachment was with a mother in the throes of grief because how could she not be? She did everything right, and yet somehow, the deep sadness of her loss permeated my brainwaves and rooted themselves as one of my core personality traits. Being loved despite something, being loved when loving someone is hard—that was my first experience with it.

Today, Jen is my best friend. I could tell her anything. She raised me and Beth with fierce love and advocacy, and I am nowhere near ready to live without her. Fuck that. I bet she felt the same way about her own mother. Maybe if I'd gotten the chance to meet Gianna Giardina, I would have called her GG. Anyway, that's all I thought about today as we wandered the streets of Palermo, where the Giardinas lived and worked.

And maybe it's that logical awareness that leads to a deeper sense of knowing, or maybe I still would have felt it if I'd just stumbled upon the Roman cathedrals, the Baroque palaces, the cobblestones glistening under the golden sun—I

*like to think I'd know either way. It's something about the
light. Some part of me has been here before.*

June 11, 2018

*The more of this earth that I explore, the more I realize I
can never see and understand it all. Today, we stopped off
in Agrigento, a city on a hill in the southwest of Sicily and
home of the ancient city of Akragas, which is part of the
Valley of the Temples. These are some of the oldest and most
well-preserved ruins in the world. Being around stuff that
old puts me in a weird head space—it makes me painfully
aware of the fear and tenderness that's underneath the
surface of my externalized modes of survivals. I always
want something to eat, or watch, or fuck, or chase, because
if I am not actively stalking something that can change the
way I feel, I'm just completely...raw. Empty with no Hope of
fullness.*

*If I wasn't constantly chasing the next thing that could
change the way I feel, I'd remember that one day, I, and
everyone I know and love, will die and cease to exist. It
would occur to me on a cellular level that Hercule's temple
took 74 years to build, a lifetime, yet thousands of years
have passed, and millions of people have lived and died
and researched and spectated, and not one of them knows
the name of a single slave that built the damn thing.*

*And yet, there's this part of me that's constantly aware of
this. It's the same part that will look out at a spectacular
view of the Amalfi Coast and envision my body careening
down a cliff, my skull splitting open on a jagged rock. And
that doesn't mean I want to jump. In fact, I want to be alive
more than I ever have before. It just means my mind is a
little broken.*

Part of life is the darkness and the doom and the broken parts inside us all. One day I hope I have a partner, not a savior but a partner, who will listen to me talk about this kind of thing and maybe even relate. Someone to share the darkness with.

And isn't it a real gift that I have the space to reflect on all of it in the first place? Life used to just happen to me, and now I can observe, learn, and express. When did that happen? Was it the day I faced my trauma on Lady Bird Lake? Or was it when I began taking myself on dates and using pen and paper to sort through my feelings about it? Maybe something simply broke open in me, for better and for worse, the day I crashed Hope. What I do know is that the writing is the integrating, and the integrating is the repairing. I think I'll keep writing.

June 14, 2018

After a daylong train ride and a three-hour flight, we have made it to our next destination. Riga is haunting, to say the least. The somber exploration and the thoughtful strolls through history are a far cry from Capri's sparkling views of the Mediterranean. It is certainly beautiful; the Art Deco buildings and cobblestone streets are insanely charming. And yet it is somehow inherently paradoxical: opulent Byzantine architecture just feet away from the simple Soviet-era barracks. The people are congenial, if a little reserved. But of course, this is compared to the almost exuberant friendliness of southern Italy, where hordes of tourists frequent more often. And I suppose reserved is a fair thing to be when you've been invaded and then occupied by the Soviets and the Nazis and then the Soviets again, all within the last 80 years. Specifically, between

1941 and 1944, the very bricks laid in the buildings and the streets bore witness to ghettos and mass graves.

In total, 93,000 Jews were killed in the Latvian Holocaust. But tell me why I didn't know that until today. Is it because our wing of the lineage left for New York before the war? Could it be that I never asked enough questions? Or is it simply because there are so very many human atrocities that if I learned about all of them in school, I'd never make it to graduation?

Today, we wandered around the museum of the Riga Ghetto. People we were related to lived off these winding streets in these small wooden houses—apparently, this area hasn't changed at all. This is where they'd eat Shabbat dinner and observe the Sabbath. Where they'd laugh and fight and work and play. We also saw the KGB building, which is now a museum.

After a lunch of rye bread and smoked fish from a corner market, we visited the Freedom Monument, a copper and granite statue symbolizing unity and independence. Because if you survive a Soviet/Nazi sandwich, you deserve a statue and whatever else you want. It was built in the 20s after the Latvian War of Independence, the first time they broke free from the Soviets. A two-man honor guard stands watch at all times, except in bad weather, a stipulation that made me and Beth giggle, but I think we were pretty hungry for something to laugh about by that point.

I can't get over this thing our tour guide at the Latvian Holocaust Museum said to us. She was an older Jewish lady who reminded me of Zeyde's mom, who I only met once before she died when I was really little. Walking with us down the narrow streets with the tour group, the guide was explaining the history, to which Beth said something like, "The sheer volume of human suffering on this planet throughout history is unthinkable." The older woman just smiled at the ground. "Well," she answered in her thick yet familiar accent, "no one human being is just like the next, but we all have exactly three things in common as dictated by the laws of nature. We are all born. We all die. And we will all know suffering somewhere in the middle."

And my life is so good today that sometimes I completely forget the suffering of years past. In the same lifetime that I yearned for death, I want nothing more than to live life to its fullest potential. But in order to do that I need to always remember just how dark it got. I am under no delusion that I can't go back there if I stop doing the inner work or start taking my new life for granted.

June 16, 2018

I can't believe we are already heading home tomorrow. We spent our last hours today walking around the little street markets and vendors, buying gifts for our friends and family back home. We needed a chill day to process the intensity of yesterday and prepare for our journey home tomorrow.

Yesterday was an experience that will be tattooed on my soul until the day I die. The sights and sounds, yes, but mainly the energy. When 25,000 human lives are ended within a nine-day period in the same vicinity, something in the air refuses to ever move on.

The Rumbula Massacre refers to the murder of 25,000 Jews by firing squad. Stationary gas chambers as a means of mass killing weren't a thing until around 1942. So instead, on November 30th and December 8th, 1941, men with guns waited in or on the path to the forest just outside the Rumbula Railway Station. Those on their way were under no delusion what fate awaited them at the front of the line. Gunshots and screams leave little to the imagination.

Up until yesterday it still just felt like all of this happened a really long time ago, and maybe when you're younger, it is a really long time ago. But I know people who remember it. Bubbe was five, Zeyde was seven. If Zeyde's parents had waited even just a little bit longer to leave for New York, they could have been in the Riga Ghetto or worse. It's something I myself have been ignorant of, and I'm from a Jewish family. In reality, it just wasn't that fucking long ago.

Today, the site is a memorial. The center is an open space in the shape of the Star of David with a large menorah in the center. Stones etched with the names of those murdered at the site surround the sculpture. Mass graves are marked on the memorial grounds, and the road leading to the memorial site is laid with markers inscribed in four languages dictating exactly what happened there.

We learned about the lives lost, and we learned about the few survivors and how they learned to create their own Hope when there was none left around them. Perhaps we lost a family member. Perhaps we lost six family members. Perhaps my great-great-grandmother's maiden name, which we found repeatedly in the registry archives, was simply very common in Riga. Or maybe someone died there whose blood, no matter how fractional, runs through our veins. I have many more questions to ask and much more digging to do.

Sometimes, in meetings, people will ask, "How free do you want to be?" This could be in reference to giving up drugs and alcohol, doing the tough but right thing, or doing the work necessary to understand and move on from your own demons. And the fucked-up part is, even with all my privilege and opportunities, sometimes my answer has been, "Meh, not that free. I think I'll act like a brat for a bit longer." And I want to shake that girl awake and say, "How dare you?" After Riga, I yearn never to take my freedom for granted ever again. I hope to be a good steward of that freedom and of the many unearned blessings in my life.

Somewhere between the joy of Capri and the horror of Rumbula is everyday life. I intend to be as grateful as possible for every second of it. And when I forget to be, I ask that the FOG remind me quickly how very blessed I truly am.

CHAPTER 27

The heat hung on that September for longer than usual and sweat dripped down the side of Amelia's face as she and Ethan loaded the last of his things into the back of a U-Haul. In the early evening sun at Wethersfield Road, she'd lost the ability to distinguish one bodily fluid from the next: sweat, tears, snot, Delilah kisses—who knew anymore?

When Amelia arrived home from her European adventure, Ethan had given her a few days to settle in and get back on Austin time before he broke the news. He'd gotten a job in New York—it started in the fall. When he told her, she burst into tears of joy and loss. Joy that Ethan had gotten his dream job working on a political campaign and would be closer to his family. Loss, because this was the end of an era, the era of Ethan and Amelia, Amelia and Ethan.

It was always, "Game night at Ethan and Amelia's!" or, "Let's all meet at Ethan and Amelia's before we head downtown." Friends would ask, "Can I have my birthday dinner at Ethan and Amelia's?" One said she came for Ethan and Amelia, but stayed for Delilah.

It couldn't last forever, but some nights, half asleep, cast in the glow of the Netflix "Are you still watching?" screen, sprawled on the couch with Delilah and him on the purple chairs pushed together into a small bed, there'd be such a sense of safety and trust that she didn't know how she'd ever let him leave. He'd become like a soft, well-worn set of sheets that smelled like home. He meant security and rest and letting down the mask she wore for the outside world.

On the front walkway she let the box of books thunk to the pavement. Backlit by low-angle sunlight as it bounced off the charming red front door, she buried her face in her hands and began to cry once again.

"God damn it, Amelia, we'll never get this done if we can't keep it together for more than five minutes." Ethan let his own box hit the pavement and wrapped his arms around her from the side. Amelia dropped her hands, tilted her head back, and let a guttural sob tear from her throat and into the quiet neighborhood.

"I know, bubba, let it out," Ethan said.

"These are the last ones," Amelia said through her chronic-for-today hiccups.

"I'll get these loaded up. Go ahead inside."

Amelia ambled up the front steps and opened the old door to let herself in. When she shut it behind her, the noise from the busy Enfield Road at the corner cut off abruptly as if it'd been sucked out of the space. The clack of Delilah's nails on the floor as she trotted towards the front of the house and the woosh of the AC seemed like the only sounds in the world. She made her way to the front room, Ethan's room. The would-be home gym, office, guest room, craft area. The empty space in her soul that he'd so effortlessly furnished.

The walls closed in, but not in a scary, *Star Wars* trash compactor kind of way, more like a tight hug or a snug winter coat. She felt bundled up. Held. Stable and sturdy. Wethersfield had brought her Ethan. And she knew that the Forces of Good hadn't brought her this far just to drop her on her head—she knew it had her best interests at heart even when the FOG was too dense to see the horizon. Her side of the sober bargain was to act as if that were true even when she didn't believe it.

The bare walls and empty floors echoed with the sound of Ethan opening and closing the front door and then walking across the hardwood to the stripped bedroom. She looked out the front window at the U-Haul parked on Wethersfield Road and took a deep breath before turning around to face him.

"That's everything," he said with a sad smile.

"You'll head out from Jamie's first thing tomorrow?"

"That's the plan."

Ethan and Jamie had been dating since the start of the summer, and they were spending his last night in town together before starting the long-distance thing. He and Amelia both had the capacity to nurture romantic relationships from a healthier place than ever, thanks to what they'd taught each other. He had been spending more time with Jamie. And she with Tate. It was natural shift, one that was right on time. He should be with his girlfriend tonight, and she should be with Tate. But that didn't make it any less bittersweet.

"Are you scared?" she asked.

"Of course. I'm scared of the new job. I'm scared of leaving my girl-friend. I'm scared of being lonely without my friends. I'm scared of going back to the cold winters."

"The campaign is lucky to have you. And your people aren't going anywhere. As far as the winters go, you're fucked." They laughed, and then Amelia teared up again. "God, why am I like this? You're literally coming back for New Year's. I'll see you in three months."

"It's a lot. It's hard to say goodbye. Not just to each other but to this moment in time. We really needed each other."

Her chin quivered. "You're a huge part of why I'm a healthy and strong person today." When moisture filled Ethan's eyes she added, "I love you, dude."

"I love you, too. So, so much."

After a few more hugs and a tearful goodbye between Ethan and Delilah, Amelia walked him to the front. She opened the charming red door and leaned against the frame. "Tell Jamie hi for me before y'all jump into three months' worth of sex in one night."

The sun had made its way to the other side of Lady Bird Lake and Mopac, casting a buttery glow over Wethersfield when Ethan meandered down the walkway for his last time as a resident. He turned and gave her one last smile before rounding the truck to the driver's seat. She stood there for a few moments after the U-Haul turned onto Enfield and faded into the golden horizon.

Before going back inside, she collected that day's mail. She sifted through letters at the dining room table until she found one from her master's program. Inside the envelope, she found the invitation to her December graduation ceremony. This was her last semester, and things in her classes and clinical internship were wrapping up nicely. It was hard to believe she was almost at the finish line.

She snapped a photo of the invitation and sent it to the Enclave Mesa Gang family group chat.

> Amelia: Save the date bitches
>
> Beth: Fuck yeah, it's when I'm home for winter break *thumbs up emoji*
>
> Jen/Mom: Language? Is it even worth saying?
>
> Jen/Mom: Can't wait. On my calendar!
>
> Dad: Wouldn't miss it for the world.

Amelia's stomach dropped the tiniest bit when she hung the invitation on the fridge with a magnet. What would working as a therapist be like post-graduation? She knew she was good at it, but she still couldn't tell if it lit her world on fire the way she dreamed it might. The way theatre once did. The way riding did for her after that. What if she had done all this work just to find out it wasn't for her?

Regardless, things with her family were going so well that she sometimes feared it was too good to be true. Both of her parents were beyond happy with their new long-term partners. They planned to spend that Thanksgiving all together, one big, happy, modern hodgepodge of a family. It wasn't the first blended gathering by any means, but it was the first holiday. There was an understandable amount of trepidation and premeditated awkwardness associated with it. Would it be a dismal failure, never to be repeated? Or a resounding success, the blueprint for every seasonal festivity to come? Perhaps somewhere in the middle—her fast-moving mind still struggled with the grey areas of life.

Delilah sat at Amelia's feet and looked up expectantly. "Is it time for dinner, smooshy girl?" The dog wagged her tail against the tile enthusiastically as Amelia scratched behind her ears. When Delilah finished her dinner, Amelia opened the back door to head outside into the fading final hour of daylight. Just as she closed the door behind them, her phone buzzed in her pocket.

> Tater Tot: So, do I need to rent a tux for the weekend, or will a suit and tie fit the bill?
>
> Amelia Bedelia: Suit and tie are fine *kissy face emoji*

These nicknames had become their thing. Tate had been her date to Jen's wedding last month and was accompanying Amelia to her father's wedding in a few days. But she really started "dating" Tate a few weeks after her trip. It was a new experience for someone to court her and get to know her without any insistence or persuasion on her part.

> Tater Tot: Cool, I'll wear the suit I wore to my prom *crying with laughter emoji*
>
> Amelia Bedelia: *eye roll emoji*

Tate loved to rub in how much younger he was. Four and a half years, to be exact. She had never dated someone younger. But she'd learned the hard way that older didn't necessarily mean wiser. Tate looked and acted older than he was; an old, gentle soul with cutting wit and an affinity for dark humor. He was certainly more mature than she was in a lot of ways.

> Tater Tot: I'll pick up Chinese food and be over around 7. Sesame chicken and veggie fried rice, no mushrooms?
>
> Amelia Bedelia: Yes, thank you *smiley face emoji* see you soon

She was still getting used to how he listened and remembered what she said. How he knew her regular order at all their favorite restaurants and never had to ask how she took her coffee. But the craziest part of the whole thing was that they hadn't fucked yet. Making out and some wandering hands, sure, but nothing else. She learned his middle name before putting her face in his crotch, and if that wasn't growth, she didn't know what was.

As Amelia watched Delilah sniff around the backyard, she thought back to the very beginning. The first date had been at a coffee shop. They'd done that much with the group a million times, but never just the two of them. So, it wasn't exactly clear they'd been on a first date until they kissed on the second one.

The second date was only a few days after the coffee shop, and they decided to watch a movie at Wethersfield. As the familiar sounds of *The Hangover* poured from the TV, Delilah hopped up between them on the couch. They left plenty of room between them for Jesus, or the dog in this instance, but they both began to absentmindedly pet Delilah while they watched Bradley Cooper corral his crew around the wrecked hotel suite in Vegas. It didn't take long for their fingers to brush against one another, and it sent a jolt of electricity through Amelia's body, gut-punching the air out of her lungs. They both jerked back quickly, surprised at the contact, but within only a few moments, they were back to testing the waters on the surface of Delilah's coat, nudging their hands closer and closer.

Delilah became a fan of Tate the second he brought the excitement of football into the house, and on that second date, the dog nuzzled her head on his knee, very pleased with the situation she'd found herself in that evening. But the sound of the neighbor's dog barking eventually roused her from the couch. Their hands were basically on top of each other by that point, and it was the moment of truth: either pull away, because their excuse had been removed, or lean into it and touch for no reason other than wanting to. Without moving their gaze from the television, they made the mutual, unspoken decision to hold hands. *Fingers laced.*

They sat there frozen and staring straight ahead for several minutes like middle schoolers seated in the row behind their parents at a movie theatre. Right as Mike Tyson punched Zach Galifianakis, Amelia and Tate both chanced a look at one another. She laughed coyly, inadvertently biting her bottom lip in the way she'd become accustomed to in these moments of tension. She waited for the inevitable—the lean-in, the mutual decision, the tentative question of pursed lips followed by open-mouthed hunger. But it didn't come. He just smiled back for a moment.

Finally, he cast his gaze down at their joined hands, then back up to meet her eyes. "Would it be alright if I kissed you?"

She gawked at him wide-eyed. No one had ever asked her that. Consent was *sexy*. "Um, yes, please."

When Tate's lips met hers, it felt like coming home. A quiet recognition. It just *fit*. Like Cinderella's glass slipper, but real and scuffed on the bottom for better traction. Was this what a kiss was supposed to feel like? What had once been a manic grappling became a quiet but heated knowing.

Amelia tilted her head to deepen the kiss because she couldn't not. As lips and tongues slid and collided, she wondered for the first time in her adult life if this was the last first kiss she'd ever have. The thought didn't cause panic or even excitement; it just nestled itself in the back of her mind like foundation settling. She smiled into the kiss and wrapped her arms around Tate's neck. The safest hands she'd ever had on her body scooped around her sides to wrap around her waist, pulling her into a bear hug. He peppered kisses around her face and neck.

Before long, she pushed him back into a seated position on the couch and straddled his waist, her body pressing into his in every possible way. That onslaught of molten lava was building towards eruption, magma filling her veins as the energy surrounding them intensified.

Earlier that day, on the phone with Lucy, she'd wondered aloud if the coffee shop had been a date, making this date number two. "How embarrassing would it be if I thought it was a date, and he didn't? I'd die of cringe."

"It's almost definitely a date. The question is, are you going to bang him? Your plans for tonight sound a little Netflix and chill, if I'm being honest."

"Well, if coffee was a date, it was officially the *first* first date I've been on without hooking up. Or kissing for that matter."

"There was no kiss?"

"No, just a goodbye hug. A long one, but a hug, nonetheless. And honestly that's just fine with me. I want to take it slow. He was my friend first, and he's important to me. I don't want to fuck it up by rushing it."

"Tell that to your fanny flutters when you're straddling his lap on the couch later."

And there she was, straddling his lap on the couch with her fanny all aflutter as their kiss grew in passion and insistence. If she didn't want this to go any further tonight, she had to say something now, before she was swept away by the desire to be as close to him as possible.

She was just about to pump the brakes when Tate pulled up, pressed their foreheads together, and took a few deep breaths before letting his head fall back on a cushion. When he lifted his head, his smile could have solved the world's most unsolvable problems, melted the iciest hearts, bridged the vastest of gaps.

"Amelia, I've wanted this for so long. But I really, really want to take it slow. Get to know you better. Ease in on the physical stuff."

Even though she wanted the same thing, had been prepared to ask for the same thing, a twinge of rejection plucked a sharp chord in her chest. The stormy cloud of "what did I do wrong" prepared to ruin the evening. The night lingered in threatening proximity to the delirious pleasure of having his lips on hers.

Seeming to read her mind, he went on. "Believe me. I'm really, *really* attracted to you. But I've always done this in the wrong order. And I can't stand the idea of fucking it up this time."

That familiar ache to be desired beyond reason dissipated, and the clouds evaporated, making way for exceptional weather. She remembered what Cathy had taught her about boundaries: We set boundaries with people in order to add value to a relationship and make it last.

"I completely agree. Sorry, still trying to rewire my brain out of thinking you not wanting to fuck me is a bad thing," she said.

A flush spread through his cheeks. "Oh, I definitely want to, um, have sex with you… that's not the issue." He let out a tense chuckle. "I just would prefer it be more than once and over an extended period of time, and I can go a little crazy once I have sex with someone."

"Like slasher crazy or needy crazy?" she teased.

"Needy crazy. I'm not murderous. I'm just a stage five clinger."

"Relatable." They smiled at each other. She was still straddling his lap, and even though this wasn't a typical way to have a conversation, it felt…natural. Comfortable. She'd take this grounded bliss over the usual heady high any day. It was as if the way his hands rested on her hips, her hips on his thighs, held the entire world together. The greatest discovery since gravity.

"But we should totally still make out," he said, breaking the pleasant yet poignant silence.

So they made out like teenagers in the backseat of the family minivan. If she wanted something she'd never had, she had to do something she'd never done. And she was so beyond ready for something new and different than what she'd become accustomed to in the dating world. She had so much love to give; it poured endlessly from the abundant well of her soul. But it never had a good place to go, a worthy landscape to nourish. This person she straddled was in no rush to drink her in, which made him worthy of knowing its true source.

At the end of the night, when they put on *The Office*—a comfort show for both of them, it turned out—she and Delilah fell asleep with their heads on Tate's lap. Just before she dozed off, she heard him speak softly. "You know, everyone always talks about Jim and Pam's love story. But the truth is, I'm just looking for the Holly to my Michael." It wasn't the cringe factor of Michael Scott that was so relatable, but the goofiness, the hard-to-match-ness. The misunderstood-ness.

She smiled as the sweet tide of sleep pulled her under. "Me too."

A month and a half later, they still hadn't slept together. Though they'd swapped enough saliva to share DNA, and he was pretty obsessed with her Glickman knockers, they'd managed to keep it PG-13ish. Abstaining hadn't been a walk in the park. But talks with women from the meetings and sessions with Tamara and Cathy validated her path when it felt like "fuck it" was the right approach. She wanted it to mean something when they had sex. She wanted them to have a strong foundation before a torrential downpour of orgasms threatened to flood the first floor.

Soon, he'd be here with Chinese food and big blue eyes that saw her how she'd always dreamed of being seen. Ever since they'd started dating, she hadn't once wondered how he felt about her; he'd made it clear with both words and actions. Gone were her days of wondering if a boy would text her back. Tate always called when he said he would. She never had to demand respect or time or attention. He gave these things freely. She'd never worked less hard for love in her life. She'd always heard love was difficult, and so she'd settled for struggle. But she was starting to believe what Trevor said on that first dog walk. Relationships can be hard work, but loving someone and letting them know it should be the easiest thing in the world.

And she had worked her ass off to be ready for a relationship like this. First the ice-cold plunge into the unknown that was early sobriety. The embarrassing affair with Liam. The year of abstinence and the focus on friendships. The willingness to look her trauma in the face and change the course of her relationship with food after a decade of disordered eating. The painstaking back-and-forth with Dakota and the way she almost lost it all. The heads down dedication to grad school. The space she'd held for her clients. The vow she made to herself over those solo, candlelit dinners. The archaeological dig into her heritage. The way she'd found her most profound strength in authenticity, in vulnerability.

Sitting and waiting for him in the backyard, she couldn't help but marvel at the happiness he brought her. But he wasn't the end-all be-all.

She felt the same awe towards the tree in her backyard, with its leaves slightly swaying and rustling in the breeze, thanks to a force she could feel but not see. She felt it towards Delilah, sprawled out on the lawn with her lamby toy and watching the squirrels play. She felt it for the hum of crickets you could only ever hear once you decided to pay attention, and the dreamsicle orange sky fading into blue above Enfield Road. And true, she couldn't wait to point it all out to Tate when he got there, couldn't wait to show him the magic. To share it. But it was still real without him confirming it so.

Amelia smiled above the fence line at a cluster of pinking clouds dreamily morphing to purple at the tattered edges. The pink brought her back to when she picked up her three-year chip last month. While thanking the people at the meeting for their support, she'd mentioned that she now missed the pink cloud of early sobriety, when the world felt new again and wonder waited around every corner.

After the meeting, a woman with over a decade of sobriety approached to congratulate her on the milestone.

"Good work, girlfriend. And remember, there are pink clouds at the beginning and end of every day. It's up to you to stop and look around long enough to notice. Never forget to ask yourself: What makes today great?"

The pink clouds floated behind the old wise tree at Wethersfield, and tomorrow, as the sun rose, they would do so again, whether or not she was awake to see it.

CHAPTER 28

Falling in love with Tate Reynolds was like dozing off when the airplane reaches cruising altitude, then waking up as you land in a new and wonderful place, ready for a new and wonderful adventure. She blinked, and she was there. He felt like sunshine. Like the sweetest nostalgic familiarity blended with the most sublime and exciting Hope. But that didn't mean she wasn't scared shitless at the same time. Could she really do this, live with a partner? A man? Mark had been her only other experience with it, a naive and ill-advised attempt at playing house. She was sober this time, which was likely to help, but still. Would this be different in all the ways she needed it to be?

Sometimes they'd be laughing at something stupid at the grocery store, or belting "Defying Gravity" in the car on the way to the Sunday night meeting. She'd remember the way Wethersfield settled around him, insisting on his presence like an enthusiastic mother insisting on the perfect pair of jeans in an Old Navy dressing room. "This one. This one. This one."

And then they'd be sitting in a church basement among friends and strangers, sharing their innermost thoughts and feelings, healing just the tiniest bit more each hour that passed.

"Just 'not drinking' isn't good enough," Tate would say to the group. "I have to be a better man. For my brothers, my parents, and my future."

"I never knew what it meant to apologize until I apologized to someone who couldn't talk," Amelia said in that meeting. "It's about changing my behavior and showing up differently. Funny how only a horse could teach me that."

It was new and scary, but the Forces of Good hadn't brought her this far only to bring her this far. She knew that. But she also knew the real test would be when Tate met Shadow Amelia. She always made an appearance and was likely the only one who could truly screw this up. It was in Amelia's nature to wonder when the other shoe would drop, but as Sadie loved to remind her, if she wanted shoes to stop falling from the sky, all she needed to do was stop throwing them in the air in the first place. She'd tossed a platform heel in the air when she moved in with Mark fresh out of high school. She hoisted a Birkenstock into the sky when she went to coffee with Liam, the halfway divorcé. She chucked a Chuck Taylor up and away when she forced that pseudo-relationship with Dakota. But with Tate? She felt grounded, as if her Ugg slip-ons were planted firmly in the earth.

Butterflies danced in her gut as Amelia led the two of them up the front walkway, her arms full of Tate's scent. He insisted on using his key for the first time. It was a stark contrast to the key experience with Dakota all those months ago—the one he used to come and go as he pleased into Wethersfield, her bed, and her life. Tate's key felt permanent. He brought his electric toothbrush and his social security card. He changed the address on his driver's license.

Delilah greeted them at the door, and the clean, crisp January air wafted through while they carried in Tate's things: a few bags filled with clothes, a guitar, his laptop, and PlayStations One through Four. After dropping his things on the dining room table, he spun her around the kitchen before hauling her into his arms and planting a messy kiss on her cheek. "Hey, roomie," he said. Delilah wagged her tail excitedly at their feet.

"Hey, roomie," she said back, wondering how she could be this deliriously happy. Because this was better than anything she'd ever imagined—if she had gotten everything she thought she wanted out of a relationship, she would have sold herself insanely short. It made her think of the duality of life; the immense suffering and how it opposed the boundless joy on the other end of the spectrum. It seemed that her own most boundless joy was this, right here between the fridge and the dishwasher, bundled up in Tate's embrace on Wethersfield Road.

She remembered a time not so long ago when she sat on the other side of it all. Suddenly, it was 2015, and the house was barren and forlorn once again. *At the exact moment her life was flashing before her eyes, someone out there was realizing they were in love, having mind-blowing sex, eating an ice cream cone, watching* The Office, *or laughing at a dirty joke. Why couldn't it be her then? Why couldn't it be her now?* Now it *was* her. She snapped back to the spot in the kitchen and sent love and light to anyone on the opposite end of things from where she stood in his arms. She knew one day she'd venture into that empty place once again for one reason or another. The good, the bad, the in between—all of it would eventually pass.

Now, in the early days of 2019, Tate began to put away his clothes in the dresser drawers she'd cleared out for him, even though he'd laughed at her when she broke it to him that she wasn't willing to give up even a portion of the walk-in closet. "What? Your suits and shit can go in the spare closet, princess!" she yelped through her tickle-attack-induced laughter.

Ever since she'd made headway with her dietician and started to unpack some of her body shame shit, she learned how much she'd been holding back on her style. She'd always loved clothing, but expression through fashion was something she thought was reserved for the skinny girls. Peplum and modest cardigans were her norm for a long time. Once she gave herself the permission she'd always longed for from others, she went hog wild with the high-waisted jeans, crop tops, waist-cinching sun dresses—all the things she thought she couldn't pull off growing up.

She was the biggest she'd ever been. It was her body as it had natu-rally arrived in this present moment as a result of eating enough food, along with moving her body in a way that felt nourishing and supportive rather than punitive. She was closing in on a size 18 and never felt more confident. More beautiful. More alive. She loved how her new wardrobe hugged her hips and announced her curves. She loved coming out of hiding. So yes, it was the biggest she'd ever been. It was also the happiest she had ever been, arguably the healthiest, and the most well and thoroughly fucked she'd ever been, too.

In fact, back in early October, when they finally had sex—after ample conversation and clean bills of sexual health—she wondered how she had ever had sex with anyone else. She'd never forget the way they huddled anxiously around their phone screens in a Whataburger parking lot, logging into the Planned Parenthood patient portal to view their test results. She'd never before experienced that kind of intimacy and transparency.

Later that same night they watched a scary movie on the couch at Wethersfield. The groans and creaks settling throughout the old house seemed to push them closer and closer together at the most opportune moments until Amelia found herself practically in Tate's lap, where she'd found herself many times before. Still, this time was different, because this time, they were ready. Well before the movie ended, she twisted around in his lap to straddle his waist, mirroring the position they'd been in not so long ago when they decided to hold off.

"I don't want to wait anymore," she'd whispered in his ear as a ripple of goosebumps splashed across his neck.

He didn't respond; he just laced his fingers through her hair until he was cradling the back of her head and pulled her in for a kiss that insisted on more. And this time, when she gave of herself, when she put her entire heart and soul into that moment because that's who she was? He cherished her. He held her. He appreciated her for her desire instead of taking advantage of it. He met her halfway and never took more than he could himself offer. Sex had never been a promise before that night.

As they made their way to the bedroom, their movements were urgent but not rushed. Because something in the air told her they had all the time in the world. It was a natural shift, much like the shift from the sex being performance-based to experience-based. Instead of focusing on how she looked in his eyes, she was lost in simply seeing and enjoying him through her own.

The way her body responded to him spoke of trust and adoration. She fell apart so beautifully and so completely beneath his touch. Her pleasure was prioritized, never placed on the back burner, much like it had been on the night with Cat. But this time, the connection had a place to go past sunrise.

After, they lay in bed, tangled up in one another, sweaty and sated with nothing but their breaths and heartbeats echoing off the French doors and back into the room.

Tate's chest rose and fell as his breathing subsided. "I feel like it's pretty cliché to say this after coming inside you for the first time, but I've honest to God been feeling this way since… and I just…" He chewed on his lower lip, coming to a stuttering halt in his words.

She rolled over so her chin rested on the back of her hand that rested on his chest. "I love you, too, dude. Have for a while now." She loved that he did theatre growing up and craved show tunes as much as she did. She loved the contradictory nature of this combined with his die-hard love of football. She loved his self-proclaimed positive nihilism—the way he was somehow the most negative yet optimistic person she'd ever known.

He laughed softly and swiped a thumb across her cheekbone. "I really do. I love you. Even when you steal my thunder."

"My bad." As she rolled onto her back, cackling, she filled the quiet room with her big, loud laugh. It had always been a rambunctious, booming sound, but she'd learned to temper it circa sixth grade. It had been expanding back into its original form since her first real belly laugh in rehab and throughout her years in sobriety. But Tate's blinding light, his boundless kindness, had busted through whatever self-consciousness remained to obscure it. She never remembered to hold back anymore.

This time, he rolled onto her and wrapped his arms around her waist, resting his head on her chest. She'd never held a man like that before

Tate. She loved that they could both be vulnerable enough to allow themselves to be cared for.

He blew out a puff of air across her torso. "I think I've been in love before to some extent, and I know you have too. But this is different." Then he said the most magical words you can hear in a new relationship. "I've never felt this way before."

"Good," she said with a hushed laugh. "'Cause me neither." A few moments passed between them. "It's like I've always had this insane amount of love inside me, and it's always been too much. It had nowhere to go before I met you. But you're worthy of it. Protective of it." The next part she didn't dare to say out loud—not because she worried about scaring him away or overwhelming him, but because she wanted to offer the FOG an opportunity to really put on a show with their love story. *You're its final destination.* She could already feel the initial descent, hear the ding of the seatbelt sign.

The remainder of October and the totality of November taught her all that sex could be. It could be hot and dirty and playful and silly and loving. Now, in January, she stood in the bedroom doorway and looked over at what was now their shared bed. Tate organized his nightstand, setting a pile of philosophy and political science books against the lamp as well as a phone charger and the framed photo of the two of them Amelia had given him for Christmas. Real-life Tate smiled back at her and lifted an eyebrow suggestively as if he could read her dirty mind.

And the truth was, she couldn't get enough of him. He touched her in a way that made her want to extract every ounce of pleasure and joy from this plane of existence. Each time he caressed her body, he caressed the deepest part of her soul. He taught her about loving someone in action, in how she showed up for them and considered them on a day-to-day basis: body, mind, and spirit.

Sex became an expression of love, but it also created a safe and respectful container for her to explore some of the things she craved but never had a healthy opportunity to express before. She could submit in the context of her safe relationship, toy with degradation and control in the height of aroused play, and then come back down to earth and be nestled in the softness of aftercare, kindness, love, and commitment. With him as her anchor, it finally felt safe to truly inquire. Mutual respect, enthusiastic consent, and ongoing communication allowed her to be used in a way she'd been ashamed of wanting before, in a way that others had exploited before running away at the first opportunity. With admiration and consideration at the center, they traversed the unknown side by side.

Amelia was pulled from her thoughts when she heard Tate talking to Delilah in the living room. "Time for dinner, mooshy woman?" The way he'd picked up on the bizarre nickname, the origins of which she honestly couldn't remember, as well as when it was dinner time, made her heart do a little skip and flip in her chest. He filled the dog bowl with kibble and set it down in its usual spot. He then made himself comfortable in his own usual spot on the far right of the couch, where a new Tate-shaped indent was forming from all their movie nights and midnight talks.

He rubbed his eyes. "I'm going to set up the office space tomorrow, I'm wiped."

"Makes sense."

They decided to turn the elusive front room into a home office to share. She couldn't wait to decorate it together, filling it with both of their passions. They were passionate people. But passion always had a way of fueling a spat sooner or later.

The previous month, in early December, they'd had their first fight. "This is it," she'd thought. "The other shoe." The one she hurled into the air when she dared to believe that she of all people could navigate a healthy and successful partnership. She remembered in her couples and relationships course learning about how in most long-term relationships, there would be an inevitable battle of the egos, where the people in the partnership would finally meet as their most scared, most wounded selves and either fight it out to the other side or go their separate ways.

"Sometimes I just need a little room to breathe, Amelia. Some time to miss you."

"If you hate spending time with me so much, then just fucking leave!"

"You're not hearing me! It's making me want to run away. I need you to hear me."

"There's the door! Run." *Hello, Shadow Amelia. I'd been expecting you.*

Every fight they'd have from then on would be some iteration of that first debacle: him feeling smothered and needing some personal space, her being offended and lashing out because she thought he was leaving, then her trying to beat him to the punch. It was all rooted in her original abandonment wound, one that he did not inflict.

But that first time, having never been in a loving and healthy relationship before, she assumed that when she yelled at him to leave, it was over. She'd kicked him out of Wethersfield into a cold December night and wept into her pillow because she didn't understand how something so good could turn bad so quickly. But a few agonizing days later, she called at two a.m. to apologize and beg him to return. One day, when her life flashed before her eyes as she lay dying, she'd see him trudging up the driveway with his duffel bag just 20 minutes after that phone call, lit by the porch lights in the middle of the night. Because he wasn't just there for a quickie, for breakup sex, or a hit-and-run, he was there because he planned to stay. She felt it solidify as he crossed the threshold into Wethersfield that night.

They seldom spent a night apart after his fateful trek up the driveway. But this was now the real deal. Tate Reynolds had a new address, and it was on Wethersfield Road. Tate organized his spare closet and chest of drawers, and Amelia stood at the sink washing the dishes from their first meal as cohabitants. It was evident that Tate was the better cook. Perhaps it was never a good idea to let a bulimic in the kitchen for too long, but Amelia seemed particularly determined to burn pasta or whatever else she tried to concoct. They enjoyed the dinner he prepared—roast chicken, macaroni and cheese, and an HEB salad kit—and huddled together at the dining room table that long ago reeked of loneliness. She rinsed the remnants of their feast down the disposal and considered how they got here. Three things happened that holiday season in the wake of their first fight that changed their lives irrevocably.

They told each other everything.

Though they'd heard bits and pieces of each other's stories in meetings, nothing but the whole truth would cut it now. Tate opened up about how college partying morphed into a cocaine- and alcohol-fueled nightmare as the control slipped through his fingers and he pushed his loved ones further and further away. He spoke of blackouts and strangers and just-barely lucky breaks and crippling depression and anxiety.

Amelia opened up about the way her heart had always been cracked and splintered, and then her parents' divorce shattered it altogether. She spoke of that horrible night with Mark, the bulimia, the crash with Hope, the endless benders of wine and weed punctuated only by toxic encounters with aberrant men. She told him everything from Toby Garrett—the first instance she allowed a boy to rule her life—to Dakota, the final instance.

They sat on the floor of the bedroom by the French doors, talking into the wee hours of the morning, knees touching, the same big blanket warming them, and witnessed each other's pain. There was no "You were doing the best you could," or "Everything happens for a reason," just "Thank you for telling me," and "I love you just the same. Maybe even more."

She introduced him to Hope.

On a Sunday morning in mid-December, somewhere in the jumble of days between her grad school diploma ceremony and her 26th birthday,

Amelia drove Tate out to Greystone Farm to meet her original soulmate. She'd wanted to make sure he really planned to stick around before introducing him. They clutched to-go coffee cups, the caffeinated warmth seeping into their bones in the chilled morning air, watching as clouds of their breath mingled with the dense early mist. A slice of bright orange light fought for purchase under a blanket of grey winter clouds behind Hope. The horse raised her big brown head with the white smudge from her patch of breakfast grass and surveyed the scene before her. Because it was not just Amelia this time, trudging through the frosty grass with a big bucket of treats. The horse seemed to assess the male form at her person's side before finally deciding to make her way to the fence.

"Wow," Tate breathed, barely audible.

It was easy to forget how big horses were until you brought around someone new to them. Amelia giggled. "She's a big girl, huh?"

"And beautiful."

"I think so. My trainer Deb makes fun of me for saying that, because her head and ears are so big and her body is so long." Amelia felt struck for the first time by the idea that Hope was not stereotypically beautiful for a horse, much like she wasn't stereotypically beautiful for a human. They were both unique and wonderfully so. Beauty was truly in the eyes of the beholder, anyway.

"Seems pretty perfect to me," Tate said, looking at the horse in awe. And then to Amelia with the same expression. No one had ever looked at her the way he did.

She climbed onto the railing. Tate climbed up after her and settled beside her. Amelia gently stroked the fur under Hope's forelock. "You know, one of my favorite things about horses is their eyes. Look, you can see our entire reflection in them, like big brown mirrors."

"Huh. You really can. Can I touch her?"

"Of course. Just don't move too fast. She loves ear scratches."

Tate smiled and reached to stroke behind Hope's furry ear, and Amelia's heart grew 100 sizes like she was the Grinch learning about the gift of Christmas down in Whoville. That was when he said to Hope, "I know I've got some big shoes to fill, ma'am. And I know I'll always play second fiddle to you, but I want you to know that I will do my best to love our girl the way she deserves and take care of her as well as you have."

The entire encounter made meeting her parents look like a joke and a half. Because she had told him who Hope was, what she meant to her, many times over. And he'd listened. Not only had he listened, he took it seriously. He'd passed maybe the most important test of all. It was made all the more evident by the way Hope nuzzled her head into Tate, searching for cookies and wiggling her nose at his pocket.

⸻

She asked him to move in.

That New Year's Eve, as 2018 made its final step toward 2019, Amelia looked around at the now familiar and joyful sights and sounds of her small house on the last night of the year and decided she wanted to have a sleepover with Tate Reynolds every day for the rest of her life. But it was likely too soon for talk of marriage; even she knew that.

So as the last 10 seconds of the year were called out by a chorus of joyful, sober voices, she shouted over the sounds at a rosy-cheeked Tate wearing in a blue button-down (the Cowboys didn't play until New Year's Day that year, mind you). "Move in with me!"

10! 9! 8! He gawked at her. "What!?"

7! 6! 5! "Move in with me!" she shouted, this time louder.

4! 3! 2! "Are you sure?"

1! "Yes, one million percent sure!!!"

Happy New Year! "I would love nothing more."

The room exploded in cheers and kisses, but all that existed was how his arms wrapped around her waist and pulled her into a bear hug in the middle of the living room. In the middle of *their* living room.

That night, after doing the dishes from their first dinner as cohabitants, she wiped off the countertops with a smile and thought back to the night she asked him to merge their lives just the littlest bit more. He had officially lived there for three hours, and she could already barely fathom a Wethersfield that didn't hold Tate's booming laugh and obscure football factoids within its walls. "Did you know that Emmett Smith has the longest streak of consecutive 1,000-yard rushing seasons in the NFL?"

Later, when they were curled up on the couch watching *The Office,* he brushed a curly strand of red hair off her cheek and tucked it behind her ear. "I couldn't love you more." He kissed her gently on her forehead. "But I probably will tomorrow." He kissed the tip of her nose. "And the next day." A kiss on the jaw. "And the day after that." Their lips met somewhere in the middle as the final piece of the Wethersfield puzzle clicked into place.

CHAPTER 29

Jen used to say that you don't truly know someone until you know them through all four seasons of the year. Amelia had taken this to heart when she took the year off from sex and dating. She did the same in getting to know Tate. And she knew Tate. She'd known Tate. She wanted to always know Tate. Through every season to come. The wins, the celebrations, the smashed goals, and the well-nourished personal growth spurts. But also, the tragedies, the losses, the missed opportunities, and the broken dreams. Did you adore someone just as much in depressed gremlin mode as you did when they were shining bright? That was real love. But boy, was it fun to watch each other shimmer and shine.

Spring

After a January and February of nesting and resting both inside and outside the four walls of Wethersfield, Plumeria and Esperanza sprang up in the garden beds, Bluebonnets began to line their daily walks with Delilah, and life together somehow became sweeter by the minute. The sweetness was in the simple intimacy of having a song stuck in your head, only to hear your partner start humming the same song because you're connected through time, space, and the sound waves of the subconscious. It was in the deep sense of comfort found in a running list of inside jokes and shared disdain for tedium and politeness. It was in the sacred routine of sharing a cup of coffee on the back porch each morning as Delilah checked on her yard.

Tate's permanent arrival on Wethersfield Road was fun and joyous, but there were inevitable growing pains. The dishes, the laundry, sleep schedules, and other household bullshit were easy enough to work through. But the original wound within Amelia still throbbed whenever she felt him pull away even the tiniest bit. Could she believe he would always return when he backed away for an hour or a day? It didn't matter if it was for emotional respite, video games with friends, a Marvel movie, or football. Maybe one day, she'd learn that the space between them preserved the relationship and made it stronger, rather than allowing it to decompose.

In the meantime, she'd have moments of crippling fear. The jump scares were one thing: her startled yelps when he put his hand on her shoulder if she hadn't heard him come into the room. Aside from more obvious trauma responses, the insidious pattern of push and pull was rooted in her traumatic past. He'd take some time for himself for a completely valid and unthreatening reason. She'd feel abandoned and rejected, then he'd take it personally and become defensive. She'd get frustrated and lash out, so he'd retreat, then she'd apologize profusely for her behavior.

Her fights with Mark had been nasty. The final one was dangerous. It was no wonder any tension between her and the partner she lived with was triggering. She worked hard in therapy with Cathy to identify those triggers and work through them. A disagreement need not involve yelling. There was such a thing as healthy fighting in a relationship, so long as both parties respected one another and remembered they were on the same team. It was them against the world, not them against each other. She worked hard to master the art of being in an argument without hitting the panic button.

Once, Tate even went with her to see Cathy for a troubleshooting couples' session. They discussed Amelia's anxious attachment style and Tate's avoidant one. They broke down the push-pull pattern to its nuts and bolts, pulling Shadow Amelia from behind the curtain to reveal the scared fifteen-year-old, desperate for love.

Cathy was patient as ever. "Lashing out is not the way we ask for love in the context of a mature relationship. Instead, try using 'I' statements. 'When you blank, I feel blank because the story I tell myself is blank.'"

Amelia cringed as she remembered what she'd yelled at Tate just last week: "No, that's fine! You don't want to hang out with me. I don't even know why you're with me in the first place! Spend tonight with the boys," she'd spat. *Oops.* That was the opposite of the right way to express herself. She admitted as much to Cathy immediately.

"Why don't you try to say the same thing using those 'I' statements?"

Amelia shifted in her seat and then began talking to Cathy. "When you—"

"Not to me, dear, to Tate."

"Right." She cleared her throat and turned her body to face his. She took in his kind eyes, his patient smile. "When you cancel plans with me to go out with your dudes, I feel rejected because the story I'm telling myself is you can't stand spending time with me, and you're on your way out the door for good."

Tate's brow furrowed. "Amelia Bedelia. That's not even a little true. But when you act like that, it does make me pull away a little bit."

Cathy interrupted gently. "'I' statements."

"Right. Sorry. Amelia, when you yell at me and accuse me of being a bad partner, I feel defensive and afraid—because the story I'm telling myself is I'm failing you by trying to take care of myself."

Cathy already knew all of Amelia's shit, but she was able to dig out Tate's fear of being bulldozed in a relationship, leaving him with no close friendships or self-esteem. He expressed his fear of relying too heavily on Amelia to have his needs met and not spending enough time nurturing the friendships he was lucky enough to have through sobriety and recovery. It all made so much more sense; they made so much more sense to *each other*.

In that session, they promised to be each other's biggest fans and fiercest confidants no matter how difficult it became to navigate what lay ahead. Even when his incessant need to play the devil's advocate made her want to rip her hair out or her constant need for attention wrung him dry. Because with unconditional love lighting their path, there was nothing they couldn't face when life inevitably threw hardship their way.

Summer

"See you next week!" Amelia shut the office door behind her last client of the week and collapsed into the large plush chair with a harrumph. After a few deep breaths, she rubbed her eyes and tried to muster the strength to pack her work bag and head out into the blazing heat that still clung to the concrete at eight in the middle of July. She'd been warned about burnout all through grad school, but she honestly thought it was only something to worry about a decade or so in. Definitely not this soon. It wasn't a dumpster fire or anything, it just... wasn't what she thought it was going to be.

She let out a sigh and hoisted herself to her feet. As she packed up her belongings, her phone started to ring in her pocket, and before even looking to see who it was, she felt like screaming, because she was absolutely, positively talked out and peopled out. She pulled out her phone to check the screen and saw that it was Sadie calling. One of her best friends in the world. As she silenced the call, she realized that after a 25-client week, she had absolutely nothing to offer the people in her real life. The thought caused tepid shame to pool in the pit of her stomach.

The most confusing part was how much she loved her clients. She absolutely adored them, every single one. But the job itself was draining beyond all belief. Amelia's boss would remind her not to take her work home with her, and she'd just gawk in return. She'd never been able to do that. Maybe she was just too sensitive, too raw, too emotional. Something had to give.

But she kept trucking forward, hoping it would all feel less overwhelming at some point. She was jealous of Tate's passion for his studies and his desire to carry them forward into teaching at the collegiate level someday. Shouldn't she feel similarly passionate about her own vocation?

When she wasn't seeing clients in the therapy office where she worked, summer brought countless weekends on the lake with Tate and her friends. Amelia had stopped wearing bikinis in high school, but this summer, she did nothing to hide her round belly from the world, and sure as sunshine, freckles sprouted across the long-covered skin. She was still bigger, but her confidence only grew as she continued her work with Tamara.

It was a relatively unique experience in the ED recovery world, healing from an eating disorder into a plus-sized body, especially in a society that was quick to prescribe disordered fad diets to people in larger bodies. In the face of these old societal norms, she worked hard to remind herself of all the ways her life had improved since she started feeding herself and moving in ways that felt good rather than punitive.

Punitive movement always made her think about the elliptical machine her parents had in one of the spare rooms growing up. She could see herself at sixteen, hungry and tired, staring lifelessly at the "calories burned" screen before school—because rehearsals would consume her entire evening, and she simply had to fit into the costume the other girls were wearing. Today she preferred weightlifting and yoga, hiking and low-stakes dance classes. Those things brought her joy.

She'd never dared to dream of a world where her partner would see her casually naked and groan, "God, I fucking love your body." But there she was, feeling sexier than ever at a size her fifteen-year-old self would have deemed worthy of suicide. She'd once heard someone in a meeting say that in recovery, we get to be the person our younger self would be proud of. Lucy leaned over at that moment and whispered, "Call me crazy, but I'm just not interested in impressing a mentally ill child." Amelia couldn't have agreed more.

Fall

That fall, she fell in love with football. Every Sunday from noon to nine, football was on the TV in the living room. She'd sometimes cheer along, and other times just cuddle up with a book at Tate's side. But the sounds of the announcers, the players, and the crowds became one of the most soothing symphonies she'd ever known. As a kid, the sounds of Sunday football meant the homework she'd put off all weekend and her dad preparing for a business trip, sucked into his Blackberry while the lull of the TV held what was left of his attention.

Football had changed, but so had Jonathan Glickman. He'd been on his own healing journey the past couple of years and was becoming more present and expressive by the day. In fact, many Sundays were spent with Tate and her father speaking about football stats and plays in a way that put the most complex rocket science to shame.

The only thing reminiscent of the Sundays of her childhood was the dread. Only now, instead of school, she dreaded going to work in the therapy office on Monday morning. Yet, she had committed to it, investing money, time, and energy to become a therapist. Could she really turn back on that? What would she even do instead? She recognized the privilege tied to employing so many resources to start a career, only to entertain thoughts of changing her mind a few years in.

Amelia explained all this one evening when she and Tate were over at the lake house with Dad and Maya watching Sunday night football. "It's too late to quit now. I think I just need to suck it up," she said as she twisted the ruby ring around her pinkie finger. "It was so cool of you and mom to pay for grad school, and I'm not about to shit all over that. It's just sometimes I feel like there's so much about my own past I need to figure out, and this job makes me feel further away from doing that because I'm always just in survival mode." She felt safe opening up in the space that used to hold so much pain from her parents' divorce. The lake house now held new memories, just like her mom and Chris's house did.

Jonathan Glickman replied without shifting his gaze from the big screen. He paused first, as the Ravens were destroying the Cowboys. "First of all, I'm just so proud of who you are, and there is nothing you can do wrong in my eyes. Don't put so much pressure on yourself. And yes, you've had it easy in some ways, but don't forget that you've experienced a mixture of both a very privileged and a very difficult life. You have enjoyed remarkable fortune in certain areas but faced significant challenges in others. Privilege doesn't mean that you can't feel pain, and it doesn't imply that you don't need time for healing. It also doesn't mean that you have a duty to spend your precious time on this earth doing what is unsatisfying or painful. Grad school wasn't a waste of time, no matter what. You're a wonderful person who brings light and joy to the world. How you shine your light makes no difference to me as long as it shines for you. And I know your mother agrees with me."

Amelia was speechless. Tears sprung up as she took in the words she never knew she needed to hear.

Later that night, as she lay in bed, she heard a voice in the back of her head. Was it the FOG, or just her anxious brain? "Write it down," she heard the voice say, to which she responded, "Write what down?"

"Write it all down. Your story will never make sense until you write it down." Then the FOG settled, and she drifted off into a restful sleep.

Winter

"Write it down," became a mantra she couldn't ignore. She needed to do something quieter, softer, easier. A job at a coffee shop or a bookstore. Because she needed the vast majority of her head space to be dedicated to writing it all down. It was during a holiday gathering with both sides of her family that she told everyone she was putting a pause on her counseling career. She explained that she wasn't happy at her job, not really. That she thought this was what she wanted, but it wasn't *all* she wanted. She wanted something more...creative. And they were supportive, if not skeptical, when she'd answer their questions about what she'd be doing instead.

"I just need to write it all down."

"Write what down?" they'd ask.

"Everything," she'd say. "The whole story."

They nodded and pretended to know what that meant. Because after her years in recovery, they trusted her to run her own life. And wasn't that a miracle? She couldn't be trusted to ride her horse sober just four years ago.

The truth was, humans and their stories drew her to counseling in the first place. But she wanted to dissect the stories, rip them apart, and then put them back together in a way that healed the loneliest of hearts.

She wanted to fully understand the Forces of Good and express how those forces were ultimately the authors of her story—how she had finally learned that if you fight against them hard enough, you can completely outrun the FOG. However, if you are fortunate enough for them to catch you, it becomes your responsibility to pursue the forces, rather than the other way around. She aspired to be a FOG chaser, not a FOG dodger. She suspected that some referred to it as Jesus, or Allah, or Spirit of the Universe, but the FOG was good enough for her.

Sometime in late December, she found herself in the room of floor-to-ceiling bookshelves. She'd lived in the house for nearly five years, but she'd just built her first fire in the quaint old fireplace. What a shame she'd never slowed down enough to enjoy a fire in her own home, but she was finally ready to pump the breaks.

She'd looked at bits and pieces of her past, but never looked at the whole thing together. There was a narrative to capture. Warmth poured off the burning wood and into the small room, and perched at her keyboard, surrounded by the large collection of books and knick-knacks she'd accumulated over the years, with only a curled-up Delilah as her witness, she began: *Wethersfield Road.*

She couldn't figure out what to say next, but after staring at the mostly blank Word document for almost an hour, she settled on the ugly truth. *Amelia Glickman would never admit it, but she secretly fantasized about near-fatal car wrecks and potentially terminal cancer diagnoses.*

And that was it. The words spilled from her fingertips in a rush of relief she knew might take years to fully realize. But as she bared her soul, a fire in her chest caught that had long been dormant. This thing, this creative spirit, this *something*. She promised to follow it until she knew what it was. Until she had written it all down.

On the last night of 2019, Amelia and Tate hosted the sober New Year's Eve party at Wethersfield, just like always. Ethan had moved back to Austin and in with his now-fiancé Jamie and both were in attendance. Lucy was getting serious with an amazing woman she'd met on a dating app in the spring, and Sadie and her partner Jed were expecting a little girl that summer. The eight of them drew closer, talking and laughing in the dining room as midnight and a fresh decade inched closer.

It was hard to imagine who they'd been just four years ago at the first Wethersfield party: just trying to figure it all out, clinging to each other for dear life as they navigated their early 20s and took comfort in the way their craziness matched up so effortlessly. People trying out the sober thing had come and gone throughout the years, but their core group remained. It was beyond special to get together each year on their friend-group-iversary.

With midnight just around the corner, Tate and Ethan began filling plastic flutes with sparkling cider as the rest of their crew chatted excitedly.

"One minute to go!" someone shouted, signaling everyone to gather where the cider was being poured in the dining room. Trevor, Amelia's high school boyfriend, and his now-husband came into the room as well. She loved introducing Tate to her most important people, and Trevor was certainly one of them, especially after helping him plan his wedding last year. She was grateful that the Forces of Good had brought them back together through her dog-walking job. Sometimes they even took Delilah and Chunk on walks together.

Tate sidled up beside her, pushing through the growing number of bodies filling the small space. "Happy almost New Year, Amelia Bedelia."

"Happy almost New Year, Tater Tot."

When it came time to count down, Tate didn't join in with the chanting. Instead, he rested his hands on her shoulders and looked into her eyes.

Ten! "So, I've been thinking," he began.

Nine! "Is now really the best time to have a conversation?" she asked, slightly annoyed.

Eight! "Um, for this one, yes."

Seven! She shouted over the crowd as it got louder. "Okay, well, make it quick!"

Six! "I've been thinking…" He rolled his eyes at her good-naturedly. "About how I want to spend the rest of my life with you." She froze.

Five! "I've known you were the one since that first night on the couch. When you and Delilah fell asleep on my lap."

Four! Amelia was speechless. Her gaze met a misty-eyed Trevor's. He winked. And she smiled at her first love before returning attention to her end game.

Three! "And being that we met here two years ago tonight."

Two! "I think it's the perfect time." She noticed Sadie standing in the corner filming on her phone; Delilah wagging her tail excitedly at their feet.

One! "Amelia Glickman…" He got down on one knee and took a small velvet box out of his pocket.

Happy New Year! "Will you marry me?" He opened the box to reveal a gorgeous yet tasteful diamond ring.

Cheers and applause erupted around them as she shouted, "Yes! Yes! Yes!" until there was no breath left in her lungs.

He slid the ring on her finger, right next to Grandma Glickman's ruby pinkie ring.

The next year floated by in a haze of love and excitement. Wedding planning, her new job at an independent bookstore, volunteering at the local animal shelter, and writing filled the days, and dinners filled the evenings, either at home together or out with family and friends. She loved the way he fit into her life, and she fit into his. It all felt like a fairy tale, but it became real when they set a date for early February the next year. Where once she struggled to conjure up a short list for a birthday dinner, invitations went out to hundreds of people she loved and cared about. Amelia Glickman, the girl who couldn't make a healthy relationship work to save her life, was getting married with the full support of her loved ones and zero chances for a dramatic last-minute objection for the sake of all involved. Their union was a good thing, a thing to celebrate. Because Tate was good and good to her. There would be no "But Amelia, he's a drug dealer. Have you lost your mind?" or "Didn't he cheat on you at least thrice?" or "Isn't he on a no-fly list?"

She couldn't stop asking herself how in the fuck she got here. But the answer was obvious. The Forces of Good, Wethersfield Road, and Hope. The way they mysteriously worked together to bring her exactly where she needed to be.

CHAPTER 30

To: drb@mcclinic.net

From: aglick1992@gmail.com

Hey Dr. B! Sorry it's been so long again. Things are bananas right now, so I'll make this quick. I'M GETTING MARRIED THIS WEEKEND! THIS IS NOT A DRILL. You'd love him. He's amazing. He encourages me to be the National Forest every day. Can you believe I've been sober for almost seven years? Crazy. I think about you all the time, and I know for a fact I wouldn't be here if it weren't for you. You are truly a Force of Good in my life.

I'm taking a break from being a therapist; it got to be a little overwhelming. I miss my clients every day, but I've felt a lot better since I quit. I'm working at a bookstore and actually kind of trying to write my own book... just for like therapeutic purposes. I don't think anyone will ever read it or anything. It started with this overwhelming urge to start from the beginning and write it all down.

Anyway, I hope you're doing amazing. Let me know if you're ever in Austin.

Love, Amelia

To: aglick1992@gmail.com

From: drb@mcclinic.net

Amelia! Congratulations! I am glad you don't have much time to update me, it means you are living the full and beautiful life you deserve.

Be well,

Dr. B.

E arly February in Austin could be anything from a balmy eighty degrees and sunny to a blustery ice storm, but much like the day she watched her Hollywood dreams shatter, their wedding day at the Four Seasons was somewhere in between. She remembered being 17, eyes catching on the manicured green lawn from where she sat in the lobby, waiting for her fate to be determined. Today the Texas winter sun shined bright, a crisp 50-degree breeze wafting off a sparkling Lady Bird Lake as Amelia Glickman's father walked her down the aisle towards a blubbering Tate waiting on the very same lawn. The deliciously dramatic notes of Freddy Mercury singing about the need for somebody to love were the perfect soundtrack.

Ethan, Sadie, Beth, and Lucy stood to the left of the altar, embodying unwavering love and support; aside from the secret middle finger Lucy flipped her with a wink from behind her bouquet causing Amelia to roll her eyes lovingly with a laugh. Trevor and his husband Josh sat hand in hand in the second row, wet eyes glistening in the sun. Her parents and their new spouses sat in the front row next to Tate's parents. Even Grandma Glickman was there, sitting next to Trevor. He'd always been her favorite.

Young Amelia Glickman believed wholeheartedly that one day, Prince Charming, or more likely, Jordan Catalano, would sweep her off her feet just in time to save the day, making her complete and whole. But she'd been mistaken. For one, at the dawn of her sexuality, she had no idea that Helen Hunt in *Twister* was even an option. But she'd also learned that two halves do not make a whole in a relationship, but rather two wholes make one separate beautiful new whole.

This was especially important in honoring and holding space for her bisexuality in the context of a heteronormative relationship—at least that's the way Cathy described it. Amelia had concluded that she was a queer woman who just happened to fall in love with a man. These things were also important to the parts of her that were the youngest and most tender. She could hold and protect those parts and fight for their independence and individuality, all while showing up as the partner that Tate deserved. In their wedding ceremony, they promised one another just that.

It was a sunny, beautiful day in 2021; only she could see the FOG and the way it hovered over the gathering so lovingly. Because inside—away from the grass, the trees, and the fresh air—up the elevator on the top floor of the very same hotel, was the spot where she thought her life had ended. Where she'd been deemed almost special enough to rise above the rest. It was the first example in her life of human rejection making up the FOG's protection. Every door that had been shut in her face had made today possible.

When Jonathan Glickman arrived at the end of the aisle that overlooked Lady Bird Lake with his daughter in tow, he gave Tate a bear hug, kissed his daughter on the cheek, and went to join the hodgepodge of their family in the front row. Tate took Amelia's hands in his and looked her up and down appreciatively. The size 18 mermaid-style gown with the plunging neckline fit her like a freaking glove. Without thinking it through, he leaned in for a kiss, to which she just giggled and said, "You can't kiss me yet!"

"Right! Sorry."

Their friends and family laughed along as joy bubbled throughout the 200-plus chairs set up on the hotel lawn. Each time she tried to cut down the guest list to a more conservative number, she couldn't do it. "Only invite people who you absolutely *have* to hug that day," Lucy suggested.

But there were so many that she and Tate needed to hug. Because she was a person in recovery; everyone who made it into her life and stayed there for any considerable amount of time was complicit in saving her life in some way. Not to mention how they continued to keep her alive and moving forward.

It was good that the guest list was big, because their love was big, her heart was big, her laugh was big, and the moment was big. Unlike those times years ago, she recognized the good fortune and privilege associated with a wedding of this size and sweep. Her gratitude poured through the space like a sun-warmed tide. The officiant, a good friend of theirs, made a joke about someone accidentally spiking the mocktails and this being a really shitty time to relapse that sent her ridiculous, gargantuan laugh echoing off the trees and nearby lake.

A glint of sunshine on the lake's surface caught her attention. Just beyond the water's bend, a Hail Mary football pass away from where she was about to say I do, stood the pedestrian bridge—the bridge where she'd finally allowed herself to grieve, the spot where she'd looked her trauma in the eyes. She could almost feel the *left, right, left, right, left* of coming to terms with her past all over again.

As she shifted her attention back to Tate, her present and her future, her painful past seemed further away than ever before. It was time to move forward with her vows:

"My dearest Tate. I couldn't tell you the moment I realized you were my person; it feels like something that has always been true but has become more and more apparent over time. We have a quantum entanglement." Tate smiled knowingly at her reference—something they heard on *Survivor* once; they'd binged all the existing seasons when he moved in last year.

"Tate, I vow to love you even when I don't like you and to always be quick to remember we are on the same team. Speaking of teams, I vow to always root for the Dallas Cowboys, even when it's really embarrassing and depressing." The crowd erupted in laughter, Tate included.

"I vow to explore the world with you hand in hand as we go on countless adventures and to appreciate the moments of quiet serenity just as much. But most of all, I vow to be your best friend, your partner in crime, and your wife for the rest of my time here on earth and beyond that if such a thing exists."

Tate wiped a tear from his cheek and began:

"Amelia, you know I'm somewhat of a positive nihilist to the tune of nothing really matters, so do whatever sets your soul on fire. Except drugs. We don't do drugs anymore." He reached out for a fist bump, and she obliged.

Something more serious crossed his face as he went on. "Amelia, *you* set my soul on fire. Our relationship hasn't been perfect, because, and I hate to break this to everyone here, we aren't perfect people. But I have been amazed time and time again by your strength as you walk through the world." He squeezed her hands in his.

"I've had a running theory for a while now that finding your person is just finding someone whose eyes you want to see the world through, and your perspective and grace is something I aspire to every day. You've shown me what it looks like to love someone not just in my heart but in how I live my everyday life."

With those words another slideshow began in her mind's eye: Tate bringing her a cup of coffee in the morning and planting a sloppy kiss on her mouth despite the morning breath. Him helping with the dishes after dinner even though he'd done all the cooking. The random flowers on random days just because.

After the officiant declared them husband and wife, Tate lifted one of his Vans and smashed the ceremonial glass. Everyone in the world they loved shouted "Mazel Tov" as the glass shattered inside the embroidered cloth pouch, shards of pure glee slicing through the atmosphere insistently.

The photos and the dinner were a blur of laughter and connection—so many hugs from so many people she adored. It all moved so fast—an overload of happiness short-circuiting her brain. They danced their first dance to "Can't Take My Eyes Off of You" by Frankie Valli and the Four Seasons, a song she used to sing in the car with her mom on the way to school. Then they partied the night away with their friends and too much caffeine. She danced with her dad to Elton John's "Your Song," and halfway through, they called Beth up to join them and all three danced together.

Their loved ones sent them off to the honeymoon suite, the day wrapped in sparklers and cheers. Full of love and wedding cake, they collapsed on the giant king bed as soon as they entered the room and just lay there.

"Wow," he said, looking up at the ceiling.

"Wow," she agreed before rolling on top of him and kicking off her own white bridal Vans. He helped her out of her mermaid gown, and they savored one another into the wee hours of the morning. After, they lounged in an enormous claw foot tub, their limbs encased in fluffy bubbles and talked through each moment of the day from start to finish.

Two days later, they caught a predawn flight to the Caribbean, kicking off the life of travel they'd always imagined for themselves. This was Tate's first time leaving the country, and she couldn't wait to share the joy of taking that first deep breath of foreign air. She sat in the window seat, Tate asleep and drooling on her shoulder. She couldn't wait to give him shit for it later. Amelia couldn't stop staring out the window at the moonlit layer of clouds between the plane and the earth's surface. It was well before sunrise, and a smattering of twinkling stars carpeted the sky.

Feeling inspired, she decided to pull out the floral journal where her journey began so long ago. Careful not to wake Tate, she adjusted her shoulder and turned to the remaining blank pages to write.

Looking out the airplane window at the fluffy clouds, I realize that all those years of getting high were an attempt to arrive here, among the stars tucked in a safe, downy cocoon. For so long, I used sex, drugs, and food to launch myself from reality into a dreamy abyss, the spiritual realm where nothing can ever hurt again. But that kind of euphoria—that escape from the pain of reality—is not of this world. I used to try desperately to tap into that slice of heaven, the slice that feels like 30,000 feet in the sky just before sunrise. I wanted life to feel like that all the time.

Now, I can accept and be grateful for the moments of heaven I do receive and not demand more than my fair share. Perhaps all we have are the pieces of heaven we hold in our hearts until we die and cross over into the real thing. Pieces like Hope, Delilah, Wethersfield Road, my family, both blood and chosen. Tate and his laugh. The stories that break us and put us back together again. All I really know is that I'm glad I didn't check out all those years ago—that I didn't quit before the miracle and swallow a bottle of pills or turn my car on in a closed garage, all because I didn't trust anyone else to take good enough care of Hope and Delilah after I left. I could have completely missed the good part.

Amelia put her pen down and looked back out the window just in time to see a streak of cosmic luminescence arcing across the sky. She had seen plenty of shooting stars, but never one at eye level. Life on earth wasn't perfect; far from it. But a front-row seat to that sacred moment when the sun and the moon shared the sky, holding onto Tate with one hand, and the FOG with the other, felt pretty damn close.

EPILOGUE: FOUR YEARS LATER

Amelia Glickman Reynolds gazed up at the vast array of photo albums, trinkets, and book spines from where she sat in front of the entirely full floor-to-ceiling bookshelves on Wethersfield Road. A contented sigh passed through her lips as her eyes landed on a framed photo of her and Tate wearing joyous smiles on a scuba diving boat in the Caribbean, their arms wrapped around one another. It was her favorite memory from the honeymoon. These shelves embodied her full, beautiful life. Books of poetry, recovery memoirs, her favorite plays, photographs of her loved ones, and textbooks from grad school filled the once vacant and chilly shelves with effortless warmth. She mustered the strength to pack it all up into the empty boxes surrounding her.

How was she supposed to pack up 10 years of memories, the puzzle pieces of who she had become? How was she supposed to extract herself from the alchemy that created her? And how was she supposed to take the two wooden urns filled with Hope and Delilah's ashes off the shelf, put them in a box, and let a truck take them to another state? The wooden boxes holding their powdered essence had remained in the same place for almost four years, and as she looked up at the vibrant evidence of a life well lived, she thought perhaps they would be the last thing she packed.

She started with the copy of *The Catcher in the Rye* she stole from rehab over a decade ago, though the copy itself looked much older than her 10 years of sobriety. She plunked it in the box and marveled at the distant memory of Holden Caufield being a strange source of comfort all those years ago. Her literary heroes had since shifted to the likes of Elizabeth Bennett and Jo March. More books followed; she stacked and maneuvered them like Tetris bricks as she let her mind wander to her two gone girls.

Delilah got sick with cancer a year after the wedding. The tools Amelia acquired throughout her recovery, the ability to set aside selfish motives and biased opinions and breathe through the pain of an impossibly hard decision, enabled her to make the loving and kind choice for her loyal companion. She took the action that broke her own heart but spared Delilah pain and suffering. She'd never stop wondering if she could have held on longer to her sweet, smooshy girl.

On that last day, Amelia laid beside Delilah on the floor in front of the purple chairs in the best patch of afternoon sun Wethersfield had to offer while Tate stroked both of their hair. After a juicy steak from Austin Land and Cattle, Delilah was injected with the drug that would stop her heart. Amelia sang her lullabies as Delilah's breathing slowed. She sunk her face into her furry neck and breathed in Delilah's kind spirit through her soft coat.

Delilah drifted off into whatever was next with the guidance of the loving in-home vet service, and a piece of Amelia's heart drifted off with her across the rainbow bridge. "I wouldn't be here if it weren't for you," was the last thing she whispered into a pointy blonde ear. And it was the truth. The FOG lovingly lifted her out of her body and took her home.

She'd never forget how Delilah looked curled up with her favorite lamby toy, so completely at peace but also so completely gone. After the vet took her away, Amelia and Tate sat on the couch in the quiet emptiness she left behind, softly crying hand in hand.

Amelia wondered how the fuck they moved forward from that. She'd never lived at Wethersfield without Delilah; the void was vast and frigid. But her recovery friends suggested that she simply do the next right thing and take care of herself.

"We should probably eat something," she said to Tate. "Do you want to get some dinner?"

"You might as well ask me if I want to go to the fucking moon," Tate replied tentatively, his voice still choked with tears. Because what were once the laws of nature, Delilah's beating heart and well-oiled routine, had vanished in an afternoon. "I barely even know what year it is."

They both burst into laughter punctuated by sobs as the tears leaked from their eyes. Grief was ridiculous like that. And it meant more to Amelia than she could say that Tate could hold the heartbreak with her.

She'd never known a harder goodbye—until two months later when Hope's health declined. Foundering can happen very quickly in horses, the coffin bone in the hoof rotating to the point of rupture, leaving them immobile and in horrific pain. But the Forces of Good made Hope's foundering slow, and painkillers kept her comfortable up until the very end.

After the discovery of her increasingly dire situation, the equine veterinarian gave Hope about a week or two at the most until her leg would break completely. That would mean pain and suffering that no animal deserved, especially Hope. Her foot was essentially a ticking time bomb, the vet said. In a case like hers, there wasn't a 'too soon' to say goodbye, only a 'too late.'

Amelia again used her acquired tools to make the best decision for her heart horse—sitting quietly and waiting for that quiet knowing one way or the other. She spent one last day with Hope in a comfy stall with lots of her favorite pillowy shavings, peppermints, and neck scratches. Then, she mustered the strength to stay while they administered the medications necessary to help her cross over.

First was a large dose of tranquilizer, meant to work as an anesthetic. This was the hardest part—watching the vet inject a fluid that made Hope wobbly—it was so much different than putting down a dog. Hope swayed on her long brown legs, the vet expertly offering his own weight to assist her to the ground. It was the only part Amelia looked away from, fearing Hope may fall. The urge to run away and hide was strong, but she breathed through it, determined to put her horse first, and that meant not letting her face death alone. Her own recovery taught her how to show up even when she was afraid.

But Hope lay down quickly and gracefully, and Amelia quickly sat by her head in the grass, stroking her mane, tears soaking her face and Hope's.

"Thank you, thank you, thank you, thank you," she whispered over and over again until the words blended together and became nonsensical. "Thank you for saving me. I will love you and miss you for the rest of my life."

The vet declared that she was no longer there, and with Hope safe in the FOG's embrace, Amelia launched herself into Tate's arms, and he took her home to Wethersfield to grieve.

The heartbreak from losing her girls felt too sacred to push away. From week to week, she felt all of it, its darkness, its depth. For months, Amelia did the bare minimum. It was all she could do just to stay sober and force herself to eat three meals a day. Her bed became a haven from the outside world once again, the comforter a shield against the harsh reality that was life without her sun and moon—how could she tell day from night with them both gone? She had never been an adult without them. But she began to make sense of it through her writing, determined to tell their stories. As the months dragged on, her heart began to heal around the atrophy they left behind.

She was grateful above all else for the time she did have with such special souls. And she began to realize that while she would miss Hope and Delilah forever, the truth was, their work was done. She became who they always knew she could be, and as time continued to march on, Amelia was sprinkled with new avenues of love and happiness as her and Tate's life got bigger and bigger. It proved that bad things would always happen no matter how good life got, but grief and joy could exist in the same heart.

The years that followed were mostly filled with happiness, but her mental health struggles didn't vanish into thin air. Even outside these tremendous losses, some days she still simply tried to get from point A to point B, a grey cloud lurking over her no matter what tools she applied.

She could usually sense it the moment she woke up, a weight on her chest that promised not to budge but apologetically encouraged her to try again tomorrow. But today, her feelings weren't facts, as cliché as that sounded. She didn't have to pull the whole world down on top of herself each time life felt overwhelming, even when she became a raw nerve, quivering and tender to every touch.

After years of marriage and more sessions with Cathy, she and Tate mastered the treks through their triggers and landmines. She could let those thoughts of running, hiding, and destroying herself drift by like the ever-changing clouds she continued to see clearer in therapy and meetings. Sometimes, she'd still look up to the sky, waiting for the shoe she knew must be careening toward the earth to ruin her happy life. And sometimes, such comfort felt dangerous. Hadn't her own parents been comfortable for over 20 years when their marriage ended? She took it one day at a time.

On the hardest of days, Tate asked her what she needed: words of affirmation, long lingering hugs, the first three seasons of *Grey's*, or a grilled cheese sandwich. Sometimes, she'd answer, "I'm having a shitty body image day, and everything is making me want to scream. Can we watch *Family Guy* and order Thai food?" Other times, her answer just existed within the fact that he was always willing to ask: "I don't know, can you just hug me and not let go?"

They grew more in love with one another, and their circle of friends and family seemed to be ever-expanding. Though she once called herself the loneliest person in the world, she could no longer be lonely if she tried. Some of her favorite moments included watching Sadie's daughter wander the magical house, finding corners to play in, basking in the natural comfort of the space.

As the years went on, Wethersfield still embraced her in the exact way she needed, like an ever-intuitive, endlessly compassionate divinity. The house opened her loving arms wide and welcomed in their friends and family, reminding them all that they were never truly alone. It held

Amelia and Tate tight to her chest, the fireplace warming their insides, quiet echoes of joy and connection lulling them into deep rest. It safely guarded growing families, creating a space to laugh and play for the children who called them Auntie Amelia and Uncle Tate. The corners were cubbies for their favorite memories. The floorboards were anchors for their wildest dreams. The whispers of Delilah's unconditional love were tucked forever into the folds of the couch. But much like she and Hope's jobs were complete, so was Wethersfield's. It was time for the house to raise another and for Amelia to move on. She now knew that the FOG would follow her anywhere. Or was it her following the FOG?

As the moving boxes filled up, she noticed a dusty journal hidden under a textbook. *Something Beautiful is on the Horizon* sparkled up at her in slightly faded gold lettering. She smiled to herself, rolling her eyes at the bitter, spoiled girl who'd first filled its pages with her heartache. When she opened that notebook, a handwritten note fell out. It was the letter from Wethersfield's previous owner. She scanned the words, remembering the first time she read them in the kitchen the day she moved in. She hadn't even known she'd kept it.

The love that grew around me here on Wethersfield Road can no longer fit within its walls. Eyes wide, heart thudding in her chest, Amelia turned to the last empty page in the old journal. She'd all but forgotten the lovely floral monstrosity. She located a pen and began to write.

> *Dear new owner,*
>
> *Welcome to Wethersfield! Don't be afraid of the weird and wonderful things you will find within her. If you feel like the walls are watching, or the creaks in the floor are professing, like the shelves and the windowsills are insisting upon themselves, or like the house itself is wrapping you in her arms, just let her. When I was 22, I moved into this house, a sad, sick, lonely person who had no idea who she was, but the previous owner left me a letter*

like this, assuring me that the energy under this roof would heal me, if I let it. The spirit of this house picked us, just like it has picked you, and she intuitively knows how much you need to be mended or bended.

This journey will be your own, but what I can offer is some general advice based on my experience here: First, believe in miracles and believe in yourself; no one else can do that for you, it's a choice you must make every single day. Next, if your foundation has a crack in it, sometimes it's best to let it crumble completely and build something new in the space it leaves behind once you clear away the debris.

And above all, open your heart. People fall in love here, with themselves, with each other, and with life itself. I am now 32 years old, and the life Wethersfield has given me within her embrace has grown so big it's pouring out the doors and windows. It's so big that I must say goodbye to a dear friend, my fairy house mother. As my husband and I prepare to welcome home our adopted daughter in the Pacific Northwest, I leave pieces of my heart here in this home where it broke and got glued back together a million times. I Hope one day you and Wethersfield have your own story to tell.

Be well,
Amelia

A story to tell. And what about her story? Hadn't she done as the FOG said and written it all down? Over the years her writing had become the way she made her mark, but what if it was also the way she could make her living? She'd written it all down for herself, but what if she dared to share? It finally felt like she was in a place to do just that.

After shutting the journal and capping her pen, she carefully removed the wooden boxes containing Hope and Delilah's ashes from the shelf, planted a kiss on each lid, and carefully sheltered them in bubble wrap. She placed them on top of the stack of books inside the last box, closed the lid, and taped down the folds. Soon, she would take them to a home somewhere new, the National Forest, where the trees grew to reach the heavens. The spirit of Wethersfield and the FOG would carry her like a ladybug on the wind.

Then, she curled up in one of the purple chairs for her last sunset on Wethersfield Road. With her laptop perched on her knees, she researched editors and publishing houses. She had to find a way to share her story. The FOG had yet to reveal the next step fully, but she knew if she kept typing, kept creating, it would burst through the haze one ray of sunshine at a time like streaks of light on the forest floor.

She would do her best to be patient with it, something that was aggressively against her nature in all other areas. Because writing made her brain quiet and set her soul on fire in a way that only riding Hope or performing ever did. All the chaos made sense, filtered down to one thought at a time. She hadn't worked as a therapist in years. After a lifetime of taking on everyone else's shit, it only made sense. She was in awe of the people who made counseling a long-term career. Thank the FOG for those people. But she'd been carried by an unseen force to her safest inevitable—whenever she wrote, it was like everything and nothing belonged to her at the same time. And writing could allow her to be an extension of the FOG in her own way.

Soon, Tate would come home from work to Wethersfield for the last time, and they would eat takeout on the dining room floor and talk about how they fell in love within its walls. He'd hold her hand while they drank sparkling cider, and even though he'd heard it a million times, he'd listen lovingly as she recounted the way she and her broken heart moved in all those years ago. How she thought she would never know true happiness during her time here on earth but had proven herself wrong when laughter began to fill the house. How the house whispered to her that she was sitting next to the love of her life that special night on the couch next to Tate. How he got down on one knee in the dining room and asked for forever, Delilah wagging her tail excitedly at their feet. And how they decided to welcome a child into their lives one night while they talked quietly in bed, the breeze blowing in through the French doors.

She picked up the journal, every page within it now scribbled with bits and pieces of her life, and opened it to the letter she just wrote. She tore it out, put it on the refrigerator door with a magnet, and tried to picture the person it would greet. Maybe they'd had their heart broken, maybe they were grieving something or someone. Maybe they had just gone through the single most traumatic event of their life so far. Maybe they just needed a change. Or maybe they'd never felt at home anywhere before, and this was their chance to build something real. There was no way to know for sure, but if she had to guess, they'd probably be just like her. *A little broken, but a lot brave.*

ACKNOWLEDGMENTS

I want to express my deepest gratitude to the people who have been my pillars of support throughout this journey. To my wonderful husband, Tanner: Thank you for your unwavering love and belief in me. You are my best friend in the world, and you make me brave enough to do crazy things, like decide to be a writer at 32. To my real-life Hope and Lilah: You really did raise me. I think about you every day, and I'm a better person because of it. To my ride-or-die family: Mom, Dad, Lizzie, Mindy, Christian, Whitney, Shelly, Brady, Wilson, Monica, Kayla, Courtney, Evan, and Kara. Your constant encouragement and support mean the world to me. I hope the loose references to our family's story make you proud. To my grandmother and all the people in our family whose blood and love run through my veins: I am who I am because of you. To my incredible friends and chosen family: Thank you for not rolling your eyes at me, at least to my face, when I told you I wanted to write a book — your faith in me has been a source of strength.

A heartfelt thank you to everyone and anyone who taught me the incredible life lessons that are sprinkled throughout this book. Especially Skylar, Melisse, Geoffrey, Jaclyn, Kim, Solis, Molly, Rusty, Sally, Dr. McNerney, Mr. Baehr, Bob, Kelly, Kate, Natalie, Katherine, Lila, Karen, Barry, Erik, Tom, Kit, Lisa, Warren, Connor, Jason, Astrid, Carrie, the Sams, the Robs, the Sarahs, the Matts, the Kelseys, Crystal, Rachel, Jack, Alyssa, Hayley, Mary, Kristin, Lauren, Kaleigh, Mia, Harrison, Scarlett, Michaela, Lindsey, Susan, Bill, and Amy. Your wisdom has shaped me in ways I can never fully express.

To Ron Seybold — my coach, editor, publisher, and friend: This book wouldn't exist without you. Thank you for believing in my vision and guiding me every step of the way.

To my goddaughter, Maisie: May you always feel the freedom to be your most authentic self, and may the world be deserving of your innate beauty and goodness.

Finally, to me: We did it, bitch.

AUTHOR BIOGRAPHY

Photo by Sam Ehrnstein Photography

Anna Binder Reardon is an ex-therapist who writes about the transformative power of vulnerability. Her stories destigmatize the struggles of mental health and normalize care and support. She writes for people who are deeply moved by the beauty of life's imperfections and the powerful journey to discover our most authentic selves. She lives in Austin, Texas, with her husband, Tanner, their Golden Retriever Jax, and their Corgi-mix Oliver. When she's not writing, she can be found reading too many books at once, planning her next travel adventure, or searching for the perfect oat milk vanilla latte. *Wethersfield Road* is her debut novel.

STAY IN TOUCH:

Website: anna-writes.com

Substack: annareardon.substack.com

Linktree: https://linktr.ee/authorabr